WHAT THE REVIEWERS SAY

"An important part of this collection is the re-issue of angry young Robert Louis Stevenson's blistering, class-conscious novella, 'The Beach of Falesa.' Also present are old seadogs and beach-combers, Maugham, Michener, Burdick, James Norman Hall, Jack London and Melville — who are hard-pressed by some literary unknowns in this strong collection. The stories are taut, unromantic, and sometimes erupt with terror, and the anthology offers a high level of excitment."

Virginia Kirkus *Bulletin*

"Like countless other stories of the Pacific Islands, the selections in this book combine all the ingredients of love, violence, adventure, mystery, spooks, and even humor."

New Haven, Conn., *Register*

"Here are fifteen superb stories of the South Seas, the lure of which has attracted many writers who found romance, drama, and humor on the golden shores."

Worcester, Mass., *Telegram*

"What I particularly liked about this anthology is the freshness of selection. The editors have wisely steered clear of the hackneyed and have given us a variety of stories which are not often presented. As a bonus there are brief biographical sketches of each author."

Trenton, New Jersey, *Times*

"Though the subject matter and mood of the stories range through all the emotions, one point seems undoubtedly clear in most of the yarns, whether in Maugham's story "Red" or in Melville's "Chola Widow" — the islands, though beautiful, are lonely and not really any place for white gentlemen seeking the unfettered tranquility the natives have as a birthright."

Camden, New Jersey, *Courier Post*

"It is impossible for the editors of any anthology of 'bests' to satisfy everyone with their selections, but with these fifteen stories of the South Pacific, A. Grove Day and Carl Stroven should come fairly close."

Atlanta, Georgia, *Journal*

"Anyone who enjoys South Sea island stories should welcome this big, new anthology compiled by two members of the English faculty at the University of Hawaii."

Nashville, *Tennessean*

"This is a heady feast of South Sea fare: rich, sensuous stories of the tropics that kept men awake at night not with indigestion but with hunger for far-off isles."

Hilo, Hawaii, *Tribune*

"Thank you, Carl Stroven and Grove Day, for reminding us that the South Seas school of writing goes a lot further back than Michener and Burdick, though both are represented in this excellent omnibus."

San Francisco *Chronicle*

Best South Sea Stories

Selected and Edited by

A. GROVE DAY *and* CARL STROVEN

Mutual Publishing

Cover photograph, F. Homes, Bishop Museum
Cover design by Jane Hopkins

Library of Congress Catalog Card Number 64-12430

ISBN 0-935180-12-5

ACKNOWLEDGMENTS AND SOURCES

"Red" by W. Somerset Maugham, copyright 1921 by Asia Publishing Company. From *The Trembling of a Leaf*, reprinted by permission of Doubleday & Company, Inc. Canadian reprint rights by permission of A. P. Watt and Son.

"The Fourth Man" by John Russell, copyright 1917 by P. F. Collier & Son, reprinted by permission of Brandt & Brandt.

"The Forgotten One" by James Norman Hall, reprinted by permission of the publisher from *On the Stream of Travel*, Houghton Mifflin Company, 1926.

"The Seed of McCoy" by Jack London, reprinted from *South Sea Tales*, copyright 1911,

"Mutiny" by James A. Michener, reprinted by permission of The Macmillan Company from *Tales of the South Pacific*. Copyright 1946, 1947, by Curtis Publishing Company. Copyright 1947 by James A. Michener.

"The Black and the White" by Eugene Burdick, reprinted by permission of the publisher from *The Blue of Capricorn*, Houghton Mifflin Company, 1961.

"The Ghost of Alexander Perks, A.B." by Robert Dean Frisbie, from *Atlantic Monthly*, May, 1931, copyright 1931 by Robert Dean Frisbie, reprinted by permission of Harold Ober Associates, Inc.

"Assignment with an Octopus," by Sir Arthur Grimble, from *We Chose the Islands*, copyright 1952, by Sir Arthur Grimble, reprinted by permission of William Morrow & Company, Inc. Canadian reprint rights by permission of John Murray (Canadian title: *A Pattern of Islands*).

"A Stinking Ghost" by Sir Arthur Grimble, from *Return to the Islands: Life and Legend in the Gilberts*, copyright 1957 by Olivia Grimble, reprinted by permission of William Morrow & Company, Inc. Canadian reprint rights by permission of John Murray.

Mutual Publishing
1215 Center Street, Suite 210
Honolulu, HI 96816
Ph (808) 732-1709
Fax (808) 734-4094
Email: mutual@lava.net
Url: http://www.pete.com/mutual

Printed in Australia

THIS BOOK CONTAINS THE COMPLETE TEXT OF THE ORIGINAL HARDBOUND EDITION

CONTENTS

CONTENTS

W. Somerset Maugham

RED

The English author W. Somerset Maugham (1874–) spent several months in 1916 visiting the islands of Polynesia. He had wanted to go to the South Seas, he said, "ever since as a youth I had read *The Ebb-Tide* and *The Wrecker*. . . . It was not only the beauty of the islands that took me, Herman Melville and Pierre Loti had prepared me for that. . . . What excited me was to meet one person after another who was new to me. . . . I filled my notebook with brief descriptions of their appearance and their character, and presently, my imagination excited by these multitudinous impressions, from a hint or incident or a happy invention, stories began to form themselves round certain of the most vivid of them."

The result was his novel, *The Moon and Sixpence* (1919), based on the life of Paul Gauguin, and a volume of six short stories, *The Trembling of a Leaf* (1921), which includes the well-known "Rain" and the story he himself has chosen as his best, "Red." It is a love story, but a cruel one, written with economy and consummate skill, with each detail a step toward the ironic conclusion.

THE SKIPPER THRUST HIS HAND INTO ONE OF HIS TROUSER pockets and with difficulty, for they were not at the sides but in front and he was a portly man, pulled out a large silver watch. He looked at it and then looked again at the declining sun. The Kanaka at the wheel gave him a glance, but did not speak. The skipper's eyes rested on the island they were approaching. A white line of foam marked the reef. He knew there was an opening large enough to get his ship through, and when they came a little nearer he counted on seeing it. They had nearly an hour of daylight still before them. In the lagoon the water was deep and they could anchor comfortably. The chief of the village which he could already see among the coconut trees was a friend of the mate's, and it would be pleasant to go ashore for the night. The mate came forward at that minute and the skipper turned to him.

"We'll take a bottle of booze along with us and get some girls in to dance," he said.

"I don't see the opening," said the mate.

He was a Kanaka, a handsome, swarthy fellow, with somewhat the look of a later Roman emperor, inclined to stoutness; but his face was fine and clean-cut.

"I'm dead sure there's one right here," said the captain, looking through his glasses. "I can't understand why I can't pick it up. Send one of the boys up the mast to have a look."

The mate called one of the crew and gave him the order. The captain watched the Kanaka climb and waited for him to speak. But the Kanaka shouted down that he could see nothing but the unbroken line of foam. The captain spoke Samoan like a native, and he cursed him freely.

"Shall he stay up there?" asked the mate.

"What the hell good does that do?" answered the captain. "The blame fool can't see worth a cent. You bet your sweet life I'd find the opening if I was up there."

He looked at the slender mast with anger. It was all very well for a native who had been used to climbing up coconut trees all his life. He was fat and heavy.

"Come down," he shouted. "You're no more use than a dead dog. We'll just have to go along the reef till we find the opening."

It was a seventy-ton schooner with paraffin auxiliary, and it ran, when there was no head wind, between four and five knots an hour. It was a bedraggled object; it had been painted white a very long time ago, but it was now dirty, dingy, and mottled. It smelt strongly of paraffin and of the copra which was its usual cargo. They were within a hundred feet of the reef now and the captain told the steersman to run along it till they came to the opening. But when they had gone a couple of miles he realized that they had missed it. He went about and slowly worked back again. The white foam of the reef continued without interruption and now the sun was setting. With a curse at the stupidity of the crew the skipper resigned himself to waiting till next morning.

"Put her about," he said. "I can't anchor here."

They went out to sea a little and presently it was quite dark. They anchored. When the sail was furled the ship began to roll a good deal. They said in Apia that one day she would roll right over; and the owner, a German-American who managed one of the largest stores, said that no money was big enough to induce him to go out in her. The cook, a Chinese in white trousers, very dirty and ragged, and a thin white tunic, came to say that supper was ready, and when the skipper went into the cabin he found the engineer already seated at table. The engineer was a long, lean man with a scraggy neck. He was dressed in blue overalls and a sleeveless jersey that showed his thin arms tattooed from elbow to wrist.

"Hell, having to spend the night outside," said the skipper.

The engineer did not answer, and they ate their supper in silence. The cabin was lit by a dim oil lamp. When they had eaten the canned apricots with which the meal finished the Chink brought them a cup of tea. The skipper lit a cigar and went on the upper deck. The island now was only a darker mass against the night. The stars were very bright. The only sound was the ceaseless breaking of the surf. The skipper sank into a deck chair and smoked idly. Presently three or four members of the crew came up and sat down. One of them had a banjo and another a concertina. They began to play, and one of them sang. The native song sounded strange on these instruments. Then to the singing a couple began to dance. It was a barbaric dance, savage and primeval, rapid, with quick movements of the hands and feet and contortions of the body; it was sensual, sexual even, but sexual without passion. It was very animal, direct, weird without mystery, natural in short, and one might almost say childlike. At last they grew tired. They stretched themselves on the deck and slept, and all was silent. The skipper lifted himself heavily out of his chair and clambered down the companion. He went into his cabin and got out of his clothes. He climbed into his bunk and lay there. He panted a little in the heat of the night.

But next morning, when the dawn crept over the tranquil sea, the opening in the reef which had eluded them the night before was seen a little to the east of where they lay. The schooner entered the lagoon. There was not a ripple on the surface of the water. Deep down among the coral rocks you saw little colored fish swim. When he had anchored his ship the skipper ate his breakfast and went on deck. The sun shone from an unclouded sky, but in the early morning the air was grateful and cool. It was Sunday, and there was a feeling of quietness, a silence as though nature were at rest, which gave him a peculiar sense of comfort. He sat, looking at the wooded coast, and felt lazy and well at ease. Presently a slow smile moved his lips and he threw the stump of his cigar into the water.

"I guess I'll go ashore," he said. "Get the boat out."

He climbed stiffly down the ladder and was rowed to a little cove. The coconut trees came down to the water's edge, not in rows, but spaced out with an ordered formality. They were like a ballet of spinsters, elderly but flippant, standing in affected attitudes with the simpering graces of a bygone age. He sauntered idly through them, along a path that could be just seen winding its tortuous way, and it led him presently to a broad creek. There was a bridge across it, but a bridge constructed of single trunks of coconut trees, a dozen of them, placed end to end and supported where they met by a forked branch driven into the bed of the creek. You walked on a smooth, round surface, narrow and slippery, and there was no support for the hand. To cross such a bridge required sure feet and a stout heart. The skipper hesitated. But he saw on the other side, nestling among the trees, a white man's house; he made up his mind and, rather gingerly, began to walk. He watched his feet carefully, and where one trunk joined on to the next and there was a difference of level, he tottered a little. It was with a gasp of relief that he reached the last tree and finally set his feet on the firm ground of the other side. He had been so intent on the difficult crossing that he never noticed anyone was watching him, and it was with surprise that he heard himself spoken to.

"It takes a bit of nerve to cross these bridges when you're not used to them."

He looked up and saw a man standing in front of him. He had evidently come out of the house that he had seen.

"I saw you hesitate," the man continued, with a smile on his lips, "and I was watching to see you fall in."

"Not on your life," said the captain, who had now recovered his confidence.

"I've fallen in myself before now. I remember, one evening I came back from shooting, and I fell in, gun and all. Now I get a boy to carry my gun for me."

He was a man no longer young, with a small beard, now somewhat gray, and a thin face. He was dressed in a singlet, without arms, and a pair of duck trousers. He wore neither shoes nor socks. He spoke English with a slight accent.

"Are you Neilson?" asked the skipper.

"I am."

"I've heard about you. I thought you lived somewheres round here."

The skipper followed his host into the little bungalow and sat down heavily in the chair that the other motioned him to take. While Neilson went out to fetch whisky and glasses he took a look round the room. It filled him with amazement. He had never seen so many books. The shelves reached from floor to ceiling on all four walls, and they were closely packed. There was a grand piano littered with music, and a large table on which books and magazines lay in disorder. The room made him feel embarrassed. He remembered that Neilson was a queer fellow. No one knew very much about him, although he had been in the islands for so many years, but those who knew him agreed that he was queer. He was a Swede.

"You've got one big heap of books here," he said, when Neilson returned.

"They do no harm," answered Neilson with a smile.

"Have you read them all?" asked the skipper.

"Most of them."

"I'm a bit of a reader myself. I have the *Saturday Evening Post* sent me regler."

Neilson poured his visitor a good stiff glass of whisky and gave him a cigar. The skipper volunteered a little information.

"I got in last night, but I couldn't find the opening, so I had to anchor outside. I never been this run before, but my people had some stuff they wanted to bring over here. Gray, d'you know him?"

"Yes, he's got a store a little way along."

"Well, there was a lot of canned stuff that he wanted over, an' he's got some copra. They thought I might just as well come over as lie idle at Apia. I run between Apia and Pago Pago mostly, but they've got smallpox there just now, and there's nothing stirring."

He took a drink of his whisky and lit a cigar. He was a taciturn man, but there was something in Neilson that made him nervous, and his nervousness made him talk. The Swede was looking at him with large dark eyes in which there was an expression of faint amusement.

"This is a tidy little place you've got here."

"I've done my best with it."

"You must do pretty well with your trees. They look fine. With copra at the price it is now. I had a bit of a plantation myself once, in Upolu it was, but I had to sell it."

He looked round the room again, where all those books gave him a feeling of something incomprehensible and hostile.

"I guess you must find it a bit lonesome here though," he said.

"I've got used to it. I've been here for twenty-five years."

Now the captain could think of nothing more to say, and he smoked in silence. Neilson had apparently no wish to break it. He looked at his guest with a meditative eye. He was a tall man, more than six feet high, and very stout. His face was red and blotchy, with a network of little purple veins on the cheeks, and his features were sunk into its fatness. His eyes were bloodshot. His neck was buried in rolls of fat. But for a fringe of long curly hair, nearly white, at the back of his head, he was quite bald; and that immense, shiny surface of forehead, which might have given him a false look of intelligence, on the contrary gave him one of peculiar imbecility. He wore a blue flannel shirt, open at the neck and showing his fat chest covered with a mat of reddish hair, and a very old pair of blue serge trousers. He sat in his chair in a heavy, ungainly attitude, his great belly thrust forward and his fat legs uncrossed. All elasticity had gone from his limbs. Neilson wondered idly what sort of man he had been in his youth. It was almost impossible to imagine that this creature of vast bulk had ever been a boy who ran about. The skipper finished his whisky, and Neilson pushed the bottle towards him.

"Help yourself."

The skipper learned forward and with his great hand seized it.

"And how come you in these parts anyways?" he said.

"Oh, I came out to the islands for my health. My lungs were bad and they said I hadn't a year to live. You see they were wrong."

"I meant, how come you to settle down right here?"

"I am a sentimentalist."

"Oh!"

Neilson knew that the skipper had not an idea what he meant, and he looked at him with an ironical twinkle in his dark eyes. Perhaps just because the skipper was so gross and dull a man the whim seized him to talk further.

"You were too busy keeping your balance to notice, when you crossed the bridge, but this spot is generally considered rather pretty."

"It's a cute little house you've got here."

"Ah, that wasn't here when I first came. There was a native hut, with its beehive roof and its pillars, overshadowed by a great tree with red flowers; and the croton bushes, their leaves yellow and red and golden, made a pied fence around it. And then all about were the coconut trees, as fanciful as women, and as vain. They stood at the water's edge and spent all day looking at their reflections. I was a young man then—

good heavens, it's a quarter of a century ago—and I wanted to enjoy all the loveliness of the world in the short time allotted to me before I passed into the darkness. I thought it was the most beautiful spot I had ever seen. The first time I saw it I had a catch at my heart, and I was afraid I was going to cry. I wasn't more than twenty-five, and though I put the best face I could on it, I didn't want to die. And somehow it seemed to me that the very beauty of this place made it easier for me to accept my fate. I felt when I came here that all my past life had fallen away, Stockholm and its university, and then Bonn: it all seemed the life of somebody else, as though now at last I had achieved the reality that our doctors of philosophy—I am one myself, you know—had discussed so much. 'A year,' I cried to myself. 'I have a year. I will spend it here and then I am content to die.'

"We are foolish and sentimental and melodramatic at twenty-five, but if we weren't perhaps we should be less wise at fifty.

"Now drink, my friend. Don't let the nonsense I talk interfere with you."

He waved his thin hand towards the bottle, and the skipper finished what remained in his glass.

"You ain't drinking nothin'," he said, reaching for the whisky.

"I am of a sober habit," smiled the Swede. "I intoxicate myself in ways which I fancy are more subtle. But perhaps that is only vanity. Anyhow, the effects are more lasting and the results less deleterious."

"They say there's a deal of cocaine taken in the States now," said the captain.

Neilson chuckled.

"But I do not see a white man often," he continued, "and for once I don't think a drop of whisky can do me any harm."

He poured himself out a little, added some soda, and took a sip.

"And presently I found out why the spot had such an unearthly loveliness. Here love had tarried for a moment like a migrant bird that happens on a ship in mid-ocean and for a little while folds its tired wings. The fragrance of a beautiful passion hovered over it like the fragrance of hawthorn in May in the meadows of my home. It seems to me that the places where men have loved or suffered keep about them always some faint aroma of something that has not wholly died. It is as though they had acquired a spiritual significance which mysteriously affects those who pass. I wish I could make myself clear." He smiled a little. "Though I cannot imagine that if I did you would understand."

He paused.

"I think this place was beautiful because here I had been loved beautifully." And now he shrugged his shoulders. "But perhaps it is only that my aesthetic sense is gratified by the happy conjunction of young love and a suitable setting."

Even a man less thick-witted than the skipper might have been forgiven if he were bewildered by Neilson's words. For he seemed faintly to laugh at what he said. It was as though he spoke from emotion that his intellect found ridiculous. He had said himself that he was a sentimentalist, and when sentimentality is joined with skepticism there is often the devil to pay.

He was silent for an instant and looked at the captain with eyes in which there was a sudden perplexity.

"You know, I can't help thinking that I've seen you before somewhere or other," he said.

"I couldn't say as I remember you," returned the skipper.

"I have a curious feeling as though your face were familiar to me. It's been puzzling me for some time. But I can't situate my recollection in any place or at any time."

The skipper massively shrugged his heavy shoulders.

"It's thirty years since I first come to the islands. A man can't figure on remembering all the folk he meets in a while like that."

The Swede shook his head.

"You know how one sometimes has the feeling that a place one has never been to before is strangely familiar. That's how I seem to see you." He gave a whimsical smile. "Perhaps I knew you in some past existence. Perhaps, perhaps you were the master of a galley in ancient Rome and I was a slave at the oar. Thirty years have you been here?"

"Every bit of thirty years."

"I wonder if you knew a man called Red?"

"Red?"

"That is the only name I've ever known him by. I never knew him personally. I never even set eyes on him. And yet I seem to see him more clearly than many men, my brothers, for instance, with whom I passed my daily life for many years. He lives in my imagination with the distinctness of a Paolo Malatesta or a Romeo. But I daresay you have never read Dante or Shakespeare?"

"I can't say as I have," said the captain.

Neilson, smoking a cigar, leaned back in his chair and looked vacantly at the ring of smoke which floated in the still air. A smile played on his lips, but his eyes were grave. Then he looked at the captain. There was in his gross obesity something extraordinarily repellent. He had the plethoric self-satisfaction of the very fat. It was an outrage. It set Neilson's nerves on edge. But the contrast between the man before him and the man he had in mind was pleasant.

"It appears that Red was the most comely thing you ever saw. I've talked to quite a number of people who knew him in those days, white men, and they all agree that the first time you saw him his beauty just took your breath away. They called him Red on account of his flaming hair. It had a natural wave and he wore it long. It must have been of that wonderful color that the pre-Raphaelites raved over. I don't think he was vain of it, he was much too ingenuous for that, but no one could have blamed him if he had been. He was tall, six feet and an inch or two—in the native house that used to stand here was the mark of his height cut with a knife on the central trunk that supported the roof—and he was made like a Greek god, broad in the shoulders and thin in the flanks; he was like Apollo, with just that soft roundness which Praxiteles gave him, and that suave, feminine grace which has in it something troubling and mysterious. His skin was dazzling white, milky, like satin; his skin was like a woman's."

"I had kind of a white skin myself when I was a kiddie," said the skipper, with a twinkle in his bloodshot eyes.

But Neilson paid no attention to him. He was telling his story now and interruption made him impatient.

"And his face was just as beautiful as his body. He had large blue eyes, very dark, so that some say they were black, and unlike most red-haired people he had dark eyebrows and long, dark lashes. His features were perfectly regular and his mouth was like a scarlet wound. He was twenty."

On these words the Swede stopped with a certain sense of the dramatic. He took a sip of whisky.

"He was unique. There never was anyone more beautiful. There was no more reason for him than for a wonderful blossom to flower on a wild plant. He was a happy accident of nature.

"One day he landed at that cove into which you must have put this morning. He was an American sailor, and he had deserted from a man-of-war in Apia. He had induced some good-humored native to give him a passage on a cutter that happened to be sailing from Apia to Safoto, and he had been put ashore here in a dugout. I do not know why he deserted. Perhaps life on a man-of-war with its restrictions irked him, perhaps he was in trouble, and perhaps it was the South Seas and these romantic islands that got into his bones. Every now and then they take a man strangely, and he finds himself like a fly in a spider's web. It may be that there was a softness of fiber in him, and these green hills with their soft airs, this blue sea, took the northern strength from him as Delilah took the Nazarite's. Anyhow, he wanted to hide himself, and he thought he would be safe in this secluded nook till his ship had sailed from Samoa.

"There was a native hut at the cove and as he stood there, wondering where exactly he should turn his steps, a young girl came out and invited him to enter. He knew scarcely two words of the native tongue and she as little English. But he understood well enough what her smiles meant, and her pretty gestures, and he followed her. He sat down on a mat and she gave him slices of pineapple to eat. I can speak of Red only from hearsay, but I saw the girl three years after he first met her, and she was scarcely nineteen then. You cannot imagine how exquisite she was. She had the passionate grace of the hibiscus and the rich color. She was rather tall, slim, with the delicate features of her race, and large eyes like pools of still water under the palm trees; her hair, black and curling, fell down her back, and she wore a wreath of scented flowers. Her hands were lovely. They were so small, so exquisitely formed, they gave your heartstrings a wrench. And in those days she laughed easily. Her smile was so delightful that it made your knees shake. Her skin was like a field of ripe corn on a summer day. Good heavens, how can I describe her? She was too beautiful to be real.

"And these two young things, she was sixteen and he was twenty, fell in love with one another at first sight. That is the real love, not the love that comes from sympathy, common interests, or intellectual community, but love pure and simple. That is the love that Adam felt for Eve when he awoke and found her in the garden gazing at him with dewy eyes. That is the love that draws the beasts to one another, and the gods. That is the love that makes the world a miracle. That is the love that gives life its pregnant meaning. You have never heard of the wise, cynical French duke who said that with two lovers there is always one who loves and one who lets himself be loved; it is a bitter truth to which most of us have to resign ourselves; but now and then there are two who love and two who let themselves be loved. Then one might fancy that the sun stands still as it stood when Joshua prayed to the God of Israel.

"And even now after all these years, when I think of these two, so young, so fair, so simple, and of their love, I feel a pang. It tears my heart just as my heart is torn when on certain nights I watch the full moon shining on the lagoon from an unclouded sky. There is always pain in the contemplation of perfect beauty.

"They were children. She was good and sweet and kind. I know nothing of him, and I like to think that then at all events he was ingenuous and frank. I like to think that his soul was as comely as his body. But I daresay he had no more soul than the creatures of the woods and forests who made pipes from reeds and bathed in the mountain streams when the world was young and you might catch sight of little fauns galloping through the glade on the back of a bearded centaur. A soul is a troublesome possession and when man developed it he lost the Garden of Eden.

"Well, when Red came to the island it had recently been visited by one of those epidemics which the white man has brought to the South Seas, and one third of the inhabitants had died. It seems that the girl had lost all her near kin and she lived now in the house of distant cousins. The household consisted of two ancient crones, bowed and wrinkled, two younger women, and a man and a boy. For a few days he stayed there. But perhaps he felt himself too near the shore, with the possibility that he might fall in with white men who would reveal his hiding place; perhaps the lovers could not bear that the company of others should rob them for an instant of the delight of being together. One morning they set out, the pair of them, with the few things that belonged to the girl, and walked along a grassy path under the coconuts, till they came to the creek you see. They had to cross the bridge you crossed, and the girl laughed gleefully because he was afraid. She held his hand till they came to the end of the first tree, and then his courage failed him and he had to go back. He was obliged to take off all his clothes before he could risk it, and she carried them over for him on her head. They settled down in the empty hut that stood here. Whether she had any rights over it (land tenure is a complicated business in the islands) or whether the owner had died during the epidemic I do not know, but anyhow no one questioned them, and they took possession. Their furniture consisted of a couple of grass mats on which they slept, a fragment of looking glass, and a bowl or two. In this pleasant land that is enough to start housekeeping on.

"They say that happy people have no history, and certainly a happy love has none. They did nothing all day long and yet the days seemed all too short. The girl had a native name, but Red called her Sally. He picked up the easy language very quickly, and he used to lie on the mat for hours while she chattered gaily to him. He was a silent fellow, and perhaps his mind was lethargic. He smoked incessantly the cigarettes which she made him out of the native tobacco and pandanus leaf, and he watched her while with deft fingers she made grass mats. Often natives would come in and tell long stories of the old days when the island was disturbed by tribal wars. Sometimes he would go fishing on the reef, and bring home a basket full of colored fish. Sometimes at night he would go out with a lantern to catch lobster. There were plantains round the hut and Sally would roast them for their frugal meal. She knew how to make delicious messes from coconuts, and the breadfruit tree by the side of the creek gave them its fruit. On feast days they killed a little pig and cooked it on hot stones. They bathed together in the creek; and in the evening they went down to the lagoon and paddled about in a dugout, with its great outrigger. The sea was deep blue, wine-colored at sundown, like the sea of Homeric Greece; but in the lagoon the color had an infinite variety, aquamarine and amethyst and emerald; and the setting sun turned it for a short moment to liquid gold. Then there was the color of the coral, brown, white, pink, red, purple; and the shapes it took were marvelous. It was like a magic garden, and the hurrying fish were like butterflies. It strangely lacked reality. Among the coral were pools with a floor of white sand and here, where the water was dazzling clear, it was very good to bathe. Then, cool and happy, they wandered back in the gloaming over the soft grass road to the creek, walking hand in hand, and now the mynah birds filled the coconut trees with their clamor. And then the night, with that great sky shining with gold, that seemed to stretch more widely than the skies of Europe, and the soft airs that blew gently through the open hut, the long night again was all too short. She was sixteen and he was barely twenty. The dawn crept in among the wooden pillars of the hut and looked at those lovely children sleeping in one another's arms. The sun hid behind the great tattered leaves of the plantains so that it might not disturb them, and then, with playful malice, shot a golden ray, like the outstretched paw of a Persian cat, on their faces. They opened their sleepy eyes and they smiled to welcome another day. The weeks lengthened into months, and a year passed. They seemed to love one another as—I hesitate to say passionately, for passion has in it always a shade of sadness, a touch of bitterness or anguish, but as wholeheartedly, as simply and naturally as on that first day on which, meeting, they had recognized that a god was in them.

"If you had asked them I have no doubt that they would have thought it impossible to suppose their love could ever cease. Do we not know that the essential element of love is a belief in its own eternity? And yet perhaps in Red there was already a very little seed, unknown to himself and unsuspected by the girl, which would in time have grown to weariness. For one day one of the natives from the cove told them that some way down the coast at the anchorage was a British whaling ship.

" 'Gee,' he said, 'I wonder if I could make a trade of some nuts and plantains for a pound or two of tobacco.'

"The pandanus cigarettes that Sally made him with untiring hands were strong and pleasant enough to smoke, but they left him unsatisfied; and he yearned on a sudden for real tobacco, hard, rank, and pungent. He had not smoked a pipe for many months. His mouth watered at the thought of it. One would have thought some premonition of harm would have made Sally seek to dissuade him, but love possessed her so completely that it never occurred to her any power on earth could take him from her. They went up into the hills together and gathered a great basket of wild oranges, green, but sweet and juicy; and they picked plantains from around the hut, and coconuts from their trees, and breadfruit and mangoes; and they carried them down to the cove. They loaded the unstable canoe with them, and Red and the native boy who had brought them the news of the ship paddled along outside the reef.

"It was the last time she ever saw him.

"Next day the boy came back alone. He was all in tears. This is the story he told. When after their long paddle they reached the ship and Red hailed it, a white man looked over the side and told them to come on board. They took the fruit they had brought with them and Red piled it up on the deck. The white man and he began to talk, and they seemed to come to some agreement. One of them went below and brought up tobacco. Red took some at once and lit a pipe.

The boy imitated the zest with which he blew a great cloud of smoke from his mouth. Then they said something to him and he went into the cabin. Through the open door the boy, watching curiously, saw a bottle brought out and glasses. Red drank and smoked. They seemed to ask him something, for he shook his head and laughed. The man, the first man who had spoken to them, laughed too, and he filled Red's glass once more. They went on talking and drinking, and presently, growing tired of watching a sight that meant nothing to him, the boy curled himself up on the deck and slept. He was awakened by a kick; and, jumping to his feet, he saw that the ship was slowly sailing out of the lagoon. He caught sight of Red seated at the table, with his head resting heavily on his arms, fast asleep. He made a movement towards him, intending to wake him, but a rough hand seized his arm, and a man, with a scowl and words which he did not understand, pointed to the side. He shouted to Red, but in a moment he was seized and flung overboard. Helpless, he swam round to his canoe which was drifting a little way off, and pushed it onto the reef. He climbed in and, sobbing all the way, paddled back to shore.

"What had happened was obvious enough. The whaler, by desertion or sickness, was short of hands, and the captain when Red came aboard had asked him to sign on; on his refusal he had made him drunk and kidnaped him.

"Sally was beside herself with grief. For three days she screamed and cried. The natives did what they could to comfort her, but she would not be comforted. She would not eat. And then, exhausted, she sank into a sullen apathy. She spent long days at the cove, watching the lagoon, in the vain hope that Red somehow or other would manage to escape. She sat on the white sand, hour after hour, with the tears running down her cheeks, and at night dragged herself wearily back across the creek to the little hut where she had been happy. The people with whom she had lived before Red came to the island wished her to return to them, but she would not; she was convinced that Red would come back, and she wanted him to find her where he had left her. Four months later she was delivered of a stillborn child, and the old woman who had come to help her through her confinement remained with her in the hut. All joy was taken from her life. If her anguish with time became less intolerable it was replaced by a settled melancholy. You would not have thought that among these people, whose emotions, though so violent, are very transient, a woman could be found capable of so enduring a passion. She never lost the profound conviction that sooner or later Red would come back. She watched for him, and every time someone crossed this slender little bridge of coconut trees she looked. It might at last be he."

Neilson stopped talking and gave a faint sigh.

"And what happened to her in the end?" asked the skipper.

Neilson smiled bitterly.

"Oh, three years afterwards she took up with another white man."

The skipper gave a fat, cynical chuckle.

"That's generally what happens to them," he said.

The Swede shot him a look of hatred. He did not know why that gross, obese man excited in him so violent a repulsion. But his thoughts wandered and he found his mind filled with memories of the past. He went back five and twenty years. It was when he first came to the island, weary of Apia, with its heavy drinking, its gambling and coarse sensuality, a sick man, trying to resign himself to the loss of the career that had fired his imagination with ambitious thoughts. He set behind him resolutely all his hopes of making a great name for himself and strove to content himself with the few poor months of careful life that was all that he could count on. He was boarding with a half-caste trader who had a store a couple of miles along the coast at the edge of a native village; and one day, wandering aimlessly along the grassy paths of the coconut groves, he had come upon the hut in which Sally lived. The beauty of the spot had filled him with a rapture so great that it was almost painful, and then he had seen Sally. She was the loveliest creature he had ever seen, and the sadness in those dark, magnificent eyes of hers affected him strangely. The Kanakas were a handsome race, and beauty was not rare among them, but it was the beauty of shapely animals. It was empty. But those tragic eyes were dark with mystery, and you felt in them the bitter complexity of the groping, human soul. The trader told him the story and it moved him.

"Do you think he'll ever come back?" asked Neilson.

"No fear. Why, it'll be a couple of years before the ship is paid off, and by then he'll have forgotten all about her. I bet he was pretty mad when he woke up and found he'd been shanghaied, and I shouldn't wonder but he wanted to fight somebody. But he'd got to grin and bear it, and I guess in a month he was thinking it the best thing that had ever happened to him that he got away from the island."

But Neilson could not get the story out of his head. Perhaps because he was sick and weakly, the radiant health of Red appealed to his imagination. Himself an ugly man, insignificant of appearance, he prized very highly comeliness in others. He had never been passionately in love, and certainly he had never been passionately loved. The mutual attraction of those two young things gave him a singular delight. It had the ineffable beauty of the Absolute. He went again to the little hut by the creek. He had a gift for languages and an energetic mind, accustomed to work, and he had already given much time to the study of the local tongue. Old habit was strong in him and he was gathering together material for a paper on the Samoan speech. The old crone who shared the hut with Sally invited him to come in and sit down. She gave him kava to drink and cigarettes to smoke. She was glad to have someone to chat with and while she talked he looked at Sally. She reminded him of the Psyche in the museum at Naples. Her features had the same clear purity of line, and though she had borne a child she had still a virginal aspect.

It was not till he had seen her two or three times that he induced her to speak. Then it was only to ask him if he had seen in Apia a man called Red. Two years had passed since his disappearance, but it was plain that she still thought of him incessantly.

It did not take Neilson long to discover that he was in love with her. It was only by an effort of will now that he prevented himself from going every day to the creek, and when he was not with Sally his thoughts were. At first, looking upon himself as a dying man, he asked only to look at her, and occasionally hear her speak, and his love gave him a wonderful happiness. He exulted in its purity. He wanted nothing from her but the opportunity to weave around her graceful person a web of beautiful fancies. But the open air, the equable temperature, the rest, the simple fare, began to have an unexpected effect on his health. His temperature did not soar at night to such alarming heights, he coughed less and began to put on weight; six months passed without his having a hemorrhage; and on a sudden he saw the possibility that he might live. He had studied his disease carefully, and the hope dawned upon him that with great care he might arrest its course. It exhilarated him to look forward once more to the future. He made plans. It was evident that any active life was out of the question, but he could live on the islands, and the small income he had, insufficient elsewhere, would be ample to keep him. He could grow coconuts; that would give him an occupation; and he would send for his books and a piano; but his quick mind saw that in all this he was merely trying to conceal from himself the desire which obsessed him.

He wanted Sally. He loved not only her beauty, but that dim soul that he divined behind her suffering eyes. He would intoxicate her with his passion. In the end he would make her forget. And in an ecstasy of surrender he fancied himself giving her too the happiness which he had thought never to know again, but had now so miraculously achieved.

He asked her to live with him. She refused. He had expected that and did not let it depress him, for he was sure that sooner or later she would yield. His love was irresistible. He told the old woman of his wishes, and found somewhat to his surprise that she and the neighbors, long aware of them, were strongly urging Sally to accept his offer. After all, every native was glad to keep house for a white man, and Neilson according to the standards of the island was a rich one. The trader with whom he boarded went to her and told her not to be a fool; such an opportunity would not come again, and after so long she could not still believe that Red would ever return. The girl's resistance only increased Neilson's desire, and what had been a very pure love now became an agonizing passion. He was determined that nothing should stand in his way. He gave Sally no peace. At last, worn out by his persistence and the persuasions, by turns pleading and angry, of everyone around her, she consented. But the day after when, exultant, he went to see her he found that in the night she had burned down the hut in which she and Red had lived together. The old crone ran towards him full of angry abuse of Sally, but he waved her aside; it did not matter; they would build a bungalow on the place where the hut had stood. A European house would really be more convenient if he wanted to bring out a piano and a vast number of books.

And so the little wooden house was built in which he had now lived for many years, and Sally became his wife. But after the first few weeks of rapture, during which he was satisfied with what she gave him, he had known little happiness. She had yielded to him, through weariness, but she had only yielded what she set no store on. The soul that he had dimly glimpsed escaped him. He knew that she cared nothing for him. She still loved Red, and all the time she was waiting for his return. At a sign from him, Neilson knew that, notwithstanding his love, his tenderness, his sympathy, his generosity, she would leave him without a moment's hesitation. She would never give a thought to his distress. Anguish seized him and he battered at that impenetrable self of hers that sullenly resisted him. His love became bitter. He tried to melt her heart with kindness, but it remained as hard as before; he feigned indifference, but she did not notice it. Sometimes he lost his temper and abused her, and then she wept silently. Sometimes he thought she was nothing but a fraud, and that soul simply an invention of his own, and that he could not get into the sanctuary of her heart because there was no sanctuary there. His love became a prison from which he longed to escape, but he had not the strength merely to open the door—that was all it needed—and walk out into the open air. It was torture and at last he became numb and hopeless. In the end the fire burned itself out and, when he saw her eyes rest for an instant on the slender bridge, it was no longer rage that filled his heart but impatience. For many years now they had lived together bound by the ties of habit and convenience, and it was with a smile that he looked back on his old passion. She was an old woman, for the women on the islands age quickly, and if he had no love for her any more he had tolerance. She left him alone. He was contented with his piano and his books.

His thoughts led him to a desire for words.

"When I look back now and reflect on that brief passionate love of Red and Sally, I think that perhaps they should thank the ruthless fate that separated them when their love seemed still to be at its height. They suffered, but they suffered in beauty. They were spared the real tragedy of love."

"I don't know exactly as I get you," said the skipper.

"The tragedy of love is not death or separation. How long do you think it would have been before one or other of them ceased to care? Oh, it is dreadfully bitter to look at a woman whom you have loved with all your heart and soul, so that you felt you could not bear to let her out of your sight, and realize that you would not mind if you never saw her again. The tragedy of love is indifference."

But while he was speaking a very extraordinary thing happened. Though he had been addressing the skipper he had not been talking to him, he had been putting his thoughts into words for himself, and with his eyes fixed on the man in front of him he had not seen him. But now an image presented itself to them, an image not of the man he saw, but of another man. It was as though he were looking into one of those distorting mirrors that make you extraordinarily squat or outrageously elongate, but here exactly the opposite took place, and in the obese, ugly old man he caught the shadowy glimpse of a stripling. He gave him now a quick, searching scrutiny. Why had a haphazard stroll brought him just to this place? A sudden tremor of his heart made him slightly breathless. An absurd suspicion seized him. What had occurred to him was impossible, and yet it might be a fact.

"What is your name?" he asked abruptly.

The skipper's face puckered and he gave a cunning chuckle. He looked then malicious and horribly vulgar.

"It's such a damned long time since I heard it that I almost forget it myself. But for thirty years now in the islands they've always called me Red."

His huge form shook as he gave a low, almost silent laugh. It was obscene. Neilson shuddered. Red was hugely amused, and from his bloodshot eyes tears ran down his cheeks.

Neilson gave a gasp, for at that moment a woman came in. She was a native, a woman of somewhat commanding presence, stout without being corpulent, dark, for the natives grow darker with age, with very gray hair. She wore a black Mother Hubbard, and its thinness showed her heavy breasts. The moment had come.

She made an observation to Neilson about some household matter and he answered. He wondered if his voice sounded as unnatural to her as it did to himself. She gave the man who was sitting in the chair by the window an indifferent glance, and went out of the room. The moment had come and gone.

Neilson for a moment could not speak. He was strangely shaken. Then he said:

"I'd be very glad if you'd stay and have a bit of dinner with me. Pot luck."

"I don't think I will," said Red. "I must go after this fellow Gray. I'll give him his stuff and then I'll get away. I want to be back in Apia tomorrow."

"I'll send a boy along with you to show you the way."

"That'll be fine."

Red heaved himself out of his chair, while the Swede called one of the boys who worked on the plantation. He told him where the skipper wanted to go, and the boy stepped along the bridge. Red prepared to follow him.

"Don't fall in," said Neilson.

"Not on your life."

Neilson watched him make his way across and when he had disappeared among the coconuts he looked still. Then he sank heavily in his chair. Was that the man who had prevented him from being happy? Was that the man whom Sally had loved all these years and for whom she had waited so desperately? It was grotesque. A sudden fury seized him so that he had an instinct to spring up and smash everything around him. He had been cheated. They had seen each other at last and had not known it. He began to laugh, mirthlessly, and his laughter grew till it became hysterical. The gods had played him a cruel trick. And he was old now.

At last Sally came in to tell him dinner was ready. He sat down in front of her and tried to eat. He wondered what she would say if he told her now that the fat old man sitting in the chair was the lover whom she remembered still with the passionate abandonment of her youth. Years ago, when he hated her because she made him so unhappy, he would have been glad to tell her. He wanted to hurt her then as she hurt him, because his hatred was only love. But now he did not care. He shrugged his shoulders listlessly.

"What did that man want?" she asked presently.

He did not answer at once. She was old too, a fat, old native woman. He wondered why he had ever loved her so madly. He had laid at her feet all the treasures of his soul, and she had cared nothing for them. Waste, what waste! And now, when he looked at her, he felt only contempt. His patience was at last exhausted. He answered her question.

"He's the captain of a schooner. He's come from Apia."

"Yes."

"He brought me news from home. My eldest brother is very ill and I must go back."

"Will you be gone long?"

He shrugged his shoulders.

John Russell

THE FOURTH MAN

John Russell (1885–1958) was born in Davenport, Iowa. After two years at Northwestern University he became a special correspondent for several New York papers. During World War I he was in charge of United States government propaganda in Great Britain and Ireland. He traveled widely in South America and Asia and during the 1920's went to the South Pacific in search of material. Three of his volumes of stories were collected under one cover and published in 1930 as *Color of the East*. The book included *The Red Mark,* 1919 (British title, *Where the Pavement Ends,* 1921); *In Dark Places,* 1922; and *Far Wandering Men,* 1928.

The following story has a surprise ending, but the surprise is not an unfair one. As in several others among Russell's well-plotted South Sea yarns, such as "Jetsam" or "The Price of the Head," the outcome is ironic but not illogical.

THE RAFT MIGHT HAVE BEEN TAKEN FOR A SWATH OF CUT SEDGE or a drifting tangle of roots as it slid out of the shadowy river mouth at dawn and dipped into the first ground swell. But while the sky brightened and the breeze came fresh offshore it picked a way among shoals and swampy islets with purpose and direction, and when at last the sun leaped up and cleared his bright eye of the morning mist it had passed the wide entrance to the bay and stood to open sea.

It was a curious craft for such a venture, of a type that survives here and there in the obscure corners of the world. The coracle maker would have scorned it. The first navigating pithecanthrope built nearly as well with his log and bush. A mat of pandanus leaves served for its sail and a paddle of *niaouli* wood for its helm. But it had a single point of real seaworthiness. Its twin floats, paired as a catamaran, were woven of reed bundles and bamboo sticks upon triple rows of bladders. It was light as a bladder itself, elastic, fit to ride any weather. One other quality this raft possessed that recommended it beyond all comfort and all safety to its present crew. It was very nearly invisible. They had only to unstep its mast and lie flat in the cup of its soggy platform and they could not be spied half a mile away.

Four men occupied the raft. Three of them were white. Their bodies had been scored with brambles and blackened with dried blood, and on wrist and ankle they bore the dark and wrinkled stain of the gyves. The hair upon them was long and matted. They wore only the rags of blue canvas uniforms. But they were whites, members of the superior race—members of a highly superior race according to those philosophers who rate the criminal aberration as a form of genius.

The fourth was the man who had built the raft and was now sailing it. There was nothing superior about him. His skin was a layer of soot. His prognathous jaw carried out the angle of a low forehead. No line of beauty redeemed his lean limbs and knobby joints. Nature had set upon him her plainest stamp of inferiority, and his only attempts to relieve it were the twist of bark about his middle and the prong of pig ivory through the cartilage of his nose. Altogether a very ordinary specimen of one of the lowest branches of the human family—the *Canaques* of New Caledonia.

The three whites sat together well forward, and so they had sat in silence for hours. But at sunrise, as if some spell had been raised by the clang of that great copper gong in the east, they stirred and breathed deep of the salt air and looked at one another with hope in their haggard faces, and then back toward the land that was now no more than a gray-green smudge behind them. "Friends," said the eldest, whose temples were bound with a scrap of crimson scarf, "Friends—the thing is done."

With a gesture like conjuring he produced from the breast

of his tattered blouse three cigarettes, fresh and round, and offered them.

"Nippers!" cried the one at his right. "True nippers—name of a little good man! And here? Doctor, I always said you were a marvel. See if they be not new from the box!"

Dr. Dubosc smiled. Those who had known him in very different circumstances about the boulevards, the lobbies, the clubs, would have known him again and in spite of all disfigurement by that smile. And here, at the bottom of the earth, it had set him still apart in the prisons, the cobalt mines, the chain gangs of a community not much given to mirth. Many a crowded lecture hall at Montpellier had seen him touch some intellectual firework with just such a twinkle behind his bristly gray brows, with just such a thin curl of lip.

"By way of celebration," he explained. "Consider. There are seventy-five evasions from Nouméa every six months, of which not more than one succeeds. I had the figures myself from Dr. Pierre at the infirmary. He is not much of a physician, but a very honest fellow. Could anybody win on that percentage without dissipating? I ask you."

"Therefore you prepared for this?"

"It is now three weeks since I bribed the night guard to get these same nippers."

The other regarded him with admiration. Sentiment came readily upon this beardless face, tender and languid, but overdrawn, with eyes too large and soft and oval too long. It was one of those faces familiar enough to the police which might serve as model for an angel were it not associated with some revolting piece of devilry. Fenayrou himself had been condemned "to perpetuity" as an incorrigible.

"Is not our doctor a wonder?" he inquired as he handed a cigarette along to the third white man. "He thinks of everything. You should be ashamed to grumble. See—we are free, after all. Free!"

The third was a gross, pock-marked man with hairless lids known sometimes as *Niniche, Trois Huit, Le Tordeur,* but chiefly among *copains* as *Perroquet*—a name derived perhaps from his beaked nose, or from some perception of his jailbird character. He was a garroter by profession, accustomed to rely upon his fists only for the exchange of amenities. Dubosc might indulge a fancy and Fenayrou seek to carry it as a pose, but The Parrot remained a gentleman of strictly serious turn. There is perhaps a tribute to the practical spirit of penal administration in the fact that while Dubosc was the most dangerous of these three and Fenayrou the most depraved, Perroquet was the one with the official reputation, whose escape would be signaled first among the "Wanted." He accepted the cigarette because he was glad to get it, but he said nothing until Dubosc passed a tin box of matches and the first gulp of *picadura* filled his lungs.

"Wait till you've got your two feet on a *pavé,* my boy. That will be the time to talk of freedom. What? Suppose there came a storm."

"It is not the season of storms," observed Dubosc.

But The Parrot's word had given them a check. Such spirits as these, to whom the land had been a horror, would be slow to feel the terror of the sea. Back there they had left the festering limbo of a convict colony, oblivion. Out here they had reached the rosy threshold of the big round world again. They were men raised from the dead, charged with all the furious appetites of lost years, with the savor of life strong and sweet on their lips. And yet they paused and looked about in quickened perception, with the clutch at the throat that takes the landsman on big waters. The spaces were so wide and empty. The voices in their ears were so strange and murmurous. There was a threat in each wave that came from the depths, a sinister vibration. None of them knew the sea. None knew its ways, what tricks it might play, what traps it might spread—more deadly than those of the jungle.

The raft was running now before a brisk chop with alternate spring and wallow, while the froth bubbled in over the prow and ran down among them as they sat. "Where is that cursed ship that was to meet us here?" demanded Fenayrou.

"It will meet us right enough." Dobosc spoke carelessly, though behind the blown wisp of his cigarette he had been searching the outer horizon with keen glance. "This is the day, as agreed. We will be picked up off the mouth of the river."

"You say," growled Perroquet. "But where is any river now? Or any mouth? Sacred name, this wind will blow us to China if we keep on."

"We dare not lie in any closer. There is a government launch at Torrien. Also the traders go armed hereabouts, ready for chaps like us. And don't imagine that the native trackers have given us up. They are likely to be following still in their proas."

"So far!"

Fenayrou laughed, for The Parrot's dread of their savage enemies had a morbid tinge.

"Take care, Perroquet. They will eat you yet."

"Is it true?" demanded the other, appealing to Dubosc. "I have heard it is even permitted these devils to keep all runaways they can capture—name of God!—to fatten on."

"An idle tale," smiled Dubosc. "They prefer the reward. But one hears of convicts being badly mauled. There was a forester who made a break from Baie du Sud and came back lacking an arm. Certainly these people have not lost the habit of cannibalism."

"Piecemeal," chuckled Fenayrou. "They will only sample you, Perroquet. Let them make a stew of your brains. You would miss nothing."

But The Parrot swore.

"Name of a name—what brutes!" he said, and by a gesture recalled the presence of that fourth man who was of their party and yet so completely separated from them that they had almost forgotten him.

The *Canaque* was steering the raft. He sat crouched at the stern, his body glistening like varnished ebony with spray. He held the steering paddle, immobile as an image, his eyes fixed upon the course ahead. There was no trace of expression on his face, no hint of what he thought or felt or whether he thought or felt anything. He seemed not even aware of their regard, and each one of them experienced somehow that twinge of uneasiness with which the white confronts his brother of color—this enigma brown or yellow or black he is fated never wholly to understand or to fathom.

"It occurs to me," said Fenayrou, in a pause, "that our friend here who looks like a shiny boot is able to steer us God knows where. Perhaps to claim the reward."

"Reassure yourself," answered Dobosc. "He steers by my order. Besides, it is a simple creature—an infant, truly, incapable of any but the most primitive reasoning."

"Is he incapable of treachery?"

"Of any that would deceive us. Also, he is bound by his duty. I made my bargain with his chief, up the river, and this one is sent to deliver us on board our ship. It is the only interest he has in us."

"And he will do it?"

"He will do it. Such is the nature of the native."

"I am glad you feel so," returned Fenayrou, adjusting himself indolently among the drier reeds and nursing the last of his cigarette. "For my part I wouldn't trust a figurehead like that for two sous. *Mazette!* What a monkey face!"

"Brute!" repeated Perroquet, and this man, sprung from some vile river-front slum of Argenteuil, whose home had been the dock pilings, the grog shop, and the jail, even this man viewed the black *Canaque* from an immeasurable distance with the look of hatred and contempt.

Under the heat of the day the two younger convicts lapsed presently into dozing. But Dubosc did not doze. His tormented soul peered out behind its mask as he stood to sweep the skyline again under shaded hand. His theory had been so precise, the fact was so different. He had counted absolutely on meeting the ship—some small schooner, one of those flitting, half-piratical traders of the copra islands that can be hired like cabs in a dark street for any questionable enterprise. Now there was no ship, and here was no crossroads where one might sit and wait. Such a craft as the catamaran could not be made to lie to.

The doctor foresaw ugly complications for which he had not prepared and whereof he must bear the burden. The escape had been his own conception, directed by him from the start. He had picked his companions deliberately from the whole forced-labor squad, Perroquet for his great strength, Fenayrou as a ready echo. He had made it plain since their first dash from the mine, during their skirmish with the military guards, their subsequent wanderings in the brush with bloodhounds and trackers on the trail—through every crisis—that he alone should be the leader.

For the others, they had understood well enough which of their number was the chief beneficiary. Those mysterious friends on the outside that were reaching half around the world to further their release had never heard of such individuals as Fenayrou and The Parrot. Dubosc was the man who had pulled the wires: that brilliant physician whose conviction for murder had followed so sensationally, so scandalously, upon his sweep of academic and social honors. There would be clacking tongues in many a Parisian salon, and white faces in some, when news should come of his escape. Ah, yes, for example, they knew the highflier of the band, and they submitted—so long as he led them to victory. They submitted, while reserving a depth of jealousy, the inevitable remnant of caste persisting still in this democracy of stripes and shame.

By the middle of the afternoon the doctor had taken certain necessary measures.

"Ho!" said Fenayrou sleepily. "Behold our colors at the masthead. What is that for, comrade?"

The sail had been lowered and in its place streamed the scrap of crimson scarf that had served Dubosc as a turban.

"To help them sight us when the ship comes."

"What wisdom!" cried Fenayrou. "Always he thinks of everything, our doctor: everything—"

He stopped with the phrase on his lips, and his hand outstretched toward the center of the platform. Here, in a damp depression among the reeds, had lain the wicker-covered bottle of green glass in which they carried their water. It was gone.

"Where is that flask?" he demanded. "The sun has grilled me like a bone."

"You will have to grill some more," said Dubosc grimly. "This crew is put on rations."

Fenayrou stared at him wide-eyed, and from the shadow of a folded mat The Parrot thrust his purpled face. "What do you sing me there? Where is that water?"

"I have it," said Dubosc.

They saw, in fact, that he held the flask between his knees, along with their single packet of food in its wrapping of coconut husk.

"I want a drink," challenged Perroquet.

"Reflect a little. We must guard our supplies like reasonable men. One does not know how long we may be floating here. . . ."

Fell a silence among them, heavy and strained, in which they heard only the squeaking of frail basketwork as their raft labored in the wash. Slow as was their progress, they were being pushed steadily outward and onward, and the last cliffs of New Caledonia were no longer even a smudge in the west, but only a hazy line. And still they had seen no moving thing upon the great round breast of the sea that gleamed in its corselet of brass plates under a brazen sun. "So that is the way you talk now?" began The Parrot, half-choking. "You do not know how long? But you were sure enough when we started."

"I am still sure," returned Dubosc. "The ship will come. Only she cannot stay for us in one spot. She will be cruising to and fro until she intercepts us. We must wait."

"Ah, good! We must wait. And in the meantime, what? Fry here in the sacred heat with our tongues hanging out while you deal us drop by drop—*hein?*"

"Perhaps."

"But no!" The garroter clenched his hands. "Blood of God, there is no man big enough to feed me with a spoon!"

Fenayrou's chuckle came pat, as it had more than once, and Dubosc shrugged.

"You laugh!" cried Perroquet, turning in fury. "But how about this lascar of a captain that lets us put to sea unprovided? What? He thinks of everything, does he? He thinks of everything! . . . Sacred *farceur*—let me hear you laugh again!"

Somehow Fenayrou was not so minded.

"And now he bids us be reasonable," concluded The Parrot. "Tell that to the devils in hell. You and your cigarettes, too. Bah—comedian!"

"It is true," muttered Fenayrou, frowning. "A bad piece of work for a captain of runaways."

But the doctor faced mutiny with his thin smile.

"All this alters nothing. Unless we would die very speedily, we must guard our water."

"By whose fault?"

"Mine," acknowledged the doctor. "I admit it. What then? We can't turn back. Here we are. Here we must stay. We can only do our best with what we have."

"I want a drink," repeated The Parrot, whose throat was afire since he had been denied.

"You can claim your share, of course. But take warning of one thing. After it is gone do not think to sponge on us—on Fenayrou and me."

"He would be capable of it, the pig!" exclaimed Fenayrou, to whom this thrust had been directed. "I know him. See here, my old, the doctor is right. Fair for one, fair for all."

"I want a drink."

Dubosc removed the wooden plug from the flask.

"Very well," he said quietly.

With the delicacy that lent something of legerdemain to all his gestures, he took out a small canvas wallet, the crude equivalent of the professional black bag, from which he drew a thimble. Meticulously he poured a brimming measure, and Fenayrou gave a shout at the grumbler's fallen jaw as he accepted that tiny cup between his big fingers. Dubosc served Fenayrou and himself with the same amount before he recorked the bottle.

"In this manner we should have enough to last us three days—maybe more—with equal shares among the three of us."

Such was his summing of the demonstration, and it passed without comment, as a matter of course in the premises, that he should count as he did—ignoring that other who sat alone at the stern of the raft, the black *Canaque,* the fourth man.

Perroquet had been outmaneuvered, but he listened sullenly while for the hundredth time Dubosc recited his easy and definite plan for their rescue, as arranged with his secret correspondents.

"That sounds very well," observed The Parrot, at last. "But what if these jokers only mock themselves of you? What if they have counted it good riddance to let you rot here? And us? Sacred name, that would be a famous jest! To let us wait for a ship and they have no ship!"

"Perhaps the doctor knows better than we how sure a source he counts upon," suggested Fenayrou slyly.

"That is so," said Dubosc, with great good humor. "My faith, it would not be well for them to fail me. Figure to yourselves that there is a safety vault in Paris full of papers to be opened at my death. Certain friends of mine could hardly afford to have some little confessions published that would be found there. . . . Such a tale as this, for instance—"

And to amuse them he told an indecent anecdote of high life, true or fictitious, it mattered nothing, so he could make Fenayrou's eyes glitter and The Parrot growl in wonder. Therein lay his means of ascendancy over such men, the knack of eloquence and vision. Harried, worn, oppressed by fears that he could sense so much more sharply than they, he must expend himself now in vulgar marvels to distract these ruder minds. He succeeded so far that when the wind fell at sunset they were almost cheerful, ready to believe that the morning would bring relief. They dined on dry biscuit and another thimbleful of water apiece and took watch by amiable agreement. And through that long, clear night of stars, whenever the one of the three who kept awake between his comrades chanced to look aft, he could see the vague blot of another figure—the naked *Canaque,* who slumbered there apart.

It was an evil dawning. Fenayrou, on the morning trick, was aroused by a foot as hard as a hoof, and started up at Perroquet's wrathful face, with the doctor's graver glance behind.

"Idler! Good-for-nothing! Will you wake at least before I smash your ribs? Name of God, here is a way to stand watch!"

"Keep off!" cried Fenayrou wildly. "Keep off. Don't touch me!"

"Eh, and why not, fool? Do you know that the ship could have missed us? A ship could have passed us a dozen times while you slept?"

"Bourrique!"

"Vache!"

They spat the insults of the prison while Perroquet knotted his great fist over the other, who crouched away catlike, his mobile mouth twisted to a snarl. Dubosc stood aside in watchful calculation until against the angry red sunrise in which they floated there flashed the naked red gleam of steel. Then he stepped between.

"Enough. Fenayrou, put up that knife."

"The dog kicked me!"

"You were at fault," said Dubosc sternly. "Perroquet!"

"Are we all to die that he may sleep?" stormed The Parrot.

"The harm is done. Listen now, both of you. Things are bad enough already. We may need all our energies. Look about."

They looked and saw the far, round horizon and the empty desert of the sea and their own long shadows that slipped slowly before them over its smooth, slow heaving, and nothing else. The land had sunk away from them in the night—some one of the chance currents that sweep among the islands had drawn them none could say where or how far. The trap had been sprung. "Good God, how lonely it is!" breathed Fenayrou in a hush.

No more was said. They dropped their quarrel. Silently they shared their rations as before, made shift to eat something with their few drops of water, and sat down to pit themselves one against another in the vital struggle that each could feel was coming—a sort of tacit test of endurance.

A calm had fallen, as it does between trades in this flawed belt, an absolute calm. The air hung weighted. The sea showed no faintest crinkle, only the maddening, unresting heave and fall in polished undulations on which the lances of the sun broke and drove in under their eyelids as white, hot splinters; a savage sun that kindled upon them with the power of a burning glass, that sucked the moisture from poor human bits of jelly and sent them crawling to the shelter of their mats and brought them out again, gasping, to shrivel anew. The water, the world of water, seemed sleek and thick as oil. They came to loathe it and the rotting smell of it, and when the doctor made them dip themselves overside they found little comfort. It was warm, sluggish, slimed. But a curious thing resulted.

While they clung along the edge of the raft they all faced inboard, and there sat the black *Canaque*. He did not join them. He did not glance at them. He sat hunkered on his heels in the way of the native, with arms hugging his knees. He stayed in his place at the stern, motionless under that shattering sun, gazing out into vacancy. Whenever they raised their eyes they saw him. He was the only thing to see.

"Here is one who appears to enjoy himself quite well," remarked Dubosc.

"I was thinking so myself," said Fenayrou.

"The animal!" rumbled Perroquet.

They observed him, and for the first time with direct interest, with thought of him as a fellow being—with the beginning of envy.

"He does not seem to suffer."

"What is going on in his brain? What does he dream of there? One would say he despises us."

"The beast!"

"Perhaps he is waiting for us to die," suggested Fenayrou with a harsh chuckle. "Perhaps he is waiting for the reward. He would not starve on the way home, at least. And he could deliver us—piecemeal."

They studied him.

"How does he do it, doctor? Has he no feeling?"

"I have been wondering," said Dubosc. "It may be that his fibers are tougher—his nerves."

"Yet we have had water and he none."

"But look at his skin, fresh and moist."

"And his belly, fat as a football!"

The Parrot hauled himself aboard.

"Don't tell me this black beast knows thirst!" he cried with a strange excitement. "Is there any way he could steal our supplies?"

"Certainly not."

"Then, name of a dog, what if he has supplies of his own hidden about?"

The same monstrous notion struck them all, and the others swarmed to help. They knocked the black aside. They searched the platform where he had sat, burrowing among the rushes, seeking some secret cache, another bottle or a gourd. They found nothing.

"We were mistaken," said Dubosc.

But Perroquet had a different expression for disappointment. He turned on the *Canaque* and caught him by the kinky mop of the hair and proceeded to give him what is known as gruel in the cobalt mines. This was a little specialty of The Parrot's. He paused only when he himself was breathless and exhausted and threw the limp, unresisting body from him.

"There, lump of dirt! That will teach you. Maybe you're not so chipper now, my boy—*hein?* Not quite so satisfied with your luck. Pig! That will make you feel . . ."

It was a ludicrous, a wanton, a witless thing. But the others said nothing. The learned Dubosc made no protest. Fenayrou had none of his usual jests at the garroter's stupidity. They looked on as at the satisfaction of a common grudge. The white trampled the black with or without cause, and that was natural. And the black crept away into his place with his hurts and his wrongs and made no sign and struck no blow. And that was natural too.

The sun declined into a blazing furnace whereof the gates stood wide, and they prayed to hasten it and cursed because it hung enchanted. But when it was gone their blistered bodies still held the heat like things incandescent. The night closed down over them like a purple bow, glazed and impermeable. They would have divided the watches again, though none of them thought of sleep, but Fenayrou made a discovery.

"Idiots!" he rasped. "Why should we look and look? A whole navy of ships cannot help us now. If we are becalmed, why so are they!"

The Parrot was singularly put out.

"Is this true?" he asked Dubosc.

"Yes, we must hope for a breeze first."

"Then, name of God, why didn't you tell us so? Why did you keep on playing out the farce?"

He pondered it for a time. "See here," The Parrot said. "You are wise, eh? You are very wise. You know things we do not and you keep them to yourself." He leaned forward to peer into the doctor's face. "Very good. But if you think you're going to use that cursed smartness to get the best of us in any way—see here, my zig, I pull your gullet out like the string of an orange—like that. What?"

Fenayrou gave a nervous giggle and Dubosc shrugged, but it was perhaps about this time that he began to regret his intervention in the knife play.

For there was no breeze and there was no ship.

By the third morning each had sunk within himself, away from the rest. The doctor was lost in a profound depression, Perroquet in dark suspicion, and Fenayrou in bodily suffering, which he supported ill. Only two effective ties still bound their confederacy. One was the flask which Dubosc had slung at his side by a strip of the wickerwork. Every move he made with it, every drop he poured, was followed by burning eyes. And he knew, and he had no advantage of them in knowing, that the will to live was working its relentless formula aboard that raft. Under his careful saving there still remained nearly half of their original store.

The other bond, as it had come to be by strange mutation, was the presence of the black *Canaque.*

There was no forgetting the fourth man now, no overlooking of him. He loomed upon their consciousness, more formidable, more mysterious, more exasperating with every hour. Their own powers were ebbing. The naked savage had yet to give the slightest sign of complaint or weakness.

During the night he had stretched himself out on the platform as before, and after a time he had slept. Through the hours of darkness and silence while each of the whites wrestled with despair, this black man had slept as placidly as a child, with easy, regular breathing. Since then he had resumed his place aft. And so he remained, unchanged, a fixed fact and a growing wonder.

The brutal rage of Perroquet, in which he had vented his distorted hate of the native, had been followed by superstitious doubts.

"Doctor," he said at last, in awed huskiness, "is this a man or a fiend?"

"It is a man."

"A miracle," put in Fenayrou.

But the doctor lifted a finger in a way his pupils would have remembered:

"It is a man," he repeated, "and a very poor and wretched example of a man. You will find no lower type anywhere. Observe his cranial angle, the high ears, the heavy bones of his skull. He is scarcely above the ape. There are educated apes more intelligent."

"Ah! Then what?"

"He has a secret," said the doctor.

That was a word to transfix them.

"A secret! But we see him—every move he makes, every instant. What chance for a secret?"

The doctor rather forgot his audience, betrayed by chagrin and bitterness.

"How pitiful!" he mused. "Here are we three—children of the century, products of civilization—I fancy none would deny that, at least. And here is this man who belongs before the Stone Age. In a set trial of fitness, of wits, of resource, is he to win? Pitiful!"

"What kind of secret?" demanded Perroquet, fuming.

"I cannot say," admitted Dubosc, with a baffled gesture. "Possibly some method of breathing, some peculiar posture that operates to cheat the sensations of the body. Such things are known among primitive peoples—known and carefully guarded—like the properties of certain drugs, the uses of hypnotism and complex natural laws. Then, again, it may be psychologic—a mental attitude persistently held. Who knows?

"To ask him? Useless. He will not tell. Why should he? We scorn him. We give him no share with us. We abuse him.

He simply falls back on his own expedients. He simply remains inscrutable—as he has always been and will always be. He never tells those innermost secrets. They are the means by which he has survived from the depth of time, by which he may yet survive when all our wisdom is dust."

"I know several very excellent ways of learning secrets," said Fenayrou as he passed his dry tongue over his lips. "Shall I begin?"

Dubosc came back with a start and looked at him.

"It would be useless. He could stand any torture you could invent. No, that is not the way."

"Listen to mine," said Perroquet, with sudden violence. "Me, I am wearied of the gab. You say he is a man? Very well. If he is a man, he must have blood in his veins. That would be, anyway, good to drink."

"No," returned Dubosc. "It would be hot. Also it would be salt. For food—perhaps. But we do not need food."

"Kill the animal, then, and throw him over!"

"We gain nothing."

"Well, sacred name, what do you want?"

"To beat him!" cried the doctor, curiously agitated. "To beat him at the game—that's what I want! For our own sakes, for our racial pride, we must, we must. To outlast him, to prove ourselves his masters. By better brain, by better organization and control. Watch him, watch him, friends—that we may ensnare him, that we may detect and defeat him in the end!"

But the doctor was miles beyond them.

"Watch?" growled The Parrot. "I believe you, old windbag. It is all one watch. I sleep no more and leave any man alone with that bottle."

To this the issue finally sharpened. Such craving among such men could not be stayed much longer by driblets. They watched. They watched the *Canaque*. They watched each other. And they watched the falling level in their flask—until the tension gave.

Another dawn upon the same dead calm, rising like a conflagration through the puddled air, cloudless, hopeless! Another day of blinding, slow-drawn agony to meet. And

Dubosc announced that their allowance must be cut to half a thimbleful.

There remained perhaps a quarter of a liter—a miserable reprieve of bare life among the three of them, but one good swallow for a yearning throat.

At sight of the bottle, at the tinkle of its limpid contents, so cool and silvery green inside the glass, Fenayrou's nerve snapped.

"More!" he begged, with pleading hands. "I die. More!"

When the doctor refused him he groveled among the reeds, then rose suddenly to his knees and tossed his arms abroad with a hoarse cry:

"A ship! A ship!"

The others spun about. They saw the thin unbroken ring of this greater and more terrible prison to which they had exchanged: and that was all they saw, though they stared and stared. They turned back to Fenayrou and found him in the act of tilting the bottle. A cunning slash of his knife had loosed it from its sling at the doctor's side. Even now he was sucking at the mouth, spilling the precious liquid—

With one sweep Perroquet caught up their paddle and flattened him, crushed him.

Springing across the prostrate man, Dubosc snatched the flask upright and put the width of the raft between himself and the big garroter who stood wide-legged, his bloodshot eyes alight, rumbling in his chest.

"There is no ship," said The Parrot. "There will be no ship. We are done. Because of you and your rotten promises that brought us here—doctor, liar, ass!"

Dubosc stood firm.

"Come a step nearer and I break bottle and all over your head."

They stood regarding each other, and Perroquet's brows gathered in a slow effort of thought.

"Consider," urged Dubosc with his quaint touch of pedantry. "Why should you and I fight? We are rational men. We can see this trouble through and win yet. Such weather cannot last for ever. Besides, there are only two of us to divide the water now."

"That is true," nodded The Parrot. "That is true, isn't it? Fenayrou kindly leaves us his share. An inheritance—what? A famous idea. I'll take mine now."

Dubosc probed him keenly.

"My share, at once, if you please," insisted Perroquet, with heavy docility. "Afterward, we shall see. Afterward."

The doctor smiled his grim and wan little smile.

"So be it."

Without relinquishing the flask he brought out his canvas wallet once more—that wallet that replaced the professional black bag—and rolled out the thimble by some swift sleight of his flexible fingers while he held Perroquet's glance with his own.

"I will measure it for you."

He poured the thimbleful and handed it over quickly, and when Perroquet had tossed it off he filled again and again.

"Four—five," he counted. "That is enough."

But The Parrot's big grip closed quietly around his wrist at the last offering and pinioned him and held him helpless.

"No, it is not enough. Now I will take the rest. Ha, wise man! Have I fooled you at last?"

There was no chance to struggle, and Dubosc did not try, only stayed smiling up at him, waiting.

Perroquet took the bottle.

"The best man wins," he remarked. "Eh, my zig? A bright notion—of yours. The—best—"

His lips moved, but no sound issued. A look of the most intense surprise spread upon his round face. He stood swaying a moment, and collapsed like a huge hinged toy when the string is cut.

Dubosc stooped and caught the bottle again, looking down at his big adversary, who sprawled in brief convulsion and lay still, a bluish scum oozing between his teeth.

"Yes, the best man wins," repeated the doctor, and laughed as he in turn raised the flask for a draft.

"The best wins!" echoed a voice in his ear.

Fenayrou, writhing up and striking like a wounded snake, drove the knife home between his shoulders.

The bottle fell and rolled to the middle of the platform,

and there, while each strove vainly to reach it, it poured out its treasure in a tiny stream that trickled away and was lost.

It may have been minutes or hours later—for time has no count in emptiness—when next a sound proceeded from that frail slip of a raft, hung like a mote between sea and sky. It was a phrase of song, a wandering strain in half tones and fluted accidentals, not unmelodious. The black *Canaque* was singing. He sang without emotion or effort, quite casually and softly to himself. So he might sing by his forest hut to ease some hour of idleness. Clasping his knees and gazing out into space, untroubled, unmoved, enigmatic to the end, he sang—he sang.

And after all, the ship came.

She came in a matter befitting the sauciest little tops'l schooner between Nuku Hiva and the Pelews—as her owner often averred and none but the envious denied—in a manner worthy, too, of that able Captain Jean Guibert, the merriest little scamp that ever cleaned a pearl bank or snapped a cargo of labor from a scowling coast. Before the first whiff out of the west came the "Petite Susanne," curtsying and skipping along with a flash of white frill by her forefoot, and brought up startled and stood shaking her skirts and keeping herself quite daintily to windward.

"And 'ere they are sure enough, by dam'!" said the polyglot Captain Jean in the language of commerce and profanity. "Zose passengers for us, hey? They been here all the time, not ten mile off—I bet you, Marteau. Ain't it 'ell? What you zink, my gar?"

His second, a tall and excessively bony individual of gloomy outlook, handed back the glasses.

"More bad luck. I never approved of this job. And now—see?—we have had our voyage for nothing. What misfortune!"

"Marteau, if that good Saint Pierre gives you some day a gold 'arp still you would holler bad luck—bad job!" retorted Captain Jean. "Do I 'ire you to stand zere and cry about ze luck? Get a boat over, and quicker zan zat!"

M. Marteau aroused himself sufficiently to take command of the boat's crew that presently dropped away to investigate.

"It is even as I thought," he called up from the quarter when he returned with his report. "I told you how it would be, Captain Jean."

"Hey?" cried the captain, bouncing at the rail. "Have you got zose passengers yet, *enfant de salaud?"*

"I have not," said Marteau in a tone of lugubrious triumph. There was nothing in the world that could have pleased him quite so much as this chance to prove Captain Jean the loser on a venture. "We are too late. Bad luck, bad luck—that calm. What misfortune! They are all dead!"

"Will you mind your business?" shouted the skipper.

"But still, the gentlemen are dead—"

"What is zat to me? All ze better, they will cost nozzing to feed."

"But how—"

"Hogsheads, my gar," said Captain Jean paternally. "Zose hogsheads in the afterhold. Fill them nicely with brine, and zere we are!" And, having drawn all possible satisfaction from the other's amazement, he sprang the nub of his joke with a grin. "Ze gentlemen's passage is all paid, Marteau. Before we left Sydney, Marteau. I contrac' to bring back three escape' convicts, and so by 'ell I do—in pickle! And now if you'll kindly get zose passengers aboard like I said an' bozzer less about ze goddam' luck, I be much oblige'. Also, zere is no green on my eye, Marteau, and you can dam' well smoke it!"

Marteau recovered himself with difficulty in time to recall another trifling detail. "There is a fourth man on board that raft, Captain Jean. He is a *Canaque*—still alive. What shall we do with him?"

"A *Canaque?"* snapped Captain Jean. "A *Canaque!* I have no word in my contrac' about any *Canaque*. . . . Leave him zere. . . . He is only a dam' nigger. He'll do well enough where he is."

And Captain Jean was right, perfectly right, for while the "Petite Susanne" was taking aboard her grisly cargo the wind freshened from the west, and just about the time she was shaping away for Australia the "dam' nigger" spread his own sail of pandanus leaves and twirled his own helm of *niaouli* wood and headed the catamaran eastward, back toward New Caledonia.

Feeling somewhat dry after his exertion, he plucked at random from the platform a hollow reed with a sharp end, and, stretching himself at full length in his accustomed place at the stern, he thrust the reed down into one of the bladders underneath and drank his fill of sweet water.

He had a dozen such storage bladders remaining, built into the floats at intervals above the water line—quite enough to last him safely home again.

James Norman Hall

THE FORGOTTEN ONE

James Norman Hall (1887–1951), an American born in Iowa, volunteered at the outbreak of World War I and served for two years in the British Army as a machine gunner. He was discharged in order to join the Lafayette Flying Corps of the French Foreign Legion in 1916. He was shot down over Germany and spent the last six months of the war as a prisoner.

A comrade of Hall's was Charles Nordhoff, and *The Lafayette Flying Corps* (1920) was the title of the first book written by one of the most notable teams of collaborators of our time. The two soon "yielded to a long-suppressed desire to sail for the South Pacific Ocean"; and after a year of roaming among the islands they settled in Tahiti, where both took Polynesian wives. They continued to write together, producing such books about the Pacific as the famed *Bounty* trilogy (1932–34), *Faery Lands of the South Seas* (1921), *The Hurricane* (1935), *The Dark River* (1938), *No More Gas* (1940), *Botany Bay* (1941), and *The High Barbaree* (1945).

Aside from the eleven volumes written with Nordhoff, Hall published a number of his own. Those with Pacific backgrounds include three books of travel essays; two novels, *Lost Island* (1944) and *The Far Lands* (1950); a collection of stories, *The Forgotten One* (1950); and an autobiography, *My Island Home* (1952).

The story of the agony of Crichton, the lone "atoll man," will remain for many years a South Sea classic. Crichton is not the usual romantic refugee from civilization. His secret is deep, and it is subtly revealed. The story has a macabre persistence that will linger in the mind of any reader.

SOMEONE, READING THIS MEMOIR, MAY RECALL MY EARLIER account of Crichton, the solitary white inhabitant of a small coral island in the Low Archipelago. The recollection would be vague at best, I fear; for although I tried to give a vivid impression both of the man and of the lonely beauty of Tanao, the island where he lives, the attempt, I know, was a failure. I spent a good deal of time over that earlier sketch, writing, rewriting, changing a word here and a phrase there, hoping to discover, either by chance or by dint of patient effort, the magic formula that would conjure up the place for some reader who would never see it. It was useless. The best I could do fell so far short of my hopes that at last I gave up in despair and ended my little story abruptly, with these words:

> The damaged whaleboat having been repaired, we rowed out to the schooner and were under way by midafternoon. For three hours I watched the island dwindling and blurring until, at sunset, it was lost to view beneath the rim of the southern horizon. Still I looked back, imagining that I could see a diminishing circle of palm-clad land—a mere speck at last—dropping farther and farther away down the reverse slope of the sea as though it were vanishing for all time from the knowledge and the concern of men.

So I closed my story. That was four years ago. I have wandered far from Tanao since then, but the memory of it has followed me everywhere: through America, England, Scotland, Denmark, Norway, Iceland. In a crowded restaurant in New York, where the waitresses shouted orders down a call-tube and the air was loud with the clatter of dishes and the hum of conversation, I have seen the palm trees of Tanao bending to the southeast trade, and Crichton sitting in the shade, far up the beach, hands clasped about his knees, looking out over the empty sea. I have walked at high noon along Princes Street in Edinburgh, and heard the "Mamma-Ruau," the old native woman from whom Crichton leased his island, singing softly to herself as she broiled fish over an open fire on the lagoon beach. In Iceland, while watching the visible music of the northern lights, I have felt the softness of the air at Tanao and the smoke of the surf on my face from the combers rising to their height and thundering over the barrier reef. The island and its two lonely inhabitants have been more real to me, often, than the streets through which I passed or the people with whom I sat at table. No effort of will was needed to call them up. They came of themselves, at strange moments, in strange places; and then, no matter where my body happened to be, my spirit seemed to leave it and fly straight to an atom of an island in the midmost Pacific.

Despite the briefness of the first visit—of two days' duration only—I must have left a part of myself at Tanao, as it is said one does wherever one goes; and it is necessary at times to revisit these shadowy, fragmentary selves left behind as one grows older. But it was not so much a lost self to which I returned at Tanao as one I had never had, and Crichton was its flesh-and-blood embodiment. He represented, to me, certain qualities I have always longed to possess, but chiefly, I think, I envied him his exceptional capacity for solitude—at least I thought it exceptional then. I am not likely to forget the day in March, 1920, when we landed at Tanao, and he found that it was, in truth, the ideal retreat he had searched for during ten years of continual wandering. It was the first time he had seen it and I chanced to be traveling on the schooner that had carried him out. The only inhabitant was the old Paumotan woman—"Mamma-Ruau" (Grandma) he always called her—who owned the place. No boats touched there except by arrangement. The lagoon had no entrance and in order to land it was necessary to ride the surf in a small boat, over one of the most dangerous reefs in the whole of the Dangerous Archipelago. All of this delighted him—but that is not the word. His joy was something so much deeper than delight that it seemed there could be no adequate expression of it. He conveyed to me—I scarcely know how—a sense of this. Life could never be long enough for him now. He was only twenty-eight, and I confess that, at times, this deep joy at the prospect of uninterrupted solitude seemed to me a little mad in a man of his age. What had life done to him that he should be so glad to leave it—to bury himself here? He did not have a guilty conscience. Five minutes of talk with him would have convinced anyone of that. Furthermore, no man with a guilty conscience would have sought out a place where he would be so terribly alone with it. I came to the conclusion—and despite what happened later I still think it the right one—that he is one of those men who love solitude as other men love beauty; that to him it is really a manifestation of beauty in its most ravishing, pitiless form.

At last the desire to return in the flesh to Tanao was no longer to be withstood. I remember precisely the moment when the ache of longing became hardest to bear and the decision to appease it was made. It was on a November evening. I was in Boston at the time, living in lodgings high up on Beacon Hill, my windows looking down one of the side streets leading to the Common and beyond to Boylston Street. I had been trying to read, gave it up, turned out the light and sat by the window. Facing me from across the Common was a huge electric sign, an arresting, exasperating device in which a series of lighted words moved endlessly out of darkness into darkness. I must have observed it before, subconsciously, but on this occasion, in order to keep from thinking I let my eyes follow the moving inscription, and my brain took the impress of it with the accuracy of a photographic plate. I believe I can still quote it, word for word: THERE IS ON SALE IN THE DRUGSTORES OF THIS CITY AN ANTISEPTIC PREPARATION ONE HUNDRED TIMES STRONGER THAN CARBOLIC ACID AND YET AS HARMLESS WHEN APPLIED TO THE HUMAN BODY AS PURE WATER. IT IS NONPOISONOUS AND DOES NOT BUBBLE WHEN APPLIED. IT ACTUALLY KILLS GERMS. IT PUTS AN END TO ACCIDENTAL POISONING AND SHOULD BE IN EVERY MEDICINE CHEST. THE NAME OF THIS ANTISEPTIC IS . . .

But neither the name nor the antiseptic itself is of any great consequence in this memoir. I left Boston that same evening, and awoke, not many weeks later, in my old room at the hotel on the water front at Papeete.

I might have left the place yesterday. The same old paper on the walls; the same mosquito netting around the bed, with the rents in it neatly drawn together; the same tin bucket, with the dent in it, by the washstand; the same dilapidated wardrobe, the shelves covered with pages from the Sydney *Bulletin* and the Auckland *Weekly News;* the same tattered hotel register dating from 1902, and the same genial, portly landlord bringing it up for me to sign before I was out of bed. We had a pleasant chat about island affairs, and in the midst of it I chanced to speak of a defective board in the floor of the veranda, and how I had nearly broken my leg there, coming in, in the dark the night before.

"Why, don't you remember that hole?" he asked, quite seriously, with genuine surprise: and I realized, clearly enough, that the fault was not his for not having it repaired, but mine for not having remembered during four years that repair was needed. How glad I was to be back in a place where life is as leisurely as that! Where all things animate and inanimate—even a hole in a veranda floor—seem to partake of a timeless, ideal existence like that of the figures on Keats's Grecian urn.

It was still quite early. Chinamen were sweeping the street with their long-handled brooms, heaping into neat piles the dead leaves and twigs and withered blossoms from the flamboyant trees, against the coming of the rubbish cart. I had a pleasant thrill of anticipation, remembering the former driver of this cart. Girot was his name, a thin, wiry little Frenchman of uncertain age. He called his horse "Banane," and carried on with her an endless, animated conversation as they wandered along the street. Were they too under the enchantment of timelessness? Yes, here they came presently, Girot barefoot as usual, walking behind the cart, carrying the two little boards with which he picked up the piles of leaves. He was in the usual costume: floppy pandanus hat, tattered undershirt, and denim overalls faded to a whitish blue by many washings. More than likely it was the same pair of overalls. Banane was a trifle bonier, if that is possible, than I had remembered her. She moved as deliberately as ever. I could count twenty-five while the wheel of the cart was making a single revolution, but Girot was reproaching her in the old manner for going too fast:

"Whoa! Whoa, *sacré nom de Balzac! Écoute, Banane! Penses-tu que nous sommes sur un champ de course? Comment? Ah, non alors! Oui, je comprends; pour toi ça ne fait rien. Mais pour moi? Je ne suis pas garçon, moi. J'ai plus de soixante ans. Maintenant nous allons jusqu'au coin de la rue—tu vois?—là! Et la prochaine fois quand je dis* 'Whoa!' *arrête-toi. Tu comprends? Bon! En route!*"

No one paid the least attention to them—no one ever did—and at last they were out of hearing. Natives were passing to and from the market with strings of fish, containers of green bamboo filled with fermented coconut sauce, and baskets of fresh-water shrimps, fruit, and vegetables. It was good to hear again their soft voices, the slither of their bare feet, to smell the humid odors of tropical vegetation; to look across the still lagoon to the island of Mooréa, fifteen miles distant, every fantastic peak outlined against the sky—all that a South Sea island should be, and surpassing my most splendid dreams of one, as a boy. I whistled for the first time in months while taking my bath—luckily there were no other guests at the hotel—then sat down in pajamas to breakfast on the upstairs veranda, just as I used to do.

While I was drinking my coffee, the landlord returned, bringing a suit of white drill I had left behind in the hurry of departure four years ago.

"I thought you would come back some time," he said, "so I didn't give it away."

In one of the pockets I found a piece of scratch paper covered with penciled notes, all of them having to do either with Crichton or his island, reminding me how completely he had engaged my interest during the time of my first sojourn in the South Seas. Among other notes I found this one, an attempt to describe him in a paragraph:

> He is one of those lonely spirits—without friends or any of the ties that make life pleasant to most of us—who wander the unpeopled places of the earth, interested in a detached way in what they see from afar or faintly hear; but looking

> quietly on, taking no part, being blessed—or cursed—by Nature with a love of silence, of the unchanging peace of great solitudes. Now and then one reads of such men in fiction, and if they live in fiction it is because of individuals like Crichton, their prototypes in reality, seen for a moment as they slip apprehensively across some bypath leading from the outside world.

Reading this again, I wondered, as I had at the time of writing it, whether it were true—whether I had not been describing a quite imaginary figure rather than an Englishman named Crichton. Well, I should know, soon. Four years had passed, ample time for anyone to test the nature of his capacities for solitude. Had Crichton found his adequate? Viewed in one light, my interest in this question seemed absurd. And yet, as I have said, or implied, here was a man, sensitive, imaginative, highly organized, who appeared to have within himself inexhaustible resources against boredom—the greatest curse that spirit is heir to. He at least was confident of having them. He would never leave Tanao, he had told me. He was sure that he could be happy there, though he were never again to see a man of his own race—a human being of any kind. It would have been hard to rest content without knowing what had happened to him.

I made a hasty breakfast and set out in the cool of the morning in search of some schooner bound for the Low Islands. Along the water front fifteen or twenty vessels from all parts of the eastern Pacific were unloading pearl shell and copra, taking in cargoes of rice and flour, lumber, tinned food, and assorted merchandise. Among them was the "Caleb Winship," the two-masted schooner that had taken Crichton to Tanao at the time when I was a passenger. Tino, her supercargo then, had since been made captain. I found him in the cabin checking over bills of lading. He is a dry, blunt man, Tino, three-quarters American blood and one-quarter Rarotongan. For all the fact that he was born among them, I doubt whether he has ever seen the islands or ever will see them; but he can tell you to a dot what each of them produces in pearl shell and copra.

"Well!" he said, holding out his hand. "Haven't seen you

for some time. Where you been keeping yourself? Living out in the country?"

I told him I had just come from America; then, after a quarter of an hour's chat of indifferent matters, I asked in a by-the-way fashion for news of Crichton.

"Crichton? Crichton? Who's— Oh! You mean that Swede —that Dane—"

"He is an Englishman," I said.

"Whoever he was. Hell, no! I haven't seen him since we was out there—you remember? The time we stove in the new whaleboat going over the reef. Funny thing," he added. "I haven't thought of him from that day to this. He might be dead, for all I know—or care, for that matter."

Now that he was reminded, it was plain that Tino was still sore on the subject of Crichton. He had consented to carry him to Tanao because he thought there was something of commercial interest in view. "He can't fool me!" I remembered him saying more than once during that voyage. "He's got something up his sleeve and I'm going to find out what it is." When he had satisfied himself that the island was as poor as it had always been, he set Crichton down either as crazy or some knave in hiding. Remembering his disgust at the loss of time in going so far out of his way, I knew that it would be useless asking him to go again. Nevertheless, I did ask, for the "Winship" was on the point of sailing for that part of the Pacific.

"What! Tanao? Not much! I'm not traveling for my health; but what do you want to go back there for, if it's any of my business?"

"I rather liked the place," I said. "You don't see such islands in my part of the world."

"Ought to be glad you don't. Why anyone should go to one of them Godforsaken little holes of his own free will, beats me. Well, that Swede can rot in his. I expect he has. He's probably dead or gone somewhere else long before this."

At the end of two weeks I was at the point of accepting this opinion. During that time I spent many hours along the water front, loafed through long afternoons at the club, the hotel, and the other favorite resorts of traders, planters, pearl buyers, and sailors. I made many discreet inquiries—never direct, interested ones—knowing how jealous for his solitude Crichton had been, how concerned lest even talk of Tanao by others should sully the purity of its loneliness. Little chance of that! "Tanao? Oh, yes! The 'Madeleine' went on the reef there—let me see, when was it? Nineteen-four, I think." That was the most recent bit of information I gathered in talk on the club veranda. As for Crichton, no one apparently, in that place where everyone is known, could tell me what had become of him. I was considering the possibility of chartering a small Paumotu cutter for a special voyage, when I met an old friend, Chan Lee, captain of a one-hundred-ton schooner belonging to a firm of his fellow countrymen. I had once made a long voyage with Chan. He is a good sailor for a Chinaman, with all the fine personal qualities of the Oriental at his best; but he carries minding-his-own-business to curious lengths. It was not until a week after I had first spoken to him of Crichton that he admitted knowing him.

"Go Tanow once year," he said, holding up a finger as though to emphasize the infrequency of his visits. "Not much copla—five ton." Then, as an afterthought apparently, "Clichton say, suppose I see you, tell you come back some time."

"What! He asked you to tell me that?"

I confess that I was pleased. Slightly as I knew Crichton, I had a warm regard for him, carefully concealed, of course; for his attitude throughout our brief acquaintanceship on the "Winship" had been merely that of fellow passengers on shipboard everywhere—pleasant, courteous, but without a hint of intimacy.

"Yes, he say that," said Chan. "Hlee year ago, now. Bimeby next week I go. You come along me?"

On the following Monday we were outward bound. Chan had a dozen islands to visit first, and during the early part of the voyage the schooner was crowded with native passengers. These were gradually dispersed, the last of them at an island one hundred and fifty miles from Tanao. Owing to alternate calms and head winds we were five days in covering the last leg of the voyage, and thirty-eight days out when we sighted the island.

Crichton need not have feared for the purity of its loneliness. It was lonelier than the sea. It seemed to have gathered to itself an esoteric kind of loneliness, peculiar to the man who lived at the heart of it. It seemed a place he had dreamed into being, created out of fancy through sheer strength of longing. And there he was, alone of his kind, and there he had been for four years without once having left it. Chan gave me this information.

"He like stay here. Stay all time. Never go 'way."

I asked whether he had taken a native wife.

"No, no womans. I want get him nice Paumotu wife. Help make copla, make him big fambly. He no want."

He had, however, imported a Chinese family—father, mother, two children, and an elderly relative of theirs—who did his housework. Chan had brought them two years before, he said. The old man had a hut on the main island, near Crichton. The others lived on a little islet across the lagoon. There was no one else except the Mamma-Ruau. She was still living, in good health. At least she had been a year ago.

"What about letters?" I asked. "And books, and papers? Does he receive many?"

"Mebbe some book. One letta evely year. Always same place. No more."

Chinamen living in exile are often lonely enough men, but even Chan seemed to wonder at this lack of correspondence. He spoke of it several times during the voyage and showed me the letter he was carrying out to Crichton. It was as impersonal in appearance as a bank note. The name and address of a London trust company was stamped on the envelope. I could imagine the nature of this one yearly communication from the outside world: "Dear Sir: You will find attached for your examination the statement of your account for the year just closed. Very respectfully," and so forth.

As I held this letter in my hand a truer conception of Crichton's isolation came to me. He was like those men

Matthew Arnold speaks of in his "Rugby Chapel"—men who die without leaving a trace behind them:

> and no one asks
> Who or what they have been
> More than he asks what waves
> In the moonlit solitudes mild
> Of the midmost ocean, have swelled,
> Foamed for a moment, and gone.

Certainly that is true of Crichton, and he is still living, in the full vigor of manhood. But beyond the borders of his own little physical world he has long been as good as dead and buried. There is Chan to think of him, and some clerk in a London banking house—once a year at least, when he sends him his statement of account—myself, and no one else. I suppose this is really what has prompted me to write of him again. Crichton would not thank me for meddling, but it gives me a quite definite feeling of relief to know that a few others, reading this sketch, will share, momentarily at least, in the task of keeping the man alive. I have guarded his anonymity, of course, as well as that of his island.

But to continue, we passed the northwestern extremity of Tanao, close inshore, between three and four in the afternoon. At that point the atoll is mostly barren reef washed over by the surf. There is but one small islet—a boy's dream of an island to be shipwrecked on. Indeed, the bones of an old vessel lie there, high and dry above the reef, bleaching in the sun—all that remains from the wreck of the "Madeleine." The island is just boy-size, not more than one hundred paces across, either way. It is of clean coral sand, as level as a floor, with thick green bush fringing it on the lagoon side. There are eight tall coconut palms, three in one clump and four in another, with one tree growing apart, holding its tuft of fronds far out over the surface of the lagoon. A pass goes through the reef at one side of the islet, but it is too narrow to permit entrance to any craft larger than a skiff or canoe. On that side an ancient pandanus tree throws a patch of deep shade on the sand. Well within the shelter of it was a thatch-roofed hut, open to the four winds; and I saw a roughhewn bench facing seaward, with its back against the trunk of the tree.

"Very likely Crichton comes here to fish," I thought, but the place was deserted now. The sunshine, of that mellow, golden quality of late afternoon, gilded the stems of the palms. I saw not even a sea bird there. Nothing moved save the trees bending to the wind and their shadows on the yellow sand.

We passed the islet all too quickly, then stood away from the reef to come in to the main island on the starboard tack. There are seven widely separated islands around the lagoon, which is five miles across at the widest point. From the mainmast crosstrees I had them all in view. Three were on the opposite side, and from that distance the trees seemed to be growing directly out of the water. Crichton lives on the largest of the seven, a fringe of land less than a mile long and some three hundred yards broad. With my glasses. I searched the shore line without result until Chan called up to me, "You no see?"

I saw them plainly enough when they were pointed out—Crichton and the Mamma-Ruau sitting just within the border of shade at the upper slope of the beach, hidden momentarily by the sunlight-filtered smoke of the surf. He had on a pair of dark glasses, and, for clothing, a pair of knee-length trousers and a soft-brimmed straw hat. The old woman was in her best black dress and hat. Both were squatting, native fashion, their chins resting on their hands. How many times I had seen them thus, in the imagination! I could hardly credit the reality of the scene before me, it had appeared so often in my dreams. The old woman was talking in an excited manner, pointing to the schooner from time to time. Once I saw her take Crichton by the shoulders and turn him till he sat directly facing us.

The sea was fairly calm here on the leeward side, but for all that the great swells looked dangerously high as they swept shoreward and toppled with a deafening crash over the ledge of the reef. We were carried across at terrific speed; the whaleboat shot down the broad slope of broken water and through the shallows, grounding almost at the point where Crichton and the Mamma-Ruau were sitting.

"O vai tera? Chan?" (Who is it? Chan?) Crichton called when he heard the keel grating and bumping over the coral.

"Yes, yes!" cried the old woman. "Don't you believe me? It is Chan and the white man who first came here with you. *Ia ora na orua!"*

She shook our hands warmly, saying *"Ia ora na orua!"* (Health to you!) again and again. This kindly Polynesian greeting seems always to have the freshness of a phrase coined yesterday. The reason is, perhaps, that among the islands friends meet after long separation, after long and often hazardous sea voyages. They are in all truth glad to see each other again.

Mamma-Ruau put her hands on my shoulders and gazed long at me, searching my face feature by feature.

"Ua tae mai oé?" (You have come?) she said, as though still in doubt that anyone from the outside world could, in reality, reach that lonely place. She had aged greatly in four years, but Crichton had not altered in the least, insofar as I could tell at first glance. He is a splendid type physically, just over six feet, broad-shouldered, deep-chested—he looked more than ever the athlete he is, in fact. The ghost of the smile I remembered curved his lips almost imperceptibly, and he spoke English in the same curious, exotic way. His eyes were concealed by the smoked glasses.

"You will forgive me for not recognizing you?" he said. "Until recently I've never taken any precaution against the glare of the sun. It was very unwise, and the result is—well, I'm nearly blind."

Mamma-Ruau, who was standing behind him, gave me a look of all but agonized appeal, as much as to say, "Don't encourage him to talk of it!"

"Rather a nuisance," he went on. "I may get over it, of course, but in six months' time I can't say there has been any change for the better. Well, enough of that. Shall we go to the house? Luckily, I know my way about after four years. I could go anywhere, blindfold."

The island as I had first seen it had been a wilderness of

brush, pandanus trees, and self-sown coconut palms. Now everything was clean and orderly, the palms thinned out to six or eight paces apart so that one had charming views in every direction. A well-shaded road, bordered with shrubbery, led from the ocean beach to the lagoon. We followed it in silence. Having greeted each other, we seemed to have nothing more to say. Mamma-Ruau had gone on ahead. Chan remained at the beach to oversee the landing of some supplies. At last, with a good deal of effort, I remarked, "You've not been idle here."

"No, there's been enough to do. I found that I needed some help at first. I had Chan bring me a dozen natives from another island. They stayed three months, clearing the land. They helped build my house, too."

I had often tried to picture Crichton's house. He had, I knew, the imagination to take full advantage of his exotic environment, and for all his years of wandering was still enough of an Englishman to be concerned about comfort. Nevertheless I was not prepared to find so spacious and homelike a dwelling. It stood on the lagoon beach at the end of the road, and was raised about three feet above the ground, the open space beneath being concealed by shrubbery. The roof of thatch was steeply pitched, and extended low over a broad veranda. Crichton stopped at the foot of the steps. For a long moment he seemed to have forgotten me; then he said: "I think I must be rather excited. I've some instructions to give Chan about my copra, and he never stops ashore unless his schooner is at anchor. Will you make yourself comfortable? You might look over the house if you care to."

A clock with a ship's-bell attachment, striking five as I entered the veranda, demanded immediate attention. "Odd!" I thought, "having a clock here." But it would be a wise precaution, perhaps, in so lonely a place. Crichton would need to live by schedule, to fill his days with self-imposed duties to be regularly performed. No doubt he did. The house gave evidence of his all but meticulous habits of mind, and of the strict obedience to his orders of his literal-minded Chinaman. Settees and cushioned chairs were as carefully arranged as pieces in an upholsterer's display window. The floors, oiled and polished, shone with a dull luster and the straw mats were precisely placed. Four shelves of books ran the length of the inner wall of the veranda. I took the opportunity offered me in Crichton's absence to make an examination of them. They had been classified and subclassified. Novelists, historians, poets, biographers, travelers, stood in the ranks of their contemporaries and in the immediate company, one would have said, most congenial to them individually. There must have been fifteen hundred volumes in his library, nothing very recent, but all of them books to live with. The margins of the pages of those I looked into were covered with penciled notes and comments, and one could see what delight, what solace, Crichton had found in their companionship. Now that he was deprived of it—but that would not bear thinking about. It would be a calamity worse than death to a man of his tastes, in his position. One section of the library contained only books on Polynesia, everything important, surely, which had been written about the islands of the eastern Pacific. There were many philological works in this section, and I remembered the interest Crichton had taken in the study of the various island dialects, speculating, with this study as a basis, on the probable routes followed during the great Polynesian migrations.

On a top shelf, bare of books, were models of ancient sailing canoes, spears and clubs of ironwood, coconut shells polished and carved with intricate designs, stone axes, and taro-mashers. The windward end of the veranda was enclosed with a wall of freshly braided palm fronds, and midway in it a section had been built to prop open, outward. Crichton's desk stood opposite this window space. The view from his chair was over an inlet from the lagoon, bordered with palms, through which now a greenish-golden sunset light sifted like impalpable dust. An open passageway led through the center of the house to a second veranda on the lagoon side. The first door to the right along this passageway—that leading to Crichton's room, no doubt—was closed. Three others, latched open, disclosed spacious, airy rooms, each of them prettily furnished as a combined bed- and sitting-room, with a wardrobe, a chest of drawers, a washstand, a reading table holding a shaded lamp, several easy chairs or sofas, and above each of the beds a shelf filled with books. These rooms, in keeping with the rest of the house, were immaculately clean and the beds made up, ready for occupancy.

Returning to the front veranda, I walked up and down, saying to myself, "What a delightful spot! What an ideal home!" conscious all the while of a feeling very like depression. I was at a loss to assign a cause for this unless it were the clock, ticking away with self-important industry as though it were the only one in existence. Within half an hour I revised my opinion as to the wisdom of having a clock. The silence was too profound for any such noisy piece of furniture. I could all but hear the steady drip-drip of the minutes and the tiny splash they made as they fell into the sea of time past. Then I found myself listening for voices—of the wife who might have been there, of Crichton's unborn children. It was that kind of a house—much too large, it seemed to me, for one man, and much too homelike for spiritual comfort under those circumstances. One would have thought that Crichton had built it for the very purpose of evoking ghostly presences; to shelter some ideal conception of a family that he preferred to the warm, living, imperfect reality. Or, perhaps, not satisfied with the superficial aspects of a solitude that would have daunted most men, he meant his house to accentuate it, to remind him of its inviolability. Certainly he had succeeded in building into it a personality as strange as his own. It seemed conscious of having been prepared for guests and to be awaiting them with the complacent assurance that they would never come.

I, too, waited—anything but complacently—for the return of my host, reproaching myself, now that it was too late, for having taken a welcome for granted. To be sure, I had been invited, but that was three years ago, and I had forgotten to ask Chan whether the invitation had ever been renewed. An hour passed and still I waited, sitting on the top step of the veranda as Crichton must have done times without number at that hour, looking down his empty roadway to the empty sea. The sun had set and the colorless light faded swiftly from the sky. The fronds of the palms, swaying gently in the last faint tremors of the breeze, came gradually to rest. In the trancelike calm of earth and air I was conscious again of the beating of the surf on the reef. Now it was measured, regular, as though it were the pulsing of the blood through the mighty heart of Solitude; now it seemed the confused roar of street traffic from a thousand cities, mingled with the voices of all humankind, flowing smoothly in soundless waves, in narrowing circles, over the rim of the world, to break audibly at last on this minute ringed shoal in the farthermost sea of Silence.

After listening to that lonely sound for at least another hour, I began to feel very uncomfortable. What had happened to my host, and where was the Mamma-Ruau? I knew that she had her own little house farther down the beach, and that Crichton, with his strict ideas of propriety, would not ask her to dine with us. Nevertheless I thought it likely that she would be somewhere about. At last I saw a glimmer of light along the passageway leading to the lagoon-side veranda. A little while afterward a gong was sounded. "That means dinner, evidently," I thought. Perhaps Crichton had returned through the groves and along the beach and was waiting for me.

I have but mentioned, thus far, Crichton's lagoon-side veranda. It is semicircular in shape and extends over shoal water to the very brink of a magnificent coral precipice. Standing at the edge of it, one looks down into a submarine garden of exquisite beauty. Gorgeously colored fish, of the most fantastic shapes, swim lazily in and out of the caves that honeycomb the precipice, and from the floor of the lagoon forests of coral arise, spreading their symmetrical branches into water as clear as air. The veranda is roofed with canvas stretched over a framework of light poles, and this covering is so constructed that it may be drawn back, by means of ropes, against the wall of the house.

Emerging from the passageway, I gave an inward gasp of astonishment at the beauty and strangeness of the scene before me. It was now deep night. The veranda lay open to the sky, and the reflections of the stars in the water were so bright and clear, it was easy to imagine that the little house was adrift, motionless, in the innermost depths of space. But what first attracted my attention was a table set for one, and holding a shaded lamp; and, standing beside it, a withered, ancient Chinaman as small and frail of body as a delicate child of ten. He was dressed in a clean cotton undershirt and a black *pareu,* and carried a napkin over his arm in quite the approved fashion. He made a striking and memorable picture, standing with his back to the starlit lagoon. The lamplight filled the hollows of his eyes with shadow, and the black *pareu* blended so perfectly with the surrounding darkness that he looked only half a Chinaman suspended motionless above two bare feet.

I bade him good evening and inquired for Crichton, but his only reply was to draw back my chair and wait for me to be seated. When I had done so I noticed a piece of folded note paper tucked under the edge of my plate. It was a message from Crichton. "I am sorry," it read, "that I cannot join you at dinner, and as Chan expects to sail early tomorrow afternoon it may be that I shall not see you again before you go. Ling Foo, my Chinaman, will look after you. Please believe that you are welcome here and feel free to use my house as though it were your own."

Ling Foo had gone to the kitchen while I was puzzling over this message. At any rate, when I looked up again he was standing at my elbow holding a covered dish which certainly he had not been holding a moment before. After he had set it down in front of me, I should not have been surprised to have seen him conjure it away again with his napkin. It required an effort of the imagination to think of that voiceless wraith of a man, who moved as soundlessly as a shadow, concerning himself in the usual manner with anything so substantial and matter-of-fact as food. Most of it was out of tins, but it had been admirably disguised in the preparation. I wish that I might have paid his art as a cook the tribute it deserved; but it was Ling's fate, apparently, to spend his days performing useless labor: airing empty rooms, making up unoccupied beds, sweeping dustless floors. He carried back the scarcely tasted food as though he had quite expected this. Then, having lighted a lamp on the front veranda and another in the room where I was to sleep, he again vanished, and that is the last I ever saw of him.

"Please believe that you are welcome here." The words kept repeating themselves in my mind. I tried to believe it, but under the circumstances nothing seemed less likely than that Crichton meant me to accept this absentee welcome in good faith. I had seen his copra, stacked on the beach, ready for loading in the morning. The island afforded nothing else in the way of cargo. What other work could there be to do which would occupy his time until after our departure? No, he did not want to see me, that was plain. I wished I had not come. I wished with all my heart that I had not come.

Having come, there was nothing for it but to remain. Impossible to return to the schooner. When I had last seen her, just after sundown, she was at least three miles offshore. Chan had no engines and would stand well out to sea during the night. I smiled, rather lugubriously, however, at the thought of my anxiety to leave an island I had dreamed of with such longing during four years. But those dreams had been concerned with the Crichton I knew, or thought I knew, on board the "Caleb Winship." Now, going back in thought over the details of that first voyage to his island, I realized how meager my knowledge of him really was. Although we had been much in each other's company, it had been a curiously silent companionship for the most part. Often for days together we scarcely spoke. I was new to the islands then, and could hardly believe that places with names and fixed positions on charts could so far surpass my most sanguine expectations. They could have thrown a glamour over one's relations with the most prosaic of fellow passengers, and whatever else he may have been Crichton was not prosaic. The mere fact of his searching out so lonely an island offered sufficient proof to the contrary. Once—it was the only occasion when he even approached making a confidence—he told me that he hoped to find Tanao a place where he could do his thinking and writing undisturbed. "What sort of thinking?" I had wanted to ask, but one could hardly venture so intimate a question without further encouragement, which he did not give. At another time, breaking an all-day silence, he had said, "I wish I had come out here years ago. They appeal to the imagination, don't you think—all these islands?" That struck me as a happy expression of one's feeling about them, for we were then in the very heart of the Archipelago, with islands all round us, and yet they did not seem real.

The glimpses I had into his mind were all of this fragmentary nature, and they were as brief as they were rare. I had taken the rest of him for granted. Even though I were justified then in doing so, who could say what might have happened to him meanwhile—what changes had taken place during four appallingly lonely years? I was not hopeful. One might love solitude at a distance and long to know it intimately; but the heart of it was too vast, surely, for one poor human waif to snuggle against with impunity, or to attempt to explore in search of the secret of its peace. I tried to put myself in Crichton's place, and succeeded so well—or so ill, I could not be sure which—that I came back with a feeling of immense relief to my proper identity; but as a result of the attempt I could understand how one might so completely lose touch with humankind that the mere thought of renewing it, even for a moment, would be unbearable.

It was not yet nine—too early to think of going to bed. I returned to the front veranda to examine at leisure some charts and sketches—the latter, Crichton's own handiwork—that hung on the wall above the bookshelves. Some of his drawings were extremely interesting. One had for title, "When the Seas Go Dry." It was a sketch in crayon of several of the atolls of the Low Archipelago as they would appear from the ocean floor if the waters should recede. Immensely high mountains, in the shape of truncated cones, were shown, with walls in many places falling almost sheer from heights of eight or ten thousand feet to the general level of the surrounding country. It was a vividly imaginative impression and true to fact at the same time. I could see that the idea had come from a chart of the islands with its data of soundings, which hung beside it. Another similar sketch showed Tanao alone, with two pygmy figures standing in the valley below, as they do in old engravings of mountain scenery, one of them pointing to the cliffs towering above them.

Having examined the drawings, I turned again to the library, taking volumes from the shelves at random, and reading a page here and there. Many of Crichton's books were in my own library, not a few of them in the same editions. It gave me an uncanny feeling to find it so. I seemed to have entered his mind, assumed his personality whether I would or no, and this sense of identity was intensified when I came upon marked passages that I too had thus noted in some of my own books. One of these was in a volume of Shelley's *Lyrics and Minor Poems,* which I chanced to open at Shelley's preface to "Alastor: or, The Spirit of Solitude." There was no marginal comment on the page, but the paragraph, underscored in pencil, was as follows:

> Among those who attempt to exist without human sympathy, the pure and tenderhearted perish through the intensity and passion of their search after its communities, when the vacancy of their spirit suddenly makes itself felt. All else, selfish, blind, and torpid, are those unforeseeing multitudes who constitute, together with their own, the lasting misery and loneliness of the world. Those who love not their fellow beings live unfruitful lives and prepare for their old age a miserable grave.

The whole of the preface had a very special interest for me under those circumstances. As for "Alastor" itself, I had not read it in several years, and it occurred to me that I could never have a more favorable opportunity than this for a sympathetic appreciation of the poem, if not for its fullest enjoyment. Therefore, drawing a chair close to the lamp, I began, and at the second stanza started reading aloud that I might better sense the sonorous beauty of the words:

> Mother of this unfathomable world!
> Favor my solemn song, for I have loved
> Thee ever, and thee only; I have watched
> Thy shadow and the darkness of thy steps,
> And my heart ever gazes on the depth
> Of thy deep mysteries. I have made my bed
> In charnels and on coffins, where black death
> Keeps record of the trophies won from thee,

Hoping to still these obstinate questionings
Of thee and thine, by forcing some lone ghost,
Thy messenger, to render up the tale
Of what we are. In lone and silent hours
When night makes a weird sound of its own stillness . . .

I had been reading for a quarter of an hour, I should say, sometimes aloud, sometimes silently, when I heard from the adjoining room a slight but very distinct noise: a drumming of fingers against the wall just back of my head. I don't believe I have ever been so curiously startled in my life before. A cry, a crash of breaking glass, a pistol fired behind my back, might have produced a more violent shock, but nothing like such an eerie one. I got up at once, blew out the light, tiptoed into my room at the other end of the veranda, and closed the door. The reaction was purely instinctive, as a child's would be upon hearing at night a sound it could not understand. Theoretically, I should then have jumped into bed and hidden under the coverlet, but instinct did not carry me so far as that. I knew well enough, of course, that Crichton was in the other room. That is to say, I knew it after hearing the noise. Before that his presence in the house had not so much as occurred to me. The fact of his sending a message had given me a sense of his remoteness. I seem to have taken it for granted that he was far away—across the lagoon, perhaps, on one of the other islands, anywhere but under his own roof.

For some time I stood, listening, in the middle of the floor; then, hearing no further sound, I sat in the darkness by the open window and gave myself up to the most disquieting reflections. I winced at the thought of having read aloud. Had I set to work deliberately, maliciously, to devise for Crichton some exquisite form of torment, I doubted whether I could have hit upon one more likely to prove successful. Deprived through his blindness of the enjoyment of his books, I had reminded him what a deprivation it was. Accustomed during four years to all but unbroken silence, he had been compelled to listen to the monotonous intonation of my voice. "Alastor" might very well be the last poem in the world so lonely a man would care to hear read, and he must have heard distinctly every word, for only a thin board partition separated the veranda from the rooms behind it. At last, irritated beyond endurance, he had let me know of his presence.

Thus I reasoned myself into a very uncomfortable frame of mind. I was tempted to go to Crichton's room; to make my apologies for having disturbed him—for having come to Tanao at all. What would have happened, I wonder, had I done so? Perhaps I then missed the greatest opportunity I am ever likely to have to be of service to a man in dire need—whether he knew it or not—of human companionship, of human sympathy. And yet it is doubtful that I should have known how to offer it or he to accept it. I might have succeeded only in creating a situation so embarrassing as to be ludicrous. At the moment—heaven knows!—I felt that I had been sufficiently meddlesome without making further advances. Then, too, his method of warning me of his presence had something scarcely human about it. He had drummed twice, very lightly, with the tips of his fingers, and after a moment of silence had repeated the sound. It is hard to convey, in words, a sense of the uncanny feeling it produced in me. If he had pounded on the wall with his fist, or if he had shouted, "In heaven's name! Stop that infernal mumbling, will you?" I should have felt that he was within reach, so to speak. And I should have felt a welcome flush of anger at churlishness that even his blindness could hardly excuse. As the matter stood, I was awed rather than angry at the strangeness of his behavior, and it seemed best to remain in my room, wearing out the rest of the night as unobtrusively as possible.

But although Ling Foo had turned the coverlet invitingly back, I did not go to bed. Instead, I sat by the window listening to the clock on the veranda striking the half-hours and the hours, each of them a little eternity in itself. I dozed off at last to be awakened out of uneasy slumber by the crowing of a cock. It was a welcome sound, for I thought day was at hand, but this was far from being the case. Paumotan chickens, like the Paumotans themselves, are seminocturnal in their habits. Roosters greet the rising of the moon as well as of the sun, and I have often heard them break into a prolonged ecstasy of crowing for no reason at all, in the middle of a starlit night. One can hardly blame them, for the nights are enchantingly beautiful; but the sound of persistent crowing may be extremely annoying if close at hand, and this cock was perched in some shrubbery just in front of the veranda. A late moon was rising, which may have been the cause of his outburst. However that may be, he kept it up. With a premonitory flapping of wings he shattered the silence time after time, waiting with seeming intent for it to heal that he might shatter it again the more effectively. I endured it as long as I could; then climbed noiselessly out of the window, that I might not have to pass Crichton's room, and walked down the lagoon beach, keeping well within the shadow of the trees.

The crowing stopped almost at once. I was in the mood to be chagrined at this, and to take as an intentional affront the habitual action of the hermit crabs—there were hundreds of them along the beach—snapping into their shells at my approach and closing their doors behind them. The land crabs, too, showed hostility in their own fashion, holding up their claws in menace, scurrying away on either side and dodging into their burrows as though fleeing a pestilence. "I'm having a strange welcome all round!" I thought. And yet the Mamma-Ruau had been friendly. I could not doubt the sincerity of her welcome, and the fact of her disappearance immediately after our arrival was easily accounted for. She had old-fashioned ideas that Crichton, I knew, encouraged as to the propriety of women sharing uninvited in the companionship of men. No doubt she had gone straight to her house to wait until she should be sent for.

Her little hut on the lagoon beach, a five-minute walk from Crichton's place, seemed as essential a feature of the landscape as the old *kahaia* tree growing near by. All was silent there. A fire of coconut husks still smoldered on the earthen floor of the back kitchen. I knocked lightly on the doorpost, and, receiving no reply, looked in. The reflections from the moonlit water made the room almost as light as day. A wooden chest for clothing stood against a wall and a sewing machine in a corner. That was all the room contained in the way of furniture except for some shell necklaces and hat wreaths and some beautifully formed branches of coral hanging on the walls. The Mamma-Ruau lay on a mat, her hands palm to palm, tucked under her cheek. She was sleeping so peacefully that I had not the heart to waken her; therefore I slipped quietly away and sat down for a time under the *kahaia* tree.

Here Crichton and I had had our first meal together upon our arrival four years ago. I recalled the story the Mamma-Ruau had told us that evening, of the spirit of the last of her children—a son of twenty, who had been drowned while fishing outside the reef of one of the neighboring islets. It appeared to her but rarely, she said, and always in the form of an enormous dog, so large that it could have picked up her little house in its teeth, like a basket. But it never offered to harm her. She would come upon it—only at the full of the moon—lying on the beach, its huge head resting on its paws. It would regard her mournfully for a long time, beating its tail on the ground. Then it would rise, take a long drink of sea water, and start at a lope up the beach. Soon it would break into a run, gathering tremendous speed, until, reaching the end of the island, it would make a flying spring, and she would last see it high in the air, clearly outlined against the moonlit sky, crossing in one gigantic leap the two-mile gap to the island where her son had been drowned.

Her manner of telling the story had made a deep impression upon me, and I had no doubt of the realness, to her, of the apparition. She was pure heathen, and believed in all sorts of spirits, good and bad. I was glad for her sake that she had missed contact with the itinerant missionaries—Seventh-Day Adventists and Latter-Day Saints—who wander through the Archipelago from time to time, seeking converts. They would have destroyed what beliefs she had without giving her anything she could honestly accept to replace them. Indeed, her mother had been converted to Christianity, but evidently she had not been at all happy in her new faith, for she had counseled her children to have nothing to do with it. She had never been sure what to believe, and shortly before her death at Tanao, many years ago, had left instructions that a little stone idol, which she had always kept, was to be set at the head of her grave, and at the foot, a slab of coral with a cross carved on it. I had seen this grave at the time of my last visit. It is in the family burying ground at the far end of the island. As day was still long distant, I decided to go there again and look at it by moonlight.

I doubt whether there is a cemetery in all the Pacific—except at the bottom of it—more impressively lonely than the one at Tanao. It lies close to the ocean beach, where, owing to the contour of the fringing reef, the sea breaks with unusual violence; and the moonlight-silvered spray drifting slowly over the land makes one think of an endless procession of ghosts. There must be fifteen or twenty graves in all, most of them now in a sadly neglected condition, overgrown with shrubs and bushes. I found the grave of Mamma-Ruau's mother. The little idol, its hands folded across its fat stomach, seemed to be gazing with stony-eyed hostility at the nearby cross.

But what interested me most was another grave, freshly prepared, ready for occupancy. It had been dug to a depth of five or six feet and carefully roofed over with sheets of corrugated iron to keep out the rain. A drainage trench surrounded it, and close by were stacked a number of large flat stones, chiseled square and the edges beveled, with which to cover over the grave at last. The headstone was ready to be set in place, and on it was carved the Mamma-Ruau's name: Fainau a Hiva. I was not greatly surprised at this, for it is not unusual for Paumotans to make preparations for death when they know that it cannot be far distant. They have no dread of it. In old age they seem rather to welcome the approach of death, and make all ready for their last long sleep. The Mamma-Ruau was merely following the custom of her people; but she was too frail, I knew, to have done this work herself. Crichton must have helped her with it, and a shiver of dismay went through me when I saw how thoroughly and painstakingly he had set about the business. It struck me that he must have found pleasure in it, as though he were thinking, "It won't be long now. I'll soon have the place to myself."

I stood for a time watching the great seventh waves crashing over the reef. The ground trembled under the ceaseless impact, and the roar of broken water was loud enough, one would think, to disturb even the profound repose of the dead. Crichton would be lying here eventually if he held fast to his voluntary exile. But that would be years hence. Meanwhile, supposing he were to go completely and permanently blind? The possibility must have presented itself to him often. Walking slowly back along the ocean beach, I again tried to persuade myself that it was my duty to go to him at once; to urge him to come away with us. His blindness gave me a good pretext. I could urge the need of his going to England or America for expert advice and treatment. Quickening my pace, I crossed the island to the lagoon beach, and, if I had been five minutes earlier, who can say what might have happened? Perhaps—but conjecturing is futile. What did happen was this: When I was within fifty yards of the house, that cock started crowing again as though it had been waiting all this while to warn Crichton of the return of his unwelcome guest. The shrill cry stopped me as effectively as a stone wall would have done. While I stood there, doubtful as to what I should do, Crichton himself emerged from the darkness of the veranda, walked down the steps, and groped among the bushes where the cock was roosting. He was lost to view for a moment, and when he reappeared I saw that he had the fowl under his arm. To my dismay he came down the beach directly toward me. I was standing in the shadow, against a tree. He passed so closely that I could have touched him, and he stopped not half a dozen paces distant. He was not now wearing the smoked glasses, and his eyes had a vacant, expressionless look. He stood for a moment gently stroking the bird; then speaking to it softly, in a half-bantering, half-aggrieved tone, "You shouldn't have made such an infernal racket," he said. "And just under my window, too! It isn't the first time either, and you know you've been warned. Now I'm going to punish you—a quite serious little punishment. You won't like it in the least."

With that he took the fowl firmly by the legs, one in each hand, and very slowly and deliberately tore it apart. I could plainly hear the smothered rending of the flesh. To say that it was a horrible sight is to say nothing at all, but more horrible still was the expression on Crichton's face. I shall not attempt to describe it. The cock gave one loud squawk, almost human in its quality of terror and pain, but Crichton soon silenced it. He bashed it again and again against the trunk of a tree until it was only a misshapen mass of bloody feathers. Then he threw it into the lagoon.

His bare chest and his face and hands were spattered with blood. Having washed carefully, he dried his body with his *pareu* and sat down on the beach in such a position that he was turned half toward me with the moon shining full in his face. I would not venture to guess how long he sat thus, quite motionless, his eyes closed, as though he were deep in reverie. At last the shadow of a frown darkened his features and he said in a passionate half-whisper, "Why did you come? Did you think I was lonely?"

For two or three seconds I was convinced that he had spoken to me direct, conscious of my presence, and it was only the shock of astonishment that prevented me from giving myself away. But his air of complete self-absorption reassured me. It was plain that he thought himself alone.

"Ah, my friend!" he went on, "you are too kind! Too considerate by far! Your companionship—your conversation—oh! Charming! No doubt! No doubt! But you will forgive a solitary man if he deprives himself—"

He broke off, and was again long silent, sitting with his arms crossed on his knees and his forehead resting against them. I was compelled to stand absolutely motionless. He could have heard the least sound I might have made. Finally, he raised his head wearily, and, speaking in a low, broken, heartsick voice, "I don't know what's to come," he said. "I don't know." A moment later he rose and walked slowly back to the house.

I never saw him again. Neither he nor the Mamma-Ruau appeared at the beach the following morning. I went out to the schooner with the first boatload of copra and, being dead tired after my all-night vigil, turned into my bunk and slept till late afternoon. When I came on deck we were headed westward and Tanao was only a faint bluish haze far to windward. Chan, the least inquisitive of men, asked no questions as to my stay ashore. In fact, as soon as we left the island it seemed to have dropped completely out of his thoughts.

But I was to hear of Crichton once more. It was at an island four hundred miles from his retreat. We stopped there for copra and spent one night at anchor in the lagoon, close to the village. Some natives had come aboard to yarn with the sailors. I was lying on deck, looking at the stars, paying little attention to their conversation until I heard Tanao mentioned.

One voice said, "Pupuré, the old woman calls him." (That was Crichton's native name.)

"Ah é!" (Ah yes!) replied a second voice. *"Tera popaa—tera taata haa-moé-hia."* (That white man—that forgotten one.)

Jack London

THE SEED OF McCOY

Jack London (1876–1916) knew well the waters over which sailed the characters in his many yarns set in the South Seas. Born in San Francisco, illegitimate son of a wandering astrologer, London began his adventures on the sea when a mere boy. In 1907, he and his wife Charmian, aboard his ketch "Snark," set out on a voyage that was to last two years and include visits to Hawaii, the Marquesas, the Society group, Samoa, Fiji, the "terrible Solomons," and other islands. London's short stories and novels with Pacific settings include *South Sea Tales* (1911), *Adventure* (1911), *The House of Pride* (1911), *A Son of the Sun* (1912), *Jerry of the Islands* (1917), and *On the Makaloa Mat* (1919).

The protagonist in "The Seed of McCoy" is a descendant of the mutineers of the "Bounty" who, led by Fletcher Christian and aided by a band of Tahitian men and women, escaped to Pitcairn Island and were not discovered for almost twenty years. Only a man of such heredity and such seafaring skill could stand the remotest chance of piloting a burning sailing ship through the perilous Paumotus.

THE "PYRENEES," HER IRON SIDES PRESSED LOW IN THE WATER by her cargo of wheat, rolled sluggishly, and made it easy for the man who was climbing aboard from out a tiny outrigger canoe. As his eyes came level with the rail, so that he could see inboard, it seemed to him that he saw a dim, almost indiscernible haze. It was more like an illusion, like a blurring film that had spread abruptly over his eyes. He felt an inclination to brush it away, and the same instant he thought that he was growing old and that it was time to send to San Francisco for a pair of spectacles.

As he came over the rail he cast a glance aloft at the tall masts, and, next, at the pumps. They were not working. There seemed nothing the matter with the big ship, and he wondered why she had hoisted the signal of distress. He thought of his happy islanders, and hoped it was not disease. Perhaps the ship was short of water or provisions. He shook hands with the captain, whose gaunt face and careworn eyes made no secret of the trouble, whatever it was. At the same moment the newcomer was aware of a faint, indefinable smell. It seemed like that of burned bread, but different.

He glanced curiously about him. Twenty feet away a weary-faced sailor was calking the deck. As his eye lingered on the man, he saw suddenly arise from under his hands a faint spiral of haze that curled and twisted and was gone. By now he had reached the deck. His bare feet were pervaded by a dull warmth that quickly penetrated the thick calluses. He knew now the nature of the ship's distress. His eyes roved swiftly forward, where the full crew of weary-faced sailors regarded him eagerly. The glance from his liquid brown eyes swept over them like a benediction, soothing them, wrapping them about as in the mantle of a great peace. "How long has she been afire, Captain?" he asked in a voice so gentle and unperturbed that it was as the cooing of a dove.

At first the captain felt the peace and content of it stealing in upon him; then the consciousness of all that he had gone through and was going through smote him, and he was resentful. By what right did this ragged beachcomber, in dungaree trousers and a cotton shirt, suggest such a thing as peace and content to him and his overwrought, exhausted soul? The captain did not reason this; it was the unconscious process of emotion that caused his resentment.

"Fifteen days," he answered shortly. "Who are you?"

"My name is McCoy," came the answer in tones that breathed tenderness and compassion.

"I mean, are you the pilot?"

McCoy passed the benediction of his gaze over the tall,

heavy-shouldered man with the haggard, unshaven face who had joined the captain.

"I am as much a pilot as anybody," was McCoy's answer. "We are all pilots here, Captain, and I know every inch of these waters."

But the captain was impatient.

"What I want is some of the authorities. I want to talk with them, and blame quick."

"Then I'll do just as well."

Again that insidious suggestion of peace, and his ship a raging furnace beneath his feet! The captain's eyebrows lifted impatiently and nervously, and his fist clenched as if he were about to strike a blow with it.

"Who in hell are you?" he demanded.

"I am the chief magistrate," was the reply in a voice that was still the softest and gentlest imaginable.

The tall, heavy-shouldered man broke out in a harsh laugh that was partly amusement, but mostly hysterical. Both he and the captain regarded McCoy with incredulity and amazement. That this barefooted beachcomber should possess such high-sounding dignity was inconceivable. His cotton shirt, unbuttoned, exposed a grizzled chest and the fact that there was no undershirt beneath. A worn straw hat failed to hide the ragged gray hair. Halfway down his chest descended an untrimmed patriarchal beard. In any slop-shop, two shillings would have outfitted him complete as he stood before them.

"Any relation to the McCoy of the 'Bounty'?" the captain asked.

"He was my great-grandfather."

"Oh," the captain said, then bethought himself. "My name is Davenport, and this is my first mate, Mr. Konig."

They shook hands.

"And now to business." The captain spoke quickly, the urgency of a great haste pressing his speech. "We've been on fire for over two weeks. She's ready to break all hell loose any moment. That's why I held for Pitcairn. I want to beach her, or scuttle her, and save the hull."

"Then you made a mistake, Captain," said McCoy. "You should have slacked away for Mangareva. There's a beautiful beach there, in a lagoon where the water is like a millpond."

"But we're here, ain't we?" the first mate demanded. "That's the point. We're here, and we've got to do something."

McCoy shook his head kindly.

"You can do nothing here. There is no beach. There isn't even anchorage."

"Gammon!" said the mate. "Gammon!" he repeated loudly, as the captain signaled him to be more soft-spoken. "You can't tell me that sort of stuff. Where d'ye keep your own boats, hey—your schooner, or cutter, or whatever you have? Hey? Answer me that."

McCoy smiled as gently as he spoke. His smile was a caress, an embrace that surrounded the tired mate and sought to draw him into the quietude and rest of McCoy's tranquil soul.

"We have no schooner or cutter," he replied. "And we carry our canoes to the top of the cliff."

"You've got to show me," snorted the mate. "How d'ye get around to the other islands, hey? Tell me that."

"We don't get around. As governor of Pitcairn, I sometimes go. When I was younger, I was away a great deal—sometimes on the trading schooners, but mostly on the missionary brig. But she's gone now, and we depend on passing vessels. Sometimes we have had as high as six calls in one year. At other times, a year, and even longer, has gone by without one passing ship. Yours is the first in seven months."

"And you mean to tell me—" the mate began.

But Captain Davenport interfered.

"Enough of this. We're losing time. What is to be done, Mr. McCoy?"

The old man turned his brown eyes, sweet as a woman's, shoreward, and both captain and mate followed his gaze around from the lonely rock of Pitcairn to the crew clustering forward and waiting anxiously for the announcement of a decision. McCoy did not hurry. He thought smoothly and slowly, step by step, with the certitude of a mind that was never vexed or outraged by life.

"The wind is light now," he said finally. "There is a heavy current setting to the westward."

"That's what made us fetch to leeward," the captain interrupted, desiring to vindicate his seamanship.

"Yes, that is what fetched you to leeward," McCoy went on. "Well, you can't work up against this current today. And if you did, there is no beach. Your ship will be a total loss."

He paused, and captain and mate looked despair at each other.

"But I will tell you what you can do. The breeze will freshen tonight around midnight—see those tails of clouds and that thickness to windward, beyond the point there? That's where she'll come from, out of the southeast, hard. It is three hundred miles to Mangareva. Square away for it. There is a beautiful bed for your ship there."

The mate shook his head.

"Come into the cabin, and we'll look at the chart," said the captain.

McCoy found a stifling, poisonous atmosphere in the pent cabin. Stray waftures of invisible gases bit his eyes and made them sting. The deck was hotter, almost unbearably hot to his bare feet. The sweat poured out of his body. He looked almost with apprehension about him. This malignant, internal heat was astounding. It was a marvel that the cabin did not burst into flames. He had a feeling as if of being in a huge bake oven where the heat might at any moment increase tremendously and shrivel him up like a blade of grass.

As he lifted one foot and rubbed the hot sole against the leg of his trousers, the mate laughed in a savage, snarling fashion.

"The anteroom of hell," he said. "Hell herself is right down there under your feet."

"It's hot!" McCoy cried involuntarily, mopping his face with a bandanna handkerchief.

"Here's Mangareva," the captain said, bending over the table and pointing to a black speck in the midst of the white blankness of the chart. "And here, in between, is another island. Why not run for that?"

McCoy did not look at the chart.

"That's Crescent Island," he answered. "It is uninhabited, and it is only two or three feet above water. Lagoon, but no entrance. No, Mangareva is the nearest place for your purpose."

"Mangareva it is, then," said Captain Davenport, interrupting the mate's growling objection. "Call the crew aft, Mr. Konig."

The sailors obeyed, shuffling wearily along the deck and painfully endeavoring to make haste. Exhaustion was evident in every movement. The cook came out of his galley to hear, and the cabin boy hung about near him.

When Captain Davenport had explained the situation and announced his intention of running for Mangareva, an uproar broke out. Against a background of throaty rumbling arose inarticulate cries of rage, with here and there a distinct curse, or word, or phrase. A shrill Cockney voice soared and dominated for a moment, crying: "Gawd! After bein' in 'ell for fifteen days—an' now 'e wants us to sail this floatin' 'ell to sea again!"

The captain could not control them, but McCoy's gentle presence seemed to rebuke and calm them, and the muttering and cursing died away, until the full crew, save here and there an anxious face directed at the captain, yearned dumbly toward the green-clad peaks and beetling coast of Pitcairn.

Soft as a spring zephyr was the voice of McCoy:

"Captain, I thought I heard some of them say they were starving."

"Ay," was the answer, "and so we are. I've had a sea biscuit and a spoonful of salmon in the last two days. We're on whack. You see, when we discovered the fire, we battened down immediately to suffocate the fire. And then we found how little food there was in the pantry. But it was too late. We didn't dare break out the lazaret. Hungry? I'm just as hungry as they are."

He spoke to the men again, and again the throat-rumbling and cursing arose, their faces convulsed and animal-like with rage. The second and third mates had joined the captain, standing behind him at the break of the poop. Their faces were set and expressionless; they seemed bored, more than anything else, by this mutiny of the crew. Captain Davenport glanced questioningly at his first mate, and that person merely shrugged his shoulders in token of his helplessness.

"You see," the captain said to McCoy, "you can't compel sailors to leave the safe land and go to sea on a burning vessel. She has been their floating coffin for over two weeks now. They are worked out, and starved out, and they've got enough of her. We'll beat up for Pitcairn."

But the wind was light, the "Pyrenees" bottom was foul, and she could not beat up against the strong westerly current. At the end of two hours she had lost three miles. The sailors worked eagerly, as if by main strength they could compel the "Pyrenees" against the adverse elements. But steadily, port tack and starboard tack, she sagged off to the westward. The captain paced restlessly up and down, pausing occasionally to survey the vagrant smoke wisps and to trace them back to the portions of the deck from which they sprang. The carpenter was engaged constantly in attempting to locate such places, and, when he succeeded, in calking them tighter and tighter.

"Well, what do you think?" the captain finally asked McCoy, who was watching the carpenter with all a child's interest and curiosity in his eyes.

McCoy looked shoreward, where the land was disappearing in the thickening haze.

"I think it would be better to square away for Mangareva. With that breeze that is coming, you'll be there tomorrow evening."

"But what if the fire breaks out? It is liable to do it any moment."

"Have your boats ready in the falls. The same breeze will carry your boats to Mangareva if the ship burns out from under."

Captain Davenport debated for a moment, and then McCoy heard the question he had not wanted to hear, but which he knew was surely coming.

"I have no chart of Mangareva. On the general chart it is only a flyspeck. I would not know where to look for the entrance into the lagoon. Will you come along and pilot her in for me?"

McCoy's serenity was unbroken.

"Yes, Captain," he said, with the same quiet unconcern with which he would have accepted an invitation to dinner: "I'll go with you to Mangareva."

Again the crew was called aft, and the captain spoke to them from the break of the poop.

"We've tried to work her up, but you see how we've lost ground. She's setting off in a two-knot current. This gentleman is the Honorable McCoy, chief magistrate and governor of Pitcairn Island. He will come along with us to Mangareva. So you see, the situation is not so dangerous. He would not make such an offer if he thought he was going to lose his life. Besides, whatever risk there is, if he of his own free will can come on board and take it, we can do no less. What do you say for Mangareva?"

This time there was no uproar. McCoy's presence, the surety and calm that seemed to radiate from him, had had its effect. They conferred with one another in low voices. There was little urging. They were virtually unanimous, and they shoved the Cockney out as their spokesman. That worthy was overwhelmed with consciousness of the heroism of himself and his mates, and with flashing eyes he cried: "By Gawd! if 'e will, we will!"

The crew mumbled its assent and started forward.

"One moment, Captain," McCoy said, as the other was turning to give orders to the mate. "I must go ashore first."

Mr. Konig was thunderstruck, staring at McCoy as if he were a madman.

"Go ashore!" the captain cried. "What for? It will take you three hours to get there in your canoe."

McCoy measured the distance of the land away, and nodded.

"Yes, it is six now. I won't get ashore till nine. The people cannot be assembled earlier than ten. As the breeze freshens up tonight, you can begin to work up against it, and pick me up at daylight tomorrow morning."

"In the name of reason and common sense," the captain

burst forth, "what do you want to assemble the people for? Don't you realize that my ship is burning beneath me?"

McCoy was as placid as a summer sea, and the other's anger produced not the slightest ripple upon it.

"Yes, Captain," he cooed in his dovelike voice, "I do realize that your ship is burning. That is why I am going with you to Mangareva. But I must get permission to go with you. It is our custom. It is an important matter when the governor leaves the island. The people's interests are at stake, and so they have the right to vote their permission or refusal. But they will give it, I know that."

"Are you sure?"

"Quite sure."

"Then if you know they will give it, why bother with getting it? Think of the delay—a whole night."

"It is our custom," was the imperturbable reply. "Also, I am the governor, and I must make arrangements for the conduct of the island during my absence."

"But it is only a twenty-four-hour run to Mangareva," the captain objected. "Suppose it took you six times that long to return to windward; that would bring you back by the end of a week."

McCoy smiled his large, benevolent smile.

"Very few vessels come to Pitcairn, and when they do, they are usually from San Francisco or from around the Horn. I shall be fortunate if I get back in six months. I may be away a year, and I may have to go to San Francisco in order to find a vessel that will bring me back. My father once left Pitcairn to be gone three months, and two years passed before he could get back. Then, too, you are short of food. If you have to take to the boats, and the weather comes up bad, you may be days in reaching land. I can bring off two canoe loads of food in the morning. Dried bananas will be best. As the breeze freshens, you beat up against it. The nearer you are, the bigger loads I can bring off. Good-by."

He held out his hand. The captain shook it, and was reluctant to let go. He seemed to cling to it as a drowning sailor clings to a life buoy.

"How do I know you will come back in the morning?" he asked.

"Yes, that's it!" cried the mate. "How do we know but what he's skinning out to save his own hide?"

McCoy did not speak. He looked at them sweetly and benignantly, and it seemed to them that they received a message from his tremendous certitude of soul.

The captain released his hand, and, with a last sweeping glance that embraced the crew in its benediction, McCoy went over the rail and descended into his canoe.

The wind freshened, and the "Pyrenees," despite the foulness of her bottom, won half a dozen miles away from the westerly current. At daylight, with Pitcairn three miles to windward, Captain Davenport made out two canoes coming off to him. Again McCoy clambered up the side and dropped over the rail to the hot deck. He was followed by many packages of dried bananas, each package wrapped in dry leaves.

"Now, Captain," he said, "swing the yards and drive for dear life. You see, I am no navigator," he explained a few minutes later, as he stood by the captain aft, the latter with gaze wandering from aloft to overside as he estimated the "Pyrenees' " speed. "You must fetch her to Mangareva. When you have picked up the land, then I will pilot her in. What do you think she is making?"

"Eleven," Captain Davenport answered, with a final glance at the water rushing past.

"Eleven. Let me see, if she keeps up that gait, we'll sight Mangareva between eight and nine o'clock tomorrow morning. I'll have her on the beach by ten, or by eleven at latest. And then your troubles will be all over."

It almost seemed to the captain that the blissful moment had already arrived, such was the persuasive convincingness of McCoy. Captain Davenport had been under the fearful strain of navigating his burning ship for over two weeks, and he was beginning to feel that he had had enough.

A heavier flaw of wind struck the back of his neck and whistled by his ears. He measured the weight of it, and looked quickly overside.

"The wind is making all the time," he announced. "The

old girl's doing nearer twelve than eleven right now. If this keeps up, we'll be shortening down tonight."

All day the "Pyrenees," carrying her load of living fire, tore across the foaming sea. By nightfall, royals and topgallant sails were in, and she flew on into the darkness, with great, crested seas roaring after her. The auspicious wind had had its effect, and fore and aft a visible brightening was apparent. In the second dogwatch some careless soul started a song, and by eight bells the whole crew was singing.

Captain Davenport had his blankets brought up and spread on top the house.

"I've forgotten what sleep is," he explained to McCoy. "I'm all in. But give me a call at any time you think necessary."

At three in the morning he was aroused by a gentle tugging at his arm. He sat up quickly, bracing himself against the skylight, stupid yet from his heavy sleep. The wind was thrumming its war song in the rigging, and a wild sea was buffeting the "Pyrenees." Amidships she was wallowing first one rail under and then the other, flooding the waist more often than not. McCoy was shouting something he could not hear. He reached out, clutched the other by the shoulder, and drew him close so that his own ear was close to the other's lips.

"It's three o'clock," came McCoy's voice, still retaining its dovelike quality, but curiously muffled, as if from a long way off. "We've run two hundred and fifty. Crescent Island is only thirty miles away, somewhere there dead ahead. There's no lights on it. If we keep running, we'll pile up, and lose ourselves as well as the ship."

"What d'ye think—heave to?"

"Yes; heave to till daylight. It will only put us back four hours."

So the "Pyrenees," with her cargo of fire, was hove to, bitting the teeth of the gale and fighting and smashing the pounding seas. She was a shell, filled with a conflagration, and on the outside of the shell, clinging precariously, the little motes of men, by pull and haul, helped her in the battle.

"It is most unusual, this gale," McCoy told the captain, in the lee of the cabin. "By rights there should be no gale at this time of the year. But everything about the weather has been unusual. There has been a stoppage of the trades, and now it's howling right out of the trade quarter." He waved his hand into the darkness, as if his vision could dimly penetrate for hundreds of miles. "It is off to the westward. There is something big making off there somewhere—a hurricane or something. We're lucky to be so far to the eastward. But this is only a little blow," he added. "It can't last. I can tell you that much."

By daylight the gale had eased down to normal. But daylight revealed a new danger. It had come on thick. The sea was covered by a fog, or, rather, by a pearly mist that was foglike in density, insofar as it obstructed vision, but that was no more than a film on the sea, for the sun shot it through and filled it with a glowing radiance.

The deck of the "Pyrenees" was making more smoke than on the preceding day, and the cheerfulness of officers and crew had vanished. In the lee of the galley the cabin boy could be heard whimpering. It was his first voyage, and the fear of death was at his heart. The captain wandered about like a lost soul, nervously chewing his mustache, scowling, unable to make up his mind what to do.

"What do you think?" he asked, pausing by the side of McCoy, who was making a breakfast of fried bananas and a mug of water.

McCoy finished the last banana, drained the mug, and looked slowly around. In his eyes was a smile of tenderness as he said: "Well, Captain, we might as well drive as burn. Your decks are not going to hold out forever. They are hotter this morning. You haven't a pair of shoes I can wear? It is getting uncomfortable for my bare feet."

The "Pyrenees" shipped two heavy seas as she swung off and put once more before it, and the first mate expressed a desire to have all that water down in the hold, if only it could be introduced without taking off the hatches. McCoy ducked his head into the binnacle and watched the course set.

"I'd hold her up some more, Captain," he said. "She's been making drift when hove to."

"I've set it to a point higher already," was the answer. "Isn't that enough?"

"I'd make it two points, Captain. This bit of a blow kicked that westerly current ahead faster than you imagine."

Captain Davenport compromised on a point and a half, and then went aloft, accompanied by McCoy and the first mate, to keep a lookout for land. Sail had been made, so that the "Pyrenees" was doing ten knots. The following sea was dying down rapidly. There was no break in the pearly fog, and by ten o'clock Captain Davenport was growing nervous. All hands were at their stations, ready, at the first warning of land ahead, to spring like fiends to the task of bringing the "Pyrenees" up on the wind. That land ahead, a surf-washed outer reef, would be perilously close when it revealed itself in such a fog.

Another hour passed. The three watchers aloft stared intently into the pearly radiance.

"What if we miss Mangareva?" Captain Davenport asked abruptly.

McCoy, without shifting his gaze, answered softly: "Why, let her drive, Captain. That is all we can do. All the Paumotus are before us. We can drive for a thousand miles through reefs and atolls. We are bound to fetch up somewhere."

"Then drive it is." Captain Davenport evidenced his intention of descending to the deck. "We've missed Mangareva. God knows where the next land is. I wish I'd held her up that other half point," he confessed a moment later. "This cursed current plays the devil with a navigator."

"The old navigators called the Paumotus the Dangerous Archipelago," McCoy said, when they had regained the poop. "This very current was partly responsible for that name."

"I was talking with a sailor chap in Sydney, once," said Mr. Konig. "He'd been trading in the Paumotus. He told me insurance was eighteen per cent. Is that right?"

McCoy smiled and nodded.

"Except that they don't insure," he explained. "The owners write off twenty per cent of the cost of their schooners each year."

"My God!" Captain Davenport groaned. "That makes the life of a schooner only five years!" He shook his head sadly, murmuring, "Bad waters! Bad waters!"

Again they went into the cabin to consult the big general chart; but the poisonous vapors drove them coughing and gasping on deck.

"Here is Moerenhout Island." Captain Davenport pointed it out on the chart, which he had spread on the house. "It can't be more than a hundred miles to leeward."

"A hundred and ten." McCoy shook his head doubtfully. "It might be done, but it is very difficult. I might beach her, and then again I might put her on the reef. A bad place, a very bad place."

"We'll take the chance," was Captain Davenport's decision, as he set about working out the course.

Sail was shortened early in the afternoon, to avoid running past in the night; and in the second dogwatch the crew manifested its regained cheerfulness. Land was so very near, and their troubles would be over in the morning.

But morning broke clear, with a blazing tropic sun. The southeast trade had swung around to the eastward, and was driving the "Pyrenees" through the water at an eight-knot clip. Captain Davenport worked up his dead reckoning, allowing generously for drift, and announced Moerenhout Island to be not more than ten miles off. The "Pyrenees" sailed the ten miles; she sailed ten miles more; and the lookouts at the three mastheads saw naught but the naked, sun-washed sea.

"But the land is there, I tell you," Captain Davenport shouted to them from the poop.

McCoy smiled soothingly, but the captain glared about him like a madman, fetched his sextant, and took a chronometer sight.

"I knew I was right," he almost shouted, when he had worked up the observation. "Twenty-one, fifty-five, south; one-thirty-six, two, west. There you are. We're eight miles to windward yet. What did you make it out, Mr. Konig?"

The first mate glanced at his own figures, and said in a low voice: "Twenty-one, fifty-five all right; but my longitude's one-thirty-six, forty-eight. That puts us considerably to leeward—"

But Captain Davenport ignored his figures with so contemptuous a silence as to make Mr. Konig grit his teeth and curse savagely under his breath.

"Keep her off," the captain ordered the man at the wheel. "Three points—steady there, as she goes!"

Then he returned to his figures and worked them over. The sweat poured from his face. He chewed his mustache, his lips, and his pencil, staring at the figures as a man might at a ghost. Suddenly, with a fierce, muscular outburst, he crumpled the scribbled paper in his fist and crushed it underfoot. Mr. Konig grinned vindictively and turned away, while Captain Davenport leaned against the cabin and for half an hour spoke no word, contenting himself with gazing to leeward with an expression of musing hopelessness on his face.

"Mr. McCoy," he broke silence abruptly. "The chart indicates a group of islands, but not how many, off there to the north'ard, or nor'-nor'westward, about forty miles—the Acteon Islands. What about them?"

"There are four, all low," McCoy answered. "First to the southeast is Matuerui—no people, no entrance to the lagoon. Then comes Tenarunga. There used to be about a dozen people there, but they may be all gone now. Anyway, there is no entrance for a ship—only a boat entrance, with a fathom of water. Vehauga and Teura-raro are the other two. No entrances, no people, very low. There is no bed for the 'Pyrenees' in that group. She would be a total wreck."

"Listen to that!" Captain Davenport was frantic. "No people! No entrances! What in the devil are islands good for?

"Well, then," he barked suddenly, like an excited terrier, "the chart gives a whole mess of islands off to the nor'west. What about them? What one has an entrance where I can lay my ship?"

McCoy calmly considered. He did not refer to the chart. All these islands, reefs, shoals, lagoons, entrances, and distances were marked on the chart of his memory. He knew them as the city dweller knows his buildings, streets, and alleys.

"Papakena and Vanavana are off there to the westward, or west-nor'westward a hundred miles and a bit more," he said. "One is uninhabited, and I heard that the people on the other had gone off to Cadmus Island. Anyway, neither lagoon has an entrance. Ahunui is another hundred miles on to the nor'-west. No entrance, no people."

"Well, forty miles beyond them are two islands?" Captain Davenport queried, raising his head from the chart.

McCoy shook his head.

"Paros and Manuhungi—no entrances, no people. Nengo-Nengo is forty miles beyond them, in turn, and it has no people and no entrance. But there is Hao Island. It is just the place. The lagoon is thirty miles long and five miles wide. There are plenty of people. You can usually find water. And any ship in the world can go through the entrance."

He ceased and gazed solicitously at Captain Davenport, who, bending over the chart with a pair of dividers in hand, had just emitted a low groan.

"Is there any lagoon with an entrance anywhere nearer than Hao Island?" he asked.

"No, Captain; that is the nearest."

"Well, it's three hundred and forty miles." Captain Davenport was speaking very slowly, with decision. "I won't risk the responsibility of all these lives. I'll wreck her on the Acteons. And she's a good ship, too," he added regretfully, after altering the course, this time making more allowance than ever for the westerly current.

An hour later the sky was overcast. The southeast trade still held, but the ocean was a checkerboard of squalls.

"We'll be there by one o'clock," Captain Davenport announced confidently. "By two o'clock at the outside. McCoy, you put her ashore on the one where the people are."

The sun did not appear again, nor, at one o'clock, was any land to be seen. Captain Davenport looked astern at the "Pyrenees'" canting wake.

"Good Lord!" he cried. "An easterly current! Look at that!"

Mr. Konig was incredulous. McCoy was noncommittal, though he said that in the Paumotus there was no reason why it should not be an easterly current. A few minutes later a squall robbed the "Pyrenees" temporarily of all her wind, and she was left rolling heavily in the trough.

"Where's that deep lead? Over with it, you there!" Captain Davenport held the lead line and watched it sag off to the northeast. "There, look at that! Take hold of it for yourself."

McCoy and the mate tried it, and felt the line thrumming and vibrating savagely to the grip of the tidal stream.

"A four-knot current," said Mr. Konig.

"An easterly current instead of a westerly," said Captain Davenport, glaring accusingly at McCoy, as if to cast the blame for it upon him.

"That is one of the reasons, Captain, for insurance being eighteen per cent in these waters," McCoy answered cheerfully. "You never can tell. The currents are always changing. There was a man who wrote books, I forget his name, in the yacht 'Casco.' He missed Takaroa by thirty miles and fetched Tikei, all because of the shifting currents. You are up to windward now, and you'd better keep off a few points."

"But how much has this current set me?" the captain demanded irately. "How am I to know how much to keep off?"

"I don't know, Captain," McCoy said with great gentleness.

The wind returned, and the "Pyrenees," her deck smoking and shimmering in the bright gray light, ran off dead to leeward. Then she worked back, port tack and starboard tack, crisscrossing her track, combing the sea for the Acteon Islands, which the masthead lookouts failed to sight.

Captain Davenport was beside himself. His rage took the form of sullen silence, and he spent the afternoon in pacing the poop or leaning against the weather shrouds. At nightfall, without even consulting McCoy, he squared away and headed into the northwest. Mr. Konig, surreptitiously consulting chart and binnacle, and McCoy, openly and innocently consulting the binnacle, knew that they were running for Hao Island. By midnight the squalls ceased, and the stars came out. Captain Davenport was cheered by the promise of a clear day.

"I'll get an observation in the morning," he told McCoy, "though what my latitude is, is a puzzler. But I'll use the

Sumner method, and settle that. Do you know the Sumner line?"

And thereupon he explained it in detail to McCoy.

The day proved clear, the trade blew steadily out of the east, and the "Pyrenees" just as steadily logged her nine knots. Both the captain and mate worked out the position on a Sumner line, and agreed, and at noon agreed again, and verified the morning sights by the noon sights.

"Another twenty-four hours and we'll be there," Captain Davenport assured McCoy. "It's a miracle the way the old girl's decks hold out. But they can't last. They can't last. Look at them smoke, more and more every day. Yet it was a tight deck to begin with, fresh-calked in 'Frisco. I was surprised when the fire first broke out and we battened down. Look at that!"

He broke off to gaze with dropped jaw at a spiral of smoke that coiled and twisted in the lee of the mizzenmast twenty feet above the deck.

"Now, how did that get there?" he demanded indignantly.

Beneath it there was no smoke. Crawling up from the deck, sheltered from the wind by the mast, by some freak it took form and visibility at that height. It writhed away from the mast, and for a moment overhung the captain like some threatening portent. The next moment the wind whisked it away, and the captain's jaw returned to place.

"As I was saying, when we first battened down, I was surprised. It was a tight deck, yet it leaked smoke like a sieve. And we've calked and calked ever since. There must be tremendous pressure underneath to drive so much smoke through."

That afternoon the sky became overcast again; and squally, drizzly weather set in. The wind shifted back and forth between southeast and northeast, and at midnight the "Pyrenees" was caught aback by a sharp squall from the southwest, from which point the wind continued to blow intermittently.

"We won't make Hao until ten or eleven," Captain Davenport complained at seven in the morning, when the fleeting promise of the sun had been erased by hazy cloud masses in the eastern sky. And the next moment he was plaintively demanding, "And what are the currents doing?"

Lookouts at the mastheads could report no land, and the day passed in drizzling calms and violent squalls. By nightfall a heavy sea began to make from the west. The barometer had fallen to 29.50. There was no wind, and still the ominous sea continued to increase. Soon the "Pyrenees" was rolling madly in the huge waves that marched in an unending procession from out of the darkness of the west. Sail was shortened as fast as both watches could work, and, when the tired crew had finished, its grumbling and complaining voices, peculiarly animal-like and menacing, could be heard in the darkness. Once the starboard watch was called aft to lash down and make secure, and the men openly advertised their sullenness and unwillingness. Every slow movement was a protest and a threat. The atmosphere was moist and sticky like mucilage, and in the absence of wind all hands seemed to pant and gasp for air. The sweat stood out on faces and bare arms, and Captain Davenport for one, his face more gaunt and careworn than ever, and his eyes troubled and staring, was oppressed by a feeling of impending calamity.

"It's off to the westward," McCoy said encouragingly. "At worst, we'll be only on the edge of it."

But Captain Davenport refused to be comforted, and by the light of a lantern read up the chapter in his *Epitome* that related to the strategy of shipmasters in cyclonic storms. From somewhere amidships the silence was broken by a low whimpering from the cabin boy.

"Oh, shut up!" Captain Davenport yelled suddenly and with such force as to startle every man on board and to frighten the offender into a wild wail of terror.

"Mr. Konig," the captain said in a voice that trembled with rage and nerves, "will you kindly step for'ard and stop that brat's mouth with a deck mop?"

But it was McCoy who went forward, and in a few minutes had the boy comforted and asleep.

Shortly before daybreak the first breath of air began to move from out the southeast, increasing swiftly to a stiff and stiffer breeze. All hands were on deck waiting for what might be behind it.

"We're all right now, Captain," said McCoy, standing close to his shoulder. "The hurricane is to the west'ard, and we are south of it. This breeze is the in-suck. It won't blow any harder. You can begin to put sail on her."

"But what's the good? Where shall I sail? This is the second day without observations, and we should have sighted Hao Island yesterday morning. Which way does it bear, north, south, east, or what? Tell me that, and I'll make sail in a jiffy."

"I am no navigator, Captain," McCoy said in his mild way.

"I used to think I was one," was the retort, "before I got into these Paumotus."

At midday the cry of "Breakers ahead!" was heard from the lookout. The "Pyrenees" was kept off, and sail after sail was loosed and sheeted home. The "Pyrenees" was sliding through the water and fighting a current that threatened to set her down upon the breakers. Officers and men were working like mad, cook and cabin boy, Captain Davenport himself, and McCoy all lending a hand. It was a close shave. It was a low shoal, a bleak and perilous place over which the seas broke unceasingly, where no man could live, and on which not even sea birds could rest. The "Pyrenees" was swept within a hundred yards of it before the wind carried her clear, and at this moment the panting crew, its work done, burst out in a torrent of curses upon the head of McCoy—of McCoy who had come on board, and proposed the run to Mangareva, and lured them all away from the safety of Pitcairn Island to certain destruction in this baffling and terrible stretch of sea. But McCoy's tranquil soul was undisturbed. He smiled at them with simple and gracious benevolence, and, somehow, the exalted goodness of him seemed to penetrate to their dark and somber souls, shaming them, and from very shame stilling the curses vibrating in their throats.

"Bad waters! Bad waters!" Captain Davenport was murmuring as his ship forged clear; but he broke off abruptly to gaze at the shoal which should have been dead astern, but which was already on the "Pyrenees'" weather quarter and working up rapidly to windward.

He sat down and buried his face in his hands. And the first mate saw, and McCoy saw, and the crew saw, what he had seen. South of the shoal an easterly current had set them down upon it; north of the shoal an equally swift westerly current had clutched the ship and was sweeping her away.

"I've heard of these Paumotus before," the captain groaned, lifting his blanched face from his hands. "Captain Moyendale told me about them after losing his ship on them. And I laughed at him behind his back. God forgive me, I laughed at him. What shoal is that?" he broke off, to ask McCoy.

"I don't know, Captain."

"Why don't you know?"

"Because I never saw it before, and because I have never heard of it. I do know that it is not charted. These waters have never been thoroughly surveyed."

"Then you don't know where we are?"

"No more than you do," McCoy said gently.

At four in the afternoon coconut trees were sighted, apparently growing out of the water. A little later the low land of an atoll was raised above the sea.

"I know where we are now, Captain." McCoy lowered the glasses from his eyes. "That's Resolution Island. We are forty miles beyond Hao Island, and the wind is in our teeth."

"Get ready to beach her then. Where's the entrance?"

"There's only a canoe passage. But now that we know where we are, we can run for Barclay de Tolley. It is only one hundred and twenty miles from here, due nor'-nor'west. With this breeze we can be there by nine o'clock tomorrow morning."

Captain Davenport consulted the chart and debated with himself.

"If we wreck her here," McCoy added, "we'd have to make the run to Barclay de Tolley in the boats just the same."

The captain gave his orders, and once more the "Pyrenees" swung off for another run across the inhospitable sea.

And the middle of the next afternoon saw despair and mutiny on her smoking deck. The current had accelerated, the wind had slackened, and the "Pyrenees" had sagged off to the west. The lookout sighted Barclay de Tolley to the eastward, barely visible from the masthead, and vainly and for hours the "Pyrenees" tried to beat up to it. Ever, like a mirage, the coconut trees hovered on the horizon, visible only from the masthead. From the deck they were hidden by the bulge of the world.

Again Captain Davenport consulted McCoy and the chart. Makemo lay seventy-five miles to the southwest. Its lagoon was thirty miles long, and its entrance was excellent. When Captain Davenport gave his orders, the crew refused duty. They announced that they had had enough of hell-fire under their feet. There was the land. What if the ship could not make it? They could make it in the boats. Let her burn, then. Their lives amounted to something to them. They had served faithfully the ship, now they were going to serve themselves.

They sprang to the boats, brushing the second and third mates out of the way, and proceeded to swing the boats out and to prepare to lower away. Captain Davenport and the first mate, revolvers in hand, were advancing to the break of the poop, when McCoy, who had climbed on top of the cabin, began to speak.

He spoke to the sailors, and at the first sound of his dovelike, cooing voice they paused to hear. He extended to them his own ineffable serenity and peace. His soft voice and simple thoughts flowed out to them in a magic stream, soothing them against their wills. Long forgotten things came back to them, and some remembered lullaby songs of childhood and the content and rest of the mother's arm at the end of the day. There was no more trouble, no more danger, no more irk, in all the world. Everything was as it should be, and it was only a matter of course that they should turn their backs upon the land and put to sea once more with hell-fire hot beneath their feet.

McCoy spoke simply; but it was not what he spoke. It was his personality that spoke more eloquently than any word he could utter. It was an alchemy of soul occultly subtle and profoundly deep—a mysterious emanation of the spirit, seductive, sweetly humble, and terribly imperious. It was illumination in the dark crypts of their souls, a compulsion of purity and gentleness vastly greater than that which resided in the shining, death-spitting revolvers of the officers.

The men wavered reluctantly where they stood, and those who had loosed the turns made them fast again. Then one, and then another, and then all of them, began to sidle awkwardly away.

McCoy's face was beaming with childlike pleasure as he descended from the top of the cabin. There was no trouble. For that matter there had been no trouble averted. There never had been any trouble, for there was no place for such in the blissful world in which he lived.

"You hypnotized 'em," Mr. Konig grinned at him, speaking in a low voice.

"Those boys are good," was the answer. "Their hearts are good. They have had a hard time, and they have worked hard, and they will work hard to the end."

Mr. Konig had no time to reply. His voice was ringing out orders, the sailors were springing to obey, and the "Pyrenees" was paying slowly off from the wind until her bow should point in the direction of Makemo.

The wind was very light, and after sundown almost ceased. It was insufferably warm, and fore and aft men sought vainly to sleep. The deck was too hot to lie upon, and poisonous vapors, oozing through the seams, crept like evil spirits over the ship, stealing into the nostrils and windpipes of the unwary and causing fits of sneezing and coughing. The stars blinked lazily in the dim vault overhead; and the full moon, rising in the east, touched with its light the myriads of wisps and threads and spidery films of smoke that intertwined and writhed and twisted along the deck, over the rails, and up the masts and shrouds.

"Tell me," Captain Davenport said, rubbing his smarting eyes, "what happened with that 'Bounty' crowd after they reached Pitcairn? The account I read said they burned the 'Bounty,' and that they were not discovered until many years later. But what happened in the meantime? I've always been curious to know. They were men with their necks in the rope.

There were some native men, too. And then there were women. That made it look like trouble right from the jump."

"There was trouble," McCoy answered. "They were bad men. They quarreled about the women right away. One of the mutineers, Williams, lost his wife. All the women were Tahitian women. His wife fell from the cliffs when hunting sea birds. Then he took the wife of one of the native men away from him. All the native men were made very angry by this, and they killed off nearly all the mutineers. Then the mutineers that escaped killed off all the native men. The women helped. And the natives killed each other. Everybody killed everybody. They were terrible men.

"Timiti was killed by two other natives while they were combing his hair in friendship. The white men had sent them to do it. Then the white men killed them. The wife of Tullaloo killed him in a cave because she wanted a white man for husband. They were very wicked. God had hidden His face from them. At the end of two years all the native men were murdered, and all the white men except four. They were Young; John Adams; McCoy, who was my great-grandfather; and Quintal. He was a very bad man, too. Once, just because his wife did not catch enough fish for him, he bit off her ear."

"They were a bad lot!" Mr. Konig exclaimed.

"Yes, they were very bad," McCoy agreed and went on serenely cooing of the blood and lust of his iniquitous ancestry. "My great-grandfather escaped murder in order to die by his own hand. He made a still and manufactured alcohol from the roots of the ti plant. Quintal was his chum, and they got drunk together all the time. At last McCoy got delirium tremens, tied a rock to his neck, and jumped into the sea.

"Quintal's wife, the one whose ear he bit off, also got killed by falling from the cliffs. Then Quintal went to Young and demanded his wife, and went to Adams and demanded his wife. Adams and Young were afraid of Quintal. They knew he would kill them. So they killed him, the two of them together, with a hatchet. Then Young died. And that was about all the trouble they had."

"I should say so," Captain Davenport snorted. "There was nobody left to kill."

"You see, God had hidden His face," McCoy said.

By morning no more than a faint air was blowing from the eastward, and, unable to make appreciable southing by it, Captain Davenport hauled up full-and-by on the port tack. He was afraid of that terrible westerly current that had cheated him out of so many ports of refuge. All day the calm continued, and all night, while the sailors, on a short ration of dried banana, were grumbling. Also, they were growing weak and complaining of stomach pains caused by the straight banana diet. All day the current swept the "Pyrenees" to the westward, while there was no wind to bear her south. In the middle of the first dogwatch, coconut trees were sighted due south, their tufted heads rising above the water and marking the low-lying atoll beneath.

"That is Taenga Island," McCoy said. "We need a breeze tonight, or else we'll miss Makemo."

"What's become of the southeast trade?" the captain demanded. "Why don't it blow? What's the matter?"

"It is the evaporation from the big lagoons—there are so many of them," McCoy explained. "The evaporation upsets the whole system of trades. It even causes the wind to back up and blow gales from the southwest. This is the Dangerous Archipelago, Captain."

Captain Davenport faced the old man, opened his mouth, and was about to curse, but paused and refrained. McCoy's presence was a rebuke to the blasphemies that stirred in his brain and trembled in his larynx. McCoy's influence had been growing during the many days they had been together. Captain Davenport was an autocrat of the sea, fearing no man, never bridling his tongue, and now he found himself unable to curse in the presence of this old man with the feminine brown eyes and the voice of a dove. When he realized this, Captain Davenport experienced a distinct shock. This old man was merely the seed of McCoy, of McCoy of the "Bounty," the mutineer fleeing from the hemp that waited him in England, the McCoy who was a power for evil in the early days of blood and lust and violent death on Pitcairn Island.

Captain Davenport was not religious, yet in that moment he felt a mad impulse to cast himself at the other's feet—and to say he knew not what. It was an emotion that so deeply stirred him, rather than a coherent thought, and he was aware in some vague way of his own unworthiness and smallness in the presence of this other man who possessed the simplicity of a child and the gentleness of a woman.

Of course he could not so humble himself before the eyes of his officers and men. And yet the anger that had prompted the blasphemy still raged in him. He suddenly smote the cabin with his clenched hand and cried:

"Look here, old man, I won't be beaten. These Paumotus have cheated and tricked me and made a fool of me. I refuse to be beaten. I am going to drive this ship, and drive and drive and drive clear through the Paumotus to China but what I find a bed for her. If every man deserts, I'll stay by her. I'll show the Paumotus. They can't fool me. She's a good girl, and I'll stick by her as long as there's a plank to stand on. You hear me?"

"And I'll stay with you, Captain," McCoy said.

During the night, light, baffling airs blew out of the south, and the frantic captain, with his cargo of fire, watched and measured his westward drift and went off by himself at times to curse softly so that McCoy should not hear.

Daylight showed more palms growing out of the water to the south.

"That's the leeward point of Makemo," McCoy said. "Katiu is only a few miles to the west. We may make that."

But the current, sucking between the two islands, swept them to the northwest, and at one in the afternoon they saw the palms of Katiu rise above the sea and sink back into the sea again.

A few minutes later, just as the captain had discovered that a new current from the northeast had gripped the "Pyrenees," the masthead lookouts raised coconut palms in the northwest.

"It is Raraka," said McCoy. "We won't make it without

wind. The current is drawing us down to the southwest. But we must watch out. A few miles farther on a current flows north and turns in a circle to the northwest. This will sweep us away from Fakarava, and Fakarava is the place for the 'Pyrenees' to find her bed."

"They can sweep all they da— all they well please," Captain Davenport remarked with heat. "We'll find a bed for her somewhere just the same."

But the situation on the "Pyrenees" was reaching a culmination. The deck was so hot that it seemed an increase of a few degrees would cause it to burst into flames. In many places even the heavy-soled shoes of the men were no protection, and they were compelled to step lively to avoid scorching their feet. The smoke had increased and grown more acrid. Every man on board was suffering from inflamed eyes, and they coughed and strangled like a crew of tuberculosis patients. In the afternoon the boats were swung out and equipped. The last several packages of dried bananas were stored in them, as well as the instruments of the officers. Captain Davenport even put the chronometer into the longboat, fearing the blowing up of the deck at any moment.

All night this apprehension weighed heavily on all, and in the first morning light, with hollow eyes and ghastly faces, they stared at one another as if in surprise that the "Pyrenees" still held together and that they still were alive.

Walking rapidly at times, and even occasionally breaking into an undignified hop-skip-and-run, Captain Davenport inspected his ship's deck.

"It is a matter of hours now, if not of minutes," he announced on his return to the poop.

The cry of land came down from the masthead. From the deck the land was invisible, and McCoy went aloft, while the captain took advantage of the opportunity to curse some of the bitterness out of his heart. But the cursing was suddenly stopped by a dark line on the water that he sighted to the northeast. It was not a squall, but a regular breeze—the disrupted tradewind, eight points out of its direction but resuming business once more.

"Hold her up, Captain," McCoy said as soon as he reached

the poop. "That's the easterly point of Fakarava, and we'll go in through the passage full-tilt, the wind abeam, and every sail drawing."

At the end of an hour, the coconut trees and the low-lying land were visible from the deck. The feeling that the end of the "Pyrenees'" resistance was imminent weighed heavily on everybody. Captain Davenport had the three boats lowered and dropped short astern, a man in each to keep them apart. The "Pyrenees" closely skirted the shore, the surf-whitened atoll a bare two cable lengths away.

"Get ready to wear her, Captain," McCoy warned.

And a minute later the land parted, exposing a narrow passage and the lagoon beyond, a great mirror, thirty miles in length and a third as broad.

"Now, Captain."

For the last time the yards of the "Pyrenees" swung around as she obeyed the wheel and headed into the passage. The turns had scarcely been made, and nothing had been coiled down, when the men and mates swept back to the poop in panic terror. Nothing had happened, yet they averred that something was going to happen. They could not tell why. They merely knew that it was about to happen. McCoy started forward to take up his position on the bow in order to conn the vessel in; but the captain gripped his arm and whirled him around.

"Do it from here," he said. "That deck's not safe. What's the matter?" he demanded the next instant. "We're standing still."

McCoy smiled.

"You are bucking a seven-knot current, Captain," he said. "That is the way the full ebb runs out of this passage."

At the end of another hour the "Pyrenees" had scarcely gained her length, but the wind freshened and she began to forge ahead.

"Better get into the boats, some of you," Captain Davenport commanded.

His voice was still ringing, and the men were just beginning to move in obedience, when the amidship deck of the "Pyrenees," in a mass of flame and smoke, was flung upward into the sails and rigging, part of it remaining there and the rest falling into the sea. The wind being abeam was what had saved the men crowded aft. They made a blind rush to gain the boats, but McCoy's voice, carrying its convincing message of vast calm and endless time, stopped them.

"Take it easy," he was saying. "Everything is all right. Pass that boy down, somebody, please."

The man at the wheel had forsaken it in a funk, and Captain Davenport had leaped and caught the spokes in time to prevent the ship from yawing in the current and going ashore.

"Better take charge of the boats," he said to Mr. Konig. "Tow one of them short, right under the quarter. . . . When I go over, it'll be on the jump."

Mr. Konig hesitated, then went over the rail and lowered himself into the boat.

"Keep her off half a point, Captain."

Captain Davenport gave a start. He had thought he had the ship to himself.

"Ay, ay; half a point it is," he answered.

Amidships the "Pyrenees" was an open, flaming furnace, out of which poured an immense volume of smoke that rose high above the masts and completely hid the forward part of the ship. McCoy, in the shelter of the mizzen shrouds, continued his difficult task of conning the ship through the intricate channel. The fire was working aft along the deck from the seat of explosion, while the soaring tower of canvas on the mainmast went up and vanished in a sheet of flame. Forward, though they could not see them, they knew that the headsails were still drawing.

"If only she don't burn all her canvas off before she makes inside," the captain groaned.

"She'll make it," McCoy assured him with supreme confidence. "There is plenty of time. She is bound to make it. And once inside, we'll put her before it; that will keep the smoke away from us and hold back the fire from working aft."

A tongue of flame sprang up the mizzen, reached hungrily for the lowest tier of canvas, missed it, and vanished. From aloft a burning shred of ropestuff fell square on the back of Captain Davenport's neck. He acted with the celerity of one stung by a bee as he reached up and brushed the offending fire from his skin.

"How is she heading, Captain?"

"Nor'west by west."

"Keep her west-nor'west."

Captain Davenport put the wheel up and steadied her.

"West by north, Captain."

"West by north she is."

"And now west."

Slowly, point by point, as she entered the lagoon, the "Pyrenees" described the circle that put her before the wind; and point by point, with all the calm certitude of a thousand years of time to spare, McCoy chanted the changing course.

"Another point, Captain."

"A point it is."

Captain Davenport whirled several spokes over, suddenly reversing and coming back one to check her.

"Steady."

"Steady she is—right on it."

Despite the fact that the wind was now astern, the heat was so intense that Captain Davenport was compelled to steal sidelong glances into the binnacle, letting go the wheel, now with one hand, now with the other, to rub or shield his blistering cheeks. McCoy's beard was crinkling and shriveling and the smell of it, strong in the other's nostrils, compelled him to look toward McCoy with sudden solicitude. Captain Davenport was letting go the spokes alternately with his hands in order to rub their blistering backs against his trousers. Every sail on the mizzenmast vanished in a rush of flame, compelling the two men to crouch and shield their faces.

"Now," said McCoy, stealing a glance ahead at the low shore, "four points up, Captain, and let her drive."

Shreds and patches of burning rope and canvas were falling about them and upon them. The tarry smoke from a smoldering piece of rope at the captain's feet set him off into a violent coughing fit, during which he still clung to the spokes.

The "Pyrenees" struck, her bow lifted, and she ground ahead gently to a stop. A shower of burning fragments, dislodged by the shock, fell about them. The ship moved ahead again and struck a second time. She crushed the fragile coral under her keel, drove on, and struck a third time.

"Hard over," said McCoy. "Hard over?" he questioned gently, a minute later.

"She won't answer," was the reply.

"All right. She is swinging around." McCoy peered over the side. "Soft, white sand. Couldn't ask better. A beautiful bed."

As the "Pyrenees" swung around, her stern away from the wind, a fearful blast of smoke and flame poured aft. Captain Davenport deserted the wheel in blistering agony. He reached the painter of the boat that lay under the quarter, then looked for McCoy, who was standing aside to let him go down.

"You first," the captain cried, gripping him by the shoulder and almost throwing him over the rail. But the flame and smoke were too terrible, and he followed hard after McCoy, both men wriggling on the rope and sliding down into the boat together. A sailor in the bow, without waiting for orders, slashed the painter through with his sheath knife. The oars, poised in readiness, bit into the water, and the boat shot away.

"A beautiful bed, Captain," McCoy murmured, looking back.

"Ay, a beautiful bed, and all thanks to you," was the answer.

The three boats pulled away for the white beach of pounded coral, beyond which, on the edge of a coconut grove, could be seen a half-dozen grass houses, and a score or more of excited natives, gazing wide-eyed at the conflagration that had come to land.

The boats grounded, and they stepped out on the white beach.

"And now," said McCoy, "I must see about getting back to Pitcairn."

James A. Michener

MUTINY

James A. Michener, whose name is almost synonymous with the South Pacific of World War II and after, was born in 1907 and grew up in "dire poverty" in Bucks County, Pennsylvania. After a period as professor and editor, in 1942 he volunteered, although a Quaker, for combat duty in the Navy. Assigned to aircraft maintenance work, he visited some fifty tropical islands. One result of his experience was his first book, *Tales of the South Pacific* (1947), source of the Broadway musical show "South Pacific."

This first volume and others such as *Return to Paradise* (1951), *Rascals in Paradise* (in collaboration with A. Grove Day, 1957), and the giant novel *Hawaii* prove Michener's right to eminence among the authors who have written about the Pacific.

The setting of "Mutiny" is Norfolk Island, a dot on the map between New Zealand and New Caledonia, an island well suited to emphasize the story's theme. First used as a prison for convicts too desperate to be handled at Botany Bay, it was evacuated when the prisoners mutinied against their jailers. It was next used for the resettlement of people from Pitcairn Island, descendants of Fletcher Christian, William McCoy, and others of the "Bounty" mutineers. And then, during World War II, an order to destroy the giant Norfolk pines that made the island a "living cathedral" brings an American naval officer close to revolt.

WHEN I RETURNED TO NOUMÉA FROM THE ISLAND OF VANIKORO, Admiral Kester called me into his office. He had one of the rooms near the gingerbread balcony on Rue General Gallieni.

He said, "We were lucky at Coral Sea. It's the next battle that counts." He waved his hand over the islands. His finger came to rest, I remember, on a large island shaped like a kidney, Guadalcanal.

"Some day we'll go into one of those islands. When we do, we've got to have a steady flow of planes from New Zealand and Australia. Now look!" Spreading his fingers wide he dragged them down the map from Bougainville, New Georgia, and Guadal. He brought them together at Santo. "We have Santo. We'll keep it. It's the key. And we can supply Santo from Nouméa. But if we ever need planes in an emergency, we must be able to fly them up to Nouméa from New Zealand and Australia." He slashed his thumb boldly from Guadalcanal to Auckland. "That's the life line.

"Now if you'll look at the air route from Nouméa to Auckland you'll see a speck in the ocean not far from the route from Australia to Nouméa. That speck's an island. It's vital. Absolutely vital!" His chin jutted out. His stubby forefinger stabbed at the map. The vital speck was Norfolk Island.

There is no other island in the South Pacific like Norfolk. Lonely and lost, it is the only island in the entire ocean where no men lived before the white man came. Surrounded by gaunt cliffs, beat upon endlessly by the vast ocean, it is a speck under the forefinger of God, or Admiral Kester.

"You'll find some Americans down there," the Admiral continued. "Building an airstrip. They're bogged down. Look." He handed me a dispatch from Norfolk: "TWO SITES CHOSEN X OPPOSITION TO BETTER SITE TERRIFIC X CAN WE IGNORE LOCAL WISHES X ADVISE X TONY FRY X."

"This man Fry," the Admiral remarked, "is a queer duck. One of the best reserves I've seen. He wouldn't bother me with details unless something important had developed. Obviously, we can ignore local opinion if we have to. The Australian government has placed responsibility for the protection of Norfolk squarely on us. We can do what we damned well want to. But it's always wisest to exercise your power with judgment. Either you do what the local people want to do, or you jolly them into wanting to do what you've got to do anyway."

He studied the map again. "They're the life lines." His broad thumb hit Guadal again. "We've got to have an airstrip on Norfolk. And a big one." He turned away from the map. "Now you run on down to Norfolk. Take the old PBY. And you tell Fry you have my full authority to settle the problem. Don't make anyone mad, if you can help it. But remember the first job: Win the war!"

The old PBY flew down from Nouméa on a day of rare beauty. We did not fly high. Below us the waves of the great ocean formed and fled in golden sunlight. There was a fair breeze from Australia, as if that mighty island were restless, and from the Tasman Sea gaunt waves, riding clear from the polar ice cap, came north and made the sea choppy. The winter sun was low, for it was now July. It hurried across the sky before us.

After six hours I saw a speck on the horizon. It grew rapidly into an island, and then into an island with jagged cliffs. Norfolk was below us. I remember clearly every detail of that first view. Not much more than ten square miles. Forbidding cliffs along all shores. A prominent mountain to the north. Fine plateau land elsewhere.

"Oughtn't to be much trouble building an airstrip there," I mused aloft. "Run it right down the plateau. Throw a cross strip about like that, and you have an all-wind landing area. Looks simple. This guy Tony Fry must have things screwed up."

"We'll land in that little bay," the pilot said.

"I don't see any," I replied.

"Between the cliffs," he said.

I looked, and where he pointed there was a small bay. Not protected from the sea, and terribly small. But a bay. "The waves look mighty high to me," I said.

"They are," he laughed. "Damned high."

He went far out to sea and came in for his landing. But he had too much speed and zoomed over the island, climbing rapidly for another attempt. We came roaring in from the tiny bay, sped over a winding hill road leading up to the plateau and then right down the imaginary line I had drawn as the logical location for the airstrip. It was then that I saw the pines of Norfolk.

For on each side of that line, like the pillars of a vast and glorious cathedral, ran the pine trees, a stately double column stretching for two miles toward the mountain. "My God," I whispered to myself. "That's it. That's the problem."

We flew to sea once more, leveled off and again tried the tricky landing. Again we had too much speed. Again we gunned the old PBY over the hill road, up to the plateau and down the pines of Norfolk. We were so low we could see along the dusty road running between the columns. An old woman in a wagon was heading down to the sea. She looked up sharply as we roared overhead. And that was my first view of Teta Christian.

We landed on the third try, bouncing our teeth out, almost. A tall, thin, somewhat stooped naval officer waved to us from the crumbling stone pier. It was Lieutenant (jg) Tony Fry, dressed in a sloppy shirt and a pair of shorts. He greeted us when we climbed ashore and said, "Glad to have you aboard, sir. Damned glad to have you aboard." He had twinkling eyes and a merry manner. "Now if you'll step over here to our shed, I'll make the welcome more sincere."

He led us through the crowd of silent islanders to a small stone cow shed not far from the pier. "But this cow shed is built of dressed stone," I said. "It's better than you see back home."

"I know," Tony said. "The convicts had to be kept busy. If there was nothing else to do, they built cow sheds."

"What convicts?" I asked.

"Gentlemen, a real welcome!" Tony produced a bottle of Scotch. I learned later that no one ever asked Tony where or how he got his whisky. He always had it.

"This island," he said to me as we drank, "is the old convict island. Everything you see along the shore was built by the convicts."

"From where?"

"From Australia. England sent her worst convicts to Australia. And those who were too tough for Australia to handle were sent over here. This isn't a pretty island," Fry said. "Or wouldn't be, if it could talk."

"Well!" I said, looking at Tony. "About this airstrip?"

He smiled at me quizzically. "Admiral Kester?" he asked.

"Yes."

He smiled again. "You came down here to see about the airstrip?" I nodded. He grinned, an infectious, lovely grin showing his white and somewhat irregular teeth. "Commander," he said. "Let's have one more drink!"

"I have a terrible premonition that the trouble is that row of pine trees," I said as he poured.

Fry didn't bat an eye. He simply grinned warmly at me and raised his glass. "To the airstrip!" he said. "Thank God it's your decision, not mine."

At this moment there was a commotion outside the shed. "It's Teta!" voices cried. A horse, panting from his gallop, drew to a halt and wagon wheels crunched in the red dust. A high voice cried out, "Where is he? Where's Tony?"

"In there! In with the new American."

"Let me in!" the high voice cried.

And into our shed burst Teta Christian, something over ninety. She had four gaunt teeth in her upper jaw and two in her lower. Her hair was thin and wispy. But her frail body was erect. She went immediately to Tony. He took her by the hand and patted her on the shoulder. "Take it easy, now, Teta," he said.

She pushed him away and stood before me. "Why do you come here to cut down the pine trees?" she asked, her high voice rising to a wail.

"I . . ."

But Tony interrupted. "Be careful what you say, Commander. It's the only adequate site on the island."

"You shut up!" old Teta blurted out. "You shut up, Tony."

"I merely came down to see what should be done," I said.

"Well, go back!" Teta cried, pushing me with her bony hand. "Get in the airplane. Go back. Leave us alone."

"We'd better get out of here," I said. "Where do I bunk?"

"That's a problem," Fry said, whimsically. "It's a damned tough problem."

"Anywhere will do me," I assured him. "Why not put up with you? I'll only be here one night."

Tony raised his eyebrows as if to say, "Want to bet on that?" He laughed again. "That's what the problem is, Commander. I sort of don't think you should live with me." He fingered his jay-gee bar on his collar flap. "I . . . I . . ."

"Hm!" I said to myself. "Woman trouble. These damned Yanks. Let them get anywhere near a dame. I suppose Fry has something lined up. Officers are worse than the men."

"Very well," I said aloud. "Anywhere will do."

I reached for my single piece of luggage, a parachute bag battered from the jungle life on Vanikoro. As I did so a chubby young girl of fifteen or sixteen came into the shed and ran up to Tony in that strange way you can spot every time. She was desperately in love with him. To my utter disgust, I noticed that she was vacant-eyed and that her lower jaw was permanently hung open.

"This is Lucy," Fry said, patting the young girl affectionately on the shoulder. Lucy looked at me and grinned. "Hello," she said.

"We could find quarters for you in the old convict houses," Tony suggested. "Down here along the shore."

I felt a bit sick at my stomach: American officers and native women. "If the convict houses are as well built as this shed, I'll be in luck," I said.

"Oh, they're much finer construction," he assured me.

"Why don't you get in the plane and fly back?" old Teta whined.

"I can drive you over in the jeep," Fry suggested.

"I'm much more interested, really, in surveying the island," I said. "Let's just drop the bag and get going."

"You tell him, Tony," Teta wailed. "You tell him the truth!"

Fry wiped his forehead. I found out later that he perspired more than any man in the Pacific. He was always looking for a cool spot or someone else to do his work. "Now look, Teta. You run along. Get us some orangeade fixed up. Get us a nice dinner for tonight." He reached in his pocket and pulled out what change he had. Mostly pennies. "Have you a buck?" he asked me. I gave him one. "You take this, Teta, and scram!" He slapped her gently on the bottom and pushed her out of the shed. We followed and climbed into his jeep. Lucy was already sitting in front.

"No, Lucy!" Fry said. "You'll have to get in back." As the girl climbed over the seats, Tony returned to the shed to speak to a group of sullen native men. In this instant a young army lieutenant hurried up to the jeep.

"Boy, are we glad to see you!" he blurted out. "It's about time somebody came down here to straighten things up. We were all ready to start building the strip when Fry called the whole thing off. You got to be firm, Commander," he whispered. "Stop all this damned nonsense. That old Teta is the worst of the lot."

I loked over my shoulder at Lucy. She was sitting there quietly, saying nothing, hearing nothing. "Don't bother about her, Commander," the lieutenant said. "She's crazier than a bedbug." Fry left the shed and the army man hurried off.

"That was the big prison," Tony said as we drove up the road from the pier. "And that's Gallows Gate. They used to hang prisoners there for everyone to see. Had a special noose that never tightened up. Just slowly strangled them. They didn't tie their feet, either. Some of them kicked for fifteen minutes. Kept guards standing about with clubs and guns. Sometime I'll tell you about what happened one day at a hanging here."

I studied the superb gate. The lava rock from which it was built was cleaner and fresher, more beautifully cut and matched than in 1847, when the magnificent structure was built. Proportioned like the body of a god, this gate was merely one of hundreds of superb pieces of construction. There were walls as beautiful as a palace at Versailles, old houses straight from the drawing boards of England, towers, block houses, salt works, chimneys, barns, a chapel, granaries, and lime pits, all built of gray lava rock, all superb and perfect. They clustered along the foreshore of Norfolk Island in grim memory of the worst convict camp England ever fostered. They moaned beneath the Norfolk pines when winds whipped in at night, for they were empty. They were dead and empty ruins. They were not rotting by the sea, for they were stronger than when they were built. But they were dead and desolate.

"I can never go past this one without stopping," Fry said. "It seems to cry out with human misery." We climbed out of the jeep beside an exquisite piece of building. "If you want to," Fry said to Lucy, "come along." The girl scrambled out and stood close to Fry as we studied the officers' bathhouse.

"They were afraid to swim in the sea," he said. "Sharks. And too many officers were drowned there by the prisoners. They'd hide behind rocks and drag the officers under the waves. So this was built." The bathhouse was a small building beside the road. Twenty steps or more, perfectly carved out of rock, descended to a flagstone bath possibly twenty-four feet square. The western end of the bath dipped slightly so that water would run free to the ocean.

The bath was a superb thing, walled with matched rock, patiently built in the perfection of men who had endless time. But it was not the bath which captivated Tony's imagination and my horror. It was the conduit by which the water of a little stream was diverted into the bath. This tunnel was six feet high. It was dug completely through the base of a small hill about three hundred feet long. It was paved with beautiful stone. It was arched like the most graceful portico ever built. Down the roof of the three-hundred-foot conduit were keystones of perfect design. And all this was buried under a hill of dirt where no man would ever see.

I studied it in horror. I thought of the endless hours and pain that went into its building, the needless perfectionism, the human misery, when a pipe would have done as well. Tony and Lucy stood beside me in the dank place as I studied the exquisite masonry. Fry spoke in the grim silence: "And when any of the stone dressers or skilled masons died, the governor sent word back to England. And the word was passed along. Then judges kept a sharp lookout for stone masons. Some were sent here for life because they stole a rabbit."

When Tony dropped me off at my quarters he coughed once or twice. "I'm terribly sorry to leave you down here," he said. "But I think this is best." Lucy was crawling over the seats to the front of the jeep.

"This will do me," I said.

"I'd have you up to my diggings," he continued. "But it would be embarrassing. It would be terribly embarrassing to you. That's the mistake I made. You see, I board with old Teta Christian. She'd love to have you stay with her. The soul of hospitality. But if you did, she'd capture you the way she has me."

"The pine trees?" I asked.

"Yes," he replied. "The only good site on the island."

"Then why don't you cut them down and build the strip?"

Fry looked at me for more than a minute. His eyes were clear and joking. He had a sharp nose and chin. He was about thirty years old and didn't give a damn about anything or anybody. He was taking my measure, and although I was his superior officer I stood at attention and tried to pass muster. Apparently I did. He punched me softly on the arm. "You see, Commander," he said. "Old Teta Christian is the granddaughter of Fletcher Christian, the mutineer. All those people at the pier were 'Bounty' people. They don't push around easy." He winked at me and left. Lucy leaned over and blew the horn as he backed the jeep into a tight circle.

" 'Bounty' people!" I said to myself. "So this is where they wound up when they left Pitcairn Island? This paradise!"

And it was a paradise! Oh, it was one of the loveliest paradises in the vast ocean. Untouched by man for aeons, it grew its noble pine trees hundreds of feet high and always straight. It developed a plateau full of glens and valleys to warm the heart of any man. It grew all manner of food and protected its secrets by forbidding cliffs. I came to Norfolk for a day. I stayed a week, and then another. And I lived in a paradise, cool, fresh, clean, and restful after the mists of Vanikoro.

Late that afternoon Tony drove down for me. I said, "We'll look the two sites over and I can fly back in the morning."

"Now don't rush things, Commander," Tony replied. "We

can study the island tomorrow. Old Teta asked a few of the 'Bounty' people in for dinner. They want to meet you. Purely social."

"Fry, I don't want to be brusque about this, but the reason I'm down here is that Admiral Kester is pretty well browned off at the shilly-shallying. There's a war on!"

"That I'm aware of," Tony replied. "I'm in it."

"So if you don't mind, I'd like to see the two sites right now. Then, if we have time, we'll stop by the old woman's."

"Very well," Fry said. I was glad to see that Lucy was not waiting for us in the jeep. The fat little moron was becoming somewhat unnerving. But as we drove past the deserted ruins of the prison, she ran out into the road. "We better take her along," Tony said. "She never says much." So he stopped the jeep and Lucy climbed in back.

"The first site," Tony said, "is at the northwestern tip of the island. Up by the cable station." We drove along the shore road to reach the place. Inland I could see one sweeping valley after another, each with its quota of pine trees tall against the late afternoon sky.

The location we had come to visit was disappointing indeed. To the east and south the mountain encroached on the potential field. Landings would be difficult. Cliffs prohibited much more than a four-thousand-foot runway. Any cross runway for alternate winds was out of the question. "Not much of a location for an airstrip," I said.

"Not too good," Tony agreed. "Want to see the other?"

"I'd like to," I answered. He drove south from the cable station until he came to a sight which made me blink my eyes. There, on this lonely island, was a chapel, a rustic gem of architecture. It was built of wood and brown stone among a grove of pines. It was so different in spirit from the precise, brutal buildings on the water front that I must have shown my surprise.

"The old Melanesian Mission," he said. "From this spot all the Hebrides and Solomons were Christianized. This is where the saints lived."

"The saints?" I asked.

"Yes. Lucy's great-uncle was one. He went north from

here. To an island called Vanikoro. The natives roasted him alive. And during his torment he kept shouting, 'God is love. Jesus saves.' The old men of the village decided there must be something to his religion after all. They set out in canoes to a nearby island and brought another missionary back. A whole village was converted. There were lots of saints around here."

"Was he . . ." I inclined my head toward the rear seat.

"Sure. They all are, more or less. Listen to names at the party tonight. Christian, Young, Quintal, Adams. Do they mean anything to you?"

"The mutineers from the 'Bounty'?" I asked. Old Matthew Quintal was a favorite of mine. I could not believe that his descendants lived and remembered that unregenerate scoundrel.

"That's right. And Nobbs and Buffet, the missionaries that followed. The mutineers have been intermarrying for more than a hundred years. I guess they're all a little nuts." The frankness of Fry's comment startled me. I turned to look at Lucy, expecting to find her in tears. She grinned at me, with her mouth open.

"This is the other site," Fry said. We were on a little hill. Before us spread the heart of the plateau, with the pines of Norfolk laid out along an ideal runway.

"I saw this from the air," I said. "Ideal. We can even run a six-thousand-foot auxiliary strip for alternate landings."

"That's right," Tony agreed.

"Let's get going tomorrow," I suggested.

"Good idea. Let's eat now." Tony threw the jeep into low and started slowly down the hill. When he reached the bottom, Lucy cried out, "Blow the horn! Blow the horn!" Fry did not obey, so Lucy leaned over the seat and pushed the button for about a minute. From a ramshackle house a host of children ran into the dusty road beside the crawling jeep. "It's Lucy! It's Lucy!" they screamed. "It's Lucy in the jeep!" Our chubby moron grinned at them, threw them kisses, and twisted the horn button. Then she sat back in her seat quietly and said no more.

When we were past the half-ruined house, Tony threw

the jeep into high and we hurried toward old Teta's farm. In doing so, we had to enter the avenue of pine trees down which I had seen Teta hurrying that morning. As we passed under their vast canopy, noise from the jeep was muffled. Eighty feet above us, on either side, tree after tree, the pines of Norfolk raised their majestic heads. There was a wind from the south, that wind that sweeps up from the Antarctic day after day. It made a singing sound among the pines. Nobody said anything, not Tony nor I nor Lucy.

I was not unhappy when we turned off the road of the pines and into a little lane. It led past some ruins that, in the midst of the South Pacific, were breath-taking. Above me rose what seemed to be a large portion of an aqueduct that might have graced the Appian Way.

"What's that?" I cried.

"Part of a series of stables," Tony replied. "The convicts were building it for the governor's horses when the lid blew off the island." I looked at the fantastic stables. Graceful, curved archways, ten or a dozen in number, had been erected in the 1850's. Now they stood immaculately clean, the stone finished with exquisite care, and arches proportioned like the temples of ancient Rome.

"For his horses?" I asked.

"That's right," Tony said. "He had to think of something to keep all the stone masons busy."

I studied this grotesque folly. Imperial ruins in Carthage and Syracuse I could understand. But this massive grandeur lost in the heart of a tiny island ages of time from anywhere!

Two hundred yards from the end of the stables we entered a garden filled with all kinds of flowers, shrubs, and fruit trees. This was Teta Christian's home. "When the 'Bounty' folk first came here, Commander," she said in her high, thin voice, "my father, Fletcher Christian, chose this place for his farm. He liked the view down that valley." She drew the curtain aside and showed me her prospect, a valley of lovely pine trees, a thin stream, and curves lost in the vales that swept down to the sea. "My father, Fletcher Christian, planted all this land. But I put in the orange trees." It was uncanny, oranges growing so luxuriantly beside the pines.

It was like having a citrus grove in Minnesota, difficult to comprehend.

"When my father, Fletcher Christian, came to this island," she said, "he and Adams Quintal looked over the land. Am I boring you, Commander?"

"Oh, no! Please, go ahead. I'm very interested."

"He and Adams Quintal looked over the land. Nobbs Buffet and Thomas Young were along. They decided that they would not live along the shore. That was prison land."

"Were there no prisoners there?" I asked.

"Oh, no! After the great mutiny all the prisoners were taken away. Two years later they gave the empty island to us. I am the last person living who came here from Pitcairn," she moaned on. "I was five years old when we sailed. I remember Pitcairn well, although some people say you can't remember that far back." She lapsed into the strange Pitcairn dialect, composed of seafaring English from the "Bounty" modified by Tahitian brought in by the girls the mutineers had stolen. Her friends argued with her for a moment or two in the impossible jargon. They were Quintals and Nobbses and Buffets and endless Christians.

"They still don't believe me," Teta laughed. "But I remember one day standing on the cliffs at Pitcairn. It was right beside the statue of the old god my father found when he came to Pitcairn . . ." Her mind wandered. I never knew whether the original Christian, that terrible-souled mutineer, was her grandfather or her great-grandfather, or someone even farther back.

"So my father, Fletcher Christian, and Adams Quintal decided that they would have nothing whatever to do with the prison lands. Let them die and bury their dead down there. Let those awful places go away. My father, Mr. Fletcher Christian, was a very good man and he helped to build the Mission that you saw today. He would not take any money for his work. My father said, 'If the Lord has given me this land and this valley, I shall give the Lord my work.' Am I boring you with this talk, Commander?"

I assured her again and again that night that I was not bored by the memories of Norfolk Island. I made my point so secure that she promised to visit me in the morning and to show me the records of the first settlement of the mutineers. Accordingly, at 0900 the jeep drove up to my quarters. Tony and Lucy were in front. Old Teta sat in the back. "We'll just go down the road a little way," she said. She led us to the largest of the remaining prison buildings. It was hidden behind a wall of superb construction. This wall was more securely built, more thoroughly protected with corner blockhouses and ramparts, than the jail itself.

"What did they keep in here?" I asked. "The murderers?"

"Oh, no!" she said in a high voice of protest. "The jail keepers lived in here."

"But that twenty-foot wall? The broken glass?"

"To keep the prisoners out. In case they mutinied. They did, too. All the time. This was an island of horror," she said.

Up past the post office old Teta led us, up two flights of stairs and into a large, almost empty room. It was the upper-council chamber, and upon its walls rested faded photographs of long-dead Christians, Buffets, Quintals, and members of the other families. Lucy stood on one foot and studied their grim faces.

Teta, however, went to an old cupboard built into the wall. From it she took a series of boxes, each thick with dust and tied with red string. She peered into several boxes and finally selected one. Banging it on the table until her white hair was lost in a cloud, she said, "This is the one." From it she took several papers and let them fall through her idle hands onto the table. I picked up one. A petition from Fletcher Christian to the governor. "And I therefore humbly beg your permission to let my white bull Jonas run wild upon the common lands. If he can get to plenty of cows, he will not have a bad temper, and since he is the best bull on the island, everybody will be better off." It was signed in an uncertain writing much different from the petition.

"This is the one," Teta said. It was another petition signed by Fletcher Christian, Adams Quintal, Nobbs Buffet, and Thomas Young: "Because God has been kind in his wisdom to bring us here, it is proposed that an avenue of pine trees that grow upon this island and nowhere else in the world be planted and if we do not live to see them tall our children will." The petition was granted.

"I ought to go out to survey the field," I said.

"Well, you needn't go till afternoon," Tony replied. "Tell the PBY to lay over another day. Some of the villagers are having a picnic lunch for us."

I attended. The more I heard of Teta's stories the more interested I became. After we had eaten and I had consumed half a dozen oranges she said, "Would you like to see the old headstones? In the cemetery?"

I was indeed interested. She led me to the cemetery, this old, old woman who would soon be there herself. It lay upon a gently rising hillside near the ocean. "In this section are the 'Bounty' people," she said. There were the white headstones, always with the same names: Quintal, Young, Adams, Christian. "I am a Quintal," she said. "I married this man." She pointed to the gravestone of Christian Nobbs Quintal. Beside it were the inevitable tiny stones: "Mary Nobbs Quintal, Aged 3 Mos." "Adams Buffet Quintal, Aged 1 Yr." "Nobbs Young Christian Quintal, Aged 8 Mos."

"My father, Fletcher Christian, is buried over there," she said. "He's not really buried there, either. He was lost at sea. And down here are the convict graves. This corner is for those that were hung." I studied the dismal relics. "Thomas Burke, Hung 18 July 1838. He struck a guard and God struck him." "Timothy O'Shea, Hung 18 July 1838. He killed a guard. May God have Mercy on his Soul." The tragic story of hatred, sudden death, breaks, and terrible revenge was perpetuated in the weathering stones. "Thomas Bates, Worcester, America, 18 Yrs. Old." The rest was lost.

"They buried the mutineers over here," old Teta whined.

I looked at the close cluster of graves. English peasant names, Irish peasants. "What did they do?" I asked.

"These are the men who killed the guards and buried their bodies in the bridge. There where we had our picnic. Bloody Bridge."

"They hung them all?"

"All of them. They hung them with the slow knot. The last

man fainted, so they waited till he came back. A prisoner cried out against this, and they beat him till he died." She looked over the graves to the restless sea. "My father, Fletcher Christian, said he wanted none of their bloody buildings. So the 'Bounty' people tore down the houses we were given along the shore. When my father said that."

It was now too late for me to inspect the airstrip that day, so I told the PBY pilot to take off early next morning and return to Nouméa without me. I would send a dispatch when I got my work done. That night I sat in Teta's house by the ruined stables and listened as she told us about the days on Pitcairn. "My father, Fletcher Christian," she said, "was known as the leader of the mutineers. But Captain Bligh was a very evil man. My father told me that Mr. Christian had to do what he did. There are some who say it is a shame Tahitian girls went to Pitcairn, too, but my father, Fletcher Christian, said that if Tahitian girls didn't go, who would? And that is a question you cannot answer. I am half-Tahitian myself. Nobody in our family has ever married outside the mutiny people. That is, the Pitcairn people. A lot of people think this is bad." She spoke to her island friends in Pitcairn, and they laughed.

"Teta!" a Mr. Quintal said. "You're drinking too much of the lieutenant's rum. You're getting drunk."

Teta leaned over and patted Fry on the arm. "Drinking a little rum isn't getting drunk," she said. Fry poured her some whisky. To Teta everything from a bottle was rum, a relic of the old seafaring days.

"What we are laughing about, Commander, is a funny old man came here some time ago. Measured all our heads. He was a German. He made pictures of who everybody married and then proved we were all crazy people. His book had pictures, too. I was one of the people that wasn't crazy, but Nobbs over there," and she pointed to an islander, "his picture was in the front of the book. He was very crazy!"

"You might as well stay here the night," Fry said, but I disagreed. I preferred to sleep in my own quarters. "As you wish." We got into the jeep and Lucy climbed in back.

"Blow the horn! Blow the horn!" she cried as we crept past

the ramshackle house. This time Tony blew the horn for her. Into the darkness tumbled a dozen childish forms. They screamed in the night, "It's Lucy! It's Lucy! In the American jeep!" In the darkness I could almost hear dumb Lucy grinning and laughing behind me.

I went up to the proposed airstrip next morning and surveyed the job that lay ahead. Tony was not visible, but the energetic young army lieutenant was wheeling his tractors into position with help supplied by the Australian government. "Well," he said. "I guess we're ready to go now."

I was about to nod when I looked over toward the Norfolk pines and there was old Teta. She was in her wagon, the reins tied to the whip. Just watching. "You can start clearing away the brush," I said.

"But the trees, Commander!"

"We'll wait a few days on that," I said.

"But damn it all, Commander! It will take us a long time to get those trees down. We can't do anything till that's done."

"I want to look over that other site, first. We can get that land cheaper."

"But my God!" the lieutenant cried. "We been through all that before."

"We'll go through it again!" I shouted.

"Yes, sir," he replied.

I walked over to study one of the trees. It was six feet through the base, had scaly bark. Its branches grew out absolutely parallel to the ground. Its leaves were like spatulas, broad and flat, yet pulpy like a water-holding cactus. In perfect symmetry it rose high into the air. I thought, "It was a tree like this that Captain Cook saw when he inspected Norfolk. He was the first man, white or black, ever known to visit the island. It was a tree like this that made him say, 'And the hospitable island will be a fruitful source of spars for our ships.' "

"I'm going down to the Mission," old Teta said as she drove up. "Would you like to ride along?" I climbed into her wagon. When we drove past Lucy's corner, that grinning girl saw us. Quick as an animal she ran to her own horse and vaulted into the saddle. Whipping him up with her heels, she soon caught up to us.

"Going to the Mission?" she asked.

"Come along," the frail old woman said. "Lucy's a good girl," Teta said. "She's not too bright."

At the Mission we tied the horse and Lucy let hers roam free. The chapel was even lovelier than I had thought from the road. Inside, it was made of colored marble, rare shells from the northern islands, wood from the Solomons, and carvings from the Hebrides. Not ornate, it was rich beyond imagination. Gold and silver flourished. Each pew end was set in mother-of-pearl patiently carved by some island craftsman. Scenes from Christ's life predominated in the intaglios, but occasionally a free Christian motif had been worked out. The translucent shell spoke of the love that had been lavished upon it.

The windows perplexed me. They reminded me of something I had seen elsewhere, but the comparison I made was so silly that I did not even admit it to myself.

"The windows," Teta said, "were made by a famous man in England and sent out here on a boat."

"Good heavens!" I said, "it is Burne-Jones." How wildly weird his ascetic figures looked in that chapel.

"Bishop Patteson built this chapel," old Teta whined on. But her memories were vague. She got the famous Melanesian missionaries all confused. She had known each of them well. Selwyn and Patteson and Paton.

"My brother, Fletcher Christian, went up north with good Bishop Selwyn," she said. "They went to Vanikoro where my uncle, Fletcher Christian, was burned alive. He converted a whole village by that. He was a very saintly man. My brother was also named Fletcher Christian. That tablet up there is to him, not to my uncle. My brother came home one day and knelt down. It was right after my father died at sea. He said, that is, my brother Fletcher Christian said, 'I am going to follow God! I am going with Bishop . . .' " She faltered. " 'I am going with Bishop Patteson.' He went up north to an island right near Vanikoro. Bali-ha'i. He was a very good missionary. Bishop Paton said of him, 'Fletcher

Christian rests with God!' He rests with God because the natives shot at him with a poisoned arrow. They shot him through the right arm. He got well, at first, but blood poisoning set in, and Bishop Patteson knew he was going to die. They prayed for my brother for three days, and all that time he twisted on the ground and cried out, 'I am saved! I am washed in the blood of the Lord.' And for three days he cried like that, and his jaws locked tight shut and he cried through his teeth, 'God is my salvation!' And on the fourth day he died." Teta sat in the now-empty Mission, deserted because its function was fulfilled. Its word had been carried north to all the islands.

"I remember in Pitcairn," she said. "We were all sick and had no medicine. The medicine of Tahiti had been forgotten, because we had no herbs. We had no food, either. My father, Fletcher Christian, went to a meeting. They decided that we must leave Pitcairn. Everybody. Not only those that wanted to go, but everybody. When we got here we were happy for a while. Enough food, at least. But in two years many of us wanted to go home. Back to Pitcairn. Some of the families did go back." Teta thought of the faraway people. "I always wanted to go back. My mother, she was a Quintal, she wanted to go home very much. But my father, Fletcher Christian, wouldn't hear of it. He said, 'God in His wisdom brought us to these flowering shores. God meant us to stay here.' We never went with the others."

Back at my quarters that afternoon I was in a confusion of thoughts. No one could tell how urgently we might need the airstrip on Norfolk, nor how soon. Suppose the Japs defeated us in some great battle in the Hebrides! In such an event the airstrip on Norfolk might be essential to our life itself. Thought of this steeled me to the inescapable conclusion. The pines of Norfolk must go. An end to this silly nonsense!

I walked slowly down to the old stone cow shed where the Army had its headquarters. "We'll start in the morning," I told them. "Get the trees out of there."

"It's only three now, sir," the eager young lieutenant said. "We could get a couple down this afternoon!"

"Time enough in the morning," I said. "Get your gear ready."

"It's been ready for two weeks," he said coldly.

I felt honor-bound to tell the islanders that the irrevocable decision had been made. I planned to do so that evening, at Teta's. I climbed the dusty road from the prison camp to the free lands and the pine-filled valleys. Fry must have been sleeping that afternoon, as he frequently did, for Lucy clattered past me on her horse, riding like a centaur, raising a fine hullabaloo. She would tear past going in one direction, then stop, wheel her big horse, and rush by me the other way. She kept this up for eight or ten sallies, never saying a word.

When I reached the avenue of pines my resolution wavered. I said, "I can't permit this thing! The loveliest monument in the South Pacific completely destroyed. No, by God! I'll do everything I can. Up to the hilt. I've got to!" And I hurried back to the prison lands, the compressed, pain-saddened shore, and sent an urgent dispatch to Admiral Kester. It was a long one. Gave the dimensions of the two fields. Told him that the north field could have no cross runway and would be hampered by the small mountain. I said there was great opposition to the central field. I closed the dispatch as follows: "REQUEST PERMISSION PROCEED NORTH FIELD."

I did not go to Teta's for dinner. I missed dinner, and was not aware of that fact. About ten o'clock that night I got my answer. It was brief, and in it I could hear many oaths from the Admiral, such as: "What are those damned fools doing down there?" and "By God, why can't they look at the goddamn' facts and make up their minds?" His dispatch had its mind made up: "RE UR 140522 X NEGATIVE X REPEAT NEGATIVE X KESTER."

But the dispatch relieved me. I clutched it in my hand and walked up the hill to the plateau where the "Bounty" people lived. I walked down the long avenue of trees and thought, "You are not dying by my hand." At the side road I turned toward Teta's house, and to my left were the grim yet lovely stables. "The stone masons had been sentenced for life. They were already out here," Tony had said. "They had to be kept busy doing something." Against the rising moon the stables of Norfolk stood silent in solemn grandeur, each stone delicately finished, each mortised joint perfect.

Teta and Tony were alone, drinking rum. Lucy, of course, sat in a corner and watched Tony all night. "My father, Fletcher Christian, was a very good sailor," Teta said. "It was a great pity for this island when he was killed at sea. It was at the Cascade Landing. There are only two places where boats can possibly land on Norfolk. It reminds me of Pitcairn in that respect. My grandfather, Fletcher Christian, said that if a man could sail in and out of Pitcairn Island, he was indeed a sailor. I have been told my father was the best sailor on either island, but he was killed at sea. At Cascade Landing, which is very rough and brutal. A very bad place to land in any weather. The waves crushed his boat and threw him on the rocks. Right at the landing. Then pulled him back out to sea and we never got the body. I think we could have found the body, but there were no other sailors as brave as my father, and no one searched for him until the storm was over."

"Bad news," I said. Tony poured old Teta another drink. Lucy came to the table and asked for some rum. "No, Lucy!" Tony said. "You go back and sit down."

"From Nouméa?" Tony asked.

"Yes. I wired the Admiral."

"I know," Tony said. "I did the same thing."

"He made the decision," I said.

"I know," Tony replied. "I passed the buck to you. And you passed it to the Admiral."

"Teta," I said quietly. "We start to take the trees down tomorrow."

The old mutineer looked at me and started to speak. No words came. She licked her six gaunt teeth and took a big drink of rum. "I remember when my father, Fletcher Christian, planted those trees," she said. "I ran along beside the men. They laid out two lines. There was no road there, then. Four men stood with poles and my father said to Adams Quintal—it was his son Christian Nobbs Quintal that I married. We were married by a missionary from the Mission. Bishop Patteson married us, and then he took my brother,

Fletcher Christian, up to the islands, where the young man died of blood poisoning. Tony, my brother died with his jaws tied shut with bands of iron. He could only speak through his teeth." The old woman dropped her head on her hands. The lamp threw an eerie glow upon her white hair.

"She's drunk again," Lucy said. "Too much rum."

"Lucy!" Fry said. "I told you to sit over there and not talk."

"We'll have to start tomorrow. In the morning," I said. I waved the dispatch at him.

"You don't have to prove it to me, Commander," Fry chuckled. "I know what you feel, exactly. It's the islanders you've got to prove it to. Save the dispatch for them."

I don't know who spread the word. I can't believe it was Teta, and Lucy was sitting tight-lipped in the corner when I left. Perhaps the islanders heard it from the Army. At any rate, early next morning a crowd of people gathered at the pine trees. As I approached with the army engineers, Nobbs Quintal, whose photograph had served as the frontispiece to the book that proved that all Norfolk "Bounty" people were degenerate, tipped his hat and asked me if he could speak. I clenched my hands and thought, "Here it comes!"

"Commander," Nobbs Quintal said. "We know the trees have to go. We know there's war. My son is at war. In Egypt. Old Teta has five grandsons in the Army. We know you've tried to change the airport. We heard about your message yesterday. But won't you wait one more day? We want to take some pictures of the trees."

They had an old box camera and some film. An American soldier had a pretty good miniature camera, and an Australian had a very good French job. All morning they took pictures of the trees. The Quintals and the Christians and the Nobbses and all the others stood beneath the trees, drove wagons along the dusty road, and made family groups. About noon Nobbs Quintal went over by the stables and hitched up Teta's wagon. The old woman appeared between the trees and looked sadly into space as she was photographed with various families and alone. The reins were wrapped about the whip post. Saliva ran into the corners of her mouth from the six teeth. Her white hair reflected the dim sunlight that pierced the green canopy. She was the last of the Pitcairn people.

All film was used up by two o'clock. The last shots were taken of Teta Christian, Tony, and me. On the very last shot Lucy ran from the crowd to stand beside Tony. In that picture her head almost covers Teta's, but the old woman leaned sideways in the wagon and peeked from behind my shoulder.

The engineers moved in. With rotary saws they cut part way through the first tree. Then two bulldozers shoved against the trunk. The great pine broke loose and almost imperceptibly started to fall. As it did so, it caught for a moment, twisted in the air like a soldier shot as he runs forward. The tree twirled, mortally wounded, and fell into a cloud of dust. Three more were destroyed in that manner.

The island people said nothing as their living cathedral was desecrated. The old "Bounty" people watched the felling of the trees as simply one more tragedy in the long series their clans had had to tolerate.

"You'll have to move back," the army engineers said. "We've got to blast the stumps."

We moved to a safe distance and watched the engineers place sticks of dynamite among the roots of each fallen tree. Then a detonator was attached and the wires gathered together at a plunger box. The charge was exploded, but nothing much happened. Just some dirt and dust in the air, with a few fragments of wood. It was not until the bulldozers came back and nudged the stumps that we saw what had happened. The roots had been destroyed. Like old hulks of men who can be pushed and bullied about the slums of a large city, the stumps of Norfolk were pushed and harried into a dump.

I could not go back to Teta's that night. I was lonely, and miserable in my loneliness. I stayed with some Australians who had built their camp near the line of trees. "It's a bloody shime," one of them said in barbarous Anzac Cockney. "One bloody line of trees on the bloody island, and we put the bloody airport there!"

Our thoughts were broken by a crashing explosion outside. We rushed to the door of our tent and saw in the moonlight a cloud of dust rising by the trees.

"Fat's in the fire!" an Australian cried.

We hurried across the field to where the explosion had taken place. We found one of the smaller bulldozers blown to bits. Dynamite. "Those dirty bastards!" an army engineer said. Then, in true military fashion, he got busy proving that it wasn't his fault. He shouted, "These things were supposed to be guarded. Sergeant! Didn't I tell you to have these guarded?" He ran toward some lights shouting, "Sergeant! Sergeant!"

I left the Australians and headed for the stone stables. As I did so, I caught a glimpse of a woman running ahead of me. I hurried as fast as I could and overtook fat Lucy. I grabbed her by the shoulders and started to shake her, but she burst into a heavy flow of tears and blubbered so that I could make nothing of her answers. I turned, therefore, toward old Teta's house and did so in time to see her door open and close. "Come along, Lucy!" I said. She scuffed her bare feet in the dust behind me.

In Teta's house Fry and the old woman were drinking rum. Teta was not puffing, but she seemed out of breath. Fry had obviously not moved for some time. "My father, Fletcher Christian," Teta said, "always told us that it did not matter whether you lived on Norfolk Island or Pitcairn Island so long as you lived in the love of God. My mother did not believe this. She said that this island was very good for people who had never lived on Pitcairn. But she could not see how a little more food and steamers from Australia could make up for the life we had on Pitcairn. She said that she would rather live there, on the cliff by the ocean, than anywhere else in the world. But when my father died at sea, she had a chance to go back to her home on Pitcairn. A boat was going there. I begged her to go on the boat and take us all. But she said, 'No. Fletcher is buried out there at sea. My place is here.' It was shortly after this that my brother, Fletcher Christian, was killed up north. Like my father he was a very saintly man. But the religion in the family was all in the men. Not the women. Although I did know Bishop Paton. He was a fine man."

The old woman droned on and on until it was obvious to me that she was drunk again from too much of Tony's rum. Toward morning she left us and went into her bedroom. I sat drumming my fingers on the table and Tony said, "Come on! We'll drive Lucy home."

"I don't want to go home!" she cried.

"Get in the jeep!" Tony commanded, adding in a low voice, "You've done enough for one night."

The crazy girl climbed in behind us. At the hill Tony drove very slowly and pushed on the horn. The reaction was delayed, but when it came it was more explosive than before. Kids from everywhere piled out of the old house and came screaming in the night. "It's Lucy!" they shouted. "Lucy comin' home in the American jeep!"

"So she blew up the bulldozer?" I asked.

"That's right," Tony said sleepily. "She and Teta."

"Fry," I said coldly. "Those two women could never in a million years figure out how to explode dynamite." A guard stopped us.

"Good evening, Commander," he said. "Saboteurs about. Blew up a half-track."

"They couldn't figure it in a million years, Tony."

"It was an old bulldozer anyway," Fry said as we drove back to Teta's. "Something somebody in the States didn't want. Commander, I can just see him, rubbing his hands and saying, 'Look! I can sell it to the guv'mint. Make money on the deal, too. And it's patriotic! You can't beat a deal like that!' Well, his tractor did a lot of good."

"We need that bulldozer for the airstrip."

"I don't think you do," Tony replied. "As a matter of fact, I'm damned sure you don't. Because that's the one that broke down this afternoon and the army man said it couldn't be fixed." He brought the jeep to a stop by Teta's fence.

"Fry," I said. "You could be court-martialed for this."

Tony turned to face me. "Who would believe you?" he asked.

"By God, man," I said grimly. "If I had the facts I'd press this case."

"With whom?" he asked. "With Ghormley? With Admiral Kester? You tell your story. Then I'll tell mine. Can you imagine the look on Kester's face? There was an old, useless bulldozer. A couple of women blew it up as a last gesture of defiance. A woman ninety and a crazy girl. That story wouldn't stand up. Especially if I said how you came here to do a job and just couldn't make up your mind to knock down a few trees. It's too fantastic, Commander. Kester would never believe that."

"I could understand your helping them, in peacetime," I said. "But this is war."

"That's when people need help, Commander!" Fry said quietly. "Not when everything is going smoothly."

"It's all so damned futile," I said, looking away toward the stone stables. "Blowing up one bulldozer."

"Commander," Fry said with quiet passion. "Right now I can see it. Some sawed-off runt of a Jew in Dachau prison. Plotting his escape. Plotting to kill the guards. Working against the Nazis. One little Hebrew. You probably wouldn't invite him to your house for dinner. He smells. So futile. One little Jew. But by God, I'm for him. I'm on his side, Commander." Fry punched me lightly on the shoulder. I hate being mauled.

"These people on Norfolk can't be dismissed lightly," he continued. "They're like the little Jew. Some smart scientists can come down here and prove they're all nuts. But do you believe it? We took down a map the other day, Teta and I. We figured where her grandsons are fighting. She can't remember whether they're grandsons or great-grandsons. All the same names. They're in Africa, Malaya, India, New Guinea, England. One was at Narvik. Crete. They may be stupid, but they know what they want. They knew what they wanted when they knocked that Nazi Bligh off his ship. They knew what they wanted when they turned their backs on the prison lands. Refused convict homes all ready, waiting for them. The saints knew what they wanted when they went north as missionaries. I'm on their side. If blowing up a broken bulldozer helps keep the spirit alive, that's O.K. with me."

Tony submitted a vague report on the bulldozer. I endorsed it and sent it on to my own files in Nouméa. I don't know where it is now. When Fry handed it to me he said, "Doesn't it seem horrible? The trees all down. We don't destroy one single memento of the prison days. Not one building do we touch. The airstrip runs twenty yards from the stone stables, but they're as safe as the Gallows Gate. We won't touch a rock of Bloody Bridge, where they buried the murdered guards, nor that obscene officers' bath. But the cathedral of the spirit, that we knock to hell."

"Fry," I said. "The Melanesian Mission's safe."

"That lousy thing!" Fry shouted. "A rustic English mission built on a savage island. A rotten, sentimental chapel with Burne-Jones' emaciated angels on an island like this. If you wanted to build an airstrip, why couldn't you have built it over there? Let the real chapel stand?"

"My father, Fletcher Christian," Teta said on my last night, when graders were working by flares to speed the airstrip. "He told us that God meant to build Norfolk this way. A man has to love the island to get here, because there are no harbors and no landings. My father said, 'A man has to fight his way ashore on this island!' That's what he was doing when the boat crashed on the rocks. Am I boring you with this, Commander?"

Eugene Burdick

THE BLACK AND THE WHITE

Eugene L. Burdick was born in Iowa in 1918 but grew up in California. After high school he earned money as a clerk, ditch digger, and truck driver until he had saved $150, enough to enter Stanford University, where he worked his way through and was graduated in 1941. Not long after that he was married, taken into the Navy, and sent to Guadalcanal. He spent twenty-six months in the Pacific as a gunnery officer aboard various types of vessels.

After a period of study in Wallace Stegner's writing class at Stanford, Burdick earned a Ph.D. from Oxford as a Rhodes scholar and became a professor of political science at the University of California. His first novel, *The Ninth Wave* (1956), won a literary fellowship. Best-sellers such as *The Ugly American* (1958) and *Fail-Safe* (1962), both written in collaboration, brought him fame. In *The Blue of Capricorn* (1961), Burdick mingles essays on Pacific subjects with short stories.

With his wife and three children, Burdick spends part of each year on the island of Mooréa, near Tahiti. That the South Seas, after more than a century of literary exploitation, can still provide material for good stories is proved by "The Black and the White," a narrative of an escapist of nowadays.

HIS NAME WAS ZOLA, ZOLA MARTIN. THAT INCREDIBLE NAME signed to an innocent letter was what first called him to my attention. That plus the fact that the letter was postmarked Tahiti and that beneath the politeness of the letter there was a rasplike indication of toughness.

He had written to criticize a sea story that I had published two years before. In that story I had described the fate of a group of survivors adrift in a sailless lifeboat. The story was based on an old incident that had turned up in British Admiralty files.

> My dear sir,
> In your otherwise excellent story you state that your survivors in a lifeboat without sails drifted northeast at the rate of three knots an hour until it was thrown up on an atoll of the Society Islands. It appears to me that this is a very unlikely circumstance.

He backed this assertion with a dazzling knowledge of the wind, currents, and waves of the Pacific. He made an intricate calculation that demonstrated that the drifting boat would have missed the most southerly of the Societies by at least one hundred miles and went on to suggest that either the Admiralty report was written by sailors who did not know their true location or, in fact, the lifeboat had been able to put on a bit of sail.

I wrote him and thanked him for his criticism. Also, because I was working on a number of other sea stories, I asked him some detailed questions about ocean and island life in Polynesia. He responded, and we began an exchange of letters that lasted several years. His letters, in English, but written in an elegant copperplate French handwriting were, at first, very distant and factual. Over the years, however, I came to know the following facts about him: Zola was fifty-five years old, he had a steady, small income from vineyards in Burgundy, was properly married in church to a Polynesian woman, had five children by her and had sent all of them to European schools.

In one of my letters to Zola I asked him, quite casually, why he had left Paris to live in Polynesia. When his reply arrived two months later, even before I opened the envelope I could tell it had been written in a different mood. The handwriting was still elegant, but somewhat more sprawling; there was a brown smudge on the envelope as if a cigarette ash had burned out on it. When I opened the letter the top half of the first page was smudged and I sensed at once that it had been blurred by spilled alcohol.

> Proust has described life in Paris and its rottenness very accurately [Zola wrote]. There is no need for me to try and improve upon him. The forced masculinity of the *bon vivants* made them seem like dandies with the minds of roosters. The simpering of the women, their endless efforts to strike a balance between seductiveness and purity, came to nauseate me. The constant grubbing for money, whether it was done by elegant men at the Bourse for millions of francs or by peddlers for a mean percentage, pervaded everything. But the basic flaw, the most awful consistency in Paris, was the true inability of anyone to love. It is no accident that Proust was a tortured homosexual. He was well aware that love in Europe is a kind of organized and shrewd torture, a device for skewering people on the twin spikes of eroticism and propriety.
>
> I came to Polynesia, to a tiny island, to escape all this. Do not conclude, my dear sir, that I am one of your Rousseau romantics. I am not. But love in these islands does have a simplicity, a spontaneity, a kindness that we Europeans have lost. Here a man can sometimes feel some of the bull-like assurance that a man should feel without being bound up in the awful artificial skeins of Western notions of marital love. Nor does he have to become involved in a slippery smart evilness of adultery. Here a man can live the life he is supposed to live: the life of the body, the life of the mind, the life of the heart. Some terrible bypath that we Europeans and you Americans have taken has been avoided here in Polynesia.

And then, quite surprisingly, he invited me to visit him. Something about the burned paper, the alcoholic sprawl, the urgency of his words made Zola more than an unknown person. I wanted to see him.

Almost by accident I did. A movie company operating at Papeete had chartered a flying boat to search for shooting locations and were going to make a sweep through the Tuamotus and Marquesas. They offered to drop me off at the Frenchman's isolated atoll and pick me up within five days. We made the flight in a World War II PBY, flown by two English pilots with mustaches, lean, handsome faces marred only by slightly bloodshot eyes caused partly by Hinano beer and partly by flying over the glare of open ocean. They both had hard Manchester accents. The plane badly needed paint and inside it was dirty, but the two engines were in magnificent shape. The two pilots tried to give the impression of flying by the seat of the pants, but actually they could both pilot and navigate beautifully. They hit the Frenchman's atoll on the nose and made a long, languid sweep of a descent that was both artistic and safe.

The atoll was the shape of a teardrop. At the heavy, rounded end the land rose fifteen or twenty feet above the surface and was covered with cultivated coconut palms. The thin point of the tear also was slightly elevated and there were signs of an inhabited native village there. The atoll was four miles long and two miles wide at the widest point. Like most atolls, only 5 to 10 per cent of the outer ring rose high enough above the water to be livable. The pilots needed only the one pass to detect a long streak of green-white water that indicated enough depth to land.

They brought the plane down exquisitely, the first contact with the water so subtle that it felt as if oil had been splashed along the keel. As we came to a standstill they cut one motor; the power of the other propeller turned us in the water and we had stopped precisely in front of the Frenchman's house. One of the pilots came back, tossed a yellow rubber life raft over and handed me a paddle. He tossed my gear down to me without saying a word, but as he pulled the hatch shut I could see that beneath his mustache he was smiling. I was only ten yards from the plane when the prop-wash caught me and pushed me halfway to shore. I knew they had done it deliberately, a final signature of their skill.

As I rowed the rest of the way in I looked at the Frenchman's house. It was the largest Tahitian-type house I had ever seen outside of Papeete. On three sides it had a long overhang of roof that formed a veranda railing that was barbed with dozens of small intricately carved *tikis.*

Every form of building has its marks of perfection. Thatch roof comes in two qualities: Pandanus or coconut thatch. Pandanus is infinitely superior. Another mark of quality is how close the spine of the thatch mats are laid together. The closer together, the more that are used, the thicker the roof, the longer it will resist the attack of wind, rain, and rats. On Zola's roof the spines of the mats were no more than a quarter inch apart. From the house down to the beach there was a lawn that was neatly clipped. Separating the house from the coconut grove was an artful arrangement of fruit trees very carefully blended for shape and color. A papaya tree by itself can have a slightly obscene look, but here the papaya trees were scattered among mangoes and frangipani trees so that they looked tall and elegant.

Zola was on the beach to meet me. He walked out into the water up to his thighs and steadied the yellow boat as I climbed out.

"Ah, ah. The literary friend from California," he said, although he must have been guessing, for I hadn't any way to tell him of my arrival.

He was a surprise. Somehow I had expected a tall, lean, somewhat withdrawn man. Zola looked much more like a rounded bourgeois shopkeeper. His face was rubicund. His manner was cheerful and friendly. He talked very fast. And he gave off the slightest odor of gin. His eyes, however, were those of the man who had written the brilliant letters. They were large, almost beautiful, a deep black. He had a birdlike energy, quick small gestures that seemed ineffectual, but were remarkably efficient. He hustled my gear out of the rubber boat and onto the veranda in a flurry of jerks, steps, tugs, and pulls before I could give him a hand.

"I would have written, but the chance to come was so sudden that I did not have time," I explained.

"And I do not have a radio," Zola said with delight. "It is a pleasure to have you. What difference would it have made if you had written? Everything would be the same. Here there is no need to prepare for a pleasure."

His curious eyes glanced over me, his mouth pulled up into a laugh. Together we pulled the boat up onto the beach.

"You have a beautiful place here," I said, waving my hand to take in the entire atoll.

"Yes, it is beautiful," Zola said quietly. "And all of this with no politics." He burst out laughing.

In our correspondence we had had a long debate on

whether or not politics figured large in the life of Polynesia. He insisted that there was no such thing. He was wrong, but that is another matter. He paused and for the first time the smile vanished from his face. "I shall also demonstrate to you that my description of love and the South Pacific is precisely as I said in my letters."

His wife was waiting for us on the veranda. I knew from his letters that her name was Toma and that she was in her early forties. Uniformly when Polynesian women have reached this age they have started to take on weight. The breasts and the thighs begin to thicken. But Toma was different. I guessed from her face that one of her parents must have been Chinese, because her cheekbones were higher and her face was thinner than those of most Polynesian women. She was also quite slim. She wore a *pareu* that had been washed often enough so that the glossy cheapness that it had when it came off the looms in France or England had disappeared. Her hair was thick and very black and was drawn up into a large, loose bun on her neck.

Zola paused for a moment at the bottom of the stairs, his arm around my shoulders, and restrained me. He bounded up the stairs, put his arm around Toma and stood smiling down triumphantly at me.

"A pretty picture, eh?" he shouted. "A picture of the East and the West and a proof that the twain shall meet. Where is your camera? It would tell you more than a thousand words of conversation or a hundred books."

I explained that I had no camera, and he roared. Toma came down the steps and shook my hand. She spoke a few words of English, just enough to say hello and to welcome me. After she had shaken hands she went up the steps ahead of me, went over to a large, fresh sprig of *tiare* that was in a jar of water, plucked one of the flowers and put it behind my right ear. Zola and I sat down in the rattan chairs to talk. Toma drew off to one side and then did a thing that is very disturbing to Occidentals, but is typically Polynesian. She studied me from head to foot, without any attempt to disguise her interest. She stared at my tennis shoes, my bare legs, my khaki shorts and shirt, my arms, my neck, and my face. Her attention was direct and obvious and was punctuated every few seconds by a nod of approval. She shook her head, however, when she came to my colored glasses as if they were somehow out of character. I knew that within a few hours she would have described my physical appearance in the greatest detail to everyone else that she met on the atoll. I have sometimes heard these descriptions of others by Polynesian women and they are uncanny in their ability to reproduce verbally the physical looks of a person. Every small spot, the length of the hair, the shape of the ears is remembered perfectly.

When Toma had finished her scrutiny she came over and asked us in French if we would like something to drink. She offered us coconut water, lime juice, or fresh pineapple juice. I settled for pineapple juice, and she turned and walked down the steps towards the cookshack. At the bottom of the steps she turned and said, "With gin?" I nodded, and she smiled broadly.

Later Toma served us an excellent Tahitian lunch: raw shrimp in lime juice, small red fish buttered and then broiled whole on hot coals, a plate of *fa-fa,* and a plate of freshly cut pineapple. There was also a large carafe of Algerian red wine. When we had finished this, Toma brought over a large tin coffeepot of very strong coffee and we sat on the veranda sipping.

Zola and I began to talk in English about the matters we had discussed in our letters. Like everyone else in the South Pacific we also exchanged gossip. That incredible gossip about people and events which stretch over an area much faster than in the United States but in which land and people are so few that events on islands thousands of miles away have a great interest for everyone. We discussed the mystery of the large Japanese tuna boat. It had arrived in the South Seas, spanking new and gleaming, from a shipbuilding yard in Japan and was to be the first effort by the Japanese to fish the tuna-rich water. It had left port on its first cruise, disappeared and was never heard of again. We gossiped about a Chinese gentleman in Nouméa who was reputed to be running opium in the South Pacific by an ingenious device. In Laos his agents mixed raw opium with paper pulp, pressed into ordinary pages, printed up into books, and then mailed to him. The eventual consumer merely had to dissolve the book pages in vinegar, and the pulp floated to the top and could be skimmed off. Left in the sun for a few days, the mixture became almost pure opium. No one knew if it were true, but it is a good story. Our conversation droned on and eventually Zola said that he wanted to take a nap.

He asked me if I would like to look through his library and led me into a large, airy room that had a view of the lagoon. He apologized for the condition of the books and pointed out that the salt air, humidity, and tiny bugs of an atoll were all highly destructive of anything as soft as paper.

"But what is here is yours," Zola said. "Treat it as your own." Those words were a mistake. If he had not uttered them, I would not have discovered his secret life.

Zola was right. The books were in very bad shape. Although he had shelved them carefully with blocks of wood between each book to allow circulation of air, the edges of the pages were brittle and came away in tiny crisp fragments as I turned the pages. By the time I had gone through a half-dozen books there was a semicircle of broken, powdered paper on the table.

Even so, the library was exciting. It contained not only works on Polynesia and all the languages of the world, but it contained typewritten manuscripts of old songs; genealogical tables of Polynesian families; beautiful little sketches, as fragile as the tracery in a butterfly's wings of long-vanished and old-fashioned huts; long verbatim records of stories that were passed on from generation to generation orally; a meticulous file of the signs that appeared on various *tikis* and *maraes* along with shrewd guesses as to what they meant. It was a magnificent example of practical scholarship done by a single man.

On a small table in the corner of the room there was a box, built very much like a cigar humidor. On the top it had a small brass plate that said "Memoirs." I opened it without a moment's hesitation. It might have been the memoirs of anyone; and, after all, Zola told me that I could look at everything. The humidor was two-thirds full of handwritten manuscripts. I recognized the handwriting as that of Zola. But oddly enough most of the memoirs were written in English instead of French. Later I sensed that he did this so that the manuscript could not be read by the natives, many of whom can read French fluently.

The first entry in the memoirs was twenty-five years old. It was written aboard the ship that carried Zola from Marseilles to Tahiti. It was only ten pages long, but it was remarkable. It was one of the most bitter, lucid, incisive, tragic, instructive commentaries on the European situation I had ever read.

With the strange clarity that is possessed by the very young or the very angry, Zola caught, in acid detail, every affectation, every depravity, every hypocrisy, every flaw of European life. In his letters to me his criticism of Europe had been abstract; here they were personalized. He described the manipulations by which his mother and sister entrapped a wealthy young Parisian who wanted to be an artist into becoming the daughter's groom and a merchant in silk. It is a commonplace occurrence, but in Zola's spare prose, it looked suddenly obscene. There was a description of a business deal in which Zola's father had outmaneuvered his best friend. It was an ordinary business deal, quite legal, but put down without the usual soft words it almost stank of rottenness; devoid of heart or even of meaning. There was a description of a family Christmas reunion, no more than seventy-five words in length, that revealed the avarice and jealousy that hung, like invisible fog, around the Christmas tree, the roasted goose, the presents, the incantations of love. There was a description of the private school Zola attended, and it was depicted as an expensive institution for squeezing the life out of children, instilling a feral competition among them, giving them a civilized veneer to hide an inculcated meanness.

It was a remarkable piece of writing, and with a bony economy it destroyed individuals, a family, a city, a culture.

Zola had also put down what he had expected to find in the South Seas. He had read the romantic novels of the South Seas, but he had also read the grim anthropological journals and reports of French administrators. He was no romantic.

He was prepared for elephantiasis, the neat line of feces along the white sand at low tide, the fact that natural beauty could become boring, the sure knowledge that there would be long periods of loneliness. Zola came to Tahiti as a bitter young man with hard, perceptive eyes, a fugitive from the intolerable, expecting no moments of grace, a searcher for himself.

When he arrived in Tahiti he spent only a few days in Papeete and then moved to the tiny village of Tautira on Tahiti. Here his eye was still sharp, his comments clear and unsentimental, but he was entranced. There was almost a mood of delirium, of enravishment, of illumination in the early pages he wrote on Tautira. The gentleness of the Tahitians, their complete lack of duplicity, the apparent absence of status were precisely what he needed to wipe out the bitter memories of life in Paris. Two entries that he made in his memoirs during this period I quickly scribbled down in my notebook:

> I return to my hut to find Kaoko rifling my sea chest. He had ignored the bundle of franc notes, but held in his hand an American box camera, and a large Swiss pocketknife with a variety of screwdrivers, blades, and other gadgets sunk in its thick handle. "I was borrowing these," Kaoko said without the slightest embarrassment.
>
> "Would you have brought them back?" I said in anger.
>
> "No, probably not," Kaoko replied. "I intended to borrow them permanently."
>
> Kaoko had not the slightest sense of guilt. I realized suddenly that he had absolutely no notion of theft . . . just as the children in Europe must be carefully indoctrinated with a notion of property before they can be made to feel guilt about theft. This man had been brought up in an environment in which there was no notion of theft. I told him that I would need both the camera and the knife and he handed them to me without even the hint of a roguish smile. He simply handed them back.

A few days later he wrote in his diary:

> Last night I slept like a dead man on the beach. I had gotten drunk on beer and wine and the dancing. I fell asleep with the stars in my eyes . . . big, explosive, pure white stars

lost in the purest blackness. When I closed my eyes, the stars still seemed to glint somewhere in my eyeballs, tiny, pleasant dots of light.

During the night I awoke slowly and there was a hand in my lava-lava. It was the hand of a girl who was crouched down beside me, staring into my face and smiling. She was perhaps thirteen years old. She was very slim and her breasts were barely large enough to hold up her *pareu.*

She bent her head close to my ear and whispered into my ear in French. She told me that the dancing had excited her especially because she had never seen a white man dancing. As she spoke her hand wandered over my legs and between them.

For a moment on that warm beach my European conscience rebelled. I felt I could not do what the child wanted. What she wanted me to do was technically a crime in every civilized country of the world. She sensed my reluctance and laughed. It was not a nervous or hysterical laugh, it was the curious laughter of an inquisitive child. I took her, and it was sheer pleasure. She made love in the style that the natives call *maori:* quick, savage, silent. At the climax her tiny body arched up, she moaned, and then her fingernails scratched down my face. It was over quickly, but it was a very skillful performance and the girl was deeply satisfied. I am not quite sure how I feel today except that I am excited.

I knew then that Zola had not intended for me to read these memoirs. It was the kind of document that is kept only for the eyes of the author. I had always been curious as to why authors would specify that certain of their letters or notes or unpublished writings be destroyed upon their death. It had always struck me as a wanton waste of talent, a reckless and selfish pouring away of creative energy. Now I understood.

I should have stopped reading but I could not. The memoirs went on to describe his meeting with Toma.

Toma came to Tautira from the atoll on which Zola was now living. She had relatives in the village and had been living with them for a year. At Zola's invitation she had moved from her relatives' house into his. They lived together for six months, and then Toma told Zola that she was pregnant. Zola insisted upon being married, and being married in a church. Toma was puzzled, but she consented. After the first child was born they went to Toma's native atoll and at once Zola decided that they would live there. After this the entries in the book became very scanty. For five years he wrote no more than a line or two a month, recording the planting of coconut palms, the amount of copra harvested, the birth of children, the arrival of books on the trading schooner. It was as if his days were so satisfying that he no longer needed the solace of the memoirs.

Six years after his arrival on the atoll, however, the entries in the memoirs began to lengthen. One of them said:

> Toma is still as attractive as when I married her. Still as kind. Still as generous. At one point she began to take on weight and I did something for which I am ashamed. I insisted that she diet and stay slim. She argued that weight is a sign of prosperity and of dignity. But she has gone along with me.

A few days later there was another entry:

> There is a blankness about Toma that disturbs me. I have been trying to teach her to read and write French, but she simply does not have the interest. She will spend ten or twelve hours a day gossiping with members of her family on some petty thing such as the name of a new child. But she will not give attention enough to learn to read or write. I am puzzled.

A month later there was a long entry:

> I think I understand Toma and through her, the Polynesian personality. She lives literally in the moment. She loves *tiare* and her eyes will light up when she sees them, but she will not plant them. She has started vegetable gardens five times at my insistence, but each time has allowed the gardens to wither. She loves radishes, but not enough to grow and fertilize and water them. Three times she has agreed to hire workers to build an outdoor privy next to the bathhouse. But each time the money has gone for calico or tobacco. Flowers, radishes, a privy . . . all of these are things of the future and Toma does not think of the future. Polynesians do not know how to calculate future pleasures. I do not know why this should exasperate me but it does.

The entry after this was the last one: "I am bored, bored, bored, bored."

Later that afternoon Zola and I went for a long walk around the island. He was cheerful and talkative and his knowledge about everything about the South Seas was monumental. The habits of fish, the diseases of coconut palms, the old histories of great Polynesian kings, where infanticide was practiced and where it was not, were only a few of the things he discussed in the greatest detail. Now, however, I listened with a new ear. Zola's encyclopedic knowledge of Polynesia no longer seemed to me to be based on a simple fascination with the people, rather I had the impression that he was trying desperately to use the facts and information to fill a great yawning chasm of despair. He threw facts into it as his Polynesian chiefs threw victims over cliffs to satisfy a dimly seen, but terribly feared, deity.

We had almost finished our walk when we met a young boy and girl walking in the opposite direction. They said hello to us and then vanished on the path. Zola turned and looked at me.

"They have just finished making love in the bushes," he said. His voice was expressionless.

"How could you tell?" I asked.

"Really it is an exercise in probability," he said "Quite literally every time a Tahitian girl or boy meet casually it leads to sexual intercourse. The only exceptions are if they are sister and brother, or if one of them is malformed. Then also the boy's face had a few scratches on it. As you probably know Polynesian women at the climax scratch the man's face. The men often do the same thing."

"I knew that, but it still surprises me," I said. "They are so gentle in everything else that you would think when they are making love that it would carry over there, too. I have never been able to understand their use of violence in sex."

Zola turned and looked out toward the sea. The tide was just starting to flood, crabs scurried about, gradually moving toward the sand like a disorganized army in retreat. The waves boomed solidly against the reef, but aside from the sound, there was only a flat layer of foam to show their force.

"For them sex is not really an act of love," Zola said. "It is a way to break tedium, a way of breaking the monotony of endless beautiful days. It is like a game, but no more than a game."

That night after dinner a strange thing happened. We ate on the veranda overlooking the lagoon, watching the water gradually change into an even, flawless green, In the center of the table was a flower-and-shell arrangement that Toma had made. It had a startling miniature beauty to it. Tiny shells, stamens of some sort of flowers, the green from the throats of wild orchids, and an edging of blue petals that had been picked from flowers.

"That is a beautiful arrangement, Toma," I said.

Toma was pleased. Zola looked down at the arrangement and smiled.

"It is a beautiful arrangement," Zola said. He watched it intently for a few moments, and the smile went from his face. He bent forward and with his hand gently pushed the tiny arrangement apart. He looked at me as he spoke to Toma.

"Put it back together, Toma," he said.

Without a word Toma leaned forward, and her fingers flicked over the diminutive shells and flowers and petals. Almost at once it was back in order. Then I realized that it was back in *exactly* the same order, it was an exact duplication of the first arrangement.

I looked up from the arrangement, and Zola was watching me. His lips were turned up in a smile, but there was something like a pleading in his eyes.

"Can you do any other arrangements?" Zola asked Toma without looking at her.

"No, this is the only arrangement I make," she said. She smiled. "They taught us this when we were children. *Mai-tai,* eh."

"Mai-tai," I replied.

"Mai-tai, and every girl on the island can do this single arrangement, and the girls of the island have been making this arrangement and no other for over four hundred years," Zola said. His voice was empty.

Zola's face was held in a tight little smile, but his eyes

were suddenly deep and black with a strange expression. I sensed that he had looked over the edge of the chasm. Between us hung the knowledge that Toma could make only one flower arrangement, could cook *poa* only one way, cook fish only one way, make love in only one way, sing in only one pattern of songs, dance one kind of dance. Anything outside of the simple patterns did not interest her. And years ago Zola had come to know all of them.

Zola and I did not discuss this during the remaining days I was on his atoll. We walked and talked constantly, but he never referred to himself. When the PBY returned I rowed the old rubber boat out to it after saying good-by to Zola and Toma. The sweat was pouring into my eyes by the time I reached the plane. I was tired. Just as I shipped my oars and looked again at Zola's house the salty drops of sweat fogged my vision. Zola seemed shrunken, small, hunched, almost bleached. He had stopped waving. Toma seemed life-sized and natural.

He was a prisoner not of a dream, but of those faded years in France that had instilled into his nerves and brain and soul an interest in questions beyond himself and beyond the day in which he existed. He had escaped only the real presence of European life; twisted through his mind like a maze of black jets were a set of conditionings and experiences that had burned into his youthful mind. From these he could never escape.

Zola is typical of a whole breed of men, of white men that live in the South Seas. Sensitive to the rawness of their native society, they flee to the apparent tranquillity of the South Pacific. But by then the damage has been done.

To every white man in the South Seas this dread knowledge of thinness, sameness, an endless unrolling of identical acts, the haunting absence of distinct personality, must some day be faced. For many it is too much to face. This is one reason why so many of the white men of the Pacific are the most quietly desperate alcoholics in the world. They have burned all their bridges; there is no path back to Paris or Dubuque or London. They must, because of pride and sometimes sloth and sometimes poverty, stay in the South Seas.

But the original vision has been cauterized over with the scars of experience. So they must be sustained by alcohol or gambling or opium or driving economic activity or, as in the case of Zola, by a frantic search for the fullest knowledge of a culture that he did not really value.

There is a lesson. If you want to live in the South Seas start early. Early, very early, our nerves become civilized. It is not easy to then slough off the coatings of civilization; they are more durable and tough than the softer stuff of primitive life.

Robert Dean Frisbie

THE GHOST OF ALEXANDER PERKS, A.B.

After being discharged from the United States Army at the end of World War I, Robert Dean Frisbie (1896–1948) arrived in Tahiti in 1920 with a disability pension, a portable typewriter, and an ambition to write a sea novel that would be as great as *Moby Dick*. In three years he sold a few articles to magazines, took a Tahitian girl to live with him, and rebuilt a thirty-foot yawl in which he intended to visit the farthest and loneliest islands of Polynesia. After a year-long voyage to the Cook Islands, Samoa, and Fiji, having run out of money, he sold his boat and settled down on Danger Island, or Puka-Puka, as the resident trader, the only white man on the island.

He married a native girl and for four years tended his trading station, read a great deal, and wrote *The Book of Puka-Puka* (1929), the first and the best of a half-dozen books that brought him a measure of fame as one of the most interesting writers on the South Seas. But he could not remain permanently settled in his island home. Often he left it to sail to other islands, taking his wife and children with him. He was a restless Ishmael, an idealist, a dreamer, a primitivist who sought peace in the South Seas but never found it.

The following short story, one of several that Frisbie published in the *Atlantic Monthly*, is a whimsical tale of a sailor's ghost that haunted a South Sea copra schooner and was addicted to playing draughts with the second mate.

THE "PIRARA" IS A GARRULOUS OLD HOOKER, PROUD OF HER departed days and fond of reminiscing to me during the night watches below. At times she is querulous, too, complaining of the cargoes of rancid copra she must carry in her old age; of the native passengers who mess up her decks, tie awnings of patchwork quilts to the rigging, and whittle their initials in the rail; or of the parsimony of her owners, who refuse to buy a new winch—the old one is in a sorry plight—or replace the rusty old foretopmast stay. She even growls at me, her mate, though the Lord knows that I do my best; but it *is* hard to keep awake on clear nights during the twelve-to-four watch.

"Lackadaisy!" she groaned tonight, breaking into my dreams. "This is a lubber's shift! Rancid copra bulging my poor old ribs; engine-room grease and bilge water washing over my kelson. Why don't you pay a little attention to the pumps? You haven't sounded my well for a week! Fine mate you are for such a lady as me!"

"That is unfair!" I cried in my sleep. "You know that I watched Six-Seas pumping during the dogwatch."

The old schooner laughed derisively. "What a fib!" she cried. "Watched, indeed! You sat on the wheel box twiddling your thumbs, and you took Six-Seas' word for it when he said the pumps had sucked!" Then sharply, not giving me time to reply: "Don't say anything! Not a word out of you! You'll only lie and make me angry, and that'll be bad for your soul and my digestion!"

She fell silent as she wallowed in a long trough; then, with a groan—more from habit than anything else, for, like all old folks, she makes much of her troubles—she rose to the top of a long sea and lumbered down the other side.

"There's another one over, thank the good Lord!" she muttered. "My, what a number of rollers there are in the ocean! It is perfectly ridiculous! I've crossed as many as seven thousand in a single day. That was on the good old Shanghai-Frisco run when beating against the northwesterlies. Ah, those were the days! No filthy copra then, but cases of silks and tea, and clean mats of rice with little tins of opium hidden in them. And in those days Captain Pester gave my spars a coat of varnish every four months, all my standing rigging was served, and the brass on my rail shone beautifully. There were no broken catheads or rusty jib-boom guys on me then."

One bell sounded. I heard it in my sleep, but refused to waken for another moment or two.

"Get up, get up!" the old schooner cried maliciously. She concluded, her voice dwindling away to a murmur that finally merged into the splash of water along her sides: "Get up and go on deck, Lazybones, and finish your sleep while you're on watch."

There was a scratching on my cabin port light; then the senile whine of old Seaside, the Kanaka second mate: "One bell! One bell! Ropati *tané!*"

I opened my eyes. The scratching continued, irritating me. Knowing it would not stop until I replied, I pounded on the bulkhead, and growled, "All right, Seaside, you old fool! I hear you!"

The scratching stopped. I jumped out of my berth, lit the lamp, and dressed. Then, turning the lamp low, I climbed on deck just as the Seth Thomas clock struck eight times and the second mate repeated the hour on the ship's bell. He was alone, with the wheel lashed, for we had given the sailors the entire night below so we could work them all day on the morrow holystoning, scraping, and oiling decks.

The old man grinned at me, exposing his three yellow wolf-fang teeth. He sat on the wheel box with the binnacle light full on his deeply wrinkled face, making his sharp little eyes glow evilly. I glanced at the compass and then went to the weather rail to feel the wind. We seemed to be keeping on our course, full and by on the port tack. Returning to Seaside, I asked: "Well, old man, how's your friend the ghost tonight?"

I was referring to Mr. Alexander Perks, A.B., the spirit that is supposed to haunt this trading schooner. Mind you, I don't believe a word of it; but the sailors claim they see the old gentleman snooping around every night, trying to get one of them to play draughts with him. Personally, I say it's all nonsense, for I have a theory that there are no such things as ghosts.

"Up and about," came from Seaside's grinning lips. "Listen, there he is now!"

"It's only the wind, Seaside, you old fool," I replied. "Only the wind moaning in the shrouds."

"It's Perks," the old man declared, his smile fading and an indignant flash appearing in his eyes. Abruptly he turned and pointed to the galley. "And there he is; I must go and have a yarn with him. I'll be back by and by."

I glanced forward. There *was* a nebulous glimmer visible through the galley door, and I could understand how a simple native like Seaside might imagine it a ghost. Of course I knew better.

"It's only the moonlight, Seaside," I said as the old man started forward. "Only the moonlight shining through the galley window."

The silly old fellow laughed in his cackling way as he crossed the midship-house deck. "It's gone now, but still the moon shines," he said. A moment later he had dropped into the waist and entered the galley, leaving me to my thoughts.

Rats and ghosts, I mused, are favorable omens to a sailor, for they always desert a ship that is doomed. There was the old "Lillah Allers," for instance, which was named after her owner's wife—the owner was his own skipper. If I remember rightly, Mrs. Allers died aboard during a blow off the Horn. Lillah must have been a terror to the captain, for she used to come on deck when the wind freshened and make suggestions about taking in the royals, reefing the t'gallants'ls, or tying up the flying jib.

"Woman," Captain Allers would say to her in his sternest tone, "thy place is below; get thee below to thy sewing!"

This would make the old lady rave, for she believed that in a tight place she was more levelheaded than the captain; also, she claimed to have presentiments that never failed her. Well, she died that night off the Horn while she was in the midst of one of her presentiments. She had rushed on deck to declare that something terrible was about to happen. Just then the spanker backed, carried away its boom tackle, and, jibbing over, caught her on the nape of the neck. She was buried in latitude 60° 18′ south; but her spirit stayed by the ship, and Captain Allers used to swear that every time the wind freshened to a gale he could see her hovering above the poop deck, gesticulating frantically, pointing aloft in an effort to give some advice about handling the ship.

"Poor old 'Lillah Allers'!" I continued my musing, thinking of the ship, not the lady. The last time Captain Allers took her out of the Golden Gate he knew he would come to grief, for the night before he had seen the ghost of his late wife, a Gladstone bag and a hatbox in her hands, walking hurriedly down the gangplank.

"The ship is doomed!" he told the mate as soon as they were out of the bay, but before they had dropped the pilot. "My wife's spirit has deserted us!"

The mate respectfully suggested that the captain might have mentioned this before they threw off their dock lines. He added that he would just step into his cabin for his gear and go ashore with the pilot; but the captain wouldn't hear of it.

Well, they dropped the pilot, hoisted the old "Lillah Allers' " kites, and sailed over the horizon, never to be seen or heard of again!

I walked to the weather rail and watched the clouds of phosphorescence rise and subside. A school of bonito was over our windward quarter, streaking the sea with parallel lines of fire. I could hear from above our masts the squawking of a tropic bird, and from the galley Seaside's whine as he cried: "Jump me, Perks! You've got to jump!" or cackling with glee as he told the ghost that he had made the king row. The poor deluded native was imagining he was playing draughts with the spirit of Able-bodied Seaman Alexander Perks!

I returned to my musings, letting my mind wander to stories of other haunted ships. There was the "Ghost Ship" of Richard Middleton that was blown into Host's turnip patch by the great gale; the "Flying Dutchman"; the "Marie Celeste"; the Maori canoe of ill omen that appears at night in the lagoon of an island before a great catastrophe is to occur. Then there was Captain Arthur Mason's "Wampa" with its mysterious Hindu stowaway, who saved the ship during a hurricane by taking orders from the ghost of the dead captain and transmitting them to the crew. Haunted ships are as common as haunted houses, for sailors are as superstitious as old women; their lives are governed by omens and presentiments. Even I, who have a theory that such things are all nonsense, find myself half-believing in them at times. There is Perks, for instance. Much though I deride his existence, it is sometimes difficult to disbelieve in him; in fact, it requires all the cogency of my theory to prove him an illusion.

"I beat him," said Seaside, as he climbed over the break of the midship house.

"Suppose you turn in instead of snooping around deck and playing checkers with imaginary specters," I replied sharply. "You'll be good for nothing tomorrow unless you get some sleep."

"Old men seldom sleep," the second mate told me, "and tonight I could never lie in my bunk, I'd be that fidgety."

"What's all the trouble?"

The old man came close to me and whispered: "We make Vostok Island tomorrow, Captain Andy says, and I'm to go ashore for birds' eggs!"

"All the more reason for you to sleep tonight."

"But Perks?"

"What about him?"

Seaside leaned against the weather rail and let his sharp little eyes wander aloft. He shook his head knowingly, and again the fatuous grin played across his mouth; but in another moment he was whispering his story to me—whispering it because, as he said, he did not want Perks to overhear.

Three years ago, according to Seaside, the "Pirara" was not a haunted ship; but one day Captain Andy decided to put into Vostok Island for sea birds' eggs, and then all the trouble started. They came along the reef in the afternoon, and Seaside was landed with some empty boxes for the eggs. The reef boat put back to the schooner, leaving him alone. The old man waded through the shallows and climbed up the beach with his boxes, untroubled by an inkling of the harrowing experience that lay ahead.

It was a dreary place, he told me, of coral formation and without more than six feet elevation on its highest point. Not a coconut tree grew there, nor a bush, nor a blade of grass; but inland the island was overgrown with great *puka* trees, whose huge, soft and porous trunks towered straight and slimy two hundred feet in the air, and there broke into a mass of foliage so dense that only a dismal leaden light seeped through, lugubrious, as is the fading refulgence of twilight. The ground swarmed with black Norwegian rats and coconut crabs, the latter a foot long, their bodies scarlet-red, their eyes protruding, their claws powerful enough to snap off a man's finger. Millions of birds roosted like owls on the limbs of the trees, squawking with a deafening clamor, leaving their perches by the thousand as the old native passed beneath them. Other than these there was no sign of life on that unearthly island.

Seaside felt the awe of the unknown gnaw his bones; his knees weakened and his skin became clammy as he picked his way deep into the jungle, climbing over the trunks of fallen giants, stumbling into crab holes, sinking into quagmires of guano and decayed vegetation. He kept clear of the trunks of the trees, for, he said, they swarmed with rats and crabs climbing to the roosting birds to feed on their eggs and young. Often he could see fights carried on between them, when the boobies would pounce on the rats that were sucking their eggs, tear them from the limbs, and hurl them to the ground; or screaming birds would dive at and circle about a coconut crab that held a fledgling in its claws. It was a horrible scene of carnage that had been carried on for thousands of years—a death struggle between the species.

On into the island went Seaside, his boxes under his arms, hunting for an open space by the eastern beach where the terns should lay their eggs. The gloom of the jungle deepened, the air became rank and nauseating with the stench of sea birds' droppings, decaying flesh, damp vegetation. And the deeper he penetrated the more alive the ground became with evil, creeping things.

Suddenly he halted in panic terror, his hair on end and his eyes bulging. Directly in front of him, hanging by a long rope of bark, was a dead man! A few rags of cloth hung to him, a sailor cap sat jauntily on his head. He must have been long dead. Seaside shuddered when he told me that one arm had dropped off; its yellowed bones lay, rat-gnawed, on the ground.

Seaside did not know how long he stood staring at the dead man; but when he did regain enough courage to move he turned with a yell, dropped his boxes, and rushed wildly through the jungle, hunting for the outer beach! He must have run in circles, for an hour passed and still he was in the depth of the island. It seemed that the jungle, with its millions of loathsome creatures feeding on one another, had no end. Twice again he came upon the dead man, each time to increase his terror and send him rushing wildly away.

Several hours passed, when suddenly, it seemed, darkness closed about him, dense and impenetrable. The blackness pressed him from all sides as though a sable shroud had been thrown over him and he had been sunk deep in the sea. He staggered a few feet forward and bumped against a tree. A rat dropped on his head and ran down his body. All about him he could hear sharp squeals, the clicking of the crabs' claws, and, above, the clamor of the birds, though they were quieter now except when a rat or a crab crept upon their young—then the air would be alive with their screams.

Seaside sank on his knees at the foot of the tree. Gradually he became calmer. "After all," he reasoned, "the crabs and the rats can't kill me; the worst that can happen will be a sleepless night on this island." He felt a little better after this, but still far from easy. He told me an hour must have passed before he saw the ghost of Able-bodied Seaman Alexander Perks.

He had been staring into the darkness, his eyes shifting from side to side, when all at once a nebulous thing formed a few yards from him, danced back and forth among the trees, and then gradually took the shape of a man. It approached to within a few feet, bowed extravagantly, and lifted its hat. Seaside said that the jungle became aglow with an eerie light which disclosed the dead man a few feet to one side, swinging slightly now, while a dozen rats below his feet were leaping into the air, trying to get at him. After this Seaside lost cognizance of things.

When he came to, there was Perks, sitting on one of the boxes that he had brought ashore for eggs, talking in the hollow tone common among ghosts. "It's a shame," he was saying, "a beastly shame!"

Seaside snapped his eyes closed and started repeating the Lord's Prayer, but still he could hear Perks muttering: "I see you've come to, now. It's about time. 'Ere I've been marooned fer four years on this blinkin' island, and the first bloke as comes 'asn't the courtesy to treat me wid common civility. So strike me pink if it ain't a shame!"

Seaside opened one eye a fraction of an inch. He noted that the specter appeared to have a kindly face; but he was far from reassured, so he snapped his eyes shut again and started trembling violently as again he went over the prayer.

"Prayin', so 'elp me, prayin'!" moaned Perks. "But I suppose it *is* queerlike to see a man o' my profession—Able-bodied Seaman I am, Alexander Perks, A.B.—on a bloomin' island like this. But it's all right, matey, I'm 'armless—only a poor marooned mariner wot's died by 'is own 'and after two years of lonely and pathetic life on this blinkin' desert island."

Seaside opened both his eyes at this, for he felt sorry for the spirit. He had seen plenty of ghosts before, and though they always filled him with terror he realized that there were both the harmless and the vicious kinds.

"It must have been lonely," he managed to gasp.

"Lonely ain't no word fer it," Perks said with a shake of his head. "It's been unsocial as 'ell. I've been livin' a retired and 'omeless life widout even a bloke to play draughts wid!"

Here Seaside saw tears stream down the poor fellow's cheeks. "You like to play draughts?" he asked, his fright now gone.

The ghost's eyes brightened with an unearthly light. "It's been my lifelong 'abit," he replied, "and even since my late and lamented end it bides by me." After a moment's silence a wistful glow appeared in his eyes; he leaned forward and asked: "Matey, you don't 'appen, let's say, to play draughts, do you? I've the most 'andsome checkerboard on the north beach, beamy and symmetrical."

Seaside told him that he played a game now and then, whereupon the ghost insisted that they go to the beach and play. Of course this suited the old native, for at least it would mean their getting out of the foul, damp air of the jungle. He rose and followed Perks, who drifted among the trees, leaving a ghostly light behind him by which Seaside could with difficulty pick his way. In the course of a half-hour they broke through the trees to the clean white outer beach, sparkling with moonlight and swept by a fine breeze from off the sea. Perks stopped before a large slab of coral.

"Ain't it 'andsome?" he asked. "I marked the squares wid octopus ink, as you can see, and my men are black shells and white ones; only when I makes a king I turns 'im over instead of pilin' one on top of t'other, they being too roundlike to stand. But I ain't 'ad a game since my sad end, it bein' against nature fer a ghost to move the men. Before my decease I played myself."

"That must have been a tiresome game," Seaside ventured.

"Strike me pink, but it was awful," Perks said; "always winning from myself, one way or t'other! It got so discouragin', never winning a game decisivelike, that I put an end to it all and done away wid myself!"

They sat with the slab between them and started a game, Seaside moving Perks's men for him. One game after the other he lost to the ghost, sometimes no more than getting a single man to the king row. The night waned, but still they played. Perks became more and more excited over the game; he would scream like a banshee when he won, and an evil glint would come into his eyes when he jumped three men at once or slipped into a saddle between two of Seaside's men. They were near the end of their twentieth game when dawn broke. Gradually Perks dissolved in the morning light, and his voice became fainter until it was lost in a scarcely audible moan that told Seaside of another game he had lost.

The old native looked up from the checkerboard. The sun was just breaking above the horizon; in the offing lay the "Pirara," her boat over the side and not twenty yards from the reef.

Seaside told me there was the devil to pay when he met Captain Andy and tried to explain why he had no birds' eggs and why he hadn't been on the reef the evening before. He mentioned something about being delayed by a ghost; but at this the captain flew off the handle, cursing all superstitious sailors to Gehenna and back again. Seaside stood it as long as he could; then slunk forward and told his story to the sailors. They all knew it was true, and sympathized mightily.

But the strange thing was that, as soon as he came on deck the next night to stand his watch, there was Alexander Perks waiting for him, smiling and bowing and lifting his hat and suggesting a game of draughts. The old gentleman had stowed away, slipping into the ship's boat under cover of daylight!

Seaside broke from his story, turned quickly and said: "All right, Perks, I'm coming."

A cold shiver ran down my back. There, not six feet away, was a strange misty thing, bowing extravagantly and lifting his hat. I shook myself to dispel the illusion; then turned aft, refusing to glance toward the thing for several moments, for I don't believe in ghosts and don't want my convictions shaken by hallucinations. When I did turn, both Seaside and the imaginary Perks were gone.

"Lackadaisy!" the old "Pirara" groaned while I was putting in my twelve-to-four watch below. "Death comes to old and young alike."

"What a hackneyed thing to say!" I replied sharply—the old hooker had nearly wakened me. "You might be a little more original."

"Patience, my son," she went on, a note of true pathos in her voice. "You should be more considerate of the dying."

"Dying?"

"Alas, yes; my day has come, and now I find myself so close to Christening Grooves that—"

"Christening Grooves! What's that?"

"Such ignorance! It's the paradise for dead ships, where every morning the ghost ships waken on the grooves of launching, stout, tight, shining with paint and varnish and polished brass. Every morning the crowds are there, watching fair maidens break bottles of champagne on the ghost ships' bows. Then everybody cheers while the band plays 'Life on the Ocean Wave,' the cameras click, and the ships slip gracefully into the water!"

"And every morning it happens all over again?"

"Every morning."

"Why do you moan about dying then?"

"Death is a sad thing," the old lady sighed. "For instance, all of you, whom I have learned to love, will probably perish at sea! Alas! You shouldn't have allowed Mr. Perks to go ashore!"

I shuddered in my sleep as I queried, "Perks ashore?"

"Of course," she replied. "He's back on Vostok Island again. He went ashore with Seaside this morning when the captain sent him after birds' eggs. Why, even the rats were trying to jump into the boat!"

"Then we're lost!" I cried in my sleep.

The old lady became sarcastic. "Don't let that trouble you," she murmured. "Fiddler's Green is quite as good a paradise for sailors as is Christening Grooves for ships."

She chuckled to herself.

"One bell! One bell! Ropati *tané!*" came Seaside's senile whine, followed by the scratching on the cabin port.

I jumped from my berth and ran on deck. "Seaside, you old fool!" I shouted. "Is it true that Perks went ashore with you?"

The old sinner grinned and nodded his head in affirmation.

Twenty-four hours later we were all in the reef boat, watching the "Pirara" plunge to Christening Grooves before we started pulling the hundred and twenty miles back to Vostok Island.

Robert Louis Stevenson

THE BEACH OF FALESÁ

After two years of voyaging throughout the Pacific islands, Robert Louis Stevenson (1850–1894) decided that the Samoan island of Upolu was the best place in all the world for him to spend the rest of his life. In 1890 he bought a tract of three hundred acres on a mountainside above the town of Apia and built a large, rambling house. He named the place "Vailima" (Five Rivers). It was there, while he was clearing undergrowth on his property, that the story of *The Beach of Falesá,* as he said, "shot through me like a bullet in one of my moments of awe, alone in that tragic jungle."

The work of writing the story, however, gave him much trouble, especially the ending; but when he had finished it he wrote to one of his friends, saying, "I believe it good; indeed, to be honest, very good." He had put into it much of what he had learned and knew was true of the islands and inhabitants, both native and white, of Polynesia. In a letter to Sidney Colvin he wrote: "It is the first realistic South Sea story; I mean with real South Sea character and details of life. Everybody else who has tried, that I have seen, got carried away by the romance, and ended in a kind of sugar-candy sham epic, and the whole effect was lost—there was no etching, no human grin, consequently no conviction. Now I have got the smell and the look of the thing a good deal. You will know more about the South Seas after you have read my little tale than if you had read a library."

CHAPTER I

A SOUTH-SEA BRIDAL

I SAW THAT ISLAND FIRST WHEN IT WAS NEITHER NIGHT NOR morning. The moon was to the west, setting, but still broad and bright. To the east, and right amidships of the dawn, which was all pink, the daystar sparkled like a diamond. The land breeze blew in our faces, and smelt strong of wild lime and vanilla; other things besides, but these were the most plain; and the chill of it set me sneezing. I should say I had been for years on a low island near the line, living for the most part solitary among natives. Here was a fresh experience; even the tongue would be quite strange to me; and the look of these woods and mountains, and the rare smell of them, renewed my blood.

The captain blew out the binnacle lamp.

"There!" said he, "there goes a bit of smoke, Mr. Wiltshire, behind the break of the reef. That's Falesá, where your station is, the last village to the east; nobody lives to windward—I don't know why. Take my glass, and you can make the houses out."

I took the glass; and the shores leaped nearer, and I saw the tangle of the woods and the breach of the surf, and the brown roofs and the black insides of houses peeped among the trees.

"Do you catch a bit of white there to the east'ard?" the captain continued. "That's your house. Coral-built, stands high, veranda you could walk on three abreast; best station in the South Pacific. When old Adams saw it, he took and shook me by the hand. 'I've dropped into a soft thing here,' says he. 'So you have,' says I, 'and time, too!' Poor Johnny! I never saw him again but the once, and then he had changed his tune—couldn't get on with the natives, or the whites, or something; and the next time we came round there, he was dead and buried. I took and put up a bit of a stick to him: 'John Adams, *obit* eighteen and sixty-eight. Go thou and do likewise.' I missed that man. I never could see much harm in Johnny."

"What did he die of?" I inquired.

"Some kind of sickness," says the captain. "It appears it took him sudden. Seems he got up in the night, and filled up on Pain Killer and Kennedy's Discovery. No go—he was booked beyond Kennedy. Then he had tried to open a case of gin. No go again—not strong enough. Then he must have turned to and run out on the veranda, and capsized over the rail. When they found him, the next day, he was clean crazy—carried on all the time about somebody watering his copra. Poor John!"

"Was it thought to be the island?" I asked.

"Well, it was thought to be the island, or the trouble, or something," he replied. "I never could hear but what it was a healthy place. Our last man, Vigours, never turned a hair. He left because of the beach—said he was afraid of Black Jack and Case and Whistling Jimmie, who was still alive at the time, but got drowned soon afterward when drunk. As for old Captain Randall, he's been here any time since eighteen forty, forty-five. I never could see much harm in Billy, nor much change. Seems as if he might live to be Old Kafoozleum. No, I guess it's healthy."

"There's a boat coming now," said I. "She's right in the pass; looks to be a sixteen-foot whale; two white men in the stern sheets."

"That's the boat that drowned Whistling Jimmie!" cried the captain; "let's see the glass. Yes, that's Case, sure enough, and the darkie. They've got a gallows' bad reputation, but you know what a place the beach is for talking. My belief, that Whistling Jimmie was the worst of the trouble; and he's gone to glory, you see. What'll you bet they ain't after gin? Lay you five to two they take six cases."

When these two traders came aboard I was pleased with the looks of them at once, or, rather, with the looks of both, and the speech of one. I was sick for white neighbors after my four years at the line, which I always counted years of prison; getting tabooed, and going down to the Speak House to see and get it taken off; buying gin and going on a break, and then repenting; sitting in the house at night with the lamp for company; or walking on the beach and wondering what kind of a fool to call myself for being where I was. There were no other whites upon my island, and when I sailed to the next, rough customers made the most of the society. Now to see these two when they came aboard was a pleasure. One was a Negro, to be sure; but they were both rigged out smart in striped pajamas and straw hats, and Case would have passed muster in a city. He was yellow and smallish, had a hawk's nose to his face, pale eyes, and his beard trimmed with scissors. No man knew his country, beyond he was of English speech; and it was clear he came of a good family and was splendidly educated. He was accomplished too; played the accordion first-rate; and give him a piece of a string or a cork or a pack of cards, and he could show you tricks equal to any professional. He could speak, when he chose, fit for a drawing room; and when he chose he could blaspheme worse than a Yankee boatswain, and talk smart to sicken a Kanaka. The way he thought would pay best at the moment, that was Case's way, and it always seemed to come natural, and like as if he was born to it. He had the courage of a lion and the cunning of a rat; and if he's not in hell today, there's no such place. I know but one good point to the man—that he was fond of his wife, and kind to her. She was a Samoa woman, and dyed her hair red—Samoa style; and when he came to die (as I have to tell of) they found one strange thing—that he had made a will, like a Christian, and the widow got the lot; all his, they said, and all Black Jack's and the most of Billy Randall's in the bargain, for it was Case that kept the books. So she went off home in the schooner "Manu'a," and does the lady to this day in her own place.

But of all this on that first morning I knew no more than a fly. Case used me like a gentleman and like a friend, made me welcome to Falesá, and put his services at my disposal, which was the more helpful from my ignorance of the natives. All the better part of the day we sat drinking better acquaintance in the cabin, and I never heard a man talk more to the point. There was no smarter trader, and none dodgier, in the islands. I thought Falesá seemed to be the right kind of a place; and the more I drank the lighter my heart. Our last trader had fled the place at half an hour's notice, taking a chance passage in a labor ship from up west. The captain, when he came, had found the station closed, the keys left with the native pastor, and a letter from the runaway, confessing he was fairly frightened of his life. Since then the firm had not been represented, and of course there was no cargo. The wind, besides, was fair, the captain hoped he could make his next island by dawn, with a good tide, and the business of landing my trade was gone about lively. There was no call for me to fool with it, Case said; nobody would touch my things, everyone was honest in Falesá, only about chickens or an odd knife or an odd stick of tobacco; and the best I could do was to sit quiet till the vessel left, then come straight to his house, see old Captain Randall, the father of the beach, take potluck, and go home to sleep when it got dark. So it was high noon, and the schooner was under way, before I set my foot on shore at Falesá.

I had a glass or two on board; I was just off a long cruise, and the ground heaved under me like a ship's deck. The world was like all new-painted; my foot went along to music; Falesá might have been Fiddler's Green, if there is such a place, and more's the pity if there isn't! It was good to foot the grass, to look aloft at the green mountains, to see the men with their green wreaths and the women in their bright dresses, red and blue. On we went, in the strong sun and the cool shadow, liking both; and all the children in the town came trotting after with their shaven heads and their brown bodies, and raising a thin kind of a cheer in our wake, like crowing poultry.

"By the bye," says Case, "we must get you a wife."

"That's so," said I; "I had forgotten."

There was a crowd of girls about us, and I pulled myself up and looked among them like a bashaw. They were all dressed out for the sake of the ship being in; and the women of Falesá are a handsome lot to see. If they have a fault, they are a trifle broad in the beam; and I was just thinking so when Case touched me.

"That's pretty," says he.

I saw one coming on the other side alone. She had been fishing; all she wore was a chemise, and it was wetted through.

She was young and very slender for an island maid, with a long face, a high forehead, and a shy, strange, blindish look, between a cat's and a baby's.

"Who's she?" said I. "She'll do."

"That's Uma," said Case, and he called her up and spoke to her in the native. I didn't know what he said; but when he was in the midst she looked up at me quick and timid, like a child dodging a blow, then down again, and presently smiled. She had a wide mouth, the lips and the chin cut like any statue's; and the smile came out for a moment and was gone. Then she stood with her head bent, and heard Case to an end, spoke back in the pretty Polynesian voice, looking him full in the face, heard him again in answer, and then with an obeisance started off. I had just a share of the bow, but never another shot of her eye, and there was no more word of smiling.

"I guess it's all right," said Case. "I guess you can have her. I'll make it square with the old lady. You can have your pick of the lot for a plug of tobacco," he added, sneering.

I suppose it was the smile that stuck in my memory, for I spoke back sharp. "She doesn't look that sort," I cried.

"I don't know that she is," said Case. "I believe she's as right as the mail. Keeps to herself, don't go round with the gang, and that. Oh, no, don't you misunderstand me—Uma's on the square." He spoke eager, I thought, and that surprised and pleased me. "Indeed," he went on, "I shouldn't make so sure of getting her, only she cottoned to the cut of your jib. All you have to do is to keep dark and let me work the mother my own way; and I'll bring the girl round to the captain's for the marriage."

I didn't care for the word marriage, and I said so.

"Oh, there's nothing to hurt in the marriage," says he. "Black Jack's the chaplain."

By this time we had come in view of the house of these three white men; for a Negro is counted a white man, and so is a Chinese! A strange idea, but common in the islands. It was a board house with a strip of rickety veranda. The store was to the front, with a counter, scales, and the finest possible display of trade: a case or two of tinned meats; a barrel of hard bread; a few bolts of cotton stuff, not to be compared with mine; the only thing well represented being the contraband firearms and liquor. "If these are my only rivals," thinks I, "I should do well in Falesá." Indeed, there was only the one way they could touch me, and that was with the guns and drink.

In the back room was old Captain Randall, squatting on the floor native fashion, fat and pale, naked to the waist, gray as a badger, and his eyes set with drink. His body was covered with gray hair and crawled over by flies; one was in the corner of his eye—he never heeded; and the mosquitoes hummed about the man like bees. Any clean-minded man would have had the creature out at once and buried him; and to see him, and think he was seventy, and remember he had once commanded a ship, and come ashore in his smart togs, and talked big in bars and consulates, and sat in club verandas, turned me sick and sober.

He tried to get up when I came in, but that was hopeless; so he reached me a hand instead, and stumbled out some salutation.

"Papa's pretty full this morning," observed Case. "We've had an epidemic here; and Captain Randall takes gin for a prophylactic—don't you, Papa?"

"Never took such a thing in my life!" cried the captain, indignantly. "Take gin for my health's sake. Mr. Wha's-ever-your-name—'s a precautionary measure."

"That's all right, Papa," said Case. "But you'll have to brace up. There's going to be a marriage—Mr. Wiltshire here is going to get spliced."

The old man asked to whom.

"To Uma," said Case.

"Uma!" cried the captain. Wha's he want Uma for? 'S he come here for his health, anyway? Wha' 'n hell's he want Uma for?"

"Dry up, Papa," said Case. " 'Tain't you that's to marry her. I guess you're not her godfather and godmother. I guess Mr. Wiltshire's going to please himself."

With that he made an excuse to me that he must move about the marriage, and left me alone with the poor wretch that was his partner and (to speak truth) his gull. Trade and station belonged both to Randall; Case and the Negro were parasites; they crawled and fed upon him like the flies, he none the wiser. Indeed, I have no harm to say of Billy Randall beyond the fact that my gorge rose at him, and the time I now passed in his company was like a nightmare.

The room was stifling hot and full of flies; for the house was dirty and low and small, and stood in a bad place, behind the village, in the borders of the bush, and sheltered from the trade. The three men's beds were on the floor, and a litter of pans and dishes. There was no standing furniture; Randall, when he was violent, tearing it to laths. There I sat and had a meal that was served us by Case's wife; and there I was entertained all day by that remains of man, his tongue stumbling among low, old jokes and long, old stories, and his own wheezy laughter always ready, so that he had no sense of my depression. He was nipping gin all the while. Sometimes he fell asleep, and awoke again, whimpering and shivering, and every now and again he would ask me why I wanted to marry Uma. "My friend," I was telling myself all day, "you must not come to be an old gentleman like this."

It might be four in the afternoon, perhaps, when the back door was thrust slowly open, and a strange old native woman crawled into the house almost on her belly. She was swathed in black stuff to her heels; her hair was gray in swatches; her face was tattooed, which was not the practice in that island; her eyes big and bright and crazy. These she fixed upon me with a rapt expression that I saw to be part acting. She said no plain word, but smacked and mumbled with her lips, and hummed aloud, like a child over its Christmas pudding. She came straight across the house, heading for me, and as soon as she was alongside, caught up my hand and purred and crooned over it like a great cat. From this she slipped into a kind of song.

"Who the devil's this?" cried I, for the thing startled me.

"It's Faavao," says Randall; and I saw he had hitched along the floor into the farthest corner.

"You ain't afraid of her?" I cried.

"Me 'fraid!" cried the captain. "My dear friend, I defy

her! I don't let her put her foot in here, only I suppose 's different today for the marriage. 'S Uma's mother."

"Well, suppose it is; what's she carrying on about?" I asked, more irritated, perhaps more frightened, than I cared to show; and the captain told me she was making up a quantity of poetry in my praise because I was to marry Uma. "All right, old lady," says I, with rather a failure of a laugh, "anything to oblige. But when you're done with my hand, you might let me know."

She did as though she understood; the song rose into a cry, and stopped; the woman crouched out of the house the same way that she came in, and must have plunged straight into the bush, for when I followed her to the door she had already vanished.

"These are rum manners," said I.

" 'S a rum crowd," said the captain, and, to my surprise, he made the sign of the cross on his bare bosom.

"Hillo!" says I, "are you a papist?"

He repudiated the idea with contempt. "Hard-shell Baptis'," said he. "But, my dear friend, the papists got some good ideas too; and th' 's one of 'em. You take my advice, and whenever you come across Uma or Faavao or Vigours, or any of that crowd, you take a leaf out o' the priests, and do what I do. Savvy?" says he, repeated the sign, and winked his dim eye at me. "No, *sir!*" he broke out again, "no papists here!" and for a long time entertained me with his religious opinions.

I must have been taken with Uma from the first, or I should certainly have fled from that house, and got into the clean air, and the clean sea, or some convenient river—though, it's true, I was committed to Case; and, besides, I could never have held my head up in that island if I had run from a girl upon my wedding night.

The sun was down, the sky all on fire, and the lamp had been some time lighted, when Case came back with Uma and the Negro. She was dressed and scented; her kilt was of fine tapa, looking richer in the folds than any silk; her bust, which was of the color of dark honey, she wore bare, only for some half a dozen necklaces of seeds and flowers; and behind her ears and in her hair she had the scarlet flowers of the hibiscus. She showed the best bearing for a bride conceivable, serious and still; and I thought shame to stand up with her in that mean house and before that grinning Negro. I thought shame, I say; for the mountebank was dressed with a big paper collar, the book he made believe to read from was an odd volume of a novel, and the words of his service not fit to be set down. My conscience smote me when we joined hands; and when she got her certificate I was tempted to throw up the bargain and confess. Here is the document. It was Case that wrote it, signatures and all, in a leaf out of the ledger:

> This is to certify that Uma, daughter of Faavao of Falesá, island of ———, is illegally married to Mr. John Wiltshire, and Mr. John Wiltshire is at liberty to send her packing when he pleases.
>
> JOHN BLACKAMOAR,
> Chaplain to the Hulks.
>
> Extracted from the Register
> by William T. Randall,
> Master Mariner.

A nice paper to put in a girl's hand and see her hide away like gold. A man might easily feel cheap for less. But it was the practice in these parts, and (as I told myself) not the least the fault of us white men, but of the missionaries. If they had let the natives be, I had never needed this deception, but taken all the wives I wished, and left them when I pleased, with a clear conscience.

The more ashamed I was, the more hurry I was in to be gone; and our desires thus jumping together, I made the less remark of a change in the traders. Case had been all eagerness to keep me; now, as though he had attained a purpose, he seemed all eagerness to have me go. Uma, he said, could show me to my house, and the three bade us farewell indoors.

The night was nearly come; the village smelt of trees and flowers and the sea and breadfruit-cooking; there came a fine roll of sea from the reef, and from a distance, among the woods and houses, many pretty sounds of men and children. It did me good to breathe free air; it did me good to be done with the captain, and see, instead, the creature at my side. I felt for all the world as though she were some girl at home in the Old Country, and forgetting myself for the minute, took her hand to walk with. Her fingers nestled into mine, I heard her breathe deep and quick, and all at once she caught my hand to her face and pressed it there. "You good!" she cried, and ran ahead of me, and stopped and looked back and smiled, and ran ahead of me again, thus guiding me through the edge of the bush, and by a quiet way, to my own house.

The truth is, Case had done the courting for me in style—told her I was mad to have her, and cared nothing for the consequences; and the poor soul, knowing that which I was still ignorant of, believed it, every word, and had her head nigh turned with vanity and gratitude. Now, of all this I had no guess; I was one of those most opposed to any nonsense about native women, having seen so many whites eaten up by their wives' relatives, and made fools of into the bargain; and I told myself I must make a stand at once, and bring her to her bearings. But she looked so quaint and pretty as she ran away and then awaited me, and the thing was done so like a child or a kind dog, that the best I could do was just to follow her whenever she went on, to listen for the fall of her bare feet, and to watch in the dusk for the shining of her body. And there was another thought came in my head. She played kitten with me now when we were alone; but in the house she had carried it the way a countess might, so proud and humble. And what with her dress—for all there was so little of it, and that native enough—what with her fine tapa and fine scents, and her red flowers and seeds, that were quite as bright as jewels, only larger—it came over me she was a kind of countess really, dressed to hear great singers at a concert, and no even mate for a poor trader like myself.

She was the first in the house; and while I was still without I saw a match flash and the lamplight kindle in the windows. The station was a wonderful fine place, coral-built, with quite a wide veranda, and the main room high and wide. My chests and cases had been piled in, and made rather of a mess; and there, in the thick of the confusion, stood Uma by the table, awaiting me. Her shadow went all the way up behind her into the hollow of the iron roof; she stood against it bright, the lamplight shining on her skin. I stopped in the door, and she looked at me, not speaking, with eyes that were eager and yet daunted; then she touched herself on the bosom.

"Me—your wifie," she said. It had never taken me like that before; but the want of her took and shook all through me, like the wind in the luff of a sail.

I could not speak if I had wanted; and if I could, I would not. I was ashamed to be so much moved about a native, ashamed of the marriage too, and the certificate she had treasured in her kilt; and I turned aside and made believe to rummage among my cases. The first thing I lighted on was a case of gin, the only one that I had brought; and partly for the girl's sake, and partly for horror of the recollections of old Randall, took a sudden resolve. I pried the lid off. One by one I drew the bottles with a pocket corkscrew, and sent Uma out to pour the stuff from the veranda.

She came back after the last, and looked at me puzzled-like.

"No good," said I, for I was now a little better master of my tongue. "Man he drink, he no good."

She agreed with this, but kept considering. "Why you bring him?" she asked, presently. "Suppose you no want drink, you no bring him, I think."

"That's all right," said I. "One time I want drink too much; now no want. You see, I no savvy, I get one little wifie. Suppose I drink gin, my little wifie be 'fraid."

To speak to her kindly was about more than I was fit for; I had made my vow I would never let on to weakness with a native, and I had nothing for it but to stop.

She stood looking gravely down at me where I sat by the open case. "I think you good man," she said. And suddenly she had fallen before me on the floor. "I belong you all-e-same pig!" she cried.

CHAPTER II

THE BAN

I came on the veranda just before the sun rose on the morrow. My house was the last on the east; there was a cape of woods and cliffs behind that hid the sunrise. To the west, a swift, cold river ran down, and beyond was the green of the village, dotted with coco palms and breadfruits and houses. The shutters were some of them down and some open; I saw the mosquito bars still stretched, with shadows of people new-awakened sitting up inside; and all over the green, others were stalking silent, wrapped in their many-colored sleeping clothes, like Bedouins in Bible pictures. It was mortal still and solemn and chilly, and the light of the dawn on the lagoon was like the shining of a fire.

But the thing that troubled me was nearer hand. Some dozen young men and children made a piece of a half-circle, flanking my house: the river divided them, some were on the near side, some on the far, and one on a boulder in the midst; and they all sat silent, wrapped in their sheets, and stared at me and my house as straight as pointer dogs. I thought it strange as I went out. When I had bathed and come back again, and found them all there, and two or three more along with them, I thought it stranger still. What could they see to gaze at in my house I wondered, and went in.

But the thought of these starers stuck in my mind, and presently I came out again. The sun was now up, but it was still behind the cape of woods. Say a quarter of an hour had come and gone. The crowd was greatly increased, the far bank of the river was lined for quite a way—perhaps thirty grown folk, and of children twice as many, some standing, some squatted on the ground, and all staring at my house. I have seen a house in a South Sea village thus surrounded, but then a trader was thrashing his wife inside, and she singing out. Here was nothing—the stove was alight, the smoke going up in a Christian manner; all was shipshape and Bristol fashion. To be sure, there was a stranger come, but they had a chance to see that stranger yesterday, and took it quiet enough. What ailed them now? I leaned my arms on the rail and stared back. Devil a wink they had in them! Now and then I could see the children chatter, but they spoke so low not even the hum of their speaking came my length. The rest were like graven images: they stared at me, dumb and sorrowful, with their bright eyes; and it came upon me things would look not much different if I were on the platform of the gallows, and these good folk had come to see me hanged.

I felt I was getting daunted, and began to be afraid I looked it, which would never do. Up I stood, made believe to stretch myself, came down the veranda stair, and strolled toward the river. There went a short buzz from one to the other, like what you hear in theaters when the curtain goes up; and some of the nearest gave back the matter of a pace. I saw a girl lay one hand on a young man and make a gesture upward with the other; at the same time she said something in the native with a gasping voice. Three little boys sat beside my path, where I must pass within three feet of them. Wrapped in their sheets, with their shaved heads and bits of topknots, and queer faces, they looked like figures on a chimney piece. Awhile they sat their ground, solemn as judges. I came up hand over fist, doing my five knots, like a man that meant business; and I thought I saw a sort of a wink and gulp in the three faces. Then one jumped up (he was the farthest off) and ran for his mammy. The other two, trying to follow suit, got foul, came to the ground together bawling, wriggled right out of their sheets, and in a moment there were all three of them scampering for their lives, and singing out like pigs. The natives, who would never let a joke slip, even at a burial, laughed and let up, as short as a dog's bark.

They say it scares a man to be alone. No such thing. What scares him in the dark or the high bush is that he can't make sure, and there might be an army at his elbow. What scares him worst is to be right in the midst of a crowd, and have no guess of what they're driving at. When that laugh stopped, I stopped too. The boys had not yet made their offing; they were still on the full stretch going the one way, when I had already gone about ship and was sheering off the other. Like a fool I had come out, doing my five knots; like a fool I went back again. It must have been the funniest thing to see, and what knocked me silly, this time no one laughed; only one old woman gave a kind of pious moan, the way you have heard Dissenters in their chapels at the sermon.

"I never saw such fools of Kanakas as your people here," I said once to Uma, glancing out of the window at the starers.

"Savvy nothing," says Uma, with a kind of disgusted air that she was good at.

And that was all the talk we had upon the matter, for I was put out, and Uma took the thing so much as a matter of course that I was fairly ashamed.

All day, off and on, now fewer and now more, the fools sat about the west end of my house and across the river, waiting for the show, whatever that was—fire to come down from heaven, I suppose, and consume me, bones and baggage. But by evening, like real islanders, they had wearied of the business, and got away, and had a dance instead in the big house of the village, where I heard them singing and clapping hands till maybe ten at night, and the next day it seemed they had forgotten I existed. If fire had come down from heaven or the earth opened and swallowed me, there would have been nobody to see the sport or take the lesson, or whatever you like to call it. But I was to find they hadn't forgot either, and kept an eye lifting for phenomena over my way.

I was hard at it both these days getting my trade in order and taking stock of what Vigours had left. This was a job that made me pretty sick, and kept me from thinking on much else. Ben had taken stock the trip before—I knew I could trust Ben—but it was plain somebody had been making free in the meantime. I found I was out by what might easily cover six months' salary and profit, and I could have kicked myself all round the village to have been such a blamed ass, sitting boozing with that Case instead of attending to my own affairs and taking stock.

However, there's no use crying over spilt milk. It was done now, and couldn't be undone. All I could do was to get what was left of it, and my new stuff (my own choice) in order, to go round and get after the rats and cockroaches, and to fix up that store regular Sydney style. A fine show I made of it; and the third morning, when I had lit my pipe and stood in the doorway and looked in, and turned and looked far up the mountain and saw the coconuts waving and posted up the tons of copra, and over the village green and saw the island dandies and reckoned up the yards of print they wanted for their kilts and dresses, I felt as if I was in the right place to make a fortune, and go home again and start a public house. There was I, sitting in that veranda, in as handsome a piece of scenery as you could find, a splendid sun, and a fine, fresh, healthy trade that stirred up a man's blood like sea bathing; and the whole thing was clean gone from me, and I was dreaming England, which is, after all, a nasty, cold, muddy hole, with not enough light to see to read by; and dreaming the looks of my public, by a cant of a broad high-road like an avenue and with the sign on a green tree.

So much for the morning, but the day passed and the devil anyone looked near me, and from all I knew of natives in other islands I thought this strange. People laughed a little at our firm and their fine stations, and at this station of Falesá in particular; all the copra in the district wouldn't pay for it (I heard them say) in fifty years, which I supposed was an exaggeration. But when the day went, and no business came at all, I began to get downhearted; and, about three in the afternoon, I went out for a stroll to cheer me up. On the green I saw a white man coming with a cassock on, by which and by the face of him I knew he was a priest. He was a good-natured old soul to look at, gone a little grizzled, and so dirty you could have written with him on a piece of paper.

"Good-day, sir," said I.

He answered me eagerly in native.

"Don't you speak any English?" said I.

"French," says he.

"Well," said I, "I'm sorry, but I can't do anything there."

He tried me a while in the French, and then again in native, which he seemed to think was the best chance. I made out he was after more than passing the time of day with me, but had something to communicate, and I listened the harder. I heard the names of Adams and Case and of Randall —Randall the oftenest—and the word *poison,* or something like it, and a native word that he said very often. I went home, repeating it to myself.

"What does *fussy-ocky* mean?" I asked of Uma, for that was as near as I could come to it.

"Make dead," said she.

"The devil it does!" says I. "Did ever you hear that Case had poisoned Johnny Adams?"

"Every man he savvy that," says Uma, scornful-like. "Give him white sand—bad sand. He got the bottle still. Suppose he give you gin, you no take him."

Now I had heard much the same sort of story in other islands, and the same white powder always to the front, which made me think the less of it. For all that, I went over to Randall's place to see what I could pick up, and found Case on the doorstep, cleaning a gun.

"Good shooting here?" says I.

"A-1," says he. "The bush is full of all kinds of birds. I wish copra was as plenty," says he—I thought, slyly—"but there don't seem anything doing."

I could see Black Jack in the store, serving a customer.

"That looks like business, though," said I.

"That's the first sale we've made in three weeks," said he.

"You don't tell me?" says I. "Three weeks? Well, well."

"If you don't believe me," he cries, a little hot, "you can go and look at the copra house. It's half-empty to this blessed hour."

"I shouldn't be much the better for that, you see," says I. "For all I can tell, it might have been whole-empty yesterday."

"That's so," says he, with a bit of a laugh.

"By the bye," I said, "what sort of a party is that priest? Seems rather a friendly sort."

At this Case laughed right out loud. "Ah!" says he, "I see what ails you now. Galuchet's been at you." *Father Galoshes* was the name he went by most, but Case always gave it the French quirk, which was another reason we had for thinking him above the common.

"Yes, I have seen him," I says. "I made out he didn't think much of your Captain Randall."

"That he don't!" says Case. "It was the trouble about poor Adams. The last day, when he lay dying, there was young Buncombe round. Ever met Buncombe?"

I told him no.

"He's a cure, is Buncombe!" laughs Case. "Well, Buncombe

took it in his head that, as there was no other clergyman about, bar Kanaka pastors, we ought to call in Father Galuchet, and have the old man administered and take the sacrament. It was all the same to me, you may suppose; but I said I thought Adams was the fellow to consult. He was jawing away about watered copra and a sight of foolery. 'Look here,' I said, 'you're pretty sick. Would you like to see Galoshes?' He sat right up on his elbow. 'Get the priest,' says he, 'get the priest; don't let me die here like a dog!' He spoke kind of fierce and eager, but sensible enough. There was nothing to say against that, so we sent and asked Galuchet if he would come. You bet he would. He jumped in his dirty linen at the thought of it. But we had reckoned without Papa. He's hard-shelled Baptist, is Papa; no papists need apply. And he took and locked the door. Buncombe told him he was bigoted, and I thought he would have had a fit. 'Bigoted!' he says. 'Me bigoted? Have I lived to hear it from a jackanapes like you?' And he made for Buncombe, and I had to hold them apart; and there was Adams in the middle, gone loony again, and carrying on about copra like a born fool. It was good as the play, and I was about knocked out of time with laughing, when all of a sudden Adams sat up, clapped his hands to his chest, and went into the horrors. He died hard, did John Adams," says Case, with a kind of a sudden sternness.

"And what became of the priest?" I asked.

"The priest?" says Case. "Oh! he was hammering on the door outside, and crying on the natives to come and beat it in, and singing out it was a soul he wished to save, and that. He was in a rare taking, was the priest. But what would you have? Johnny had slipped his cable; no more Johnny in the market; and the administration racket clean played out. Next thing, word came to Randall that the priest was praying upon Johnny's grave. Papa was pretty full, and got a club, and lit out straight for the place, and there was Galoshes on his knees, and a lot of natives looking on. You wouldn't think Papa cared that much about anything, unless it was liquor; but he and the priest stuck to it two hours, slanging each other in native, and every time Galoshes tried to kneel down Papa went for him with the club. There never were such larks in Falesá. The end of it was that Captain Randall knocked over with some kind of a fit or stroke, and the priest got in his goods after all. But he was the angriest priest you ever heard of, and complained to the chiefs about the outrage, as he called it. That was no account, for our chiefs are Protestant here; and, anyway, he had been making trouble about the drum for morning school, and they were glad to give him a wipe. Now he swears old Randall gave Adams poison or something, and when the two meet they grin at each other like baboons."

He told this story as natural as could be, and like a man that enjoyed the fun; though now I come to think of it after so long, it seems rather a sickening yarn. However, Case never set up to be soft, only to be square and hearty, and a man all round; and, to tell the truth, he puzzled me entirely.

I went home and asked Uma if she were a *Popey,* which I had made out to be the native word for Catholic.

"E le ai!" says she. She always used the native when she meant "no" more than usually strong, and, indeed, there's more of it. "No good *Popey,*" she added.

Then I asked her about Adams and the priest, and she told me much the same yarn in her own way. So that I was left not much farther on, but inclined, upon the whole, to think the bottom of the matter was the row about the sacrament, and the poisoning only talk.

The next day was a Sunday, when there was no business to be looked for. Uma asked me in the morning if I was going to "pray"; I told her she bet not, and she stopped home herself, with no more words. I thought this seemed unlike a native, and a native woman, and a woman that had new clothes to show off; however, it suited me to the ground, and I made the less of it. The queer thing was that I came next door to going to church after all, a thing I'm little likely to forget. I had turned out for a stroll, and heard the hymn tune up. You know how it is. If you hear folk singing, it seems to draw you; and pretty soon I found myself alongside the church. It was a little, long, low place, coral-built, rounded off at both ends like a whaleboat, a big native roof on the top of it, windows without sashes and doorways without doors.

I stuck my head into one of the windows, and the sight was so new to me—for things went quite different in the islands I was acquainted with—that I stayed and looked on. The congregation sat on the floor on mats, the women on one side, the men on the other, all rigged out to kill—the women with dresses and trade hats, the men in white jackets and shirts. The hymn was over; the pastor, a big buck Kanaka, was in the pulpit, preaching for his life; and by the way he wagged his hand, and worked his voice, and made his points, and seemed to argue with the folk, I made out he was a gun at the business. Well, he looked up suddenly and caught my eye, and I give you my word he staggered in the pulpit; his eyes bulged out of his head, his hand rose and pointed at me like as if against his will, and the sermon stopped right there.

It isn't a fine thing to say for yourself, but I ran away; and, if the same kind of a shock was given me, I should run away again tomorrow. To see that palavering Kanaka struck all of a heap at the mere sight of me gave me a feeling as if the bottom had dropped out of the world. I went right home, and stayed there, and said nothing. You might think I would tell Uma, but that was against my system. You might have thought I would have gone over and consulted Case; but the truth was I was ashamed to speak of such a thing, I thought everyone would blurt out laughing in my face. So I held my tongue, and thought all the more; and the more I thought, the less I liked the business.

By Monday night I got it clearly in my head I must be tabooed. A new store to stand open two days in a village and not a man or woman come to see the trade, was past believing.

"Uma," said I, "I think I'm tabooed."

"I think so," said she.

I thought a while whether I should ask her more, but it's a bad idea to set natives up with any notion of consulting them, so I went to Case. It was dark, and he was sitting alone, as he did mostly, smoking on the stairs.

"Case," said I, "here's a queer thing. I'm tabooed."

"Oh, fudge!" says he; " 'tain't the practice in these islands."

"That may be, or it mayn't," said I. "It's the practice where

I was before. You can bet I know what it's like; and I tell it you for a fact, I'm tabooed."

"Well," said he, "what have you been doing?"

"That's what I want to find out," said I.

"Oh, you can't be," said he; "it ain't possible. However, I'll tell you what I'll do. Just to put your mind at rest, I'll go round and find out for sure. Just you waltz in and talk to Papa."

"Thank you," I said, "I'd rather stay right out here on the veranda. Your house is so close."

"I'll call Papa out here, then," says he.

"My dear fellow," I says, "I wish you wouldn't. The fact is, I don't take to Mr. Randall."

Case laughed, took a lantern from the store, and set out into the village. He was gone perhaps a quarter of an hour, and he looked mighty serious when he came back.

"Well," said he, clapping down the lantern on the veranda steps, "I would never have believed it. I don't know where the impudence of these Kanakas'll go next; they seem to have lost all idea of respect for whites. What we want is a man of war—a German, if we could—they know how to manage Kanakas."

"I *am* tabooed, then?" I cried.

"Something of the sort," said he. "It's the worst thing of the kind I've heard of yet. But I'll stand by you, Wiltshire, man to man. You come round here tomorrow about nine, and we'll have it out with the chiefs. They're afraid of me, or they used to be; but their heads are so big by now, I don't know what to think. Understand me, Wiltshire; I don't count this your quarrel," he went on, with a great deal of resolution, "I count it all of our quarrel, I count it the White Man's Quarrel, and I'll stand to it through thick and thin, and there's my hand on it."

"Have you found out what's the reason?" I asked.

"Not yet," said Case. "But we'll fire them down tomorrow."

Altogether I was pretty well pleased with his attitude, and almost more the next day, when we met to go before the chiefs, to see him so stern and resolved. The chiefs awaited us in one of their big oval houses, which was marked out to us from a long way off by the crowd about the eaves, a hundred strong if there was one—men, women, and children. Many of the men were on their way to work and wore green wreaths, and it put me in thoughts of the first of May at home. This crowd opened and buzzed about the pair of us as we went in, with a sudden angry animation. Five chiefs were there; four mighty, stately men, the fifth old and puckered. They sat on mats in their white kilts and jackets; they had fans in their hands, like fine ladies; and two of the younger ones wore Catholic medals, which gave me matter of reflection. Our place was set, and the mats laid for us over against these grandees, on the near side of the house; the midst was empty; the crowd, close at our backs, murmured and craned and jostled to look on, and the shadows of them tossed in front of us on the clean pebbles of the floor. I was just a hair put out by the excitement of the commons, but the quiet, civil appearance of the chiefs reassured me, all the more when their spokesman began and made a long speech in a low tone of voice, sometimes waving his hand toward Case, sometimes toward me, and sometimes knocking with his knuckles on the mat. One thing was clear: there was no sign of anger in the chiefs.

"What's he been saying?" I asked, when he had done.

"Oh, just that they're glad to see you, and they understand by me you wish to make some kind of complaint, and you're to fire away, and they'll do the square thing."

"It took a precious long time to say that," said I.

"Oh, the rest was sawder and *bonjour* and that," said Case. "You know what Kanakas are."

"Well, they don't get much *bonjour* out of me," said I. "You tell them who I am. I'm a white man, and a British subject, and no end of a big chief at home; and I've come here to do them good, and bring them civilization; and no sooner have I got my trade sorted out than they go and taboo me, and no one dare come near my place! Tell them I don't mean to fly in the face of anything legal; and if what they want's a present, I'll do what's fair. I don't blame any man looking out for himself, tell them, for that's human nature; but if they think they're going to come any of their native ideas over me, they'll find themselves mistaken. And tell them plain that I demand the reason of this treatment as a white man and a British subject."

That was my speech. I knew how to deal with Kanakas: give them plain sense and fair dealing, and—I'll do them that much justice—they knuckle under every time. They haven't any real government or any real law, that's what you've got to knock into their heads; and even if they had, it would be a good joke if it was to apply to a white man. It would be a strange thing if we came all this way and couldn't do what we pleased. The mere idea has always put my monkey up, and I rapped my speech out pretty big. Then Case translated it—or made believe to, rather—and the first chief replied, and then a second, and a third, all in the same style—easy and genteel, but solemn underneath. Once a question was put to Case, and he answered it, and all hands (both chiefs and commons) laughed out aloud, and looked at me. Last of all, the puckered old fellow and the big young chief that spoke first started in to put Case through a kind of catechism. Sometimes I made out that Case was trying to fence, and they stuck to him like hounds, and the sweat ran down his face, which was no very pleasant sight to me, and at some of his answers the crowd moaned and murmured, which was a worse hearing. It's a cruel shame I knew no native, for (as I now believe) they were asking Case about my marriage, and he must have had a tough job of it to clear his feet. But leave Case alone; he had the brains to run a parliament.

"Well, is that all?" I asked, when a pause came.

"Come along," says he, mopping his face; "I'll tell you outside."

"Do you mean they won't take the taboo off?" I cried.

"It's something queer," said he. "I'll tell you outside. Better come away."

"I won't take it at their hands," cried I. "I ain't that kind of a man. You don't find me turn my back on a parcel of Kanakas."

"You'd better," said Case.

He looked at me with a signal in his eye; and the five chiefs looked at me civilly enough, but kind of pointed; and the people looked at me and craned and jostled. I remembered the folks that watched my house, and how the pastor had jumped in his pulpit at the bare sight of me; and the whole business seemed so out of the way that I rose and followed Case. The crowd opened again to let us through, but wider than before, the children on the skirts running and singing out, and as we two white men walked away they all stood and watched us.

"And now," said I, "what is all this about?"

"The truth is I can't rightly make it out myself. They have a down on you," says Case.

"Taboo a man because they have a down on him!" I cried. "I never heard the like."

"It's worse than that, you see," said Case. "You ain't tabooed—I told you that couldn't be. The people won't go near you, Wiltshire, and there's where it is."

"They won't go near me? What do you mean by that? Why won't they go near me?" I cried.

Case hesitated. "Seems they're frightened," says he, in a low voice.

I stopped dead short. "Frightened?" I repeated. "Are you gone crazy, Case? What are they frightened of?"

"I wish I could make out," Case answered, shaking his head. "Appears like one of their tomfool superstitions. That's what I don't cotton to," he said. "It's like the business about Vigours."

"I'd like to know what you mean by that, and I'll trouble you to tell me," says I.

"Well, you know, Vigours lit out and left all standing," said he. "It was some superstition business—I never got the hang of it; but it began to look bad before the end."

"I've heard a different story about that," said I, "and I had better tell you so. I heard he ran away because of you."

"Oh! well, I suppose he was ashamed to tell the truth," says Case; "I guess he thought it silly. And it's a fact that I packed him off. 'What would you do, old man?' says he. 'Get,' says I, 'and not think twice about it.' I was the gladdest kind of man to see him clear away. It ain't my notion to turn my back on a mate when he's in a tight place, but there was that much trouble in the village that I couldn't see where it might likely end. I was a fool to be so much about with Vigours. They cast it up to me today. Didn't you hear Maea—that's the young chief, the big one—ripping out about 'Vika'? That was him they were after. They don't seem to forget it, somehow."

"This is all very well," said I, "but it don't tell me what's wrong; it don't tell me what they're afraid of—what their idea is."

"Well, I wish I knew," said Case. "I can't say fairer than that."

"You might have asked, I think," says I.

"And so I did," says he. "But you must have seen for yourself, unless you're blind, that the asking got the other way. I'll go as far as I dare for another white man; but when I find I'm in the scrape myself, I think first of my own bacon. The loss of me is I'm too good-natured. And I'll take the freedom of telling you you show a queer kind of gratitude to a man who's got into all this mess along of your affairs."

"There's a thing I'm thinking of," said I. "You were a fool to be so much about with Vigours. One comfort, you haven't been much about with me. I notice you've never been inside my house. Own up now; you had word of this before?"

"It's a fact I haven't been," said he. "It was an oversight, and I am sorry for it, Wiltshire. But about coming now, I'll be quite plain."

"You mean you won't?" I asked.

"Awfully sorry, old man, but that's the size of it," says Case.

"In short, you're afraid?" says I.

"In short, I'm afraid," says he.

"And I'm still to be tabooed for nothing?" I asked.

"I tell you you're not tabooed," said he. "The Kanakas won't go near you, that's all. And who's to make 'em? We traders have a lot of gall, I must say; we make these poor Kanakas take back their laws, and take up their taboos, and that, whenever it happens to suit us. But you don't mean to say you expect a law-obliging people to deal in your store whether they want to or not? You don't mean to tell me you've got the gall for that? And if you had, it would be a queer thing to propose to me. I would just like to point out to you, Wiltshire, that I'm a trader myself."

"I don't think I would talk of gall if I was you," said I. "Here's about what it comes to, as well as I can make out: None of the people are to trade with me, and they're all to trade with you. You're to have the copra, and I'm to go to the devil and shake myself. And I don't know any native, and you're the only man here worth mention that speaks English, and you have the gall to up and hint to me my life's in danger, and all you've got to tell me is you don't know why!"

"Well, it *is* all I have to tell you," said he. "I don't know—I wish I did."

"And so you turn your back and leave me to myself! Is that the position?" says I.

"If you like to put it nasty," says he. "I don't put it so. I say merely, 'I'm going to keep clear of you; or, if I don't I'll get in danger for myself.' "

"Well," says I, "you're a nice kind of a white man!"

"Oh, I understand; you're riled," said he. "I would be myself. I can make excuses."

"All right," I said, "go and make excuses somewhere else. Here's my way, there's yours!"

With that we parted, and I went straight home, in a hot temper, and found Uma trying on a lot of trade goods like a baby.

"Here," I said, "you quit that foolery! Here's a pretty mess to have made, as if I wasn't bothered enough anyway! And I thought I told you to get dinner!"

And then I believe I gave her a bit of the rough side of my tongue, as she deserved. She stood up at once, like a sentry to his officer; for I must say she was always well brought up, and had a great respect for whites.

"And now," says I, "you belong round here, you're bound to understand this. What am I tabooed for, anyway? Or, if I ain't tabooed, what makes the folks afraid of me?"

She stood and looked at me with eyes like saucers.

"You no savvy?" she gasps at last.

"No," said I. "How would you expect me to? We don't have any such craziness where I come from."

"Ese no tell you?" she asked again.

(*Ese* was the name the natives had for Case; it may mean foreign, or extraordinary; or it might mean a mummy apple; but most like it was only his own name misheard and put in a Kanaka spelling.)

"Not much," said I.

"D—n Ese!" she cried.

You might think it funny to hear this Kanaka girl come out with a big swear. No such thing. There was no swearing in her—no, nor anger; she was beyond anger, and meant the word simple and serious. She stood there straight as she said it. I cannot justly say that I ever saw a woman look like that before or after, and it struck me mum. Then she made a kind of an obeisance, but it was the proudest kind, and threw her hands out open.

"I 'shamed," she said. "I think you savvy. Ese he tell me you savvy, he tell me you no mind, tell me you love me too much. Taboo belong me," she said, touching herself on the bosom, as she had done upon our wedding night. "Now I go 'way, taboo he go 'way too. Then you get too much copra. You like more better, I think. *Tofá, alii,"* says she in the native—"Farewell, chief!"

"Hold on!" I cried. "Don't be in such a hurry."

She looked at me sidelong with a smile. "You see, you get copra," she said, the same as you might offer candies to a child.

"Uma," said I, "hear reason. I didn't know, and that's a fact; and Case seems to have played it pretty mean upon the pair of us. But I do know now, and I don't mind; I love you too much. You no go 'way, you no leave me, I too much sorry."

"You no love me," she cried, "you talk me bad words!" And she threw herself in a corner of the floor, and began to cry.

Well, I'm no scholar, but I wasn't born yesterday, and I thought the worst of that trouble was over. However, there she lay—her back turned, her face to the wall—and shook with sobbing like a little child, so that her feet jumped with it. It's strange how it hits a man when he's in love; for there's no use mincing things; Kanaka and all, I was in love with her, or just as good. I tried to take her hand, but she would none of that. "Uma," I said, "there's no sense in carrying on like this. I want you stop here, I want my little wifie, I tell you true."

"No tell me true," she sobbed.

"All right," says I, "I'll wait till you're through with this." And I sat right down beside her on the floor, and set to smooth her hair with my hand. At first she wriggled away when I touched her; then she seemed to notice me no more; then her sobs grew gradually less, and presently stopped; and the next thing I knew, she raised her face to mine.

"You tell me true? You like me stop?" she asked.

"Uma," I said, "I would rather have you than all the copra in the South Seas," which was a very big expression, and the strangest thing was that I meant it.

She threw her arms about me, sprang close up, and pressed her face to mine, in the island way of kissing, so that I was all wetted with her tears, and my heart went out to her wholly. I never had anything so near me as this little brown bit of a girl. Many things went together, and all helped to turn my head. She was pretty enough to eat; it seemed she was my only friend in that queer place; I was ashamed that I had spoken rough to her: and she was a woman, and my wife, and a kind of a baby besides that I was sorry for; and the salt of her tears was in my mouth. And I forgot Case and the natives; and I forgot that I knew nothing of the story, or only remembered it to banish the remembrance; and I forgot that I was to get no copra, and so could make no livelihood; and I forgot my employers, and the strange kind of service I was doing them, when I preferred my fancy to their business; and I forgot even that Uma was no true wife of mine, but just a maid beguiled, and that in a pretty shabby style. But that is to look too far on. I will come to that part of it next.

It was late before we thought of getting dinner. The stove was out, and gone stone cold; but we fired up after a while, and cooked each a dish, helping and hindering each other, and making a play of it like children. I was so greedy of her nearness that I sat down to dinner with my lass upon my knee, made sure of her with one hand, and ate with the other. Aye, and more than that. She was the worst cook I suppose God made; the things she set her hand to, it would have sickened an honest horse to eat of; yet I made my meal that day on Uma's cookery, and can never call to mind to have been better pleased.

I didn't pretend to myself, and I didn't pretend to her. I saw I was clean gone; and if she was to make a fool of me, she must. And I suppose it was this that set her talking, for now she made sure that we were friends. A lot she told me, sitting in my lap and eating my dish, as I ate hers, from foolery—a lot about herself and her mother and Case, all which would be very tedious, and fill sheets if I set it down in Beach de Mar, but which I must give a hint of in plain English, and one thing about myself that had a very big effect on my concerns, as you are soon to hear.

It seems she was born in one of the Line Islands; had been only two or three years in these parts, where she had come with a white man, who was married to her mother and then died; and only the one year in Falesá. Before that they had been a good deal on the move, trekking about after the white man, who was one of those rolling stones that keep going round after a soft job. They talk about looking for gold at the end of a rainbow; but if a man wants an employment that'll last him till he dies, let him start out on the soft-job hunt. There's meat and drink in it too, and beer and skittles, for you never hear of them starving, and rarely see them sober; and as for steady sport, cockfighting isn't in the same county with it. Anyway, this beachcomber carried the woman and her daughter all over the shop, but mostly to out-of-the-way islands, where there were no police, and he thought, perhaps, the soft job hung out. I've my own view of this old party; but I was just as glad he had kept Uma clear of Apia and Papeete and these flash towns. At last he struck Falealii on this island, got some trade—the Lord knows how!—muddled it all away in the usual style, and died worth next to nothing, bar a bit of land at Falesá that he had got for a bad debt, which was what put it in the minds of the mother and daughter to come there and live. It seems Case encouraged them all he could, and helped to get their house built. He was very kind those days, and gave Uma trade, and there is no doubt he had his eye on her from the beginning. However, they had scarce settled, when up turned a young man, a native, and wanted to marry her. He was a small chief, and had some fine mats and old songs in his family, and was "very pretty," Uma said; and, altogether, it was an extraordinary match for a penniless girl and an out-islander.

At the first word of this I got downright sick with jealousy.

"And you mean to say you would have married him?" I cried.

"Ioe, yes," said she. "I like too much!"

"Well!" I said. "And suppose I had come round after?"

"I like you more better now," said she. "But suppose I marry Ioane, I one good wife. I no common Kanaka. Good girl!" says she.

Well, I had to be pleased with that; but I promise you I didn't care about the business one little bit. And I liked the end of that yarn no better than the beginning. For it seems this proposal of marriage was the start of all the trouble. It seems, before that, Uma and her mother had been looked down upon, of course, for kinless folk and out-islanders, but nothing to hurt; and, even when Ioane came forward, there was less trouble at first than might have been looked for. And then, all of a sudden, about six months before my coming, Ioane backed out and left that part of the island, and from that day to this Uma and her mother had found themselves alone. None called at their house—none spoke to them on the roads. If they went to church, the other women drew their mats away and left them in a clear place by themselves. It was a regular excommunication, like what you read of in the Middle Ages; and the cause or sense of it beyond guessing.It was some *talo pepelo,* Uma said, some calumny; and all she knew of it was that the girls who had been jealous of her luck with Ioane used to twit her with his desertion, and cry out, when they met her alone in the woods, that she would never be married. "They tell me no man he marry me. He too much 'fraid," she said.

The only soul that came about them after this desertion was Master Case. Even he was chary of showing himself, and turned up mostly by night; and pretty soon he began to table his cards and make up to Uma. I was still sore about Ioane, and when Case turned up in the same line of business I cut up downright rough.

"Well," I said, sneering, "and I suppose you thought Case 'very pretty' and 'liked too much'?"

"Now you talk silly," said she. "White man, he come here, I marry him all-e-same Kanaka; very well then, he marry me all-e-same white woman. Suppose he no marry, he go 'way, woman he stop. All-e-same thief, empty hand, Tonga-heart—no can love! Now you come marry me. You big heart—you no 'shamed island-girl. That thing I love you far too much. I proud."

I don't know that ever I felt sicker all the days of my life. I laid down my fork, and I put away the "island-girl"; I didn't seem somehow to have any use for either, and I went and walked up and down in the house, and Uma followed me with her eyes, for she was troubled, and small wonder! But troubled was no word for it with me. I so wanted, and so feared, to make a clean breast of the sweep that I had been.

And just then there came a sound of singing out of the sea; it sprang up suddenly clear and near, as the boat turned the headland, and Uma, running to the window, cried out it was "Misi" come upon his rounds.

I thought it was a strange thing I should be glad to have a missionary; but, if it was strange, it was still true.

"Uma," said I, "you stop here in this room, and don't budge a foot out of it till I come back."

CHAPTER III

THE MISSIONARY

As I came out on the veranda, the mission boat was shooting for the mouth of the river. She was a long whale-boat, painted white; a bit of an awning astern; a native pastor crouched on the wedge of poop, steering; some four-and-twenty paddles flashing and dipping, true to the boat-song; and the missionary under the awning, in his white clothes, reading in a book; and set him up! It was pretty to see and hear; there's no smarter sight in the islands than a missionary boat with a good crew and a good pipe to them; and I considered it for half a minute with a bit of envy perhaps, and then strolled down toward the river.

From the opposite side there was another man aiming for the same place, but he ran and got there first. It was Case; doubtless his idea was to keep me apart from the missionary, who might serve me as interpreter; but my mind was upon other things. I was thinking how he had jockeyed us about the marriage, and tried his hand on Uma before; and at the sight of him rage flew into my nostrils.

"Get out of that, you low, swindling thief!" I cried.

"What's that you say?" says he.

I gave him the word again, and rammed it down with a good oath. "And if ever I catch you within six fathoms of my house," I cried, "I'll clap a bullet in your measly carcass."

"You must do as you like about your house," said he, "where I told you I have no thought of going; but this is a public place."

"It's a place where I have private business," said I. "I have no idea of a hound like you eavesdropping, and I give you notice to clear out."

"I don't take it, though," says Case.

"I'll show you then," said I.

"We'll have to see about that," said he.

He was quick with his hands, but he had neither the height nor the weight, being a flimsy creature alongside a man like me, and, besides, I was blazing to that height of wrath that I could have bit into a chisel. I gave him first the one and then the other, so that I could hear his head rattle and crack, and he went down straight.

"Have you had enough?" cries I. But he only looked up white and blank, and the blood spread upon his face like wine upon a napkin. "Have you had enough?" I cried again. "Speak up, and don't lie malingering there, or I'll take my feet to you."

He sat up at that, and held his head—by the look of him

you could see it was spinning—and the blood poured on his pajamas.

"I've had enough for this time," says he, and he got up staggering, and went off by the way that he had come.

The boat was close in; I saw the missionary had laid his book to one side, and I smiled to myself. "He'll know I'm a man, anyway," thinks I.

This was the first time, in all my years in the Pacific, I had ever exchanged two words with any missionary, let alone asked one for a favor. I didn't like the lot, no trader does; they look down upon us, and make no concealment; and besides, they're partly Kanakaized, and suck up with natives instead of with other white men like themselves. I had on a rig of clean, striped pajamas—for, of course, I had dressed decent to go before the chiefs; but when I saw the missionary step out of his boat in the regular uniform, white duck clothes, pith helmet, white shirt and tie, and yellow boots to his feet, I could have bunged stones at him. As he came nearer, queering me pretty curious (because of the fight, I suppose), I saw he looked mortal sick, for the truth was he had a fever on, and had just had a chill in the boat.

"Mr. Tarleton, I believe?" says I, for I had got his name.

"And you, I suppose, are the new trader?" says he.

"I want to tell you first that I don't hold with missions," I went on, "and that I think you and the likes of you do a sight of harm, filling up the natives with old wives' tales and bumptiousness."

"You are perfectly entitled to your opinions," says he, looking a bit ugly, "but I have no call to hear them."

"It so happens that you've got to hear them," I said. "I'm no missionary, nor missionary-lover; I'm no Kanaka, nor favorer of Kanakas—I'm just a trader; I'm just a common, low, God-damned white man and British subject, the sort you would like to wipe your boots on. I hope that's plain!"

"Yes, my man," said he. "It's more plain than creditable. When you are sober, you'll be sorry for this."

He tried to pass on, but I stopped him with my hand. The Kanakas were beginning to growl. Guess they didn't like my tone, for I spoke to that man as free as I would to you.

"Now, you can't say I've deceived you," said I, "and I can go on. I want a service—I want two services, in fact; and, if you care to give me them, I'll perhaps take more stock in what you call your Christianity."

He was silent for a moment. Then he smiled. "You are rather a strange sort of man," says he.

"I'm the sort of man God made me," says I. "I don't set up to be a gentleman," I said.

"I am not quite so sure," said he. "And what can I do for you, Mr. ———?"

"Wiltshire," I says, "though I'm mostly called Welsher; but Wiltshire is the way it's spelt, if the people on the beach could only get their tongues about it. And what do I want? Well, I'll tell you the first thing. I'm what you call a sinner—what I call a sweep—and I want you to help me make it up to a person I've deceived."

He turned and spoke to his crew in the native. "And now I am at your service," said he, "but only for the time my crew are dining. I must be much farther down the coast before night. I was delayed at Papa-Malulu till this morning, and I have an engagement in Falealii tomorrow night."

I led the way to my house in silence, and rather pleased with myself for the way I had managed the talk, for I like a man to keep his self-respect.

"I was sorry to see you fighting," says he.

"Oh, that's part of the yarn I want to tell you," I said. "That's service number two. After you've heard it you'll let me know whether you're sorry or not."

We walked right in through the store, and I was surprised to find Uma had cleared away the dinner things. This was so unlike her ways that I saw she had done it out of gratitude, and liked her the better. She and Mr. Tarleton called each other by name, and he was very civil to her seemingly. But I thought little of that; they can always find civility for a Kanaka, it's us white men they lord it over. Besides, I didn't want much Tarleton just then. I was going to do my pitch.

"Uma," said I, "give us your marriage certificate." She looked put out. "Come," said I, "you can trust me. Hand it up."

She had it about her person, as usual; I believe she thought it was a pass to heaven, and if she died without having it handy she would go to hell. I couldn't see where she put it the first time, I couldn't see now where she took it from; it seemed to jump into her hand like that Blavatsky business in the papers. But it's the same way with all island women, and I guess they're taught it when young.

"Now," said I, with the certificate in my hand, "I was married to this girl by Black Jack, the Negro. The certificate was wrote by Case, and it's a dandy piece of literature, I promise you. Since then I've found that there's a kind of cry in the place against this wife of mine, and so long as I keep her I cannot trade. Now, what would any man do in my place, if he was a man?" I said. "The first thing he would do is this, I guess." And I took and tore up the certificate and bunged the pieces on the floor.

"Aué!" (Alas!) cried Uma, and began to clap her hands; but I caught one of them in mine.

"And the second thing that he would do," said I, "if he was what I would call a man and you would call a man, Mr. Tarleton, is to bring the girl right before you or any other missionary, and to up and say: 'I was wrong-married to this wife of mine, but I think a heap of her, and now I want to be married to her right.' Fire away, Mr. Tarleton. And I guess you'd better do it in native; it'll please the old lady," I said, giving her the proper name of a man's wife upon the spot.

So we had in two of the crew for to witness, and were spliced in our house; and the parson prayed a good bit, I must say—but not so long as some—and shook hands with the pair of us.

"Mr. Wiltshire," he says, when he had made out the lines and packed off the witnesses, "I have to thank you for a very lively pleasure. I have rarely performed the marriage ceremony with more grateful emotions."

That was what you would call talking. He was going on, besides, with more of it, and I was ready for as much taffy as he had in stock, for I felt good. But Uma had been taken up something half through the marriage, and cut straight in.

"How your hand he get hurt?" she asked.

"You ask Case's head, old lady," says I.

She jumped with joy, and sang out.

"You haven't made much of a Christian of this one," says I to Mr. Tarleton.

"We didn't think her one of our worst," says he, "when she was at Falealii; and if Uma bears malice I shall be tempted to fancy she has good cause."

"Well, there we are at service number two," said I. "I want to tell you our yarn, and see if you can let a little daylight in."

"Is it long?" he asked.

"Yes," I cried; "it's a goodish bit of a yarn!"

"Well, I'll give you all the time I can spare," says he, looking at his watch. "But I must tell you fairly, I haven't eaten since five this morning, and unless you can let me have something, I am not likely to eat again before seven or eight tonight."

"By God, we'll give you dinner!" I cried.

I was a little caught up at my swearing, just when all was going straight; and so was the missionary, I suppose, but he made believe to look out of the window, and thanked us.

So we ran him up a bit of a meal. I was bound to let the old lady have a hand in it, to show off, so I deputized her to brew the tea. I don't think I ever met such tea as she turned out. But that was not the worst, for she got round with the salt box, which she considered an extra European touch, and turned my stew into sea water. Altogether, Mr. Tarleton had a devil of a dinner of it; but he had plenty of entertainment by the way, for all the while that we were cooking, and afterward, when he was making believe to eat, I kept posting him up on Master Case and the beach of Falesá, and he putting questions that showed he was following close.

"Well," said he at last, "I am afraid you have a dangerous enemy. This man Case is very clever and seems really wicked. I must tell you I have had my eye on him for nearly a year, and have rather had the worst of our encounters. About the time when the last representative of your firm ran so suddenly away, I had a letter from Namu, the native pastor, begging me to come to Falesá at my earliest convenience, as his flock were all 'adopting Catholic practices.' I had great confidence in Namu; I fear it only shows how easily we are deceived. No one could hear him preach and not be persuaded he was a man of extraordinary parts. All our islanders easily acquire a kind of eloquence, and can roll out and illustrate, with a great deal of vigor and fancy, second-hand sermons; but Namu's sermons are his own, and I cannot deny that I have found them means of grace. Moreover, he has a keen curiosity in secular things, does not fear work, is clever at carpentering, and has made himself so much respected among the neighboring pastors that we call him, in a jest which is half-serious, the Bishop of the East. In short, I was proud of the man; all the more puzzled by his letter, and took an occasion to come this way. The morning before my arrival, Vigours had been sent on board the 'Lion,' and Namu was perfectly at his ease, apparently ashamed of his letter, and quite unwilling to explain it. This, of course, I could not allow, and he ended by confessing that he had been much concerned to find his people using the sign of the cross, but since he had learned the explanation his mind was satisfied. For Vigours had the Evil Eye, a common thing in a country of Europe called Italy, where men were often struck dead by that kind of devil, and it appeared the sign of the cross was a charm against its power.

" 'And I explain it, Misi,' said Namu, 'in this way: the country in Europe is a *Popey* country, and the devil of the Evil Eye may be a Catholic devil, or, at least, used to Catholic ways. So then I reasoned thus: if this sign of the cross were used in a *Popey* manner it would be sinful, but when it is used only to protect men from a devil, which is a thing harmless in itself, the sign too must be harmless. For the sign is neither good nor bad. But if the bottle be full of gin, the gin is bad; and if the sign made in idolatry be bad, so is the idolatry.' And, very like a native pastor, he had a text apposite about the casting out of devils.

" 'And who has been telling you about the Evil Eye?' I asked.

"He admitted it was Case. Now, I am afraid you will think me very narrow, Mr. Wiltshire, but I must tell you I was displeased, and cannot think a trader at all a good man to advise or have an influence upon my pastors. And, besides, there had been some flying talk in the country of old Adams, and his being poisoned, to which I had paid no great heed; but it came back to me at the moment.

" 'And is this Case a man of a sanctified life?' I asked.

"He admitted he was not; for, though he did not drink, he was profligate with women, and had no religion.

" 'Then,' said I, 'I think the less you have to do with him the better.'

"But it is not easy to have the last word with a man like Namu. He was ready in a moment with an illustration. 'Misi,' said he, 'you have told me there were wise men, not pastors, not even holy, who knew many things useful to be taught—about trees, for instance, and beasts, and to print books, and about the stones that are burned to make knives of. Such men teach you in your college, and you learn from them, but take care not to learn to be unholy. Misi, Case is my college.'

"I knew not what to say. Mr. Vigours had evidently been driven out of Falesá by the machinations of Case and with something not very unlike the collusion of my pastor. I called to mind it was Namu who had reassured me about Adams and traced the rumor to the ill will of the priest. And I saw I must inform myself more thoroughly from an impartial source. There is an old rascal of a chief here, Faiaso, whom I dare say you saw today at the council; he has been all his life turbulent and sly, a great fomenter of rebellions, and a thorn in the side of the mission and the island. For all that he is very shrewd, and, except in politics or about his own misdemeanors, a teller of the truth. I went to his house, told him what I had heard, and besought him to be frank. I do not think I had ever a more painful interview. Perhaps you will understand me, Mr. Wiltshire, if I tell you that I am perfectly serious in these old wives' tales with which you reproached me, and as anxious to do well for these islands as you can be to please and to protect your pretty wife. And you are to remember that I thought Namu a paragon, and was proud of the man as one of the first ripe fruits of the mission. And now I was informed that he had fallen in a sort of dependence upon Case. The beginning of it was not corrupt; it began, doubtless, in fear and respect, produced by trickery and pretense; but I was shocked to find that another element had been lately added, that Namu helped himself in the store, and was believed to be deep in Case's debt. Whatever the trader said, that Namu believed with trembling. He was not alone in this; many in the village lived in a similar subjection; but Namu's case was the most influential, it was through Namu that Case had wrought most evil; and with a certain following among the chiefs, and the pastor in his pocket, the man was as good as master of the village. You know something of Vigours and Adams, but perhaps you have never heard of old Underhill, Adams' predecessor. He was a quiet, mild old fellow, I remember, and we were told he had died suddenly: white men die very suddenly in Falesá. The truth, as I now heard it, made my blood run cold. It seems he was struck with a general palsy, all of him dead but one eye, which he continually winked. Word was started that the helpless old man was now a devil, and this vile fellow Case worked upon the natives' fears, which he professed to share, and pretended he durst not go into the house alone. At last a grave was dug, and the living body buried at the far end of the village. Namu, my pastor, whom I had helped to educate, offered up a prayer at the hateful scene.

"I felt myself in a very difficult position. Perhaps it was my duty to have denounced Namu and had him deposed. Perhaps I think so now, but at the time it seemed less clear. He had a great influence, it might prove greater than mine. The natives are prone to superstition; perhaps by stirring them up I might but ingrain and spread these dangerous fancies. And Namu besides, apart from this novel and accursed influence, was a good pastor, an able man, and spiritually minded. Where should I look for a better? How was I to find as good? At that moment, with Namu's failure fresh in my view, the work of my life appeared a mockery; hope was dead in me. I would rather repair such tools as I had than go abroad in quest of others that must certainly prove worse; and a scandal is, at the best, a thing to be avoided when humanly possible. Right or wrong, then, I determined on a quiet course. All that night I denounced and reasoned with the erring pastor, twitted him with his ignorance and want of faith, twitted him with his wretched attitude, making clean the outside of the cup and platter, callously helping at a murder, childishly flying in excitement about a few childish, unnecessary, and inconvenient gestures; and long before day I had him on his knees and bathed in the tears of what seemed a genuine repentance. On Sunday I took the pulpit in the morning, and preached from First Kings, nineteenth, on the fire, the earthquake, and the voice, distinguishing the true spiritual power, and referring with such plainness as I dared to recent events in Falesá. The effect produced was great, and it was much increased when Namu rose in his turn and confessed that he had been wanting in faith and conduct, and was convinced of sin. So far, then, all was well; but there was one unfortunate circumstance. It was nearing the time of our 'May' in the island, when the native contributions to the missions are received; it fell in my duty to make a notification on the subject, and this gave my enemy his chance, by which he was not slow to profit.

"News of the whole proceedings must have been carried to Case as soon as church was over, and the same afternoon he made an occasion to meet me in the midst of the village. He came up with so much intentness and animosity that I felt it would be damaging to avoid him.

" 'So,' says he, in native, 'here is the holy man. He has been preaching against me, but that was not in his heart. He has been preaching upon the love of God; but that was not in his heart, it was between his teeth. Will you know what was in his heart?' cries he. 'I will show it to you!' And, making a snatch at my hand, he made believe to pluck out a dollar, and held it in the air.

"There went that rumor through the crowd with which Polynesians receive a prodigy. As for myself, I stood amazed. The thing was a common conjuring trick that I have seen performed at home a score of times; but how was I to convince the villagers of that? I wished I had learned legerdemain instead of Hebrew, that I might have paid the fellow out with his own coin. But there I was; I could not stand there silent, and the best I could find to say was weak.

" 'I will trouble you not to lay hands on me again,' said I.

" 'I have no such thought,' said he, 'nor will I deprive you of your dollar. Here it is,' he said, and flung it at my feet. I am told it lay where it fell three days."

"I must say it was well played," said I.

"Oh! He is clever," said Mr. Tarleton, "and you can now see for yourself how dangerous. He was a party to the horrid death of the paralytic; he is accused of poisoning Adams; he drove Vigours out of the place by lies that might have led to murder; and there is no question but he has now made up his mind to rid himself of you. How he means to try we have no guess; only be sure, it's something new. There is no end to his readiness and invention."

"He gives himself a sight of trouble," says I. "And after all, what for?"

"Why, how many tons of copra may they make in this district?" asked the missionary.

"I dare say as much as sixty tons," says I.

"And what is the profit to the local trader?" he asked.

"You may call it three pounds," said I.

"Then you can reckon for yourself how much he does it for," said Mr. Tarleton. "But the more important thing is to defeat him. It is clear he spread some report against Uma, in order to isolate and have his wicked will of her. Failing of that, and seeing a new rival come upon the scene, he used her in a different way. Now, the first point to find out is about Namu. Uma, when people began to leave you and your mother alone, what did Namu do?"

"Stop away all-e-same," says Uma.

"I fear the dog has returned to his vomit," said Mr. Tarleton. "And now what am I to do for you? I will speak to Namu, I will warn him he is observed; it will be strange if he allows anything to go on amiss when he is put upon his guard. At the same time, this precaution may fail, and then you must turn elsewhere. You have two people at hand to whom you might apply. There is, first of all, the priest, who might protect you by the Catholic interest; they are a wretchedly small body, but they count two chiefs. And then there is old Faiaso. Ah! If it had been some years ago you would have needed no one else; but his influence is much reduced, it has gone into Maea's hands, and Maea, I fear, is one of Case's jackals. In fine, if the worst comes to the worst, you must send up or come yourself to Falealii, and, though I am not due at this end of the island for a month, I will just see what can be done."

So Mr. Tarleton said farewell; and half an hour later the crew were singing and the paddles flashing in the missionary boat.

CHAPTER IV

DEVIL-WORK

Near a month went by without much doing. The same night of our marriage Galoshes called round, and made himself mighty civil, and got into a habit of dropping in about dark and smoking his pipe with the family. He could talk to Uma, of course, and started to teach me native and French at the same time. He was a kind old buffer, though the dirtiest you would wish to see, and he muddled me up with foreign languages worse than the Tower of Babel.

That was one employment we had, and it made me feel less lonesome; but there was no profit in the thing, for though the priest came and sat and yarned, none of his folks could be enticed into my store, and if it hadn't been for the other occupation I struck out, there wouldn't have been a pound of copra in the house. This was the idea: Faavao (Uma's mother) had a score of bearing trees. Of course we could get no labor, being all as good as tabooed, and the two women and I turned to and made copra with our own hands. It was copra to make your mouth water when it was done—I never understood how much the natives cheated me till I had made that four hundred pounds of my own hand—and it weighed so light I felt inclined to take and water it myself.

When we were at the job a good many Kanakas used to put in the best of the day looking on, and once that nigger turned up. He stood back with the natives and laughed and did the big don and the funny dog, till I began to get riled.

"Here, you nigger!" says I.

"I don't address myself to you, sah," says the nigger. "Only speak to gen'le'um."

"I know," says I, "but it happens I was addressing myself to you, Mr. Black Jack. And all I want to know is just this: did you see Case's figurehead about a week ago?"

"No, sah," says he.

"That's all right, then," says I, "for I'll show you the own brother to it, only black, in the inside of about two minutes."

And I began to walk toward him, quite slow, and my hands down; only there was trouble in my eye, if anybody took the pains to look.

"You're a low, obstropulous fellow, sah," says he.

"You bet!" says I.

By that time he thought I was about as near as convenient, and lit out so it would have done your heart good to see him travel. And that was all I saw of that precious gang until what I am about to tell you.

It was one of my chief employments these days to go pot-hunting in the woods, which I found (as Case had told me) very rich in game. I have spoken of the cape that shut up the village and my station from the east. A path went about the end of it, and led into the next bay. A strong wind blew here daily, and as the line of the barrier reef stopped at the end of the cape, a heavy surf ran on the shores of the bay. A little cliffy hill cut the valley in two parts, and stood close on the beach; and at high water the sea broke right on the face of it, so that all passage was stopped. Woody mountains hemmed the place all round; the barrier to the east was particularly steep and leafy, the lower parts of it, along the sea, falling in sheer black cliffs streaked with cinnabar; the upper part lumpy with the tops of the great trees. Some of the trees were bright green, and some red, and the sand of the beach as black as your shoes. Many birds hovered round the bay, some of them snow-white; and the flying fox (or vampire) flew there in broad daylight, gnashing its teeth.

For a long while I came as far as this shooting, and went

no farther. There was no sign of any path beyond, and the coco palms in the front of the foot of the valley were the last this way. For the whole "eye" of the island, as natives call the windward end, lay desert. From Falesá round about to Papa-Malulu, there was neither house, nor man, nor planted fruit tree; and the reef being mostly absent, and the shores bluff, the sea beat direct among crags, and there was scarce a landing place.

I should tell you that after I began to go in the woods, although no one appeared to come near my store, I found people willing enough to pass the time of day with me where nobody could see them; and as I had begun to pick up native, and most of them had a word or two of English, I began to hold little odds and ends of conversation, not to much purpose, to be sure, but they took off the worst of the feeling, for it's a miserable thing to be made a leper of.

It chanced one day, toward the end of the month, that I was sitting in this bay in the edge of the bush, looking east, with a Kanaka. I had given him a fill of tobacco, and we were making out to talk as best we could; indeed, he had more English than most.

I asked him if there was no road going eastward.

"One time one road," said he. "Now he dead."

"Nobody he go there?" I asked.

"No good," said he. "Too much devil he stop there."

"Oho!" says I, "got-um plenty devil, that bush?"

"Man devil, woman devil; too much devil," said my friend. "Stop there all-e-time. Man he go there, no come back."

I thought if this fellow was so well posted on devils and spoke of them so free, which is not common, I had better fish for a little information about myself and Uma.

"You think me one devil?" I asked.

"No think devil," said he, soothingly. "Think all-e-same fool."

"Uma, she devil?" I asked again.

"No, no; no devil. Devil stop bush," said the young man.

I was looking in front of me across the bay, and I saw the hanging front of the woods pushed suddenly open, and Case, with a gun in his hand, step forth into the sunshine on the black beach. He was got up in light pajamas, near white, his gun sparkled, he looked mighty conspicuous; and the land crabs scuttled from all around him to their holes.

"Hullo, my friend!" says I, "you no talk all-e-same true. Ese he go, he come back."

"Ese no all-e-same; Ese *Tiapolo,*" says my friend; and, with a "Good-by," slunk off among the trees.

I watched Case all around the beach, where the tide was low; and let him pass me on the homeward way to Falesá. He was in deep thought, and the birds seemed to know it, trotting quite near him on the sand, or wheeling and calling in his ears. When he passed me I could see by the working of his lips that he was talking to himself, and what pleased me mightily, he had still my trade-mark on his brow. I tell you the plain truth: I had a mind to give him a gunful in his ugly mug, but I thought better of it.

All this time, and all the time I was following home, I kept repeating that native word, which I remembered by "Polly, put the kettle on and make us all some tea," tea-a-pollo.

"Uma," says I, when I got back, "what does *Tiapolo* mean?"

"Devil," says she.

"I thought *aitu* was the word for that," I said.

"Aitu 'nother kind of devil," said she; "stop bush, eat Kanaka. Tiapolo big chief devil, stop home; all-e-same Christian devil."

"Well, then," said I, "I'm no farther forward. How can Case be Tiapolo?"

"No all-e-same," said she. "Ese belong Tiapolo. Tiapolo too much like; Ese all-e-same his son. Suppose Ese he wish something, Tiapolo he make him."

"That's mighty convenient for Ese," says I. "And what kind of things does he make for him?"

Well, out came a rigmarole of all sorts of stories, many of which (like the dollar he took from Mr. Tarleton's head) were plain enough to me, but others I could make nothing of; and the thing that most surprised the Kanakas was what surprised me least—namely, that he would go in the desert among all the *aitus.* Some of the boldest, however, had accompanied him, and had heard him speak with the dead and give them orders, and, safe in his protection, had returned unscathed. Some said he had a church there, where he worshiped Tiapolo, and Tiapolo appeared to him; others swore that there was no sorcery at all, that he performed his miracles by the power of prayer, and the church was no church, but a prison, in which he had confined a dangerous *aitu.* Namu had been in the bush with him once, and returned glorifying God for these wonders. Altogether, I began to have a glimmer of the man's position, and the means by which he had acquired it, and, though I saw he was a tough nut to crack, I was noways cast down.

"Very well," said I, "I'll have a look at Master Case's place of worship myself, and we'll see about the glorifying."

At this Uma fell in a terrible taking; if I went in the high bush I should never return; none could go there but by the protection of Tiapolo.

"I'll chance it on God's," said I. "I'm a good sort of a fellow, Uma, as fellows go, and I guess God'll con me through."

She was silent for a while. "I think," said she, mighty solemn—and then, presently—"Victoreea, he big chief?"

"You bet!" said I.

"He like you too much?" she asked again. I told her, with a grin, I believed the old lady was rather partial to me.

"All right," said she. "Victoreea he big chief, like you too much. No can help you here in Falesá; no can do—too far off. Maea he be small chief—stop here. Suppose he like you—make you all right. All-e-same God and Tiapolo. God he big chief—got too much work. Tiapolo he small chief—he like too much make-see, work very hard."

"I'll have to hand you over to Mr. Tarleton," said I. "Your theology's out of its bearings, Uma."

However, we stuck to this business all the evening, and, with the stories she told me of the desert and its dangers, she came near frightening herself into a fit. I don't remember half a quarter of them, of course, for I paid little heed; but two come back to me kind of clear.

About six miles up the coast there is a sheltered cove they

call "Fanga-anaana"—the haven full of caves. I've seen it from the sea myself, as near as I could get my boys to venture in; and it's a little strip of yellow sand, black cliffs overhang it, full of the black mouths of caves; great trees overhang the cliffs, and dangle-down lianas; and in one place, about the middle, a big brook pours over in a cascade. Well, there was a boat going by here, with six young men of Falesá, "all very pretty," Uma said, which was the loss of them. It blew strong, there was a heavy head sea, and by the time they opened Fanga-anaana, and saw the white cascade and the shady beach, they were all tired and thirsty, and their water had run out. One proposed to land and get a drink, and, being reckless fellows, they were all of the same mind except the youngest. Lotu was his name; he was a very good young gentleman, and very wise; and he held out that they were crazy, telling them the place was given over to spirits and devils and the dead, and there were no living folk nearer than six miles the one way, and maybe twelve the other. But they laughed at his words, and, being five to one, pulled in, beached the boat, and landed. It was a wonderful pleasant place, Lotu said, and the water excellent, They walked round the beach, but could see nowhere any way to mount the cliffs, which made them easier in their mind; and at last they sat down to make a meal on the food they had brought with them. They were scarce set, when there came out of the mouth of one of the black caves six of the most beautiful ladies ever seen; they had flowers in their hair, and the most beautiful breasts, and necklaces of scarlet seeds; and began to jest with these young gentlemen, and the young gentlemen to jest back with them, all but Lotu. As for Lotu, he saw there could be no living woman in such a place, and ran, and flung himself in the bottom of the boat, and covered his face, and prayed. All the time the business lasted Lotu made one clean break of prayer, and that was all he knew of it, until his friends came back, and made him sit up, and they put to sea again out of the bay, which was now quite deserted, and no word of the six ladies. But, what frightened Lotu most, not one of the five remembered anything of what had passed, but they were all like drunken men, and sang and laughed in the boat, and skylarked. The wind freshened and came squally, and the sea rose extraordinary high; it was such weather as any man in the islands would have turned his back to and fled home to Falesá; but these five were like crazy folk, and cracked on all sail and drove their boat into the seas. Lotu went to the bailing; none of the others thought to help him, but sang and skylarked and carried on, and spoke singular things beyond a man's comprehension, and laughed out loud when they said them. So the rest of the day Lotu bailed for his life in the bottom of the boat, and was all drenched with sweat and cold sea water; and none heeded him. Against all expectation, they came safe in a dreadful tempest to Papa-Malulu, where the palms were singing out, and the coconuts flying like cannon balls about the village green; and the same night the five young gentlemen sickened, and spoke never a reasonable word until they died.

"And do you mean to tell me you can swallow a yarn like that?" I asked.

She told me the thing was well known, and with handsome young men alone it was even common; but this was the only case where five had been slain the same day and in a company by the love of the women-devils; and it had made a great stir in the island, and she would be crazy if she doubted.

"Well, anyway," says I, "you needn't be frightened about me. I've no use for the women-devils. You're all the women I want, and all the devil too, old lady."

To this she answered there were other sorts, and she had seen one with her own eyes. She had gone one day alone to the next bay, and, perhaps, got too near the margin of the bad place. The boughs of the high bush overshadowed her from the cant of the hill, but she herself was outside on a flat place, very stony and growing full of young mummy-apples four and five feet high. It was a dark day in the rainy season, and now there came squalls that tore off the leaves and sent them flying, and now it was all still as in a house. It was in one of these still times that a whole gang of birds and flying foxes came pegging out of the bush like creatures frightened. Presently after she heard a rustle nearer hand, and saw, coming out of the margin of the trees, among the mummy-apples, the appearance of a lean gray old boar. It seemed to think as it came, like a person; and all of a sudden, as she looked at it coming, she was aware it was no boar, but a thing that was a man with a man's thoughts. At that she ran, and the pig after her, and as the pig ran it holla'd aloud, so that the place rang with it.

"I wish I had been there with my gun," said I. "I guess that pig would have holla'd so as to surprise himself."

But she told me a gun was of no use with the like of these, which were the spirits of the dead.

Well, this kind of talk put in the evening, which was the best of it; but of course it didn't change my notion, and the next day, with my gun and a good knife, I set off upon a voyage of discovery. I made, as near as I could, for the place where I had seen Case come out; for if it was true he had some kind of establishment in the bush I reckoned I should find a path. The beginning of the desert was marked off by a wall, to call it so, for it was more of a long mound of stones. They say it reaches right across the island, but how they know it is another question, for I doubt if anyone has made the journey in a hundred years, the natives sticking chiefly to the sea and their little colonies along the coast, and that part being mortal high and steep and full of cliffs. Up to the west side of the wall the ground has been cleared, and there are coco palms and mummy-apples and guavas, and lots of sensitive. Just across, the bush begins outright; high bush at that, trees going up like the masts of ships, and ropes of liana hanging down like a ship's rigging, and nasty orchids growing in the forks like funguses. The ground where there was no underwood looked to be a heap of boulders. I saw many green pigeons that I might have shot, only I was there with a different idea. A number of butterflies flopped up and down along the ground like dead leaves; sometimes I would hear a bird calling, sometimes the wind overhead, and always the sea along the coast.

But the queerness of the place it's more difficult to tell of, unless to one who has been alone in the high bush himself. The brightest kind of a day it is always dim down there. A man can see to the end of nothing; whichever way he looks the wood shuts up, one bough folding with another like the fingers of your hand; and whenever he listens he hears always something new—men talking, children laughing, the strokes of an ax a far way ahead of him, and sometimes a sort of a quick, stealthy scurry near at hand that makes him jump and look to his weapons. It's all very well for him to tell himself that he's alone, bar trees and birds; he can't make out to believe it; whichever way he turns the whole place seems to be alive and looking on. Don't think it was Uma's yarns that put me out; I don't value native talk a fourpenny-piece; it's a thing that's natural in the bush, and that's the end of it.

As I got near the top of the hill, for the ground of the wood goes up in this place steep as a ladder, the wind began to sound straight on, and the leaves to toss and switch open and let in the sun. This suited me better; it was the same noise all the time, and nothing to startle. Well, I had got to a place where there was an underwood of what they call wild coconut—mighty pretty with its scarlet fruit—when there came a sound of singing in the wind that I thought I had never heard the like of. It was all very fine to tell myself it was the branches; I knew better. It was all very fine to tell myself it was a bird; I knew never a bird that sang like that. It rose and swelled, and died away and swelled again; and now I thought it was like someone weeping, only prettier; and now I thought it was like harps; and there was one thing I made sure of, it was a sight too sweet to be wholesome in a place like that. You may laugh if you like; but I declare I called to mind the six young ladies that came, with their scarlet necklaces, out of the cave at Fanga-anaana, and wondered if they sang like that. We laugh at the natives and their superstitions; but see how many traders take them up, splendidly educated white men, that have been bookkeepers (some of them) and clerks in the old country. It's my belief a superstition grows up in a place like the different kind of weeds; and as I stood there and listened to that wailing I twittered in my shoes.

You may call me a coward to be frightened; I thought myself brave enough to go on ahead. But I went mighty carefully, with my gun cocked, spying all about me like a hunter, fully expecting to see a handsome young woman sitting somewhere in the bush, and fully determined (if I did) to try her with a charge of duck shot. And sure enough, I had not gone far when I met with a queer thing. The wind came on the top of the wood in a strong puff, the leaves in front of me burst open, and I saw for a second something hanging in a tree. It was gone in a wink, the puff blowing by and the leaves closing. I tell you the truth: I had made up my mind to see an *aitu;* and if the thing had looked like a pig or a woman, it wouldn't have given me the same turn. The trouble was that it seemed kind of square, and the idea of a square thing that was alive and sang knocked me sick and silly. I must have stood quite a while; and I made pretty certain it was right out of the same tree that the singing came. Then I began to come to myself a bit.

"Well," says I, "if this is really so, if this is a place where there are square things that sing, I'm gone up anyway. Let's have my fun for my money."

But I thought I might as well take the off-chance of a prayer being any good; so I plumped on my knees and prayed out loud; and all the time I was praying the strange sounds came out of the tree, and went up and down, and changed, for all the world like music, only you could see it wasn't human—there was nothing there that you could whistle.

As soon as I had made an end in proper style, I laid down my gun, stuck my knife between my teeth, walked right up to that tree and began to climb. I tell you my heart was like ice. But presently, as I went up, I caught another glimpse of the thing, and that relieved me, for I thought it seemed like a box; and when I had got right up to it I near fell out of the tree with laughing.

A box it was, sure enough, and a candle box at that, with the brand upon the side of it; and it had banjo strings stretched so as to sound when the wind blew. I believe they call the thing a Tyrolean [1] harp, whatever that may mean.

"Well, Mr. Case," said I, "you frightened me once, but I defy you to frighten me again," I says, and slipped down the tree, and set out again to find my enemy's head office, which I guessed would not be far away.

[1] Æolian.

The undergrowth was thick in this part; I couldn't see before my nose, and must burst my way through by main force and ply the knife as I went, slicing the cords of the lianas and slashing down whole trees at a blow. I call them trees for the bigness, but in truth they were just big weeds, and sappy to cut through like carrot. From all this crowd and kind of vegetation, I was just thinking to myself, the place might have once been cleared, when I came on my nose over a pile of stones, and saw in a moment it was some kind of a work of man. The Lord knows when it was made or when deserted, for this part of the island has lain undisturbed since long before the whites came. A few steps beyond I hit into the path I had been always looking for. It was narrow, but well beaten, and I saw that Case had plenty of disciples. It seems, indeed it was, a piece of fashionable boldness to venture up here with the trader, and a young man scarce reckoned himself grown till he had got his breech tattooed, for one thing, and seen Case's devils for another. This is mighty like Kanakas: but, if you look at it another way, it's mighty like white folks, too.

A bit along the path I was brought to a clear stand, and had to rub my eyes. There was a wall in front of me, the path passing it by a gap; it was tumbledown and plainly very old, but built of big stones very well laid; and there is no native alive today upon that island that could dream of such a piece of building! Along all the top of it was a line of queer figures, idols or scarecrows, or whatnot. They had carved and painted faces ugly to view, their eyes and teeth were of shell, their hair and their bright clothes blew in the wind, and some of them worked with the tugging. There are islands up west where they make these kind of figures till today; but if ever they were made in this island, the practice and the very recollection of it are now long forgotten. And the singular thing was that all these bogies were as fresh as toys out of a shop.

Then it came in my mind that Case had let out to me the first day that he was a good forger of island curiosities—a thing by which so many traders turn an honest penny. And with that I saw the whole business, and how this display served the man a double purpose: first of all, to season his curiosities, and then to frighten those that came to visit him.

But I should tell you (what made the thing more curious) that all the time the Tyrolean harps were harping round me in the trees, and even while I looked, a green-and-yellow bird (that, I suppose, was building) began to tear the hair off the head of one of the figures.

A little farther on I found the best curiosity of the museum. The first I saw of it was a longish mound of earth with a twist to it. Digging off the earth with my hands, I found underneath tarpaulin stretched on boards, so that this was plainly the roof of a cellar. It stood right on the top of the hill, and the entrance was on the far side, between two rocks, like the entrance to a cave. I went as far in as the bend, and, looking round the corner, saw a shining face. It was big and ugly, like a pantomime mask, and the brightness of it waxed and dwindled, and at times it smoked.

"Oho!" says I, "luminous paint!"

And I must say I rather admired the man's ingenuity. With a box of tools and a few mighty simple contrivances he had made out to have a devil of a temple. Any poor Kanaka brought up here in the dark, with the harps whining all round him, and shown that smoking face in the bottom of a hole, would make no kind of doubt but he had seen and heard enough devils for a lifetime. It's easy to find out what Kanakas think. Just go back to yourself anyway around from ten to fifteen years old, and there's an average Kanaka. There are some pious, just as there are pious boys; and the most of them, like the boys again, are middling honest and yet think it rather larks to steal, and are easy scared, and rather like to be so. I remember a boy I was at school with at home who played the Case business. He didn't know anything, that boy; he couldn't do anything; he had no luminous paint and no Tyrolean harps; he just boldly said he was a sorcerer, and frightened us out of our boots, and we loved it. And then it came in my mind how the master had once flogged that boy, and the surprise we were all in to see the sorcerer catch it and hum like anybody else. Thinks I to myself: "I must find some way of fixing it so for Master Case." And the next moment I had my idea.

I went back by the path, which, when once you had found it, was quite plain and easy walking; and when I stepped out on the black sands, who should I see but Master Case himself. I cocked my gun and held it handy, and we marched up and passed without a word, each keeping the tail of his eye on the other; and no sooner had we passed than we each wheeled round like fellows drilling, and stood face to face. We had each taken the same notion in his head, you see, that the other fellow might give him the load of his gun in the stern.

"You've shot nothing," says Case.

"I'm not on the shoot today," said I.

"Well, the devil go with you for me," says he.

"The same to you," says I.

But we stuck just the way we were; no fear of either of us moving.

Case laughed. "We can't stop here all day, though," said he.

"Don't let me detain you," says I.

He laughed again. "Look here, Wiltshire, do you think me a fool?" he asked.

"More of a knave, if you want to know," says I.

"Well, do you think it would better me to shoot you here, on this open beach?" said he. "Because I don't. Folks come fishing every day. There may be a score of them up the valley now, making copra; there might be half a dozen on the hill behind you, after pigeons; they might be watching us this minute, and I shouldn't wonder. I give you my word I don't want to shoot you. Why should I? You don't hinder me any. You haven't got one pound of copra but what you made with your own hands, like a Negro slave. You're vegetating—that's what I call it—and I don't care where you vegetate, nor yet how long. Give me your word you don't mean to shoot me, and I'll give you a lead and walk away."

"Well," said I, "you're frank and pleasant, ain't you? And I'll be the same. I don't mean to shoot you today. Why should I? This business is beginning; it ain't done yet, Mr. Case. I've given you one turn already. I can see the marks of my knuckles on your head to this blooming hour, and I've more cooking for you. I'm not a paralee, like Underhill. My name ain't Adams, and it ain't Vigours; and I mean to show you that you've met your match."

"This is a silly way to talk," said he. "This is not the talk to make me move on with."

"All right," said I, "stay where you are. I ain't in any hurry, and you know it. I can put in a day on this beach and never mind. I ain't got any copra to bother with. I ain't got any luminous paint to see to."

I was sorry I said that last, but it whipped out before I knew. I could see it took the wind out of his sails, and he stood and stared at me with his brow drawn up. Then I suppose he made up his mind he must get to the bottom of this.

"I take you at your word," says he, and turned his back, and walked right into the devil's bush.

I let him go, of course, for I had passed my word. But I watched him as long as he was in sight, and after he was gone lit out for cover as lively as you would want to see, and went the rest of the way home under the bush, for I didn't trust him sixpence worth. One thing I saw, I had been ass enough to give him warning, and that which I meant to do I must do at once.

You would think I had had about enough excitement for one morning, but there was another turn waiting me. As soon as I got far enough round the cape to see my house I made out there were strangers there; a little farther, and no doubt about it. There was a couple of armed sentinels squatting at my door. I could only suppose the trouble about Uma must have come to a head, and the station been seized. For aught I could think, Uma was taken up already, and these armed men were waiting to do the like with me.

However, as I came nearer, which I did at top speed, I saw there was a third native sitting on the veranda like a guest, and Uma was talking with him like a hostess. Nearer still I made out it was the big young chief, Maea, and that he was smiling away and smoking. And what was he smoking? None of your European cigarettes fit for a cat, not even the genuine big, knock-me-down native article that a fellow can really put in the time with if his pipe is broke—but a cigar, and one of my Mexicans at that, that I could swear to. At sight of this my heart started beating, and I took a wild hope in my head that the trouble was over, and Maea had come round.

Uma pointed me out to him as I came up, and he met me at the head of my own stairs like a thorough gentleman.

"Vilivili," said he, which was the best they could make of my name, "I pleased."

There is no doubt when an island chief wants to be civil he can do it. I saw the way things were from the word go. There was no call for Uma to say to me: "He no 'fraid Ese now, come bring copra." I tell you I shook hands with that Kanaka like as if he was the best white man in Europe.

The fact was, Case and he had got after the same girl, or Maea suspected it, and concluded to make hay of the trader on the chance. He had dressed himself up, got a couple of his retainers cleaned and armed to kind of make the thing more public, and, just waiting till Case was clear of the village, came round to put the whole of his business my way. He was rich as well as powerful. I suppose that man was worth fifty thousand nuts per annum. I gave him the price of the beach and a quarter cent better, and as for credit, I would have advanced him the inside of the store and the fittings besides, I was so pleased to see him. I must say he bought like a gentleman: rice and tins and biscuits enough for a week's feast, and stuffs by the bolt. He was agreeable besides; he had plenty fun to him; and we cracked jests together, mostly through the interpreter, because he had mighty little English, and my native was still off-color. One thing I made out: he could never really have thought much harm of Uma; he could never have been really frightened, and must just have made believe from dodginess, and because he thought Case had a strong pull in the village and could help him on.

This set me thinking that both he and I were in a tightish place. What he had done was to fly in the face of the whole village, and the thing might cost him his authority. More than that, after my talk with Case on the beach, I thought it might very well cost me my life. Case had as good as said he would pot me if ever I got any copra; he would come home to find the best business in the village had changed hands, and the best thing I thought I could do was to get in first with the potting.

"See here, Uma," says I, "tell him I'm sorry I made him wait, but I was up looking at Case's Tiapolo store in the bush."

"He want savvy if you no 'fraid?" translated Uma.

I laughed out. "Not much!" says I. "Tell him the place is a blooming toy shop! Tell him in England we give these things to the kid to play with."

"He want savvy if you hear devil sing?" she asked next.

"Look here," I said, "I can't do it now, because I've got no banjo strings in stock; but the next time the ship comes round I'll have one of these same contraptions right here in my veranda, and he can see for himself how much devil there is to it. Tell him, as soon as I can get the strings I'll make one for his pickaninnies. The name of the concern is a Tyrolean harp; and you can tell him the name means in English that nobody but damn' fools give a cent for it."

This time he was so pleased he had to try his English again. "You talk true?" says he.

"Rather!" said I. "Talk all-e-same Bible. Bring out a Bible here, Uma, if you've got such a thing, and I'll kiss it. Or, I'll tell you what's better still," says I, taking a header, "ask him if he's afraid to go up there himself by day."

It appeared he wasn't; he could venture as far as that by day and in company.

"That's the ticket, then!" said I. "Tell him the man's a fraud and the place foolishness, and if he'll go up there tomorrow he'll see all that's left of it. But tell him this, Uma, and mind he understands it: If he gets talking it's bound to come to Case, and I'm a dead man! I'm playing his game, tell him, and if he says one word my blood will be at his door and be the damnation of him here and after."

She told him, and he shook hands with me up to the hilt, and, says he: "No talk. Go up tomollow. You my friend?"

"No, sir," says I, "no such foolishness. I've come here to

trade, tell him, and not to make friends. But, as to Case, I'll send that man to glory!"

So off Maea went, pretty well pleased, as I could see.

CHAPTER V

NIGHT IN THE BUSH

Well, I was committed now; Tiapolo had to be smashed up before next day, and my hands were pretty full, not only with preparations, but with argument. My house was like a mechanics' debating society. Uma was so made up that I shouldn't go into the bush by night, or that, if I did, I was never to come back again. You know her style of arguing: you've had a specimen about Queen Victoria and the devil; and I leave you to fancy if I was tired of it before dark.

At last I had a good idea. "What was the use of casting my pearls before her?" I thought; some of her own chopped hay would be likelier to do the business.

"I'll tell you what, then," said I. "You fish out your Bible, and I'll take that up along with me. That'll make me right."

She swore a Bible was no use.

"That's just your Kanaka ignorance," said I. "Bring the Bible out."

She brought it, and I turned to the title page, where I thought there would likely be some English, and so there was. "There!" said I. "Look at that! '*London: Printed for the British and Foreign Bible Society, Blackfriars,*' and the date, which I can't read, owing to its being in these X's. There's no devil in hell can look near the Bible Society, Blackfriars. Why, you silly," I said, "how do you suppose we get along with our own *aitus* at home! All Bible Society!"

"I think you no got any," said she. "White man, he tell me you no got."

"Sounds likely, don't it?" I asked. "Why would these islands all be chock full of them and none in Europe?"

"Well, you no got breadfruit," said she.

I could have torn my hair. "Now, look here, old lady,"

said I, "you dry up, for I'm tired of you. I'll take the Bible, which'll put me as straight as the mail, and that's the last word I've got to say."

The night fell extraordinary dark, clouds coming up with sundown and overspreading all; not a star showed; there was only an end of a moon, and that not due before the small hours. Round the village, what with the lights and the fires in the open houses, and the torches of many fishers moving on the reef, it kept as gay as an illumination; but the sea and the mountains and woods were all clean gone. I suppose it might be eight o'clock when I took the road, laden like a donkey. First there was that Bible, a book as big as your head, which I had let myself in for by my own tomfoolery. Then there was my gun, and knife, and lantern, and patent matches, all necessary. And then there was the real plant of the affair in hand, a mortal weight of gunpowder, a pair of dynamite fishing-bombs, and two or three pieces of slow match that I had hauled out of the tin cases and spliced together the best way I could; for the match was only trade stuff, and a man would be crazy that trusted it. Altogether, you see, I had the materials of a pretty good blowup! Expense was nothing to me; I wanted that thing done right.

As long as I was in the open, and had the lamp in my house to steer by, I did well. But when I got to the path, it fell so dark I could make no headway, walking into trees and swearing there, like a man looking for the matches in his bedroom. I knew it was risky to light up, for my lantern would be visible all the way to the point of the cape, and as no one went there after dark, it would be talked about, and come to Case's ears. But what was I to do? I had either to give the business over and lose caste with Maea, or light up, take my chance, and get through the thing the smartest I was able.

As long as I was on the path I walked hard, but when I came to the black beach I had to run. For the tide was now nearly flowed; and to get through with my powder dry between the surf and the steep hill took all the quickness I possessed. As it was, even the wash caught me to the knees, and I came near falling on a stone. All this time the hurry I was in, and the free air and smell of the sea, kept my spirits lively; but when I was once in the bush and began to climb the path I took it easier. The fearsomeness of the wood had been a good bit rubbed off for me by Master Case's banjo strings and graven images, yet I thought it was a dreary walk, and guessed, when the disciples went up there, they must be badly scared. The light of the lantern, striking among all these trunks and forked branches and twisted rope-ends of lianas, made the whole place, or all that you could see of it, a kind of a puzzle of turning shadows. They came to meet you, solid and quick like giants, and then spun off and vanished; they hove up over your head like clubs, and flew away into the night like birds. The floor of the bush glimmered with dead wood, the way the matchbox used to shine after you had struck a lucifer. Big, cold drops fell on me from the branches overhead like sweat. There was no wind to mention; only a little icy breath of a land breeze that stirred nothing; and the harps were silent.

The first landfall I made was when I got through the bush of wild coconuts, and came in view of the bogies on the wall. Mighty queer they looked by the shining of the lantern, with their painted faces and shell eyes, and their clothes, and their hair hanging. One after another I pulled them all up and piled them in a bundle on the cellar roof, so as they might go to glory with the rest. Then I chose a place behind one of the big stones at the entrance, buried my powder and the two shells, and arranged my match along the passage. And then I had a look at the smoking head, just for good-by. It was doing fine.

"Cheer up," says I. "You're booked."

It was my first idea to light up and be getting homeward; for the darkness and the glimmer of the dead wood and the shadows of the lantern made me lonely. But I knew where one of the harps hung; it seemed a pity it shouldn't go with the rest; and at the same time I couldn't help letting on to myself that I was mortal tired of my employment, and would like best to be at home and have the door shut. I stepped out of the cellar and argued it fore and back. There was a sound of the sea far down below me on the coast; nearer hand not a leaf stirred; I might have been the only living creature this side of Cape Horn. Well, as I stood there thinking, it seemed the bush woke and became full of little noises. Little noises they were, and nothing to hurt; a bit of a crackle, a bit of a rush; but the breath jumped right out of me and my throat went as dry as a biscuit. It wasn't Case I was afraid of, which would have been common sense; I never thought of Case; what took me, as sharp as the colic, was the old wives' tales—the devil-women and the man-pigs. It was the toss of a penny whether I should run; but I got a purchase on myself, and stepped out, and held up the lantern (like a fool) and looked all round.

In the direction of the village and the path there was nothing to be seen; but when I turned inland it's a wonder to me I didn't drop. There, coming right up out of the desert and the bad bush—there, sure enough, was a devil-woman, just as the way I had figured she would look. I saw the light shine on her bare arms and her bright eyes, and there went out of me a yell so big that I thought it was my death.

"Ah! No sing out!" says the devil-woman, in a kind of a high whisper. "Why you talk big voice? Put out light! Ese he come."

"My God almighty, Uma, is that you?" says I.

"Ioe" (yes), says she. "I come quick. Ese here soon."

"You come along?" I asked. "You no 'fraid?"

"Ah, too much 'fraid!" she whispered, clutching me. "I think die."

"Well," says I, with a kind of a weak grin. "I'm not the one to laugh at you, Mrs. Wiltshire, for I'm about the worst scared man in the South Pacific myself."

She told me in two words what brought her. I was scarce gone, it seems, when Faavao came in, and the old woman had met Black Jack running as hard as he was fit from our house to Case's. Uma neither spoke nor stopped, but lit right out to come and warn me. She was so close at my heels that the lantern was her guide across the beach, and afterward, by the glimmer of it in the trees, she got her line uphill. It was only when I had got to the top or was in the cellar that she wandered—Lord knows where!—and lost a sight of precious time, afraid to call out lest Case was at the heels of her, and falling in the bush, so that she was all knocked and bruised. That must have been when she got too far to the southward, and how she came to take me in the flank at last and frighten me beyond what I've got the words to tell of.

Well, anything was better than a devil-woman, but I thought her yarn serious enough. Black Jack had no call to be about my house, unless he was set there to watch; and it looked to me as if my tomfool word about the paint, and perhaps some chatter of Maea's, had got us all in a clove hitch. One thing was clear: Uma and I were here for the night; we daren't try to go home before day, and even then it would be safer to strike round up the mountain and come in by the back of the village, or we might walk into an ambuscade. It was plain, too, that the mine should be sprung immediately, or Case might be in time to stop it.

I marched into the tunnel, Uma keeping tight hold of me, opened my lantern, and lit the match. The first length of it burned like a spill of paper, and I stood stupid, watching it burn, and thinking we were going aloft with Tiapolo, which was none of my views. The second took to a better rate, though faster than I cared about; and at that I got my wits again, hauled Uma clear of the passage, blew out and dropped the lantern, and the pair of us groped our way into the bush until I thought it might be safe, and lay down together by a tree.

"Our lady," I said, "I won't forget this night. You're a trump, and that's what's wrong with you."

She bumped herself close up to me. She had run out the way she was, with nothing on her but her kilt; and she was all wet with the dews and the sea on the black beach, and shook straight on with cold and the terror of the dark and the devils.

"Too much 'fraid," was all she said.

The far side of Case's hill goes down near as steep as a precipice into the next valley. We were on the very edge of it, and I could see the dead wood shine and hear the sea sound far below. I didn't care about the position, which left me no retreat, but I was afraid to change. Then I saw I had made a worse mistake about the lantern, which I should have left lighted, so that I could have had a crack at Case when he stepped into the shine of it. And since I hadn't had the wit to do that, it seemed a senseless thing to leave the good lantern to blow up with the graven images. The thing belonged to me, after all, and was worth money, and might come in handy. If I could have trusted the match, I might have run in still and rescued it. But who was going to trust to the match? You know what trade is. The stuff was good enough for Kanakas to go fishing with, where they've got to look lively anyway, and the most they risk is only to have their hand blown off. But for anyone that wanted to fool around a blowup like mine that match was rubbish.

Altogether the best I could do was to lie still, see my shotgun handy, and wait for the explosion. But it was a solemn kind of a business. The blackness of the night was like solid; the only thing you could see was the nasty bogy glimmer of the dead wood, and that showed you nothing but itself; and as for sounds, I stretched my ears till I thought I could have heard the match burn in the tunnel, and that bush was silent as a coffin. Now and then there was a bit of a crack; but whether it was near or far, whether it was Case stubbing his toes within a few yards of me, or a tree breaking miles away, I knew no more than the babe unborn.

And then, all of a sudden, Vesuvius went off. It was a long time coming; but when it came (though I say it that shouldn't) no man could ask to see a better. At first it was just a son of a gun of a row, and a spout of fire, and the wood lighted up so that you could see to read. And then the trouble began. Uma and I were half-buried under a wagonful of earth, and glad it was no worse, for one of the rocks at the entrance of the tunnel was fired clean into the air, fell within a couple of fathoms of where we lay, and bounded over the edge of the hill, and went pounding down into the next valley. I saw I had rather undercalculated our distance, or overdone the dynamite and powder, which you please.

And presently I saw I had made another slip. The noise of the thing began to die off, shaking the island; the dazzle was over; and yet the night didn't come back the way I expected. For the whole wood was scattered with red coals and brands from the explosion; they were all round me on the flat, some had fallen below in the valley, and some stuck and flared in the treetops. I had no fear of fire, for these forests are too wet to kindle. But the trouble was that the place was all lit up–not very bright, but good enough to get a shot by; and the way the coals were scattered, it was just as likely Case might have the advantage as myself. I looked all round for his white face, you may be sure; but there was not a sign of him. As for Uma, the life seemed to have been knocked right out of her by the bang and blaze of it.

There was one bad point in my game. One of the blessed graven images had come down all afire, hair and clothes and body, not four yards away from me. I cast a mighty noticing glance all round; there was still no Case, and I made up my mind I must get rid of that burning stick before he came, or I should be shot there like a dog.

It was my first idea to have crawled, and then I thought speed was the main thing, and stood half up to make a rush. The same moment, from somewhere between me and the sea, there came a flash and a report, and a rifle bullet screeched in my ear. I swung straight round and up with my gun, but the brute had a Winchester, and before I could as much as see him his second shot knocked me over like a ninepin. I seemed to fly in the air, then came down by the run and lay half a minute, silly; and then I found my hands empty, and my gun had flown over my head as I fell. It makes a man mighty wide awake to be in the kind of box that I was in. I scarcely knew where I was hurt, or whether I was hurt or not, but turned right over on my face to crawl after my weapon. Unless you have tried to get about with a smashed leg you don't know what pain is, and I let out a howl like a bullock's.

This was the unluckiest noise that ever I made in my life. Up to then Uma had stuck to her tree like a sensible woman, knowing she would be only in the way; but as soon as she heard me sing out she ran forward. The Winchester cracked again, and down she went.

I had sat up, leg and all, to stop her; but when I saw her tumble I clapped down again where I was, lay still, and felt the handle of my knife. I had been scurried and put out before. No more of that for me. He had knocked over my girl, I had got to fix him for it; and I lay there and gritted my teeth, and footed up the chances. My leg was broke, my gun was gone. Case had still ten shots in his Winchester. It looked a kind of hopeless business. But I never despaired nor thought upon despairing: that man had got to go.

For a goodish bit not one of us let on. Then I heard Case begin to move nearer in the bush, but mighty careful. The image had burned out, there were only a few coals left here and there, and the wood was main dark, but had a kind of a low glow in it like a fire on its last legs. It was by this that I made out Case's head looking at me over a big tuft of ferns, and at the same time the brute saw me and shouldered his Winchester. I lay quite still, and as good as looked into the barrel: it was my last chance, but I thought my heart would have come right out of its bearings. Then he fired. Lucky for me it was no shotgun, for the bullet struck within an inch of me and knocked the dirt in my eyes.

Just you try and see if you can lie quiet, and let a man take a sitting shot at you and miss you by a hair. But I did, and lucky, too. A while Case stood with the Winchester at the port-arms; then he gave a little laugh to himself and stepped round the ferns.

"Laugh!" thought I. "If you had the wit of a louse you would be praying!"

I was all as taut as a ship's hawser or the spring of a watch, and as soon as he came within reach of me I had him by the ankle, plucked the feet right out from under him, laid him out, and was upon the top of him, broken leg and all, before he breathed. His Winchester had gone the same road as my shotgun; it was nothing to me—I defied him now. I'm a pretty strong man anyway, but I never knew what strength was till I got hold of Case. He was knocked out of time by the rattle he came down with, and threw up his hands together, more like a frightened woman, so that I caught both of them with my left. This wakened him up, and he fastened his teeth in my forearm like a weasel. Much I cared. My leg gave me all the pain I had any use for, and I drew my knife and got it in the place.

"Now," said I, "I've got you; and you're gone up, and a good job too! Do you feel the point of that? That's for Underhill! And there's for Adams! And now here's for Uma, and that's going to knock your blooming soul right out of you!"

With that I gave him the cold steel for all I was worth. His body kicked under me like a spring sofa; he gave a dreadful kind of a long moan, and lay still.

"I wonder if you're dead? I hope so!" I thought, for my head was swimming. But I wasn't going to take chances; I had his own example too close before me for that; and I tried to draw the knife out to give it him again. The blood came over my hands, I remember, hot as tea; and with that I fainted clean away, and fell with my head on the man's mouth.

When I came to myself it was pitch dark; the cinders had burned out; there was nothing to be seen but the shine of the dead wood, and I couldn't remember where I was nor why I was in such pain, nor what I was all wetted with. Then it came back, and the first thing I attended to was to give him the knife again a half a dozen times up to the handle. I believe he was dead already, but it did him no harm and did me good.

"I bet you're dead now," I said, and then I called to Uma.

Nothing answered, and I made a move to go and grope for her, fouled my broken leg, and fainted again.

When I came to myself the second time the clouds had all cleared away, except a few that sailed there, white as cotton. The moon was up—a tropic moon. The moon at home turns a wood black, but even this old butt-end of a one showed up that forest as green as by day. The night birds—or, rather, they're a kind of early-morning bird—sang out with their long, falling notes like nightingales. And I could see the dead man, that I was still half-resting on, looking right up into the sky with his open eyes, no paler than when he was alive; and a little way off Uma tumbled on her side. I got over to her the best way I was able, and when I got there she was broad awake and crying, and sobbing to herself with no more noise than an insect. It appears she was afraid to cry out loud, because of the *aitus.* Altogether she was not much hurt, but scared beyond belief; she had come to her senses a long while ago, cried out to me, heard nothing in reply, made out we were both dead, and had lain there ever since, afraid to budge a finger. The ball had ploughed up her shoulder, and she had lost a main quantity of blood; but I soon had that tied up the way it ought to be with the tail of my shirt and a scarf I had on, got her head on my sound knee and my back against a trunk, and settled down to wait for morning. Uma was for neither use nor ornament, and could only clutch hold of me and shake and cry. I don't suppose there was ever anybody worse scared, and, to do her justice, she had had a lively night of it. As for me, I was in a good bit of pain and fever, but not so bad when I sat still; and every time I looked over to Case I could have sung and whistled. Talk about meat and drink! To see that man lying there dead as a herring filled me full.

The night birds stopped after a while; and then the light began to change, the east came orange, the whole wood began to whir with singing like a musical box, and there was the broad day.

I didn't expect Maea for a long while yet; and, indeed, I thought there was an off-chance he might go back on the whole idea and not come at all. I was the better pleased when, about an hour after daylight, I heard sticks smashing and a lot of Kanakas laughing and singing out to keep their courage up. Uma sat up quite brisk at the first word of it; and presently we saw a party come stringing out of the path, Maea in front, and behind him a white man in a pith helmet. It was Mr. Tarleton, who had turned up late last night in Falesá, having left his boat and walked the last stage with a lantern.

They buried Case upon the field of glory, right in the hole where he had kept the smoking head. I waited till the thing was done; and Mr. Tarleton prayed, which I thought tomfoolery, but I'm bound to say he gave a pretty sick view of the dear departed's prospects, and seemed to have his own ideas of hell. I had it out with him afterward, told him he had scamped his duty, and what he had ought to have done was to up like a man and tell the Kanakas plainly Case was damned, and a good riddance; but I never could get him to see it my way. Then they made me a litter of poles and carried me down to the station. Mr. Tarleton set my leg, and made a regular missionary splice of it, so that I limp to this day. That done, he took down my evidence, and Uma's, and Maea's, wrote it all out fine, and had us sign it; and then he got the chiefs and marched over to Papa Randall's to seize Case's papers.

All they found was a bit of a diary, kept for a good many years, and all about the price of copra, and chickens being stolen, and that; and the books of the business and the will I told you of in the beginning, by both of which the whole thing (stock, lock, and barrel) appeared to belong to the Samoa woman. It was I that bought her out at a mighty reasonable figure, for she was in a hurry to get home. As for Randall and the black, they had to tramp; got into some kind of a station on the Papa-Malulu side; did very bad business, for the truth is neither of the pair was fit for it, and lived mostly on fish, which was the means of Randall's death. It seems there was a nice shoal in one day, and Papa went after them with the dynamite; either the match burned too fast, or Papa was full, or both, but the shell went off (in the usual way) before he threw it, and where was Papa's hand? Well, there's nothing to hurt in that; the islands up north are all full of one-handed men like the parties in the *Arabian Nights;* but either Randall was too old, or he drank too much, and the short and the long of it was that he died. Pretty soon after, the nigger was turned out of the island for stealing from white men, and went off to the west, where he found men of his own color, in case he liked that, and the men of his own color took and ate him at some kind of a corroboree, and I'm sure I hope he was to their fancy!

So there was I, left alone in my glory at Falesá; and when the schooner came round I filled her up, and gave her a deck cargo half as high as the house. I must say Mr. Tarleton did the right thing by us; but he took a meanish kind of a revenge.

"Now, Mr. Wiltshire," said he, "I've put you all square with everybody here. It wasn't difficult to do, Case being gone; but I have done it, and given my pledge besides that you will deal fairly with the natives. I must ask you to keep my word."

Well, so I did. I used to be bothered about my balances, but I reasoned it out this way. We all have queerish balances, and the natives all know it and water their copra in a proportion so that it's fair all round; but the truth is, it did use to bother me, and, though I did well in Falesá, I was half-glad when the firm moved me on to another station, where I was under no kind of a pledge and could look my balances in the face.

As for the old lady, you know her as well as I do. She's only the one fault. If you don't keep your eye lifting she would give away the roof off the station. Well, it seems it's natural in Kanakas. She's turned a powerful big woman now, and could throw a London bobby over her shoulder. But that's natural in Kanakas, too, and there's no manner of doubt that she's an A-1 wife.

Mr. Tarleton's gone home, his trick being over. He was the best missionary I ever struck, and now, it seems, he's parsonizing down Somerset way. Well, that's best for him; he'll have no Kanakas there to get loony over.

My public house? Not a bit of it, nor ever likely. I'm stuck here, I fancy. I don't like to leave the kids, you see: and—there's no use talking—they're better here than what they would be in a white man's country, though Ben took the eldest up to Auckland, where he's being schooled with the best. But what bothers me is the girls. They're only half-castes, of course; I know that as well as you do, and there's nobody thinks less of half-castes than I do; but they're mine, and about all I've got. I can't reconcile my mind to their taking up with Kanakas, and I'd like to know where I'm to find the whites?

Lloyd Osbourne

A SON OF EMPIRE

The stepson of Robert Louis Stevenson, Lloyd Osbourne (1868–1947) accompanied his mother and stepfather on several voyages to the Pacific islands. They settled at Vailima, in Samoa, where in his early twenties Osbourne became a "white chief," with a retinue of native warriors. He learned the craft of storytelling by collaborating with Stevenson on three books —*The Wrong Box* (1889), *The Wrecker* (1892), and *The Ebb-Tide* (1894). After Stevenson's death he remained in Samoa as American vice-consul until 1897, when he went to New York to make his living as a writer. Two books—*The Queen vs. Billy* (1900) and *Wild Justice* (1906, 1921)—comprise Osbourne's short stories of the South Seas. One of the best of these is "A Son of Empire," the story of Mr. Clemm, the renegade who set himself up as resident commissioner on the island of Rakahanga and for a time had everything going his way.

RAKAHANGA IS A DOT OF AN ISLAND IN THE MID-PACIFIC, AND so far from anywhere that it doesn't belong to a group—as most islands do—but is all by its lonesome in the heave and roll of the emptiest ocean in the world. In my time it was just big enough to support two traders, not counting old man Fosby, who had sort of retired and laid down life's burden in a Kanaka shack, where if he did anything at all it was making bonito hooks for his half-caste family or playing the accordion with his trembly old fingers.

It was me and Stanley Hicks that divided the trade of the place, which was poor to middling, with maybe a couple of hundred tons of copra a year and as much pearl shell as the natives cared to get. It was deep shell, you understand, and sometimes a diver went down and never came up, and you could see him shimmering down below like the back of a shark, as dead as a doornail. Nobody would dive after that, and a whole year might pass with the Kanakas still holding back unless there was a church assessment or a call for something special like a sewing machine or a new boat. It averaged anywhere from five tons to sixty, and often, as I said, nothing at all.

I had got rooted in Rakahanga, and so had Stanley Hicks, and though we both had ideas of getting away and often talked of it, we never did—being like people half-asleep in a feather bed, with life drifting on unnoticed, and the wind rustling in the palms, and one summer day so like another that you lost count of time altogether.

You would have to go far to see a prettier island than Rakahanga, or nicer, friendlier, finer-looking people; and when I say they never watered their copra on us, nor worked any of those heartbreaking boycotts to bring prices down, you can realize how much out of the beaten track it was and how little they had yet learned of civilization. They were too simple and easygoing for their own good and that's a fact, for they allowed David, the Tongan pastor, to walk all over them, which he did right royal with his great, fat, naked feet; and when anything didn't please this here David nor the deacons, they stuck him or her in the coral jail and locked the door on him—or her—as the case might be and usually was.

We were what might be called a republic, having no king and being supposed to be ruled by the old men, who met from time to time in a wickerwork building that looked more like a giant clothesbasket than anything resembling a house. Yes, Rakahanga was an independent country, and no flag floated over us but our own—or would have if we had had one, which we hadn't. Of course Stanley and I knew it could not last like this forever, and even the natives weren't unprepared for our being annexed some day by a passing man-of-war—though all hoped it would go on as it was, with nobody interfering with us nor pasting proclamations on trees. It is all very fine to see "GOD SAVE THE QUEEN" *or* "VIVE LA REPUBLIQUE" at the bottom of a proclamation, but Stanley and I knew it meant taxes and licenses and penal servitude if you did this or failed to do that, and all those other blessings that are served out to a Pacific island when one of the great powers suddenly discovers it on the map.

Our republic was more in name than anything else, for old David, the missionary, ruled the island with a rod of iron, and was so crotchety and tyrannical that no Kanaka could call his soul his own. Every night at nine he stood out in front of his house and rang a hand bell, and then woe betide anyone who didn't go to bed instanter and shut up, no matter if it were in the full of the moon and they in the middle of a game of cards or yarning sociable on an upturned boat.

One had to get up just as military and autocratic—and as for dancing, why, the word itself could hardly be said, let alone the actual thing, which meant the jail every time and a dose of the pastor's whip thrown in extra. It was a crime to miss church, and a crime to flirt or make love, and the biggest crime of all was not to come up handsome with church offerings when they were demanded. If you will believe me it was a crime to *grieve* too much if somebody died—if the dead person were married that is, and if you were of the opposite sex and not closely related!

As I said before, the natives were so easygoing that they took it all lying down, and allowed this here David to swell into a regular despot, though there must have been coming on two thousand of them, and him with nothing but his bell and his whip and his big roaring voice. Naturally he did not dare interfere with us white men, though Stanley and I toed the line more than we liked for the sake of business and keeping clear of his ill will. The only one who wasn't scared of the old Tartar, and stood right up to him, was a hulking big Fijian, named Peter Jones. Nobody knew how he came by that name, for there wasn't a white drop in his body, he being unusually dark and powerful and full of the Old Nick, and with a mop of hair on him like you never saw, it was that thick and long and stood out on end all round his head, which was the Fiji fashion of wearing it.

Peter could lick his weight in wildcats, as the saying goes, and was always ready to do it at the fall of a hat. He was a bullying, overbearing individual and had terrorized his way into a family and married their daughter, helping himself promiscuous, besides, to anything he fancied, with nobody daring to cross him nor complain. Stanley and I were afraid of him and that's the truth, and gave him a little credit for peace and quietness' sake, which was well worth an occasional can of beef or a fathom or two of Turkey cotton.

Once, when there was a ship in, he got most outrageously drunk, and rolled about the village, singing and yelling—swigging from the bottle he carried and stumbling after the girls, trying to hug them. If ever there was a scandal in Rakahanga it was the sight of this six-foot-three of raving, roaring savage, roughhousing the place upside down and bellowing insults at the top of his lungs. But nothing was done to stop him till the liquor took its course, and then old David, he gathered the parliament about him, and ran him into the jail with a one-two-three, like a sack of oats.

But Peter Jones was none of your stand-up-at-the-altar-and-repent boys, being a white man by training, if not by blood, and after he had sobered up, what if his wife didn't smuggle him in a knife, and what if he didn't dig his way out! Yes, sir, that's what Peter Jones did—dug through the gravel floor and tunneled out, rising from the grave, so to speak, to the general uproar and hullabaloo of the entire settlement. Then—no one stopping him—he armed himself with an old Springfield rifle and an ax and a crowbar, and the cry went up he was going to murder the pastor, with the children running along in front and the women screaming.

But Peter wasn't gunning for any missionary, which even in Rakahanga might have had a nasty comeback—the natives being mild but not cowards, and beginning to buzz like hornets and reach for their sharktooth spears. No, what Peter was inflamed against was the coral jail, which he set at most ferocious with crowbar and ax until it was nothing but a heap of rubbish. Then he shot holes through the galvanized roofing, and burned it in a blazing fire along of the iron-studded door and window framing. By this time the missionary was trying to raise the multitude against Peter, but they were none too fond of the coral jail themselves and did nothing but hoot and shout like a pack of boys at a circus, which indeed it was and enough to make you split your sides laughing. After that Peter was let alone and nobody dared cross him, no matter what he did.

But this is all by the way to give you an idea of what Rakahanga was like, and make the rest of the yarn the easier to understand. I shall always feel sorry all my life that Stanley and I were off fishing on the windward side of the island and thereby missed Clemm's arrival in the lagoon, which was well over before we got there, with the stern of a ten-oared boat heading for a man-of-war, and Clemm himself standing kind of helpless on the beach in the midst of all his chests and boxes and bedding.

He made a splendid appearance in his white clothes and shirt and pipe-clayed shoes and pith helmet, being a short, thickset man with gray hair and a commanding look. When we came running up he spoke to us very grand, though genial, saying: "Gentlemen, I am the new resident deputy commissioner, and I call on you to assist me raise the flag and annex this island in the name of her Royal and Imperial Majesty, Queen Victoria!"

At this he took his hat off, and we did the same, though I am an American, and then went on to tell us that he had just been landed by H.M.S. "Ringarooma" to take possession of the island, and would we kindly inform the natives and escort him to the king.

On learning we were a republic and that it would take time to assemble the old men, he condescended to accept my hospitality for a spell, and was most pleased and gracious at the little we could do in his honor. Meanwhile messengers were sent to gather in the chiefs and tell them the great news, and how the Commissioner was soon coming to meet them in the "Speak-house," as the natives called the wickerwork. Mr. Clemm said the "Ringarooma" had been sent under hurry orders to annex right and left in order to forestall the

French, who had broken their international agreement and were hoisting their flag all over the place. He also explained that was the reason why the man-of-war could not stop, it being a neck-and-neck race between her and the French which could reach the Tokelaus first. Between drinks he likewise showed us his commission, which was written very big and imposing on crinkly paper, with seals, where he was called "Our well-beloved and right trusty James Howard Fitzroy Clemm, Esquire,"—as well as the flag he had brought with him, which was an eight-by-twelve-ensign, with the halyards all ready to run it up.

I can tell you Stanley and I were mighty proud to escort the Deputy Commissioner to the Parliament, which we did slow and stately in our best pajamas, with the natives reverencing him as he passed and eying us two most respectful. The old men were there in rows, and also David, the pastor, who took the interpreting out of my hands and as usual hogged the whole show. Perhaps it was as well he did, for he had a splendid voice and a booming way of speaking that suited the grandeur of the occasion.

Then Mr. Clemm's commission was read aloud, first by him in English and then by David in Kanaka, and afterwards the Commissioner made a rousing speech, all about the loving English and the low, contemptible French, and at the end he asked everybody to hold up his right hand who wished to be a loyal, faithful, obedient subject of the Great Queen.

Up shot every hand most grateful at the narrow escape they had had of being French; and then outside it was again repeated, even the children holding up their little paws, and the flag hoisted temporary to a coconut palm amid shouts of rejoicing led off by Stanley and me and Peter Jones, who had followed along after us.

The next question was where to lodge the Commissioner till a proper house could be built for him, and he showed he wasn't a gentleman to be trifled with by cutting short their jabber, and choosing Fono's, which was the finest in the settlement, and ordering him to clear out, bag and baggage—which Fono didn't want to do and objected very crossly till Peter Jones snatched up a rock and ran at him like he meant to pound his head in. This pleased Mr. Clemm so much that he right off appointed Peter marshal of his court at a salary of forty dollars a month, and put him in charge of shifting his things into his new quarters.

I took the liberty of warning Mr. Clemm against the Fijian, but he only threw back his head and told me most cutting to kindly mind my own business. But any rancor I might have felt at this disappeared when he made me clerk of the court, and Stanley tax collector, each at a salary of sixty dollars a month, with David "Native Adviser and Official Interpreter" at the same figure.

This was the beginning of the new government, with everything old done away with, and the first official sign of it was a brand-new, white-painted flagpole with crosstrees and ratlines in front of the fine big house that was next built for the Commissioner to live in. The natives had to do this for nothing, supplying forty men, turn and turn about, though the galvanized iron, hardware, paint, varnish and whatnot were bought of Stanley and me, and paid for in taxes. It was a very fine place when done, with a broad veranda in front and an inner court behind, where Mr. Clemm used to lie in a striped hammock, waited on hand and foot.

But I fancy the wicked French couldn't have taxed the Kanakas any harder than Mr. Clemm did, which was the best thing in the world for them, considering how slack they were by nature and not given to doing anything they could help. It only needed a little attention to double the copra crop of the island, not to speak of shell—so that the taxes were a blessing in disguise, the natives being better off than they had ever been before. Of course they didn't like it and put up a great deal of opposition till Mr. Clemm raised a Native Constabulary of seven men, commanded by Peter Jones, and all of them armed any way he could, including Stanley's shotgun and my Winchester repeater, old man Fosby's Enfield and several rusty Springfields pounced on here and there as against the law to own them.

They were tricked out very smart in red lava-lavas and white drill coats, and being all of them of the obstreperous, no-good class like Peter, they were soon the terror of the island. Not that Mr. Clemm didn't keep them tight in hand, but when it came to an order of court or any backwardness in taxes he never seemed to care much whom they plundered and beat, which was what they reveled in and thirsted for the chance of.

Old David was the first to feel the weight of authority, and I believe his job of Native Adviser was merely a plan to keep him in good humor till Mr. Clemm was ready to squash him, which Mr. Clemm did three months later most emphatic. The Kanakas were forbidden to contribute to the church, and the pastor's private laws were abolished, and there was no more excommunicating nor jail for church members nor any curfew either. The natives went wild with joy—all except a few old soreheads that are always to be found in every community—and the only folks who were now forced to go to church were the Native Constabulary, who lined up regular to keep tab on what the missionary preached, and arrest him for sedition in case he let his tongue run away with him.

In private, however, old David made all the trouble he dared, and tried to hearten up his followers by saying there would be a day of reckoning for Mr. Clemm when the missionary vessel arrived on her annual visit—at which the Commissioner pretended to laugh but couldn't hide he was worried. Leastways he asked a raft of questions about the "Evangel of Hope," and that with a ruminating look, and about the character of the people in charge, which were Captain Bins and the Reverend T. J. Simpkins. The "Evangel of Hope" never stayed any longer than to land a few stores and hymnbooks for the pastor and take off what copra and shell he had acquired by way of church subscriptions. At that time she was about due in two months, and we all laughed at the empty larder she was going to find; though, as I said, Mr. Clemm seemed worried, remarking it was hard to be misrepresented and slandered when his only thought was for the good of the island.

He was certainly upsetting things very lively and bossed the island like it belonged to him. If the natives could play all they wanted, now that David was deposed, they had bumped into something they had never known before and that was—work. The Commissioner couldn't abide laziness in a Kanaka, and went at them terrific, building a fine road around the island and another across it, with bridges and culverts, where he used to ride of a sundown in a buggy he had bought off Captain Sachs of the "H. L. Tiernan," with men tugging him instead of horses, and the Native Constabulary trotting along in the rear like a royal progress.

He built a fine-appearing wharf, too, and an improved jail with a cement floor, and heaven help anybody who threw fish guts on the shore or didn't keep his land as clean as a new pin. There was a public well made in the middle of the settlement, with cement steps and a white-painted fence to keep away the pigs, and the natives, though they hated to work, were proud, too, of what they had done, and I doubt if they had ever been so prosperous or freer of sickness. I know Stanley and I doubled our trade, in spite of having to take out heavy licenses, which meant that not only we, but everybody else, were that much better off. Petty thieving disappeared entirely, and likewise all violence, and one of the Commissioner's best reforms was a land court where titles were established and boundaries marked out, that stopping the only thing the Kanakas ever seriously quarreled about. Six months of the Commissioner had revolutionized the island, and few would have cared to go back to the old, loose days when your only Supreme Court was the rifle hanging on your wall.

Well, it grew nearer and nearer for the "Evangel of Hope" to arrive, and Mr. Clemm he began to do a most extraordinary thing, which was nothing else than a large cemetery! Yes, sir, that's what Mr. Clemm did, tearing down five or six houses for the purpose on the lagoon side, nigh the wharf, and planting rows on rows of white headstones, with low mounds at each, representing graves. There must have been a couple of hundred of them, and often it was a whitewashed cross instead of a stone or maybe a pointed stake —the whole giving the impression of a calamity that had suddenly overtaken us.

It was no good asking him what it was for; the Commissioner wasn't a man to be questioned when he didn't want to be; all he said was that Stanley and I were to stick inside our stores when the ship came and not budge an inch till we were told. With us orders were orders, but the Kanakas were panicky with terror, and that cemetery with nobody in it seemed to them like tempting Providence. It took all of Mr. Clemm's authority to keep them quiet, and it got out that the Commissioner was expecting the end of the world, and the graves were for those that wouldn't go to heaven! Kanakas are like that, you know—spreading the silliest rumors and making a lot out of nothing—though in this case they couldn't be blamed for being considerable scared. But Mr. Clemm knew how to turn everything to account, and on the principle that the church was the safest place to be found in on the Day of Judgment, ordered that everybody should go there the moment he fired three pistol shots from his veranda. I noticed, however, that the Native Constabulary seemed to be taking the end of the world mighty calm, which looked like they had been tipped off ahead for something quite different.

But the meaning of the cemetery appeared later when one morning, along of ten or so, my little boy came running in to say the "Evangel" was sighted in the pass. Of course, I stuck indoors, mindful of instructions, though that didn't prevent me from looking out of my upper window and taking in all that happened. The first was a tremendous yellow flag raised on the Commissioner's staff, and the second were those three pistol shots which were to announce the Day of Judgment. Then you ought to have seen the settlement scoot! There was a rush for the church like the animals at the Ark, though old David, the pastor, wasn't any Noah. Him and the deacons were led down to the jail and locked in, and then Peter Jones and his constables divided into two parties—three of them returning to the church, while the other three with Peter got a boat ready, with another yellow flag in the stern.

By this time the missionary vessel was well up under a spanking spread of canvas, with the water hissing at her bows and parting white and sparkling in a way dandy to watch. You could almost feel her shiver at the sight of Peter's yellow flag rowing towards her, and through the glass I noticed a big commotion aboard, with half a dozen racing up the rigging and making signs at those below. It was plainer than words that they had seen the cemetery and were struck of a heap, which was no wonder considering how new and calamitous it looked, with them rows on rows of neat little headstones and nicely mounded graves.

She never even dropped her anchor nor lowered her gangway, but hove to, short; and when Peter came up he was made to lay on his oars and keep his distance, yelling what he had to say with both hands at his face while the captain he yelled back with a speaking trumpet. Of course I didn't hear a word, but it was easy enough to put two and two together, remembering the sea meaning of a yellow flag, which is seldom else than smallpox. Yes, that was why we had all took and died in the new cemetery, and that was why the settlement looked so lifeless and deserted! After no end of a powwow they hoisted out a boat, and when it was loaded to the gunwales with stores and cases, it was cast off for Peter to pick up and take in tow. It held half a ton of medical comforts, and I often had the pleasure of drinking some of them afterwards on Mr. Clemm's veranda, where we all agreed it was prime stuff and exactly suited to our complaints.

What old David thought of it all through the bars of the coral jail can only be left to the imagination. He had been banking on the "Evangel" to turn the scales against Mr. Clemm, and there she was heading out of the lagoon again, not to return for another year! We celebrated it that night with medical comforts unstinted, while the natives they celebrated, too, thankful to find the world still here and the Day of Judgment postponed. Old David wrote a red-hot protest, countersigned by the deacons, and not knowing what else to do with it, sealed it in a demijohn and threw it into the sea, where like enough it still is, bobbing around undelivered to the missionary society and still waiting for the angels to take charge of it.

Mr. Clemm's next move was to start building a small cutter of twenty tons, which he named the "Felicity" and charged to the government as an official yacht. Old man Fosby had been a shipwright in years gone by, and under his direction the

Kanakas made a mighty fine job of the little vessel, which was fitted up regardless and proved to be remarkably fast and weatherly. She was the apple of the Commissioner's eye, with a crew of four in uniform, and a half-caste Chinaman named Henry for captain, whom he had persuaded to desert from a German schooner where he was mate. Mr. Clemm was so fond of taking short cruises in the "Felicity" that we never gave his coming and going much thought, till one day he went off and never came back! Yes, sir; clean disappeared over the horizon and was never seen again from that day to this, nor the party with him, which included several very fine-looking young women!

The natives took it like the loss of a father, which indeed it was, Mr. Clemm being a grand man and universally beloved—kindly yet strict, and always the soul of justice. After giving him up altogether for lost, we put seals on his private effects, and Peter Jones took charge of the government, advised by Stanley and me. It showed the splendid influence Mr. Clemm had had that Peter had become quite a model, and instead of breaking loose was all on the side of law and order. Our idea was to hold the fort until a new Commissioner might be sent, and the only slight change we made was to double our salaries. The natives had grown so used to civilized government that they made no trouble, and we three might have been governing the island yet if a man-of-war hadn't suddenly popped in.

It was the "Ringarooma," the selfsame ship that had landed Mr. Clemm some eighteen months before, and Stanley and I were the first to board her, meeting the captain at the break of the poop, just when he had come down from the bridge.

"I have the honor to report the disappearance of Deputy Commissioner James Howard Fitzroy Clemm," said I. "He sailed from here on March sixteenth in the government yacht 'Felicity,' and has never been seen nor heard from since."

The captain, who was a sharp, curt man, looked puzzled.

"I don't know what you're talking about," he said, as abrupt as a thunderbolt.

"Why, sir, you landed him yourself," said Stanley, "and the

same day he took possession of the island and hoisted the British flag."

"Annexed us," said I.

The captain frowned very angry, like if we were making sport of him we should fast rue it.

"I never landed anybody here but a fellow named Baker," he said. "I deported him from the Ellice Islands for sedition, bigamy, selling gin to the natives, suspected arson, and receiving stolen goods. If he called himself a deputy commissioner he was a rank impostor, and had no more authority to annex this island than you have."

Months afterwards we learned that instead of being lost in the "Felicity" like we all had thought, Clemm had turned pirate in a small way down to the westward till the natives took and ate him at Guadalcanal.

Charles Warren Stoddard

A PRODIGAL IN TAHITI

Charles Warren Stoddard (1843–1909) began his literary career in the 1860's as one of the San Francisco group of writers that included Bret Harte, Mark Twain, and Ambrose Bierce. In 1870, after two visits to Hawaii, where he fell in love with island life, he sailed on a French naval transport to Tahiti. His experiences of several months there, in penniless vagabondage, provided the material for "A Prodigal in Tahiti," one of the stories in his best-known book, *South-Sea Idyls* (1873).

Twenty years after accepting "A Prodigal in Tahiti" for the *Atlantic Monthly,* where it first appeared, William Dean Howells wrote to Stoddard, saying, "I think, now, that there are few such delicious bits of literature in the language"; and later Howells included it in his anthology, *The Great Modern American Short Stories* (1920).

LET THIS CONFESSION BE TOPPED WITH A VIGNETTE DONE IN broad, shadowless lines and few of them—something like this:

A little, flyblown room, smelling of garlic; I cooling my elbows on the oily slab of a table (breakfast for one), and looking through a window at a glaring, whitewashed fence high enough to shut out the universe from my point of sight. Yet it hid not all, since it brought into relief a panting cock (with one leg in a string), which had so strained to compress itself into a doubtful inch of shade that its suspended claw clutched the air in real agony.

Having dazzled my eyes with this prospect, I turned gratefully to the vanities of life that may be had for two francs in Tahiti. *Vide* bill of fare: one fried egg, like the eye of some gigantic albino; potatoes hollowed out bombshell fashion, primed with liver sausage, very ingenious and palatable; the naked corpse of a fowl that cared not to live longer, from appearances, yet looked not happy in death.

Item: Wonder if there *is* a more ghastly spectacle than a chicken cooked in the French style; its knees dawn up on its breast like an Indian mummy, while its blue-black, parboiled, and melancholy visage tearfully surveys its own unshrouded remains. After a brief season of meditation I said, and I trust I meant it, "I thank the Lord for all these blessings." Then I gave the corpse of the chicken Christian burial under a fold of the window curtain, disposed of the fried eye of the albino, and transformed myself into a mortar for the time being, taking potato-bombshells according to my caliber.

There was claret all the while and plenty of butterless roll, a shaving of cheese, a banana, black coffee, and cognac, when I turned again to dazzle myself with the white fence, and saw with infinite pity—a sentiment perhaps not unmixed with a suspicion of cognac or some other temporary humanizing element—I saw for a fact that the poor cock had wilted, and lay flat in the sun like a last year's duster. That was too much for me. I wheeled toward the door where gleamed the bay with its lovely ridges of light; canoes drifting over it drew the eye after them irresistibly; I heard the ship calkers on the beach making their monotonous clatter, and the drone of the bareheaded fruit sellers squatted in rows, chatting indolently, with their eyes half shut. I could think of nothing but bees humming over their own sweet wares.

About this time a young fellow at the next table, who had scarcely a mouthful of English at his command, implored me to take beer with him; implying that we might, if desirable, become as tight as two bricks. I declined, much to his admiration, he regarding my refusal as a clear case of moral courage, whereas it arose simply and solely from my utter inability to see his treat and go him one better.

A grown person in Tahiti has an eating hour allotted to him twice a day, at 10 A.M. and 5 P.M. My time being up, I returned to the store in an indifferent frame of mind, and upon entering the presence of my employer, who had arrived a moment before me, I was immediately covered with the deep humiliation of servitude and withdrew to an obscure corner; while Monsieur and some naval guests took absinthe unblushingly, which was, of course, proper enough in them. Call it by what name you will, you cannot sweeten servility to my taste. Then why was I there and in bondage? The spirit of adventure that keeps life in us, yet comes near to worrying it out of us now and then, lured me with my handful of dollars to the Garden of the Pacific. "You can easily get work," said someone who had been there and didn't want it. If work I must, why not better there than here? thought I; and the less money I take with me the surer am I to seek that which might not attract me under other circumstances. A few letters that proved almost valueless; an abiding trust in Providence, afterward somewhat shaken, I am sorry to state, which convinces me that I can no longer hope to travel as a shorn lamb; considerable confidence in the good feeling of my fellow men, together with the few dollars above referred to—comprised my all when I set foot on the leaf-strewn and shady beach of Papeete.

Before the day was over I saw my case was almost hopeless; I was one too many in a very meager congregation of foreigners. In a week I was desperate, with poverty and disgrace brooding like evil spirits on either hand. Every ten minutes someone suggested something that was almost immediately suppressed by the next man I met, to whom I applied for further information. Teach, said one: there wasn't a pupil to be had in the dominion. Clerkships were out of the question likewise. I might keep store, if I could get anything to put in it; or go farther, as someone suggested, if I had money enough to get there. I thought it wiser to endure the ills I had than fly to others that I knew not of. In this state I perambulated the green lanes of Papeete, conscious that I was drawing down tons of immaterial sympathy from hearts of various nationalities, beating to the music of regular salaries in hard cash, and the inevitable ringing of their daily dinner bell; and I continued to perambulate under the same depressing avalanches for a fortnight or more—a warning to the generation of the inexperienced that persists in sowing itself broadcast upon the edges of the earth, and learns too late how hard a thing it is to take root under the circumstances.

One gloomy day I was seized in the market place and led before a French gentleman who offered me a bed and board for such manual compensation as I might be able to give him in his office during the usual business hours, namely, from daybreak to some time in the afternoon, unless it rained, when business was suspended, and I was dropped until fair weather should set that little world wagging again.

I was invited to enter into the bosom of his family, in fact, to be *one* of them, and no single man could ask to be more; to sit at his table and hope for better days, in which diversion he proposed to join me with all his soul.

With an emotion of gratitude and a pang at being thus early a subject of charity, I began business in Papeete and learned within the hour how sharper than most sharps it is to know only your own mother tongue when you're away from home.

Nightly I walked two hot and dusty miles through groves of breadfruit and colonnades of palms to my new master's. I skirted, with loitering steps, a placid sea whose crystalline depths sheltered leagues and leagues of sun-painted corals, where a myriad fish, dyed like the rainbow, sported unceasingly. Springs gushed from the mountain, singing their song of joy; the winds sang in the dark locks of the sycamore, while the palm boughs clashed like cymbals in rhythmical accompaniment; glad children chanted their choruses, and I alone couldn't sing, nor hum, nor whistle, because it doesn't pay to work for your board, and settle for little necessities out of your own pocket, in any latitude that I ever heard of.

We lived in a grove of ten thousand coco palms crowning a hill slope to the west. How all-sufficient it sounds as I write it now, but how little I cared then, for many reasons! My cottage had prior tenants, who disputed possession with me—winged tenants who sought admission at every cranny and frequently obtained it in spite of me; these were not angels, but hens. My cottage had been a granary until it got too poor a receptacle for grains, and a better shelter left it open to the barn fowls until I arrived. They hated me, these hungry chickens; they used to sit in rows on the window sill and stare me out of countenance. A wide bedstead, corded with thongs, did its best to furnish my apartment. A narrow, a very narrow and thin ship's mattress, that had been a bed of torture for many a seasick soul before it descended to me; a flat pillow like a pancake; a condemned horse blanket contributed by a good-natured Kanack who raked it from a heap of refuse in the yard, together with two sacks of rice, the despair of those hens in the window, were all I could boast of. With this inventory I strove (by particular request) to be one of those who were comfortable enough in the château adjoining. Summoned peremptorily to dinner, I entered a little latticed *salon,* connected with the château by a covered walk, discovered Monsieur seated at table and already served with soup and claret; the remainder of the company helped themselves as they best could; and I saw plainly enough that the family bosom was so crowded already, that I might seek in vain to wedge myself into any corner of it, at least until some vacancy occurred.

After dinner, sat on a sack of rice in my room, while it grew dark and Monsieur received calls; wandered down to the beach at the foot of the hill and lay a long time on a bed of leaves, while the tide was out and the crabs clattered along shore and were very sociable. Natives began to kindle their evening fires of coconut husks; smoke, sweet as incense, climbed up to the plumes of the palm trees and was lost among the stars. Morsels of fish and breadfruit were offered me by the untutored savage, who welcomed me to his frugal meal and desired that I should at least taste before he broke his fast. Canoes shot out from dense, shadowy points, fishers standing in the bows with a poised spear in one hand; a blazing palm branch held aloft in the other shed a warm glow of light over their superb nakedness. Bathed by the sea, in a fresh, cool spring, and returned to my little coop, which was illuminated by the glare of fifty floating beacons; looking back from the door I could see the dark outlines of the torchbearers and hear their signal calls above the low growl of the reef a half-mile farther out from shore. It was a blessing to lie awake in my little room and watch the flicker of those fires; to think how Tahiti must look on a cloudless night from some heavenly altitude—the ocean still as death, the procession of fishermen sweeping from point to point within the reef, till the island, flooded with starlight and torchlight, lies like a green sea-garden in a girdle of flame.

A shrill bell called me from my bed at dawn. I was not unwilling to rise, for half the night I lay like a saint on the tough thongs, having turned over in sleep, thereby missing the mattress entirely. Made my toilet at a spring on the way into town; saw a glorious sunrise that was as good as breakfast, and found the whole earth and sea and all that in them is singing again while I listened and gave thanks for that privilege. At 10 A.M. I went to breakfast in the small restaurant where I have sketched myself at the top of this chronicle, and whither we may return and begin over again if it please you.

I was about to remark that probably most melancholy and homesickness may be cured or alleviated by a wholesome meal of victuals; but I think I won't, for, on referring to my notebook, I find that within an hour after my return to the store I was as heartsick as ever and wasn't afraid to say so. It is scarcely to be wondered at: the sky was dark; aboard a schooner some sailors were making that doleful whine peculiar to them, as they hauled in to shore and tied up to a tree in a sifting rain; then everything was ominously still, as though something disagreeable were about to happen; thereupon I doubled myself over the counter like a half-shut jackknife, and burying my face in my hands, said to myself, "Oh, to be alone with Nature! her silence is religion and her sounds sweet music." After which the rain blew over, and I was sent with a handcart and one underfed Kanack to a wharf half a mile away to drag back several loads of potatoes. We two hungry creatures struggled heroically to do our duty. Starting with a multitude of sacks it was quite impossible to proceed with, we grew weaker the farther we went, so that the load had to be reduced from time to time, and I believe the amount of potatoes deposited by the way considerably exceeded the amount we subsequently arrived at the store with.

Finding life a burden, and seeing the legs of the young fellow in harness with me bend under him in his frantic efforts to get our cart out of a rut without emptying it entirely, I resolved to hire a substitute at my own expense, and save my remaining strength for a new line of business. Thus I was enabled to sit on the wharf the rest of the afternoon and enjoy myself devising new means of subsistence and watching the natives swim.

Someone before me found a modicum of sweets in his cup of bitterness, and in a complacent hour set the good against the evil in single entry, summing up the same to his advantage. I concluded to do it myself, and did it, thus:

Evil.	Good.
I find myself in a foreign land with no one to love and none to love me.	But I may do as I please in consequence, and it is nobody's business save my own.
I am working for my board and lodging (no extras), and find it very unprofitable.	But I may quit as soon as I feel like it, and shall have no occasion to dun my employer for back salary so long as I stop with him.
My clothes are in rags. I shall soon be without a stitch to my back.	But the weather is mild and the fig tree flourisheth. Moreover, many a good savage has gone naked before me.
I get hungry before breakfast and feel faint after dinner. What are two meals a day to a man of my appetite?	But fasting is saintly. Day by day I grow more spiritual, and shall shortly be a fit subject for translation to that better world which is doubtless the envy of all those who have lost it by overeating and drinking.

Nothing can exceed the satisfaction with which I read and reread this philosophical summary, but I had relapses every few minutes so long as I lived in Tahiti. I remember one Sunday morning, a day I had all to myself, when I cried out of the depths and felt better after it. It was a real Sunday. The fowls confessed it by the indifference with which they picked up a grain of rice now and then, as though they weren't hungry. The family were moving about in an unnatural way; some people are never themselves on the Lord's day. The canoes lay asleep off upon the water, evidently conscious of the long hours of rest they were sure of having. To sum it all, it seemed as though the cover had been taken off from the earth, and the angels were sitting in big circles looking at us. Our clock had run down, and I found myself half an hour too early at Mass. Some diminutive native children talked together with infinite gesticulation, like little old men. At every lag in the conversation, two or three of them would steal away to the fence that surrounded the church and begin diligently counting the pickets thereof. They were evidently amazed at what they considered a singular coincidence, namely, that the number of pickets, beginning at the front gate and counting to the right, tallied exactly with the do. do. beginning at the do. do. and counting to the left; while they were making repeated efforts to get at the heart of this mystery, the priest rode up on horseback, dismounted in our midst, and we all followed him into chapel to Mass.

A young Frenchman offered me holy water on the tips of his fingers, and I immediately decided to confide in him to an unlimited extent if he gave me the opportunity. It was a serious disappointment when I found, later, that we didn't know six words in any common tongue. Concluded to be independent and walked off by myself. Got very lonesome immediately. Tried to be meditative, philosophical, botanical, conchological, and in less than an hour gave it up—homesick again, by Jove!

Strolled to the beach and sat a long time on a bit of wreck partly embedded in the sand; consoled by the surpassing radiance of sunset, wondered how I could ever have repined, but proceeded to do it again as soon as it grew dark. Some natives drew near, greeting me kindly. They were evidently lovers; talked in low tones, deeply interested in the most trivial things, such as a leaf falling into the sea at our feet and floating stem up, like a bowsprit; he probably made some poetic allusion to it, may have proposed braving the seas with her in a shallop as fairylike, for both fell adreaming and were silent for some time, he worshiping her with fascinated eyes, while she, womanlike, pretended to be all unconscious of his admiration.

Silently we sat looking over the sea at Mooréa, just visible in the light of the young moon, like a spirit brooding upon the waters—till I broke the spell by saying "Good night," which was repeated in a chorus as I withdrew to my coop and found my feathered guests had beaten in the temporary barricade erected in the broken window, entered, and made themselves at home during my absence—a fact that scarcely endeared the spot to me. Next morning I was unusually merry; couldn't tell why, but tried to sing as I made my toilet at the spring; laughed nearly all the way into town, saying my prayers, and blessing God, when I came suddenly upon a horseshoe in the middle of the road. Took it as an omen and a keepsake; horseshoes aren't shed everywhere nor for everybody. I thought it the prophecy of a change, and at once canceled my engagement with my employer without having set foot into his house farther than the dining room, or made any apparent impression upon the adamantine bosom of his family.

After formally expressing my gratitude to Monsieur for his renewed offers of hospitality, I turned myself into the street, and was once more adrift in the world. For the space of three minutes I was wild with joy at the thought of my perfect liberty. Then I grew nervous, began to feel unhappy, nay, even guilty, as though I had thrown up a good thing. Concluded it was rash of me to leave a situation where I got two meals and a mattress, with the privilege of washing at my own expense. Am not sure that it wasn't unwise, for I had no dinner that afternoon; and having no bed either, I crept into the veranda of a house to let and dozed till daybreak.

There was but one thing to live for now, namely, to see as much of Tahiti as possible, and at my earliest convenience return like the prodigal son to that father who would doubtless feel like killing something appropriate as soon as he saw me coming. I said as much to a couple of Frenchmen, brothers, who are living a dream life over yonder, and whose wildest species of dissipation for the last seven years has been to rise at intervals from their settees in the arbor, go deliberately to the farther end of the garden, and eat several mangoes in cold blood.

To comprehend Tahiti, a man must lose himself in forests whose resinous boughs are knotted with ribbons of sea grass; there, overcome by the music of sibilant waters sifting through the antlers of the coral, he is supposed to sink upon drifts of orange blossoms, only to be resuscitated by the spray of an approaching shower crashing through the green solitudes like an army with chariots—so those brothers said, with a mango poised in each hand; and they added that I should have an official document addressed to the best blood in the kingdom, namely, Forty Chiefs of Tahiti, who would undoubtedly entertain me with true barbarian hospitality, better the world knows not. There was a delay for some reason; I, rather impatient, and scarcely hoping to receive so graceful a compliment from headquarters, trudged on alone with a light purse and an infinitesimal bundle of necessities, caring nothing for the weather nor the number of miles cleared per day, since I laid no plans save the one, to see as much as I might with the best grace possible, keeping an eye on the road for horseshoes. Through leagues of verdure I wandered, feasting my five senses and finding life a holiday at last. There were numberless streams to be crossed, where I loafed for hours on the bridges, satisfying myself with sunshine. Not a savage in the land was freer than I. No man could say to me, "Why stand ye here idle?" for I could continue to stand as long as I liked and as idly as it pleased me in spite of him! There were bridgeless streams to be forded; but the Tahitian is a nomad continually wandering from one edge of his fruitful world to the other; moreover, he is the soul of peace toward men of good will; I was invariably picked up by some bare-backed Hercules, who volunteered to take me over the water on his brawny brown shoulders, and could have easily taken two like me. It was good to be up there while he strode through the swift current, for I felt that he was perfectly able to carry me to the ends of the earth without stopping, and that sense of reliance helped to reassure my faith in humanity.

As I wandered, from most native houses came the invitation to enter and eat. Night after night I found my bed in the corner of some dwelling whither I had been led by the master of it, with unaffected grace. It wasn't simply showing me to a spare room, but rather unrolling the best mat and turning everything to my account so long as it pleased me to tarry. Sometimes the sea talked in its sleep not a rod from the house; frequently the mosquitoes accepted me as a delicacy and did their best to dispose of me. Once I awoke with a headache, the air was so dense with the odor of orange blossoms.

There was frequently a strip of blue bay that ebbed and flowed languidly and had to be lunched with; or a very deep and melodious spring, asking for an interview, and, I may add, always getting it. I remember one miniature castle built in the midst of a grassy Venice by the shore. Its moats, shining with goldfish, were spanned with slender bridges; toy fences of bamboo enclosed the rarer clumps of foliage; and there was such an air of tranquillity pervading it I thought I must belong there. Something seemed to say, "Come in." I went in, but left very soon; the place was so fairylike, I felt as though I were liable to step through it and come out on some other side, and I wasn't anxious for such a change.

I ate when I got hungry a very good sort of a meal, consisting usually of a tiny piglet cooked in the native fashion, swathed in succulent leaves and laid between hot stones till ready for eating; breadfruit, like mashed potato, but a great deal better; orange tea and coco milk—surely enough for two or three francs. Took a sleep whenever sleep came along, resting always till the clouds or a shadow from the mountain covered me so as to keep cool and comfortable. Natives passed me with salutations. A white man now and then went by barely nodding, or more frequently eying me with suspicion and giving me as much of his dust as he found convenient. In the wider fellowship of nature I forswore all blood relations and blushed for those representatives of my own color as I footed it right royally. Therefore I was enabled to scorn the fellow who scorned me while he flashed the steel hoofs of his charger in my face and dashed on to the village we were both approaching with the dusk.

What a spot it was! A long lane as green as a spring meadow, lying between wall-like masses of foliage whose deep arcades were frescoed with blossoms and festooned with vines. It seemed a pathway leading to infinity, for the blood-red bars of sunset glared at its farther end as though Providence had placed them there to keep out the unregenerated. Not a house visible all this time, nor a human, though I was in the heart of the hamlet. Passing up the turf-cushioned road I beheld on either hand, through a screen of leaves, a log spanning a rivulet that was softly singing its monody; at the end of each log the summerhouse of some Tahitian, who sat in his door smoking complacently. It was a picture of still life with a suggestion of possible motion; a village to put into a greenhouse, water, and keep fresh forever. Let me picture it once more—one mossy street between two babbling brooks, and every house thereof set each in its own moated wilderness. This was Papeali.

Like rows of cages full of chirping birds, those bamboo huts were distributed up and down the street. As I walked I knew something would cause me to turn at the right time and find a new friend ready to receive me, for it always does. So I walked slowly and without hesitation or impatience until I turned and met him coming out of his cage, crossing the rill by his log and holding out his hand to me in welcome. Back we went together, and I ate and slept there as though it had been arranged a thousand years ago; perhaps it was! There was racket up at the farther end of the lane, by the chief's house; songs and nose-flutings upon the night air; moreover, a bonfire, and doubtless much nectar—too much, as usual, for I heard such cheers as the soul gives when it is careless of consequences, and caught a glimpse of the joys of barbarism such as even we poor Christians cannot wholly withstand, but turning our backs think we are safe enough. Commend me to him who has known temptation and not shunned it, but actually withstood it!

It was the dance, as ever it is the dance where all the aspirations of the soul find expression in the body; those bodies that are incarnate souls or those that are spiritualized bodies, inseparable, whatever they are, for the time being. The fire glowed fervently; bananas hung out their tattered banners like decorations; palms rustled their silver plumes aloft in the moonlight; the sea panted upon its sandy bed in heavy sleep; the night-blooming cereus opened its waxen chambers and gave forth its treasured sweets. Circle after circle of swart savage faces were turned upon the flame-lit arena where the dancers posed for a moment with their light drapery gathered about them and held carelessly in one hand. Anon the music chimed forth—a reiteration of chords caught from the birds' treble and the wind's bass; full and resounding syllables, richly poetical, telling of orgies and of the mysteries of the forbidden revels in the charmed valleys of the gods, hearing which it were impossible not to be wrought to madness; and the dancers thereat went mad, dancing with infinite gesticulation, dancing to whirlwinds of applause till the undulation of their bodies was serpentine, and at last in frenzy they shrieked with joy, threw off their garments, and were naked as the moon. So much for a vision that kept me awake till morning; when I plodded on in the damp grass and tried to forget it, but couldn't exactly, and never have to this hour. Went on and on over more bridges spanning still-flowing streams of silver, past springs that lay like great crystals framed in moss under dripping, fern-clad cliffs that the sun never reaches. Came at last to a shining, whitewashed fort, on an eminence that commands the isthmus connecting the two hemispheres of Tahiti, where down I dropped into a narrow valley full of wind and discord and a kind of dreary neglect that made me sick for any other place. More refreshment for the wayfarer, but to be paid for by the dish, and therefore limited. Was obliged to hate a noisy fellow with too much bushy black beard and a freckled nose, and to like another who eyed me kindly over his absinthe, having first mixed a glass for me. A native asked me where I was going; being unable to give any satisfactory answer, he conducted me to his canoe, about a mile distant, where he cut a sapling for a mast, another for a gaff, twisted, in a few moments, a cord of its fibrous bark, rigged a sail of his sleeping blanket, and we were shortly wafted onward before a light breeze between the reef and shore.

Three of us, with a bull pup in the bows, dozed under the afternoon sun. He of the paddle awoke now and then to shift sail, beat the sea impetuously for a few seconds, and fall asleep again. Voices roused me occasionally, greetings from colonies of indolent Kanacks on shore, whose business it was to sit there till they got hungry, laughing weariness to scorn.

Close upon our larboard bow lay one of the islands that had bewitched me as I paced the shore but a few days previous; under us the measureless gardens of the sea unmasked a myriad imperishable blossoms, centuries old some of them, but as fair and fresh as though born within the hour. All that afternoon we drifted between sea and shore, and beached at sunset in a new land. Footsore and weary, I approached a stable from which thrice a week stages were dispatched to Papeete.

A modern pilgrim finds his scrip cumbersome, if he has any, and deems it more profitable to pay his coachman than his cobbler.

I climbed to my seat by the jolly French driver, who was continually chatting with three merry nuns sitting just back of us, returning to the convent in Papeete after a vacation retreat among the hills. How they enjoyed the ride, as three children might! and were quite wild with delight at meeting a corpulent *père,* who smiled amiably from his saddle and offered to show them the interior of the pretty chapel at Faaa (only three *a*'s in that word)—the very one I grew melancholy in when I was a man of business.

So they hurled themselves madly from the high seat, one after the other, scorning to touch anything so contaminating as a man's hand, though it looked suicidal, as the driver and I agreed while the three were at prayers by the altar. Whipping up over the road townward, I could almost recognize my own footprints left since the time I used to take the dust in my face three mornings a week from the wheels of that very vehicle as I footed it in to business. Passing the spring, my toilet of other days, drawing to the edge of the town, we stopped being jolly and were as proper as befitted travelers. We looked over the wall of the convent garden as we drove up to the gate, and saw the mother superior hurrying down to us with a cumbersome chair for the relief of the nuns, but before she reached us they had cast themselves to earth again in the face of destiny, and there was kissing, crying, and commotion as they withdrew under the gateway like so many doves seeking shelter. When the gate closed after them, I heard them all cooing at once, but the world knows nothing further.

Where would I be dropped? asked the driver. In the middle of the street, please you, and take half my little whole for your ride, sir! He took it, dropped me where we stood, and drove away, I pretending to be very much at my ease. God help me and all poor hypocrites!

I sought a place of shelter, or rather retirement, for the air is balm in that country. There was an old house in the middle of a grassy lawn on a bystreet; two of its rooms were furnished with a few papers and books, and certain gentlemen who contribute to its support lounge in when they have leisure for reading or a chat. I grew to know the place familiarly. I stole a night's lodging on its veranda in the shadow of a passion vine; but, for fear of embarrassing some early student in pursuit of knowledge, I passed the second night on the floor of the dilapidated cookhouse, where the ants covered me. I endured the tortures of one who bares his body to an unceasing shower of sparks; but I survived.

There was, in this very cookhouse, a sink six feet in length and as wide as a coffin; the third night I lay like a galvanized corpse with his lid off till a rat sought to devour me, when I took to the streets and walked till morning. By this time the president of the club, whose acquaintance I had the honor of, tendered me the free use of any portion of the premises that might not be otherwise engaged. With a gleam of hope I began my explorations. Up a narrow and winding stair I found a spacious loft. It was like a mammoth tent, a solitary center pole its only ornament. Creeping into it on all fours, I found a fragment of matting, a dry crust, an empty soda bottle—footprints on the sands of time.

"Poor soul!" I gasped; "where did *you* come from? What *did* you come for? Whither, oh, whither, have you flown?"

I might have added, how did you manage to get there? But

the present was so important a consideration, I had no heart to look beyond it. The next ten nights I passed in the silent and airy apartment of my anonymous predecessor. Ten nights I crossed the unswept floor that threatened at every step to precipitate me into the reading room below. With a faint heart and hollow stomach I threw myself upon my elbow and strove to sleep. I lay till my heart stopped beating, my joints were wooden, and my four limbs corky beyond all hope of reanimation. There the mosquito reveled, and it was a promising place for centipedes.

At either end of the building an open window admitted the tip of a banana leaf; up their green ribs the sprightly mouse careered. I broke the backbones of these banana leaves, though they were the joy of my soul and would have adorned the choicest conservatory in the land. Day was equally unprofitable to me. My best friends said, "Why not return to California?" Everyone I met invited me to leave the country at my earliest convenience. The American consul secured me a passage, to be settled for at home, and my career in that latitude was evidently at an end. In my superfluous confidence in humanity I had announced myself as a correspondent for the press. It was quite necessary that I should give some plausible reason for making my appearance in Tahiti friendless and poor. Therefore, I said plainly, "I am a correspondent, friendless and poor," believing that anyone would see truth in the face of it, with half an eye. "Prove it," said one who knew more of the world than I. Then flashed upon me the alarming fact that I couldn't prove it, having nothing whatever in my possession referring to it in the slightest degree. It was a fatal mistake that might easily have been avoided, but was too well established to be rectified.

In my chagrin I looked to the good old bishop for consolation. Approaching the Mission House through sunlit cloisters of palms, I was greeted most tenderly. I would have gladly taken any amount of holy orders for the privilege of ending my troublous days in the sweet seclusion of the Mission House.

As it was, I received a blessing, an autograph, and a "Godspeed" to some other part of creation. Added to this I learned how the address to the Forty Chiefs of Tahiti in behalf of the foreign traveler, my poor self, had been dispatched to me by a special courier, who found me not; and doubtless the fetes I heard of and was forever missing marked the march of that messenger, my proxy, in his triumphal progress.

In my innocent degradation it was still necessary to nourish the inner man. There is a market in Papeete where, under one broad roof, three-score hucksters of both sexes congregate long before daylight, and, while a few candles illumine their wares, patiently await custom. A half-dozen coolies with an eye to business serve hot coffee and chocolate at a dime per cup to any who choose to ask for it. By 7 A.M. the market is so nearly sold out that only the more plentiful fruits of the country are to be obtained at any price. A prodigal cannot long survive on husks, unless he have coffee to wash them down. I took my cup of it, with two spoonfuls of sugar and ants dipped out of a cigar box, and a crust of bread into the bargain, sitting on a bench in the market place, with a coolie and a Kanack on either hand.

It was not the coffee nor the sugared ants that I gave my dime for, but rather the privilege of sitting in the midst of men and women who were willing to accept me as a friend and helpmate without questioning my ancestry, and any one of whom would go me halves in the most disinterested manner. Then there was sure to be some superb fellow close at hand, with a sensuous lip curled under his nostril, a glimpse of which gave me a dime's worth of satisfaction and more, too. Having secreted a French roll (five cents) all hot, under my coat, and gathered the bananas that would fall in the yard so seasonably, I made my day as brief and comfortable as possible by filling up with water from time to time.

The man who has passed a grimy chophouse, wherein a frowzy fellow sat at his cheap spread, without envying the frowzy fellow his cheap spread, cannot truly sympathize with me.

The man who has not felt a great hollow in his stomach, which he found necessary to fill at the first fountain he came to, or go over on his beam-ends for lack of ballast, cannot fall upon my neck and call me brother.

At daybreak I haunted those street fountains, waiting my turn while French cooks filled almost fathomless kegs, and coolies filled pot-bellied jars, and Kanacks filled their hollow bamboos that seemed fully a quarter of a mile in length. There I meekly made my toilet, took my first course of breakfast, rinsed out my handkerchiefs and stockings, and went my way. The whole performance was embarrassing, because I was a novice and a dozen people watched me in curious silence. I had also a boot with a suction in the toe; there is dust in Papeete; while I walked that boot loaded and discharged itself in a manner that amazed and amused a small mob of little natives who followed me in my free exhibition, advertising my shooting-boot gratuitously.

I was altogether shabby in my outward appearance, and cannot honestly upbraid any resident of the town for his neglect of me. I know that I suffered the agony of shame and the pangs of hunger; but they were nothing to the utter loneliness I felt as I wandered about with my heart on my sleeve, and never a bite from so much as a daw.

Did you ever question the possibility of a man's temporary transformation under certain mental, moral, or physical conditions? There are seasons when he certainly isn't what he was, yet may be more and better than he has been, if you give him time enough.

I began to think I had either suffered this transformation or been maliciously misinformed as to my personality. Was I truly what I represented myself to be, or had I been a living deception all my days? No longer able to identify myself as anyone in particular, it occurred to me that it would be well to address a few lines to the gentleman I had been in the habit of calling "Father," asking for some particulars concerning his absent son. I immediately drew up this document ready for mailing:

MOSQUITO HALL, CENTIPEDE AVENUE, PAPEETE.

DEAR SIR: A nondescript awaits identification at this office. Answers to the names at the foot of this page, believes himself to be your son, to have been your son, or about to be something equally near and dear to you. He can repeat several chapters of the New Testament at the shortest notice; recites most of the Catechism and Commandments; thinks he would recognize two sisters and three brothers at sight, and know his mother with his eyes shut.

He likewise confesses to the usual strawberry mark in fast colors. If you will kindly send by return mail a few dollars, he will clothe, feed, and water himself, and return immediately to those arms which, if his memory does not belie him, have more than once sheltered his unworthy frame. I have, dear sir, the singular fortune to be the article above described.

The six months which would elapse before I could hope for an answer would probably have found me past all recognition, so I ceased crying to the compassionate bowels of Tom, Dick, and Harry, waiting with haggard patience the departure of the vessel that was to bear me home with a palpable C.O.D. tacked on to me. Those last hours were brightened by the delicate attentions of a few good souls who learned, too late, the shocking state of my case. Thanks to them, I slept well thereafter in a real bed, and was sure of dinners that wouldn't rattle in me like a withered kernel in an old nutshell.

I had but to walk to the beach, wave my lily hand, heavily tanned about that time, when lo! a boat was immediately dispatched from the plump little corvette "Cheveret"; where the tricolor waved triumphantly from sunrise to sunset, all the year round.

Such capital French dinners as I had there, such offers of bed and board and boundless sympathy as were made me by those dear fellows who wore the gold lace and had a piratical-looking cabin all to themselves, were enough to wring a heart that had been nearly wrung out in its battle with life in Tahiti.

No longer I walked the streets as one smitten with the plague, or revolved in envious circles about the market place, where I could have got my fill for a half dollar, but had neither the one nor the other. No longer I went at daybreak to swell the procession at the waterspout; or sat on the shore, the picture of despair, waiting sunrise, finding it my sole happiness to watch a canoe load of children drifting out upon the bay, singing like a railful of larks; nor walked solitarily through the night up and down the narrow streets wherein the gendarmes had learned to pass me unnoticed, with my hat under my arm and my heart in my throat. Those delicious moons always seduced me from my natural sleep, and I sauntered through the coco groves whose boughs glistened like row after row of crystals, whose shadows were as mosaics wrought in blocks of silver.

I used to nod at the low, whitewashed "calabooses" fairly steaming in the sun, wherein Herman Melville got some chapters of *Omoo*.

Over and over again I tracked the ground of that delicious story, saying to the breadfruit trees that had sheltered him, "Shelter me also, and whoever shall follow after, so long as your branches quiver in the wind!"

O reader of *Omoo,* think of "Motoo-Otoo," actually looking warlike in these sad days, with a row of new cannons around its edge, and pyramids of balls as big as coconuts covering its shady center.

Walking alone in those splendid nights I used to hear a dry, ominous coughing in the huts of the natives. I felt as though I were treading upon the brinks of half-dug graves, and I longed to bring a respite to the doomed race.

One windy afternoon we cut our stern hawser in a fair wind and sailed out of the harbor; I felt a sense of relief, and moralized for five minutes without stopping. Then I turned away from all listeners and saw those glorious green peaks growing dim in the distance; the clouds embraced them in their profound secrecy; like a lovely mirage Tahiti floated upon the bosom of the sea. Between sea and sky was swallowed up vale, garden, and waterfall; point after point crowded with palms; peak above peak in that eternal crown of beauty; and with them the nation of warriors and lovers falling like the leaf, but, unlike it, with no followers in the new season.

Sir Arthur Grimble

ASSIGNMENT WITH AN OCTOPUS

A graduate of Cambridge University, with further education in France and Germany, Arthur Grimble (1888–1956) entered the British Colonial Service as a cadet in 1914. On his first assignment he was sent to the Gilbert and Ellice Islands Protectorate in the Pacific, the most remote and least visited outpost of the British Empire. There he remained, except for one furlough in England, for the next nineteen years, seven of which he served as the resident commissioner for the island colony. Devoted to his native charges, he mastered their language and lore and earned their trust and friendship to a degree seldom granted a government official.

In later years, Grimble was transferred to the Atlantic island of St. Vincent, appointed governor of Seychelles, and knighted in 1938. Ten years later he retired on a pension to England. In his leisure, he wrote stories of his experiences in the Gilbert and Ellice Islands and broadcast them over the B.B.C. Their remarkable success prompted him to publish them in an equally engaging book, *A Pattern of Islands,* 1953 (entitled *We Chose the Islands* in the American edition). A second series was published posthumously, *Return to the Islands,* 1957.

Two stories, one from each of those books, are offered here. The first, a gripping narrative of a dangerous adventure, shows how far Grimble would go to hold the respect of the natives; the second is an absorbing ghost story, believed by the natives and, evidently, half-believed by the author himself.

I CERTAINLY SHOULD NEVER HAVE VENTURED OUT ALONE FOR pure sport, armed with nothing but a knife, to fight a tiger shark in its own element. I am as little ashamed of that degree of discretion as the big-game hunter who takes care not to attack a rhinoceros with a shotgun. The fear I had for the larger kinds of octopus was quite different. It was a blind fear, sick with disgust, unreasoned as a child's horror of darkness. Victor Hugo was the man who first brought it up to the level of my conscious thought. I still remember vividly the impression left on me as a boy of fourteen by that account in *Les Travailleurs de la Mer* of Gilliatt's fight with the monster that caught him among the rocks of the Douvres. For years after reading it, I tortured myself with wondering however I could behave with decent courage if faced with a giant at once so strong and so loathsome. My commonest nightmare of the period was of an octopuslike Presence poised motionless behind me, towards which I dared not turn, from which my limbs were too frozen to escape. But that phase did pass before I left school, and the Thing lay dormant inside me until a day at Tarawa.

Before I reached Tarawa, however, chance gave me a swift glimpse of what a biggish octopus could do to a man. I was wading at low tide one calm evening on the lip of the reef at Ocean Island when a Baanaban villager, back from fishing, brought his canoe to land within twenty yards of where I stood. There was no more than a show of breaking seas, but the water was only knee-deep, and this obliged the fisherman to slide overboard and handle his lightened craft over the jagged edge. But no sooner were his feet upon the reef than he seemed to be tied to where he stood. The canoe was washed shorewards ahead of him, while he stood with legs braced, tugging desperately away from something. I had just time to see a tapering, grayish-yellow rope curled around his right wrist before he broke away from it. He fell sprawling into the shallow water; the tapered rope flicked writhing back into the foam at the reef's edge. The fisherman picked himself up and nursed his right arm. I had reached him by then. The octopus had caught him with only the tip of one tentacle, but the terrible hold of the few suckers on his wrist had torn the skin whole from it as he wrenched himself adrift.

The old navigators of the Gilberts used to talk with fear of a gigantic octopus that inhabited the seas between Samoa and the Ellice Islands. They said its tentacles were three spans long and thicker at the base than the body of a full-grown man—a scale of measurements not out of keeping with what is known of the atrocious monster called *Octopus apollyon.* There were some who stated that this foul fiend of the ocean was also to be found in the waters between Onotoa, Tamana, and Arorae in the southern Gilberts. But I never came across a man who had seen one, and the biggest of the octopus breed I ever saw with my own eyes had tentacles only a little over six feet long. It was a member of the clan *Octopus vulgaris,* which swarms in all the lagoons. An average specimen of this variety is a dwarf beside *Octopus apollyon*s laid out flat, it has a total spread of no more than nine or ten feet; but it is a wicked-looking piece of work, even in death, with those disgusting suckers studding its arms and bulging, filmed eyes staring out of the mottled Gorgon face.

Possibly, if you can watch objectively, the sight of *Octopus vulgaris* searching for crabs and crayfish on the floor of the lagoon may move you to something like admiration. You cannot usually see the dreadful eyes from a water glass straight above its feeding ground, and your feeling for crustaceans is too impersonal for horror at their fate between pouncing suckers and jaws. There is real beauty in the rich change of its colors as it moves from shadow to sunlight, and the gliding ease of its arms as they reach and flicker over the rough rocks fascinates the eye with its deadly grace. You feel that if only the creature would stick to its grubbing on the bottom, the shocking ugliness of its shape might even win your sympathy, as for some poor Caliban in the enchanted garden of the lagoon. But it is no honest grubber in the open. For every one of its kind that you see crawling below you, there are a dozen skulking in recesses of the reef that falls away like a cliff from the edge where you stand watching. When *Octopus vulgaris* has eaten its fill of the teeming crabs and crayfish, it seeks a dark cleft in the coral face, and anchors itself there with a few of the large suckers nearest to its body. Thus shielded from attack in the rear, with tentacles gathered to pounce, it squats glaring from the shadows, alert for anything alive to swim within striking distance. It can hurl one or all of those whiplashes forward with the speed of dark lightning, and once its scores of suckers, rimmed with hooks for grip on slippery skins, are clamped about their prey, nothing but the brute's death will break their awful hold.

But that very quality of the octopus that most horrifies the imagination—its relentless tenacity—becomes its undoing when hungry man steps into the picture. The Gilbertese happen to value certain parts of it as food, and their method of fighting it is coolly based upon the one fact that its arms never change their grip. They hunt for it in pairs. One man acts as the bait, his partner as the killer. First, they swim eyes-under at low tide just off the reef, and search the crannies of the submarine cliff for sight of any tentacle that may flicker out for a catch. When they have placed their quarry, they land on the reef for the next stage. The human bait starts the real game. He dives and tempts the lurking brute by swimming a few strokes in front of its cranny, at first a little beyond striking range. Then he turns and makes straight for the cranny, to give himself into the embrace of those waiting arms. Sometimes nothing happens. The beast will not always respond to the lure. But usually it strikes.

The partner on the reef above stares down through the pellucid water, waiting for his moment. His teeth are his only weapon. His killing efficiency depends on his avoiding every one of those strangling arms. He must wait until his partner's body has been drawn right up to the entrance of the cleft. The monster inside is groping then with its horny mouth against the victim's flesh, and sees nothing beyond it. That point is reached in a matter of no more than thirty seconds after the decoy has plunged. The killer dives, lays hold of his pinioned friend at arm's length, and jerks him away from the cleft; the octopus is torn adrift from the anchorage of its proximal suckers, and clamps itself the more fiercely to its prey. In the same second, the human bait gives a kick which brings him, with quarry annexed, to the surface.

He turns on his back, still holding his breath for better buoyancy, and this exposes the body of the beast for the kill. The killer closes in, grasps the evil head from behind, and wrenches it away from its meal. Turning the face up towards himself, he plunges his teeth between the bulging eyes, and bites down and in with all his strength. That is the end of it. It dies on the instant; the suckers release their hold; the arms fall away; the two fishers paddle with whoops of delighted laughter to the reef, where they string the catch to a pole before going to rout out the next one.

Any two boys of seventeen, any day of the week, will go out and get you half a dozen octopuses like that for the mere fun of it. Here lies the whole point of this story. The hunt is, in the most literal sense, nothing but child's play to the Gilbertese.

As I was standing one day at the end of a jetty in Tarawa lagoon, I saw two boys from the near village shouldering a string of octopuses slung on a pole between them. I started to wade out in their direction, but before I hailed them they had stopped, planted the carrying-pole upright in a fissure and, leaving it there, swum off the edge for a while with faces submerged, evidently searching for something underwater. I had been only a few months at Tarawa, and that was my first near view of an octopus hunt. I watched every stage of it from the dive of the human bait to the landing of the dead catch. When it was over, I went up to them. I could hardly believe that in those few seconds, with no more than a frivolous-looking splash or two on the surface, they could have found, caught, and killed the creature they were now stringing up before my eyes. They explained the amusing simplicity of the thing.

"There's only one trick the decoy-man must never forget," they said, "and that's not difficult to remember. If he is not wearing the water spectacles of the Men of Matang, he must cover his eyes with a hand as he comes close to the *kika* (octopus), or the suckers might blind him." It appeared that the ultimate fate of the eyes was not the thing to worry about; the immediate point was that the sudden pain of a sucker clamping itself to an eyeball might cause the bait to expel his breath and inhale sea water; that would spoil his buoyancy, and he would fail then to give his friend the best chance of a kill.

Then they began whispering together. I knew in a curdling flash what they were saying to each other. Before they turned to speak to me again, a horrified conviction was upon me. My damnable curiosity had led me into a trap from which there was no escape. They were going to propose that I should take a turn at being the bait myself, just to see how delightfully easy it was. And that is precisely what they did. It did not even occur to them that I might not leap at the offer. I was already known as a young Man of Matang who liked swimming, and fishing, and laughing with the villagers; I had just shown an interest in this particular form of hunting; naturally, I should enjoy the fun of it as much as they did. Without even waiting for my answer, they gleefully ducked off the edge of the reef to look for another octopus—a fine fat one—*mine*. Left standing there alone, I had another of those visions. . . .

It was dusk in the village. The fishers were home, I saw the cooking fires glowing orange-red between the brown lodges. There was laughter and shouted talk as the women prepared the evening meal. But the laughter was hard with scorn. "What?" they were saying. "Afraid of a *kika?* The young Man of Matang? Why, even our boys are not afraid of a *kika!*" A curtain went down and rose again on the residency; the Old Man was talking. "A leader? You? The man who funked a schoolboy game? We don't leave your sort in charge of districts." The scene flashed to my uncles. "Returned empty," they said. "We always knew you hadn't got it in you. Returned empty . . ."

Of course it was all overdrawn, but one fact was beyond doubt: the Gilbertese reserved all their most ribald humor for physical cowardice. No man gets himself passed for a leader anywhere by becoming the butt of that kind of wit. I decided I would rather face the octopus.

I was dressed in khaki slacks, canvas shoes, and a short-armed singlet. I took off the shoes and made up my mind to shed the singlet if told to do so; but I was wildly determined to stick to my trousers throughout. Dead or alive, said a voice within me, an official minus his pants is a preposterous object, and I felt I could not face that extra horror. However, nobody asked me to remove anything.

I hope I did not look as yellow as I felt when I stood to take the plunge; I have never been so sick with funk before or since. "Remember, one hand for your eyes," said someone from a thousand miles off, and I dived.

I do not suppose it is really true that the eyes of an octopus shine in the dark; besides, it was clear daylight only six feet down in the limpid water; but I could have sworn the brute's eyes burned at me as I turned in towards his cranny. That dark glow—whatever may have been its origin—was the last thing I saw as I blacked out with my left hand and rose into his clutches. Then, I remember chiefly a dreadful sliminess with a herculean power behind it. Something whipped round my left forearm and the back of my neck, binding the two together. In the same flash, another something slapped itself high on my forehead, and I felt it crawling down inside the back of my singlet. My impuse was to tear at it with my right hand, but I felt the whole of that arm pinioned to my ribs. In most emergencies the mind works with crystal-clear impersonality. This was not even an emergency, for I knew myself perfectly safe. But my boyhood nightmare was upon me. When I felt the swift constriction of those disgusting arms jerk my head and shoulders in towards the reef, my mind went blank of every thought save the beastliness of contact with that squat head. A mouth began to nuzzle below my throat, at the junction of the collar bones. I forgot there was anyone to save me. Yet something still directed me to hold my breath.

I was awakened from my cowardly trance by a quick, strong pull on my shoulders, back from the cranny. The cables around me tightened painfully, but I knew I was adrift from the reef. I gave a kick, rose to the surface and turned on my back with the brute sticking out of my chest like a tumor. My mouth was smothered by some flabby moving horror. The suckers felt like hot rings pulling at my skin. It was only two seconds, I suppose, from then to the attack of my deliverer, but it seemed like a century of nausea.

My friend came up between me and the reef. He pounced, pulled, bit down, and the thing was over—for everyone but me. At the sudden relaxation of the tentacles, I let out a great breath, sank, and drew in the next underwater. It took the united help of both boys to get me, coughing, heaving, and pretending to join in their delighted laughter, back to the reef. I had to submit there to a kind of war dance around me, in which the dead beast was slung whizzing past my head from one to the other. I had a chance to observe then that it was not by any stretch of fancy a giant, but just plain average. That took the bulge out of my budding self-esteem. I left hurriedly for the cover of the jetty, and was sick.

Sir Arthur Grimble

A STINKING GHOST

THERE WERE FIVE EUROPEAN HOUSES SCATTERED THROUGH THE whispering glades of the palm forest on Betio station in 1923. Two of these had been put up by myself in 1916; the other three were much older; and every one of them, according to the people of Betio village next door, was haunted. The basic trouble was not, I gathered, that they had all happened to be built on prehaunted ground; there wasn't a foot of soil anywhere up the creeping length of Tarawa that wasn't the lurking place of one fiend or another, and you had to take these as you found them. It was how you dealt with them when you laid out your ground plan and built your house that really mattered. If you didn't turn on the proper spells—and how could you if you were a white man?—it followed as a matter of course that the ghosts or the elementals got in.

One of the two bungalows that I had built had been occupied without delay by an earth spirit called Na Kun, who showed himself in the form of a noddy. He croaked "Kun-kun-kun" at you in the dark of night, and aimed his droppings at your eye, and blinded you for life if he made a bull's-eye of it. The other house had a dog on its front veranda: not just a *kamea* (that is, a "come-here"), as the white man's dogs were called, but a *kiri*—one of the breed the ancestors had brought with them out of the west when, shortly after the creation of the world by Naareau the Elder, they came to settle on Tarawa. I could never make out why everyone was so frightened of this beast. He never *did* anything, simply *was* in the house. For my own purposes, I came to the conclusion that he was like the "mopoke" in the celebrated Australian story, so deceptive that what I occasionally thought I saw on the front veranda and took to be something else actually was what I took it for, namely, a mongrel of the old *kiri* strain from the village.

There was a cheerful tale among the villagers that, round about 1910, an aged friend of mine, a widely loved sorcerer who dealt in what was called the magic of kindness (meaning any kind of ritual or charm not intended to hurt anybody) had posted one of his familiars, the apparition of a gray heron, on the front veranda of a decrepit bungalow near the hospital. His intent, so the story went, was to get hold of a few medical secrets for the improvement of his repertoire of curative potions, especially those which had to do with the revitalization of flagging manhood. But his constructive plan was most untimely frustrated when the resident medical officer was tranferred to another house, only just built, but nevertheless already haunted by a hag with two heads. This unpleasant creature made a most frightful scene when the wizard tried to take the new premises over for his inquisitive bird. I learned all these facts from a glorious burlesque show put up for me one Saturday night by the lads, young and old, of Betio village. The miming of the demon lady's fury, her inhospitable gestures, the rout of the sorcerer, and the total desolation of the heron left all of us, including the venerable gentleman himself, helpless with laughter. But, in the last analysis, behind all the mirth of that roaring crowd, there wasn't a soul present except myself who didn't accept both the familiar and the demon for cold and often terrifying fact.

The oldest house on our station, the one we called the old residency, was a pleasant, two-floored structure near the lagoonside haunted by a nameless white beachcomber. This ghost was held in peculiar dread by the villagers, because they regarded it as earthbound for ever, its body having been murdered and left unburied on the beach for the Betio dogs to devour. That kind of revenant was always more *iowawa* (malicious) than any other, everyone believed.

The unhappy man, so the story ran, had been killed on the

site of the residency with a glass bottle by a fellow beachcomber named Tom, a generation or so before the coming of the British flag in 1892, which is to say, somewhere back in the late 1860's. Nothing else was remembered of him except that he was wearing a sailor's dark shore clothes and thick black boots when he came by his death. Or, at least, that is how his ghost was said to be dressed whenever it allowed itself to be seen about the house.

The villagers talked about him so much and with such conviction that Europeans began to accept the haunt as a fact. It is hard to resist belief in such things when you are lonely and the whole air around you palpitates with horrified credulity. Good Father Guichard of the Sacred Heart Mission, bless him, came down-lagoon fifteen miles when Olivia and I arrived at Tarawa in 1916, especially to warn us against living in the house. But we did live there. We couldn't see why the poor ghost, if it existed, should want to do us any harm. So we had our beds and the baby's cot on the airy gable veranda where he was supposed to walk, clump-clump, in his great thick boots; and all the time we were there, we never saw or heard a thing or had the smallest feeling of his unseen presence.

But when I was transferred to the central Gilberts in 1917, I found a house that gave me quite different sensations. That was the district officer's transit quarters on Tabiteuea, built by George Murdoch, my predecessor in the central islands. It used to stand in a rustling grove of coconut palms by the lagoon beach, a hundred yards or so north of Utiroa village and about the same distance south of the big, whitewashed island prison. It was an airily built, two-roomed shelter of local thatch and timber, a heavenly cool refuge from the ferocious glare of sea and sand beyond the grove. I found it a cheerful place, too, all through the daylight hours, with the talkative Utiroa villagers padding back and forth along the road that passed it to landward. It changed, though, when darkness fell and the village slept. An uneasiness came upon it then. Or perhaps it was I who changed—I don't know—only I couldn't pass a night there without being haunted by a thought that something was on the edge of happening: something so imminently near, I always felt, that if nothing but one gossamer-fold of the darkness could be stripped aside, I should see what it was. The idea would come back and back at me as I sat reading or writing. Once or twice, it pulled me up out of sleep, wide-awake on the instant, thinking, "Here it is!" But if it was, it never showed itself.

Had this been all, I should never have had the place pulled down. Not even the horrifying odor that visited me there one night would have sufficed of itself to drive me to that extreme. You don't destroy a house built by your predecessor—especially an old stager like George Murdoch—for the sole reason that it was once, for about thirty seconds in your experience, invaded by a smell you couldn't explain. It was what George himself said to me afterwards, when I told him (among other things) how my dog had behaved, that set me looking for another site.

The dog was my terrier, Smith. He was lying in the draft of the roadside doorway one night, while I sat reading. I wasn't deeply absorbed because I was worried about Anterea, an old friend of mine, who lay ill in the village—so ill I was sure he wouldn't last the night. Perhaps that made me particularly susceptible to whatever it was. Anyhow, I felt myself suddenly gripped, as I sat, by a more than usually disturbing sense of that imminent something. It had never had any particular direction before, but now it seemed to impend from the roadway. I was aware, also, of having to fight a definite dread of it this time, instead of greeting it with a kind of incredulous expectancy. I sprang up, staring nervously out into the dark beyond the door. And then I noticed Smith. Hackles bristling, gums bared, he was backing step by step away from the door, whimpering and trembling as he backed.

"Smith!" I called. He gave me one quick, piteous look, turned tail and bolted, yelping as if I had kicked him, through the seaward door. I heard him begin to howl on the beach, just as that unspeakable odor came sweeping into the room, wave upon wave of the breath of all corruption, from the road.

Plain anger seized me as I stood. That was natural, I think.

I had made myself a fine figure of fun, for whoever was outside, leaping to my feet and goggling like a scared rabbit through the doorway, a glorious butt for this nasty trick. It hurt: I forgot Smith and dashed out into the road. But there wasn't a clue for eye, or ear, or nose in the hissing darkness under the wind-blown palms. I found nobody and nothing, until my running feet brought me to the fringe of Utiroa village; and there I heard a sound that stripped me of all my anger. It was the noise of women wailing and men chanting, mixed with the rhythmic thud-thud of heavy staves on the ground. I couldn't mistake it. A Gilbertese *bomaki* ceremony was in full swing: some villager's departing soul was being ritually sped on its difficult road from earth to paradise. I knew then that my old friend Anterea had not lasted the night, and I lost all heart for my silly chase.

There was no taint on the air of the house when I got back. I fell asleep untroubled by anything but my own sadness. But Smith stayed out on the beach, and I couldn't persuade him to remain indoors after dark for the few more days I spent on Tabiteuea.

The rest of the story is George Murdoch's. He had settled down to trading on Kuria Island after his retirement from the administrative service, so I took the next chance I could of running across to tell him of my feelings about the house, and Smith's queer behavior, and the fetid smell someone had put across me.

"So he's been making friends with you, has he?" said George reflectively when I had finished. And, instead of answering when I asked who "he" might be, he went on, "From about the middle of Utiroa village to a bit north of the prison—that's his beat. Aye, he's a stinking old nuisance. But mind you, there's no real harm in him."

"He," in short, according to George, was an absurd ghost known to the villagers as *Tewaiteaina,* or One Leg, whose habit for several centuries it had been to walk—or, rather, hop—that particular stretch of Tabiteuea, every night of the year without exception, scaring everybody stiff who saw him go by. George spoke of him with a sort of affectionate irritation, as if he really existed. It was too ridiculous.

"But, Mr. Murdoch," I interrupted, "there's a ghost for every yard of the Gilberts, if you swallow all that village stuff!"

He eyed me humorously. "But there's only one ghost who stinks, young fella-me-lad, and that's old One Leg. Not that he plays that trick often, mind you. Just sometimes, for friendship's sake. Now, if you'll stop interrupting, I'll tell you. . . .

"I'd heard nothing about him when I had the prison and the resthouse built where they are," he went on, "otherwise, I might have chosen somewhere else. Or I might not. What's the odds, anyway? The creature's harmless. So there I was one dark, still night, with a prison nicely full of grand, strong lads up the road, and myself sitting all serene in the resthouse, enjoying a page or two of the King's Regulations. I say I was all serene, you'll note. The house had stood three years, and I'd never been troubled by the something's-going-to-happen notion you've made such a point of. Sheer nonsense that, I'm telling you straight!"

"Yes, Mr. Murdoch," I said humbly.

"Well, you'll grow out of it, I suppose," he comforted me. "So there I sat, a grown man, with not one childish fancy to make a fool of me, when in from the roadway crashed that stinking thing and hit me like a wall. Solid. A fearful stench. You were right about that. Corruption and essence of corruption from the heart of all rottenness—that's what I said to myself as I fought my way through it to the door. . . . How did I know it came from the road, you say? What does that matter—I *did* know; so don't interrupt me with your questions.

"I'll admit the uncanny suddenness of it gave me the shudders at first. But I was angry, like you, by the time I reached the road. I thought some son of a gun was taking a rise out of me. So I dashed back into the house, snatched up a hurricane lamp and started running hell for leather towards the prison. The reek was as thick as a fog that way, and I followed my nose.

"I hadn't gone far, though, before I heard a patter and a rush from ahead, and a great ox of a prison guard came charging full tilt out of the darkness and threw himself at me, gibbering like a cockatoo. As I struggled out of his clutches, I caught something about someone called One Leg who'd gone hop-hopping past him into the prison yard. Well . . . there was my clue. 'Is it One Leg that raised this stink?' I shouted. 'Yes,' he screamed back. 'One Leg . . . the ghost!' I only stayed to call him a blanky fool and belted on.

"But I wasn't quick enough to catch up with the trouble. When I got near the prison yard, something else had started. The whole crowd inside the men's lockup had gone mad . . . raving mad . . . yelling their heads off . . . and the noise of them flinging themselves against the door was like thunder. I knew the padlock wouldn't last if that went on; I heard it crack like a pistol as I came up to the yard entrance; and, begum, before you could say knife, I was down under the feet of a maniac mob stampeding out into the bush.

"I picked myself up and made a beeline for the lockup; ran halfway down the gangway between the beds, swinging my lamp around; found not a soul there; charged out again to Anterea's house in the corner of the yard—why, what's the matter now?"

I had sat bolt upright and exclaimed, "Anterea?" When I repeated it, he said, "Yes, the head warder. Retired before your time, but he's still going strong in Utiroa. One of the few who never gave a damn for old One Leg. Would you believe it? He was sleeping like a baby when I got to him. Hadn't heard a sound and said he couldn't smell a thing, though the place was still humming fit to knock you down. But he got going quick enough when I told him the news. He and I hunted the bush for those poor idiots till the crack of dawn. They came in willingly enough at sunup—all but Arikitaua, that's to say—and we had a fine powwow together round Anterea's shack, waiting for him to turn up. That's when I got all the dope about One Leg.

"They'd all seen him hopping up the gangway between the beds, so they claimed. There wasn't a light, but they'd seen him. 'Fiddle!' I said to that, and Anterea backed me. So, just for the hell of it, I turned on him then, and asked him what of the smell I'd smelt and he hadn't; and immediately about half of them butted in to say they hadn't smelt it, either; and, by the same token, the other half had. It was all very puzzling until somebody explained that One Leg only brought his saintly odor along for the particular friends of the deceased, and then, of course, it was as clear as mud. 'Which deceased?' I wanted to know. 'Oh, anyone who dies within the limits of his beat,' says my clever friend. 'He turns it on as soon as the soul has left the body.'

"You could have knocked me down with a feather if there had been a corpse in sight. But there wasn't. So I said a few words and left them to think up another story. I had a mind to go and inquire in the village after our missing number, Arikitaua . . . an Utiroa man. . . . I liked him a lot. But I hadn't gone fifty steps, when a new hullabaloo from the lockup stopped me in my tracks. I thought they were starting another One Leg stunt. But it was only poor Arikitaua this time. Yes . . . there he was—rolled off his bed on the floor up against the far end wall—where my lamp hadn't reached him —quite dead. I reckon it was just heart disease."

We sat silent a long time; then George said reflectively, "What with this and that, I'm surprised you didn't hear of a friend's death in Utiroa after the old stinker put it across you."

I told him then of Anterea.

"Well . . . well . . . think of that now," said George, ". . . and Anterea an unbeliever. Kind of friendly, I call it. There never was any real harm in old One Leg."

He was furious when I had a new resthouse built on the other side of the island—as furious as a man might be who has led you up the garden path to his own confusion. But he never would admit he'd been pulling my leg. And then again, what was it that scared my dog so?

Frank T. Bullen

THE WHALE IN THE CAVE

Left an orphan in early boyhood, Frank T. Bullen (1857–1915), after several years of dodging about London as a ragged street Arab "with wits sharpened by the constant fight for food," went to sea when he was thirteen, sailing to all parts of the world. In 1875, stranded and penniless in New Bedford, Massachusetts, he signed on an American whaling ship bound for a voyage to the Pacific Ocean. Years later, after he had left the sea for a clerk's job in London, he told the story of that voyage in *The Cruise of the Cachalot* (1899), his first book, which ranks next to Melville's *Moby Dick* among the classic narratives of whaling.

The selection that follows, in effect a self-contained short story, relates an exciting adventure that befell Bullen and some of his shipmates in one of the ship's whaleboats while they were exploring the coast of Vau-Vau, an island in the Tongan Group.

JUST WHEN THE DELIGHTFUL DAYS WERE BEGINNING TO PALL upon us, a real adventure befell us, which, had we been attending strictly to business, we should not have encountered. For a week previous we had been cruising constantly without ever seeing a spout, except those belonging to whales out at sea, whither we knew it was folly to follow them. We tried all sorts of games to while away the time, which certainly did hang heavy, the most popular of which was for the whole crew of the boat to strip, and, getting overboard, be towed along at the ends of short warps, while I sailed her. It was quite mythological—a sort of rude reproduction of Neptune and his attendant Tritons. At last, one afternoon as we were listlessly lolling (half-asleep, except the lookout man) across the thwarts, we suddenly came upon a gorge between two cliffs that we must have passed before several times, unnoticed. At a certain angle it opened, disclosing a wide sheet of water, extending a long distance ahead. I put the helm up, and we ran through the passage, finding it about a boat's length in width and several fathoms deep, though overhead the cliffs nearly came together in places. Within, the scene was very beautiful, but not more so than many similar ones we had previously witnessed. Still, as the place was new to us, our languor was temporarily dispelled, and we paddled along, taking in every feature of the shores with keen eyes that let nothing escape. After we had gone on in this placid manner for maybe an hour, we suddenly came to a stupendous cliff—that is, for those parts—rising almost sheer from the water for about a thousand feet. Of itself it would not have arrested our attention, but at its base was a semicircular opening, like the mouth of a small tunnel. This looked alluring, so I headed the boat for it, passing through a deep channel between two reefs that led straight to the opening. There was ample room for us to enter, as we had lowered the mast; but just as we were passing through, a heave of the unnoticed swell lifted us unpleasantly near the crown of this natural arch. Beneath us, at a great depth, the bottom could be dimly discerned, the water being of the richest blue conceivable, which the sun, striking down through, resolved into some most marvelous color schemes in the path of its rays. A delicious sense of coolness, after the fierce heat outside, saluted us as we entered a vast hall, whose roof rose to a minimum height of forty feet, but in places could not be seen at all. A sort of diffused light, weak, but sufficient to reveal the general contour of the place, existed—let in, I supposed, through some unseen crevices in the roof or walls. At first, of course, to our eyes fresh from the fierce glare outside, the place seemed wrapped in impenetrable gloom, and we dared not stir lest we should run into some hidden danger. Before many minutes, however, the gloom lightened as our pupils enlarged, so that, although the light was faint, we could find our way about with ease. We spoke in low tones, for the echoes were so numerous and resonant that even a whisper gave back from those massy walls in a series of recurring hisses, as if a colony of snakes had been disturbed.

We paddled on into the interior of this vast cave, finding everywhere the walls rising sheer from the silent, dark waters, not a ledge or a crevice where one might gain foothold. Indeed, in some places there was a considerable overhang from above, as if a great dome whose top was invisible sprang from some level below the water. We pushed ahead until the tiny semicircle of light through which we had entered was only faintly visible; and then, finding there was nothing to be seen except what we were already witnessing, unless we cared to go on into the thick darkness, which extended apparently into the bowels of the mountain, we turned and started to go back. Do what we would, we could not venture to break the solemn hush that surrounded us as if we were shut within the dome of some vast cathedral in the twilight.

So we paddled noiselessly along for the exit, till suddenly an awful, inexplicable roar set all our hearts thumping fit to break our bosoms. Really, the sensation was most painful, especially as we had not the faintest idea whence the noise came or what had produced it. Again it filled that immense cave with its thunderous reverberations; but this time all the sting was taken out of it, as we caught sight of its author. A goodly bull humpback had found his way in after us, and the sound of his spout, exaggerated a thousand times in the confinement of that mighty cavern, had frightened us all so that we nearly lost our breath. So far, so good; but, unlike the old nigger, though we were "doin' blame well," we did not "let blame well alone." The next spout that intruder gave, he was right alongside of us. This was too much for the semisavage instincts of my gallant harpooner, and before I had time to shout a caution he had plunged his weapon deep into old Blowhard's broad back.

I should like to describe what followed, but, in the first place, I hardly know; and, in the next, even had I been cool and collected, my recollections would sound like the ravings of a fevered dream. For of all the hideous uproars conceivable, that was, I should think, about the worst. The big mammal seemed to have gone frantic with the pain of his wound, the surprise of the attack, and the hampering confinement in which he found himself. His tremendous struggles caused such a commotion that our position could only be compared to that of men shooting Niagara in a cylinder at night. How we kept afloat, I do not know. Someone had the gumption to cut the line, so that by the radiation of the disturbance we presently found ourselves close to the wall, and trying to hold the boat in to it with our finger tips. Would he never be quiet? we thought, as the thrashing, banging, and splashing still went on with unfailing vigor. At last, in, I suppose, one supreme effort to escape, he leaped clear of the water like a salmon. There was a perceptible hush, during which we shrank together like unfledged chickens on a frosty night; then, in a never-to-be-forgotten crash that ought to have brought down the massy roof, that mountainous carcass fell. The consequent violent upheaval of the water should have smashed the boat against the rocky walls, but that final catastrophe was mercifully spared us. I suppose the rebound was sufficient to keep us a safe distance off.

A perfect silence succeeded, during which we sat speechless, awaiting a resumption of the clamor. At last Abner broke the heavy silence by saying, "I doan' see the do'way any mo' at all, sir." He was right. The tide had risen, and that half-moon of light had disappeared, so that we were now prisoners for many hours, it not being at all probable that we should be able to find our way out during the night ebb. Well, we were not exactly children, to be afraid of the dark, although there is considerable difference between the velvety darkness of a dungeon and the clear, fresh night of the open air. Still, as long as that beggar of a whale would only keep quiet or leave the premises, we should be fairly comfortable. We waited and waited until an hour had passed, and then came to the conclusion that our friend was either dead or gone out, as he gave no sign of his presence.

That being settled, we anchored the boat, and lit pipes, preparatory to passing as comfortable a night as might be under the circumstances, the only thing troubling me being the anxiety of the skipper on our behalf. Presently the blackness beneath was lit up by a wide band of phosphoric light, shed in the wake of no ordinary-sized fish, probably an immense shark. Another and another followed in rapid succession, until the depths beneath were all ablaze with brilliant foot-wide ribands of green glare, dazzling to the eye and bewildering to the brain. Occasionally, a gentle splash or ripple alongside, or a smart tap on the bottom of the boat, warned us how thick the concourse was that had gathered below. Until that weariness that no terror is proof against set in, sleep was impossible, nor could we keep our anxious gaze from that glowing inferno beneath, where one would have thought all the population of Tartarus were holding high revel. Mercifully, at last we sank into a fitful slumber, though fully aware of the great danger of our position. One upward rush of any of those ravening monsters, happening to strike the frail shell of our boat, and a few fleeting seconds would have sufficed for our obliteration as if we had never been.

But the terrible night passed away, and once more we saw the tender, iridescent light stream into that abode of dread. As the day strengthened, we were able to see what was going on below, and a grim vision it presented. The water was literally alive with sharks of enormous size, tearing with never-ceasing energy at the huge carcass of the whale lying on the bottom, who had met his fate in a singular but not unheard-of way. At that last titanic effort of his he had rushed downward with such terrific force that, striking his head on the bottom, he had broken his neck. I felt very grieved that we had lost the chance of securing him; but it was perfectly certain that before we could get help to raise him, all that would be left on his skeleton would be quite valueless to us. So with such patience as we could command we waited near the entrance until the receding ebb made it possible for us to emerge once more into the blessed light of day. I was horrified at the haggard, careworn appearance of my crew, who had all, excepting the two Kanakas, aged perceptibly during that night of torment. But we lost no time in getting back to the ship, where I fully expected a severe wigging for the scrape my luckless curiosity had led me into. The captain, however, was very kind, expressing his pleasure at seeing us all safe back again, although he warned me solemnly against similar investigations in future. A hearty meal and a good rest did wonders in removing the severe effects of our adventure, so that by next morning we were all fit and ready for the day's work again.

Louis Becke

AT A KAVA-DRINKING

Few men, and no writers, knew the real South Seas of the last century as well as Louis Becke (1855–1913), an Australian. He went to sea at the age of fourteen, was in Samoa during the civil wars, and from there was sent under sealed orders to deliver a leaky ketch to Bully Hayes, the notorious South Sea buccaneer, then cruising the Marshalls in his brig "Leonora." Persuaded by Hayes to serve as his supercargo, Becke was a survivor of the "Leonora" when it went down in a storm off the island of Kusaie. After being tried in Australia as Hayes's accomplice and acquitted, Becke spent many years as a South Sea trader in the Ellice, Gilbert, New Britain, and other island groups "from Rapa to Palau." Then, at the age of thirty-eight, married and broke in Sydney, he turned to writing the stories he knew firsthand from his life in the islands. As a successful writer he lived most of his remaining years in London, turning out more than thirty books. The best of these are among the earliest: *By Reef and Palm* (1894), *The Ebbing of the Tide* (1895), *Pacific Tales* (1896), and *Rodman the Boatsteerer* (1898).

Although even the best of Louis Becke's stories are lacking in technical skill and the polish of better-trained writers, they are spare and direct and deliver an impact on the reader. Of his books James A. Michener has written: "Around the world, men who have wandered the Pacific go back again and again to the works of Louis Becke, and as they leaf through the graceless stories of this awkward man, suddenly they are gripped in a veritable typhoon of nostalgia. . . . Louis Becke is the laureate of the prosaic, the curator of things as they actually were."

THE FIRST COOL BREATHS OF THE LAND BREEZE, CHILLED BY ITS passage through the dew-laden forest, touched our cheeks softly that night as we sat on the trader's veranda, facing the white, shimmering beach, smoking and watching the native children at play, and listening for the first deep boom of the wooden *logo* or bell that would send them racing homewards to their parents and evening prayer.

"There it is," said our host, who sat in the farthest corner, with his long legs resting by the heels on the white railing; "and now you'll see them scatter."

The loud cries and shrill laughter came to a sudden stop as the boom of the *logo* reached the players, and then a clear, boyish voice reached us—*"Ua ta le logo"* (the bell has sounded). Like smoke before the gale the lithe, half-naked figures fled silently in twos and threes between the coconuts, and the beach lay deserted.

One by one the lights gleamed brightly through the trees as the women piled the fires in each house with broken coconut shells. There was but the faintest breath of wind, and through the open sides of most of the houses not enough to flicker the steady light, as the head of the family seated himself (or herself) close to the fire, and hymnbook in hand, led off the singing. Quite near us was a more pretentious-looking structure than the others, and looking down upon it we saw that the graveled floor was covered with fine, clean mats, and arranged all round the sides of the house were a number of camphorwood boxes, always—in a Samoan house—the outward and visible sign of a well-to-do man. There was no fire lighted here; placed in the center of the one room there stood a lamp with a gorgeous-looking shade, of many colors. This was the chief's house, and the chief of Aleipata was one of the strong men of Samoa—both politically and physically. Two of our party on the veranda were strangers to Samoa; and they drew their chairs nearer, and gazed with interest at the chief and his immediate following as they proceeded with their simple service. There were quite a number of the *aualuma* (unmarried women) of the village present in the chief's house that evening, and as their tuneful voices blended in an evening hymn—*"Matou te nau e faafetai"*—we wished that instead of four verses there had been ten.

"Can you tell us, Lester," said one of the strangers to our host, "the meaning of the last words? They came out so clearly that I believe I've caught them," and to our surprise he sang the last line:

Ia matou moe tau ia te oe.

"Well, now, I don't know if I can. Samoan hymns puzzle me; you see the language used in addressing the Deity is vastly different to that used ordinarily; but I take it that the words you so correctly repeated mean, 'Let us sleep in peace with Thee.' Curious people, these Samoans," he muttered, more to himself than for us: "soon be as hypocritical as the average white man. 'Let us sleep in peace with Thee,' and that fellow (the chief), his two brothers, and about a paddockful of young Samoan bucks haven't slept at all for this two weeks. All the night is spent in counting cartridges, melting lead for bullets, and cleaning their arms, only knocking off for a drink of kava. Well, I suppose," he continued, turning to us, "they're all itching to fight, and as soon as the U.S.S. 'Resacca' leaves Apia they'll commence in earnest, and us poor devils of traders will be left here doing nothing and cursing this infernal love of fighting, which is inborn with Samoans and a part of their natural cussedness which, if the Creator hadn't given it to them, would have put many a dollar into my pocket."

"Father," said a voice that came up to us from the gloom of the young coconuts' foliage at the side of the house, "Felipe is here, and wants to know if he may come up and speak to the *alii papalagi* (white gentlemen)."

"Right you are, Felipe, my lad," said the trader in a more than usually kind voice, "bring him up, Atalina, and then run away to the chief's and get some of the *aua-luma* to come over with you and make a bowl of kava.

"Now, Doctor L——," Lester continued, addressing himself to one of his guests, the surgeon of an American war vessel then stationed in Samoa and a fellow countryman of his, "I'll show you as fine a specimen of manhood and intelligence as God ever made, although he has got a tanned hide."

The native that ascended the steps and stood before us with his hat in his hand, respectfully saluting, was indeed, as Lester called him, "a fine specimen." Clothed only in a blue-and-white lava-lava, or waistcloth, his clean-cut limbs, muscular figure, and skin like polished bronze stood revealed in the full light that now flooded room and veranda from the lamp lit in the sitting room. The finely plaited Manihiki hat held in his right hand seemed somewhat out of place with the rest of his attire and was evidently not much worn. Probably Felipe had merely brought it for the occasion, as a symbol to us of his superior tastes and ideas.

He shook hands with us all round, and then, at Lester's invitation, followed us inside, and sat down cross-legged on the mats and courteously awaited us to talk to him. The American surgeon offered him a cigar, which he politely declined; and he produced from the folds of his lava-lava a bundle of banana-leaf cigarettes, filled with strong tobacco. One of these, at a nod from the trader, he lit, and commenced to smoke.

In a few minutes we heard the crunching of the graveled path under bare feet, and then some three or four of the *aualuma*—the kava-chewing girls—ascended the steps and took up their position by the huge wooden kava bowl. As the girls, under the careful supervision of the trader's wife, prepared the drink, we fell into a general conversation.

"I wonder now," said the doctor to the trader, "that you, Lester, who by your own showing are by no means infatuated with the dreamy monotony of island life, can yet stay here, year after year, seeing nothing and hearing nothing of the world that lies outside these lonely islands. Have you no desire at all to go back again into the world?"

A faint movement—the index of some rapidly passing emotion—for a moment disturbed the calm, placid features of Lester, as he answered quietly: "No, Doctor, I don't think it's likely I'll ever see the outside world, as you call it, again. I've had my hopes and ambitions, like everyone else; but they didn't pan out as I expected . . . and then I became Lester the Trader; and as Lester the Trader I'll die, have a whitey-brown crowd at my funeral, and if you came here ten years afterwards the people couldn't even tell you where I was planted."

The doctor nodded. "Just so. Like all native races, their affections and emotions are deep but transient—no better in that way than the average American nigger."

The kava was finished now, and was handed round to us by the slender, graceful hands of the trader's little daughter. As Felipe, the last to drink, handed back the *ipu* to the girl, his eyes lit up, and he spoke to our host, addressing him, native fashion, by his Christian name, and speaking in his own tongue.

"How is it, Tiaki (Jack), that I hear thee tell these thy friends that we of the brown skins have but shallow hearts and forget quickly? Dost think that if, when thy time comes, and thou goest, that thy wife and child will not grieve? Hast thou not heard of our white man who, when he died, yet left his name upon our hearts? And yet we were in those days heathens and followers of our own gods."

The trader nodded kindly and turned to us. "Do you want to hear a yarn about one of the old style of white men that used to live like fighting cocks in Samoa? Felipe here has rounded on me for saying that his countrymen soon forget, and has brought up this wandering *papalagi tafea* (beachcomber) as an instance of how the natives will stick to a man once he proves himself a man."

"It was the tenth year after the Cruel Captain with the three ships had anchored in Apia,* and when we of Aleipata were at war with the people of Fagaloa. In those days we had no white man in this town and longed greatly to get one. But they were few in Samoa then; one was there at Tiavea, who had fled from a man-of-war of England, one at Saluafata, and perhaps one or two more at Tutuila or Savaii—that was all.

"My father's name was Lauati. He, with his mother, lived on the far side of the village, away from the rest of the houses.

* Commodore Wilkes, in command of the famous United States Exploring Expedition, 1836–40. He was a noted martinet, and was called *Le Alii Saua* (the Cruel Captain).

There were no others living in the house with them, for my father's mother was very poor, and all day long she labored—sometimes at making mats and sometimes at beating out *siapo* (tapa) cloth. As the mats were made, and the tapa was bleached, and figures and patterns drawn upon it, she rolled them up and put them away overhead on the beams of the house, for she was eaten up with poverty, and these mats and tapa cloth was she gathering together so that she might be able to pay for my father's tattooing. And as she worked on the shore, so did my father toil on the sea, for although he was not yet tattooed he was skilled more than any other youth in *sisu atu* (bonito-catching). Sometimes the chief, who was a greedy man, would take all his fish and leave him none for himself to take home to his house. Sometimes he would give him one, and then my father would cut off a piece for his mother and take the rest and sell it for taro and breadfruit. And all this time he worked, worked with his mother, so that he would have enough to pay for his tattooing, for to reach his age and not be tattooed is thought a disgrace.

"Now, in the chief's house was a young girl named Uluvao. She used to meet my father by stealth, for the chief—who was her uncle—designed to give her in marriage to a man of Siumu, who was a little chief, and had asked him for her. So Uluvao, who dreaded her uncle's wrath, would creep out at night from his house and, going down to the beach, swim along the shore till she came to the lonely place where my father lived. His mother would await her coming on the beach, and then these three would sit together in the house and talk. If a footstep sounded, then the girl would flee, for she knew her uncle's club would soon bite into my father's brain did he know of these stolen meetings.

"One day it came about that a great *fono* (meeting) was to be held at Falealili; and Tuialo the chief and many other chiefs and their *tulafale,* or talking men, set out to cross the mountains to Falealili. Six days would they be away, and Uluvao and my father rejoiced; for they could now meet and speak openly, for the fear of the chief's face was not before them, and the people of the village knew my father loved the girl, so when they saw them together they only smiled or else turned their faces another way. That night in the big council house there was a great number of the young men and women gathered together; and they danced and sang, and much kava was drunk. Presently the sister of the chief, who was a woman with a bitter tongue, came to the house, and saw and mocked at my father, and called him a 'naked wretch.' (Thou knowest, Tiaki, if a man be not tattooed we called him naked.)

" 'Alas!' said my father, 'I am poor; oh, lady, how can I help it?'

"The old woman's heart softened. 'Get thee out upon the sea and catch a fat turtle for a gift to my brother, and thou shalt be tattooed when he returns,' she said.

"The people laughed, for they knew that turtle were not to be caught at a silly woman's bidding. But my father rose up and went out into the darkness towards his house. As he walked on the sand his name was called, and Uluvao ran by his side.

" 'Lauati,' she said, 'let me come with thee. Let us hasten and get thy canoe, and seek a turtle on Nu'ulua and Nu'utele, for the night is dark, and we may find one.'

"My father took her hand, and they ran and launched the canoe.

"My father paddled; Uluvao sat in the bow of the canoe. The night was very dark, and she was frightened, for in the waters hereabout are many *tanifa,* the thick, short shark, that will leap out of the water and fall on a canoe and crush it, so that those who paddle may be thrown out and devoured. And as she trembled she looked out at the shore of the two islands, which were now close to, and said to my father, 'Lo! What is this? I see a light as of a little fire.'

"Lauati ceased to paddle and looked. And there, between the trunks of the coconuts, he saw the faint gleam of a little fire, and something, as of a figure, that moved.

"The girl Uluvao had a quick wisdom. 'Ah,' said she, 'perhaps it is the war canoes (*taumualua*) from Falifa. Those dogs hath learnt that all our men are gone away to Falealili to the *fono,* and they have come here to the islands to eat and rest, so that they may fall upon our town when it is dawn, and slay us all. Let us back, ere it is too late.'

"But as she spoke she looked into the water, and my father looked too; and they both trembled. Deep down in the blackness of the sea was it that they saw—yet it quickly came nearer and nearer, like unto a great flame of white fire. It was a *tanifa*. Like flashes of lightning did my father dash his paddle into the water and urge the canoe to the land, for he knew that when the *tanifa* had come to the surface it would look and then dive, and when it came up again would spring upon and devour them both.

" 'It is better to give our heads to the men of Falifa than for us to go into the belly of the shark,' he said, 'and it may be we can land and they see us not.' And so with fear gnawing at their vitals the canoe flew along, and the streak of fire underneath was close upon them when they struck the edge of the coral and knew they were safe.

"They dragged the canoe over the reef and then got in again, and paddled softly along till they passed the light of the fire, and then they landed on a little beach about a hundred *gafa* (fathoms) away. Then again Uluvao, who was a girl of wisdom, spoke.

" 'Listen,' she said, 'O man of my heart. Let us creep through the bushes and look. It may be that these men of Falifa are tired and weary, and sleep like hogs. Take thou, then, O Lauati, thy shark club and knife from the canoe, and perchance we may fall upon one that sleepest away from the rest, then shalt thou strike, and thou and I drag him away into the bushes and take his head. Then, ere it is well dawn, we will be back in the town, and Tuialo will no longer keep me from thee, for the head of a Falifa man will win his heart better than a fat turtle, and I will be wife to thee.'

"My father was pleased at her words. So they crept like snakes along the dewy ground. When they came to a jagged boulder covered with vines, that was near unto the fire, they looked and saw but one man, and, lo! he was a *papalagi*—a white man. And then, until it was dawn, my father and the girl hid behind the jagged rock and watched.

"The white man was sitting on the sand, with his face

clasped in his hands. At his feet lay another man, with his white face turned up to the sky, and those that watched saw that he was dead. He who sat over the dead man was tall and thin, and his hands were like the talons of the great fish eagle, so thin and bony were they. His garments were ragged and old, and his feet were bare; and as my father looked at him his heart became pitiful, and he whispered to Uluvao, 'Let us call out. He is but weak, and I can master him if he springs upon me. Let us speak.'

"But Uluvao held him back. 'Nay,' she said, 'he may have a gun and shoot.'

"So they waited till the sun rose.

"The white man stood and looked about. Then he walked down to the beach, and my father and the girl saw lying on the rocks a little boat. The man went to the side, and put in his hand and brought out something in his hand, and came back and sat down again by the face of the dead. He had gone to the boat for food, and my father saw him place a biscuit to his mouth and commence to eat. But ere he swallowed any it fell from his hand upon the sand and he threw himself upon the body of the dead man and wept, and his tears ran down over the face that was cold and were drunk up by the sand.

"Then Uluvao began to weep, and my father stood up and called out to the white man, '*Talofa!*'

"He gazed at them and spoke not, but let them come close to him, and pointing to him who lay on the sand, he covered his face with his hands and bowed his head. Then Lauati ran and climbed a coconut tree and brought him two young nuts and made him drink, and Uluvao got broad leaves and covered over the face of the dead from the hot sun. Not one word of our tongue could he speak, but yet from signs that he made Lauati and the girl knew that he wished to bury the dead man. So they two dug a deep grave in the sand, far up on the bank, where it lay soft and deep and covered with vines. When it was finished they lifted the dead white man and laid him beside it. And as they looked upon him the other came and knelt beside it and spoke many words into the ear that heard not, and Uluvao wept again to see his grief. At last they laid him in the grave and all three threw in the sand and filled it up.

"Then these two took the strange white man by the hand and led him away into a little hut that was sometimes used by those who came to the island to fish. They made him eat and then sleep, and while he slept they carried up the things out of the boat and put them in the house beside him.

"When the sun was high in the heavens, the white man awoke, and my father took his hand and pointed to the boat, and then to the houses across the sea. He bent his head and followed, and they all got into the boat, and hoisted the sail. When the boat came close to the passage of Aleipata, the people ran from out their houses, and stood upon the beach and wondered. And Lauati and Uluvao laughed and sang, and called out: 'Ho, ho, people! we have brought a great gift—a white man from over the sea. Send word quickly to Tuialo that he may return and see this our white man,' and, as the boat touched the sand, the old woman, the sister of Tuialo, came up, and said to Lauati, 'Well hast thou done, O lucky one! Better is this gift of a white man than many turtle.'

"Then she took the stranger to her house, and pigs and fowls were killed and yams and taro cooked and a messenger sent to Tuialo to hasten back quickly, and see this gift from the gods. For they were quick to see that in the boat were muskets and powder and bullets, and all the people rejoiced, for they thought that this white man could mend for them many guns that were broken and useless, and help them to fight against the men of Falifa.

"In two days Tuialo came back, and he made much of the white man, and Uluvao he gave to my father for wife. And for the white man were the softest mats and the best pieces of *siapo,* and he lived for nearly the space of two years in the chief's house. And all this time he worked at making boats and mending the broken guns and muskets, and little by little the words of our tongue came to him, and he learned to tell us many things. Yet at nighttime he would always come to my father's house and sit with him and talk, and sometimes Uluvao would make kava for him and my father.

"At about the end of the second year, there came a whale-ship, and Tuialo and the white man, whom we called *Tui-fana* (the gun-mender), went out to her, and took with them many pigs and yams to exchange for guns and powder. When the buying and selling was over, the captain of the ship gave Tui-fana a gun with two barrels—bright was it and new, and Tuialo, the chief, was eaten up with envy, and begged his white man for the gun, but he said: 'Nay, not now; when we are in the house we will talk.'

"Like a swarm of flies, the people gathered round the council house to see the guns and the powder and the swords that had been brought from the ship. And in the middle of the house sat Tui-fana with the gun with two barrels in his hand.

"When all the chiefs had come in and sat down, Tuialo came. His face was smiles, but his heart was full of bitterness towards Tui-fana, and as he spoke to the people and told them of the words that had been spoken by the captain of the ship, he said, 'And see this white man, this Tui-fana, who hath grown rich among us, is as greedy as a Tongan, and keepeth for himself a new gun with two barrels.'

"The white stood up and spoke: 'Nay, not greedy am I. Take, O chief, all I have; my house, my mats, my land, and the wife thou gavest me, but yet would I say, "Let me keep this gun with the two barrels." '

"Tuialo was eaten up with greed, yet was his mind set on the gun, so he answered, 'Nay, that were to make thee as poor as when thou comest to us. Give me the gun, 'tis all I ask.'

" 'It is not mine to give,' he answered. Then he rose and spoke to the people. 'See,' said he, 'Tuialo, the chief, desires this gun, and I say it is not mine to give, for to Lauati did I promise such a gun a year gone by. This, then, will I do. Unto Tuialo will I give my land, my house, and all that is mine, but to Lauati I give the gun, for so I promised.'

"Then fierce looks passed between the chief and the white man, and the people surged together to and fro, for they were divided, some for the fear of the chief, and some for the love of the white man. But most were for that Lauati should keep the gun. And so Tuialo, seeing that the people's hearts were against him, put on a smooth face, and came to the white man and said:

" 'Thou art as a son to me. Lauati shall keep the gun, and thou shalt keep thy house and lands. I will take nothing from thee. Let us be forever friends.'

"Then the white said to the chief, 'O chief, gladly will I give thee all I have, but this man, Lauati, is as my brother, and I promised–'

"But Tuialo put his hand on the white man's mouth and said, 'Say no more, my son; I was but angered.'

"Yet see now his wickedness. For that night, when my father and Uluvao, my mother, were sitting with the white man and his wife and drinking kava, there suddenly sprang in upon them ten men, who stood over them with clubs poised. They were the body-men of Tuialo.

" 'Drink thy kava,' said one to the white man, 'and then come out to die.'

"Ah, he was a man! He took the cup of kava from the hands of his wife's sister, and said:

" 'It is well. All men must die. But yet would I see Tuialo before the club falls.'

"The chief but waited outside, and he came.

" 'Must I die?' said the white man.

" 'Aye,' said Tuialo. 'Two such as thee and I cannot live at the same time. Thou art almost as great a man as I.'

"The white man bent his head. Then he put out his hand to my father and said, 'Farewell, O my friend.'

"Lauati, my father, fell at the chief's feet. 'Take thou the gun, O chief, but spare his life.'

"Tuialo laughed. 'The gun will I take, Lauati, but his life I must have also.'

" 'My life for his,' said my father.

" 'And mine,' said Uluvao, my mother.

" 'And mine also,' said Manini, the white man's wife; and both she and Taulaga, her sister, bent their knees to the chief.

"The white man tried to spring up, but four strong men held him.

"Then Tuialo looked at the pair who knelt before him. He stroked his club, and spoke to his body-men.

" 'Bring them all outside.' They went together to the beach. 'Brave talkers ye be,' said he; 'who now will say, "I die for the white man"?'

" 'Nay, heed them not, Tuialo,' said the white man. 'On me alone let the club fall.'

"But the chief gave him no answer, looking only at my father and the three women.

" 'My life,' said Taulaga, the girl; and she knelt on the sand.

"The club swung round and struck her on the side of her head, and it beat it in. She fell, and died quickly.

" 'Oho,' mocked Tuialo, 'is there but one life offered for so great a man as Tiu-fana?'

"Lauati fell before him. 'Spare me not, O chief, if my life but saves his.'

"And again the club swung, and Lauati, my father, died too; and as he fell his blood mixed with that of Taulaga.

"And then Uluvao and Manini, placing some little faith in his mocking words, knelt, and their blood too poured out on the ground, and the three women and my father lay in a heap together.

"Now I, Felipe, was but a child, and when my mother had gone to kneel under the club she had placed me under a *fetan* tree nearby. The chief's eye fell on me, and a man took me up and carried me to him.

"Then the white man said, 'Hurt not the child, O chief, or I curse thee before I die, and thou wastest away.'

"So Tuialo spared me.

"Then the chief came to the white man, and the two who held his hands pulled them well apart, and Tuialo once more swung his blood-dyed club. It fell, and the white man's head fell upon his breast."

Herman Melville

NORFOLK ISLE AND THE CHOLA WIDOW

Herman Melville (1819–91), "meditative Magian rover" from New York, whose name is foremost in Pacific literature, transmuted his four years of life on the waters and islands of that ocean into his greatest books. He left New Bedford as a crewman on the whaler "Acushnet" early in 1841, and after eighteen months at sea deserted from the ship and lived for some weeks in friendly captivity among the natives in the valley of Typee on one of the Marquesas Islands. Taken off by a wandering Australian whaler, he cast his lot with the mutinous crew and was soon put ashore in Tahiti. After a random, beachcombing life there and on the neighboring island of Mooréa, he boarded a Nantucket whaler that carried him to Hawaii, where several months later he enlisted as a foremast hand on the American naval frigate "United States."

It was in this ship, after a long Pacific cruise, that he returned home to begin writing the books—based mainly on his experiences in the Pacific—that make him famous today: *Typee* (1846); *Omoo* (1847); *Mardi* (1849); *White-Jacket* (1850); *Moby Dick* (1851); and *The Piazza Tales* (1856).

The scene of this story is not the Norfolk of Michener's "Mutiny" but, instead, one of the cindery volcanic islands of the Galápagos group, named for the giant turtles collected there by early ships voyaging in the Pacific. Melville, who visited those islands at least once, wrote a series of ten sketches about them entitled *The Encantadas or Enchanted Isles*. Of these the best is the story of the Chola girl left alone on desolate Norfolk. Its concluding scene, in which Hunilla rides a small gray ass toward her native Peruvian village and "eyes the jointed workings of the beast's armorial cross," seemed to James Russell Lowell to be "the finest touch of genius he had seen in prose."

FAR TO THE NORTHEAST OF CHARLES'S ISLE, SEQUESTERED FROM the rest, lies Norfolk Isle; and, however insignificant to most voyagers, to me, through sympathy, that lone island has become a spot made sacred by the strangest trials of humanity.

It was my first visit to the Encantadas. Two days had been spent ashore in hunting tortoises. There was not time to capture many; so on the third afternoon we loosed our sails. We were just in the act of getting under way, the uprooted anchor yet suspended and invisibly swaying beneath the wave, as the good ship gradually turned her heel to leave the isle behind, when the seaman who heaved with me at the windlass paused suddenly, and directed my attention to something moving on the land, not along the beach, but somewhat back, fluttering from a height.

In view of the sequel of this little story, be it here narrated how it came to pass, that an object that partly from its being so small was quite lost to every other man on board, still caught the eye of my handspike companion. The rest of the crew, myself included, merely stood up to our spikes in heaving, whereas, unwontedly exhilarated, at every turn of the ponderous windlass, my belted comrade leaped atop of it, with might and main giving a downward, thewy, perpendicular heave, his raised eye bent in cheery animation upon the slowly receding shore. Being high lifted above all others was the reason he perceived the object, otherwise unperceivable; and this elevation of his eye was owing to the elevation of his spirits; and this again—for truth must out—to a dram of Peruvian *pisco,* in guerdon for some kindness done, secretly administered to him that morning by our mulatto steward. Now, certainly, *pisco* does a deal of mischief in the world; yet seeing that in the present case it was the means, though indirect, of rescuing a human being from the most dreadful fate, must we not also needs admit that sometimes *pisco* does a deal of good?

Glancing across the water in the direction pointed out, I saw some white thing hanging from an inland rock, perhaps half a mile from the sea.

"It is a bird; a white-winged bird; perhaps a—no; it is—it is a handkerchief!"

"Aye, a handkerchief!" echoed my comrade, and with a louder shout apprised the captain.

Quickly now—like the running out and training of a great gun—the long cabin spyglass was thrust through the mizzen rigging from the high platform of the poop; whereupon a human figure was plainly seen upon the inland rock, eagerly waving towards us what seemed to be the handkerchief.

Our captain was a prompt, good fellow. Dropping the glass, he lustily ran forward, ordering the anchor to be dropped again; hands to stand by a boat, and lower away.

In a half-hour's time the swift boat returned. It went with six and came with seven; and the seventh was a woman.

It is not artistic heartlessness, but I wish I could but draw in crayons; for this woman was a most touching sight; and crayons, tracing softly melancholy lines, would best depict the mournful image of the dark-damasked Chola widow.

Her story was soon told, and though given in her own strange language was as quickly understood; for our captain from long trading on the Chilean coast was well versed in the Spanish. A Cholo, or half-breed Indian woman of Payta in Peru, three years gone by, with her young new-wedded husband Felipe, of pure Castilian blood, and her one only Indian brother, Truxill, Hunilla had taken passage on the main in a French whaler, commanded by a joyous man; which vessel, bound to the cruising grounds beyond the Enchanted Isles, proposed passing close by their vicinity. The object of the little party was to procure tortoise oil, a fluid which for its great purity and delicacy is held in high estimation wherever known; and it is well known all along this part of the Pacific coast. With a chest of clothes, tools, cooking utensils, a rude apparatus for trying out the oil, some casks of biscuit, and other things, not omitting two favorite dogs, of which faithful animal all the Cholos are very fond, Hunilla and her companions were safely landed at their chosen place; the Frenchman, according to the contract made ere sailing, engaged to take them off upon returning from a four months' cruise in the westward seas; which interval the three adventurers deemed quite sufficient for their purposes.

On the isle's lone beach they paid him in silver for their passage out, the stranger having declined to carry them at all except upon that condition; though willing to take every means to insure the due fulfillment of his promise. Felipe had striven hard to have this payment put off to the period of the ship's return. But in vain. Still they thought they had, in another way, ample pledge of the good faith of the Frenchman. It was arranged that the expenses of the passage home should not be payable in silver, but in tortoises; one hundred tortoises ready captured to the returning captain's hand. These the Cholos meant to secure after their own work was done, against the probable time of the Frenchman's coming back; and no doubt in prospect already felt, that in those hundred tortoises—now somewhere ranging the isle's interior—they possessed one hundred hostages. Enough: the vessel sailed; the gazing three on shore answered the loud glee of the singing crew; and ere evening, the French craft was hull down in the distant sea, its masts three faintest lines which quickly faded from Hunilla's eye.

The stranger had given a blithesome promise, and anchored it with oaths; but oaths and anchors equally will drag; naught else abides on fickle earth but unkept promises of joy. Contrary winds from out unstable skies, or contrary moods of his more varying mind, or shipwreck and sudden death in solitary waves; whatever was the cause, the blithe stranger never was seen again.

Yet, however dire a calamity was here in store, misgivings of it ere due time never disturbed the Cholos' busy minds, now all intent upon the toilsome matter which had brought them hither. Nay, by swift doom coming like the thief at night, ere seven weeks went by, two of the little party were removed from all anxieties of land or sea. No more they sought to gaze with feverish fear, or still more feverish hope, beyond the present's horizon line; but into the furthest future their own silent spirits sailed. By persevering labor beneath that burning sun, Felipe and Truxill had brought down to their hut many scores of tortoises, and tried out the oil, when, elated with their good success, and to reward themselves for such hard work, they, too hastily, made a catamaran, or Indian raft, much used on the Spanish main, and merrily started on a fishing trip, just without a long reef with many jagged gaps, running parallel with the shore, about half a mile from it. By some bad tide or hap, or natural negligence of joyfulness (for though they could not be heard, yet by their gestures they seemed singing at the time), forced in deep water against that iron bar, the ill-made catamaran was overset, and came all to pieces; when dashed by broad-chested swells between their broken logs and the sharp teeth of the reef, both adventurers perished before Hunilla's eyes.

Before Hunilla's eyes they sank. The real woe of this event passed before her sight as some sham tragedy on the stage. She was seated in a rude bower among the withered thickets, crowning a lofty cliff, a little back from the beach. The thickets were so disposed, that in looking upon the sea at large she peered out from among the branches as from the lattice of a high balcony. But upon the day we speak of here, the better to watch the adventure of those two hearts she loved, Hunilla had withdrawn the branches to one side, and held them so. They formed an oval frame, through which the bluely boundless sea rolled like a painted one. And there, the invisible painter painted to her view the wave-tossed and disjointed raft, its once-level logs slantingly upheaved, as raking masts, and the four struggling arms undistinguishable among them; and then all subsided into smooth-flowing creamy waters, slowly drifting the splintered wreck; while first and last, no sound of any sort was heard. Death in a silent picture; a dream of the eye; such vanishing shapes as the mirage shows.

So instant was the scene, so trancelike its mild pictorial effect, so distant from her blasted bower and her common sense of things, that Hunilla gazed and gazed, nor raised a finger or a wail. But as good to sit thus dumb, in stupor staring on that dumb show, for all that otherwise might be done. With half a mile of sea between, how could her two enchanted arms aid those four fated ones? The distance long, the time one sand. After the lightning is beheld, what fool shall stay the thunderbolt? Felipe's body was washed ashore, but Truxill's never came; only his gay, braided hat of golden straw—that same sunflower thing he waved to her, pushing from the strand—and now, to the last gallant, it still saluted her. But Felipe's body floated to the marge, with one arm encirclingly outstretched. Lockjawed in grim death, the lover-husband softly clasped his bride, true to her even in death's dream. Ah, Heaven, when man thus keeps his faith, wilt Thou be faithless who created the faithful one? But they cannot break faith who never plighted it.

It needs not to be said what nameless misery now wrapped the lonely widow. In telling her own story she passed this almost entirely over, simply recounting the event. Construe the comment of her features as you might, from her mere words little would you have weened that Hunilla was herself the heroine of the tale. But not thus did she defraud us of our tears. All hearts bled that grief could be so brave.

She but showed us her soul's lid, and the strange ciphers thereon engraved; all within, with pride's timidity, was withheld. Yet was there one exception. Holding out her small olive hand before her captain, she said in mild and slowest Spanish, "*Señor,* I buried him," then paused, struggled as against the writhed coilings of a snake, and cringing suddenly, leaped up, repeating in impassioned pain, "I buried him, my life, my soul!"

Doubtless, it was by half-unconscious, automatic motions of her hands, that this heavy-hearted one performed the final office for Felipe, and planted a rude cross of withered sticks —no green ones might be had—at the head of that lonely grave, where rested now in lasting uncomplaint and quiet haven he whom untranquil seas had overthrown.

But some dull sense of another body that should be interred, of another cross that should hallow another grave—unmade as yet—some dull anxiety and pain touching her undiscovered brother, now haunted the oppressed Hunilla. Her hands fresh from the burial earth, she slowly went back to the beach, with unshaped purposes wandering there, her spellbound eye bent upon the incessant waves. But they bore nothing to her but a dirge, which maddened her to think that murderers should mourn. As time went by, and these things came less dreamingly to her mind, the strong persuasions of her Romish faith, which sets peculiar store by consecrated urns, prompted her to resume in waking earnest that pious search that had but been begun as in somnambulism. Day after day, week after week, she trod the cindery beach, till at length a double motive edged every eager glance. With equal longing she now looked for the living and the dead; the brother and the captain; alike vanished, never to return. Little accurate note of time had Hunilla taken under such emotions as were hers, and little, outside herself, served for calendar or dial. As to poor Crusoe in the selfsame sea, no saint's bell pealed forth the lapse of week or month; each day went by unchallenged; no chanticleer announced those sultry dawns, no lowing herds those poisonous nights. All wonted and steadily recurring sounds, human or humanized by sweet fellowship with man, but one stirred that torrid trance—the cry of dogs; save which naught but the rolling sea invaded it, an all-pervading monotone; and to the widow that was the least loved voice she could have heard.

No wonder, that as her thoughts now wandered to the unreturning ship, and were beaten back again, the hope against hope so struggled in her soul, that at length she desperately said, "Not yet, not yet; my foolish heart runs on too fast." So she forced patience for some further weeks. But to those whom earth's sure indraft draws, patience or impatience is still the same.

Hunilla now sought to settle precisely in her mind, to an hour, how long it was since the ship had sailed; and then, with the same precision, how long a space remained to pass. But this proved impossible. What present day or month it was she could not say. Time was her labyrinth, in which Hunilla was entirely lost.

And now follows—

Against my own purposes a pause descends upon me here. One knows not whether nature doth not impose some secrecy upon him who has been privy to certain things. At least, it is to be doubted whether it be good to blazon such. If some books are deemed most baneful and their sale forbid, how, then, with deadlier facts, not dreams of doting men? Those whom books will hurt will not be proof against events. Events, not books, should be forbid. But in all things man sows upon the wind, which bloweth just there whither it listeth; for ill or good, man cannot know. Often ill comes from the good, as good from ill.

When Hunilla—

Dire sight it is to see some silken beast long dally with a golden lizard ere she devour. More terrible, to see how feline Fate will sometimes dally with a human soul, and by a nameless magic make it repulse a sane despair with a hope which is but mad. Unwittingly I imp this catlike thing, sporting with the heart of him who reads; for if he feel not he reads in vain.

—"The ship sails this day, today," at last said Hunilla to herself; "this gives me certain time to stand on; without certainty I go mad. In loose ignorance I have hoped and hoped; now in firm knowledge I will but wait. Now I live and no longer perish in bewilderings. Holy Virgin, aid me! Thou wilt waft back the ship. Oh, past length of weary weeks —all to be dragged over—to buy the certainty of today, I freely give ye, though I tear ye from me!"

As mariners, tossed in tempest on some desolate ledge, patch them a boat out of the remnants of their vessel's wreck, and launch it in the selfsame waves, see here Hunilla, this lone shipwrecked soul, out of treachery invoking trust. Humanity, thou strong thing, I worship thee, not in the laureled victor, but in this vanquished one.

Truly Hunilla leaned upon a reed, a real one; no metaphor: a real Eastern reed. A piece of hollow cane, drifted from unknown isles, and found upon the beach, its once jagged ends rubbed smoothly even as by sandpaper; its golden glazing gone. Long ground between the sea and land, upper and nether stone, the unvarnished substance was filed bare, and wore another polish now, one with itself, the polish of its agony. Circular lines at intervals cut all round this surface, divided it into six panels of unequal length. In the first were scored the days, each tenth one marked by a longer and deeper notch; the second was scored for the number of sea-fowl eggs for sustenance, picked out from the rocky nests; the third, how many fish had been caught from the shore; the fourth, how many small tortoises found inland; the fifth, how many days of sun; the sixth, of clouds; which last, of the two, was the greater one. Long night of busy numbering, misery's mathematics, to weary her too-wakeful soul to sleep; yet sleep for that was none.

The panel of the days was deeply worn—the long tenth notches half-effaced, as alphabets of the blind. Ten thousand times the longing widow had traced her finger over the bamboo—dull flute, which played on, gave no sound—as if counting birds flown by in air would hasten tortoises creeping through the woods.

After the one-hundred-and-eightieth day no further mark was seen; that last one was the faintest, as the first the deepest.

"There were more days," said our captain; "many, many more; why did you not go on and notch them, too, Hunilla?"

"Señor, ask me not."

"And meantime, did no other vessel pass the isle?"

"Nay, *Señor;*—but—"

"You do not speak; but *what,* Hunilla?"

"Ask me not, *Señor."*

"You saw ships pass, far away; you waved to them; they passed on;—was that it, Hunilla?"

"Señor, be it as you say."

Braced against her woe, Hunilla would not, durst not trust the weakness of her tongue. Then when our captain asked whether any whaleboats had—

But no, I will not file this thing complete for scoffing souls to quote, and call it firm proof upon their side. The half shall here remain untold. Those two unnamed events which befell Hunilla on this isle, let them abide between her and her God. In nature, as in law, it may be libelous to speak some truths.

Still, how it was that, although our vessel had lain three days anchored nigh the isle, its one human tenant should not have discovered us till just upon the point of sailing, never to revisit so lone and far a spot, this needs explaining ere the sequel come.

The place where the French captain had landed the little party was on the farther and opposite end of the isle. There, too, it was that they had afterwards built their hut. Nor did the widow in her solitude desert the spot where her loved ones had dwelt with her, and where the dearest of the twain now slept his last long sleep, and all her plaints awaked him not, and he of husbands the most faithful during life.

Now, high broken land rises between the opposite extremities of the isle. A ship anchored at one side is invisible from the other. Neither is the isle so small, but a considerable company might wander for days through the wilderness of one side, and never be seen, or their halloos heard, by any stranger holding aloof on the other. Hence Hunilla, who naturally associated the possible coming of ships with her own part of the isle, might to the end have remained quite ignorant of the presence of our vessel, were it not for a mysterious presentiment, borne to her, so our mariners averred, by this isle's enchanted air. Nor did the widow's answer undo the thought.

"How did you come to cross the isle this morning, then, Hunilla?" said our captain.

"Señor, something came flitting by me. It touched my cheek, my heart, *Señor."*

"What do you say, Hunilla?"

"I have said, *Señor,* something came through the air."

It was a narrow chance. For when in crossing the isle Hunilla gained the high land in the center, she must then for the first have perceived our masts, and also marked that their sails were being loosed, perhaps even heard the echoing chorus of the windlass song. The strange ship was about to sail, and she behind. With all haste she now descends the height on the hither side, but soon loses sight of the ship among the sunken jungles at the mountain's base. She struggles on through the withered branches, that seek at every step to bar her path, till she comes to the isolated rock, still some way from the water. This she climbs, to reassure herself. The ship is still in plainest sight. But now, worn out with over-tension. Hunilla all but faints; she fears to step down from her giddy perch; she is fain to pause, there where she is, and as a last resort catches the turban from her head, unfurls and waves it over the jungles towards us.

During the telling of her story the mariners formed a voiceless circle round Hunilla and the captain; and when at length the word was given to man the fastest boat, and pull round to the isle's thither side, to bring away Hunilla's chest and the tortoise oil, such alacrity of both cheery and sad obedience seldom before was seen. Little ado was made. Already the anchor had been recommitted to the bottom, and the ship swung calmly to it.

But Hunilla insisted upon accompanying the boat as indispensable pilot to her hidden hut. So, being refreshed with the best the steward could supply, she started with us. Nor did ever any wife of the most famous admiral, in her husband's barge, receive more silent reverence of respect than poor Hunilla from this boat's crew.

Rounding many a vitreous cape and bluff, in two hours' time we shot inside the fatal reef; wound into a secret cove, looked up along a green many-gabled lava wall, and saw the island's solitary dwelling.

It hung upon an impending cliff, sheltered on two sides by tangled thickets, and half-screened from view in front by juttings of the rude stairway, which climbed the precipice from the sea. Built of canes, it was thatched with long, mildewed grass. It seemed an abandoned hayrick, whose haymakers were now no more. The roof inclined but one way; the eaves coming to within two feet of the ground. And here was a simple apparatus to collect the dews, or rather doubly-distilled and finest winnowed rains, which, in mercy or in mockery, the night skies sometimes drop upon these blighted Encantadas. All along beneath the eaves, a spotted sheet, quite weather-stained, was spread, pinned to short, upright stakes, set in the shallow sand. A small clinker, thrown into the cloth, weighed its middle down, thereby straining all moisture into a calabash placed below. This vessel supplied each drop of water ever drunk upon the isle by the Cholos. Hunilla told us the calabash would sometimes, but not often, be half filled overnight. It held six quarts, perhaps. "But," said she, "we were used to thirst. At sandy Payta, where I live, no shower from heaven ever fell; all the water there is brought on mules from the inland vales."

Tied among the thickets were some twenty moaning tortoises, supplying Hunilla's lonely larder; while hundreds of vast tableted black bucklers, like displaced, shattered tombstones of dark slate, were also scattered round. These were the skeleton backs of those great tortoises from which Felipe and Truxill had made their precious oil. Several large calabashes and two goodly kegs were filled with it. In a pot nearby were the caked crusts of a quantity which had been permitted to evaporate. "They meant to have strained it off next day," said Hunilla, as she turned aside.

I forgot to mention the most singular sight of all, though the first that greeted us after landing.

Some ten small, soft-haired, ringleted dogs, of a beautiful breed, peculiar to Peru, set up a concert of glad welcomings when we gained the beach, which was responded to by Hunilla. Some of these dogs had, since her widowhood, been born upon the isle, the progeny of the two brought from Payta. Owing to the jagged steeps and pitfalls, tortuous thickets, sunken clefts, and perilous intricacies of all sorts in the interior, Hunilla, admonished by the loss of one favorite among them, never allowed these delicate creatures to follow her in her occasional birds'-nests climbs and other wanderings; so that, through long habituation, they offered not to follow, when that morning she crossed the land, and her own soul was then too full of other things to heed their lingering behind. Yet, all along she had so clung to them, that, besides what moisture they lapped up at early daybreak from the small scoop-holes among the adjacent rocks, she had shared the dew of her calabash among them; never laying by any considerable store against those prolonged and utter droughts which, in some disastrous seasons, warp these isles.

Having pointed out, at our desire, what few things she would like transported to the ship—her chest, the oil, not omitting the live tortoises that she intended for a grateful present to our captain—we immediately set to work, carrying them to the boat down the long, sloping stair of deeply shadowed rock. While my comrades were thus employed, I looked and Hunilla had disappeared.

It was not curiosity alone, but, it seems to me, something different mingled with it, that prompted me to drop my tortoise, and once more gaze slowly around. I remembered the husband buried by Hunilla's hands. A narrow pathway led into a dense part of the thickets. Following it through many mazes, I came out upon a small, round, open space, deeply chambered there.

The mound rose in the middle; a bare heap of finest sand, like that unverdured heap found at the bottom of an hour-glass run out. At its head stood the cross of withered sticks; the dry, peeled bark still fraying from it; its transverse limb tied up with rope, and forlornly adroop in the silent air.

Hunilla was partly prostrate upon the grave; her dark head bowed, and lost in her long, loosened Indian hair; her hands extended to the cross-foot, with a little brass crucifix clasped between; a crucifix worn featureless, like an ancient graven knocker long plied in vain. She did not see me, and I made no noise, but slid aside and left the spot.

A few moments ere all was ready for our going, she reappeared among us. I looked into her eyes, but saw no tear. There was something that seemed strangely haughty in her air, and yet it was the air of woe. A Spanish and an Indian grief, which would not visibly lament. Pride's height in vain abased to proneness on the rack; nature's pride subduing nature's torture.

Like pages the small and silken dogs surrounded her, as she slowly descended towards the beach. She caught the two most eager creatures in her arms—*"Tita mía! Tomotita mía!"* —and fondling them, inquired how many could we take on board.

The mate commanded the boat's crew; not a hardhearted man, but his way of life had been such that in most things, even in the smallest, simple utility was his leading motive.

"We cannot take them all, Hunilla; our supplies are short; the winds are unreliable; we may be a good many days going to Tumbez. So take those you have, Hunilla; but no more."

She was in the boat; the oarsmen, too, were seated, all save one, who stood ready to push off and then spring himself. With the sagacity of their race, the dogs now seemed aware that they were in the very instant of being deserted upon a barren strand. The gunwales of the boat were high; its prow —presented inland—was lifted; so owing to the water, which they seemed instinctively to shun, the dogs could not well leap into the little craft. But their busy paws hard scraped the prow, as it had been some farmer's door shutting them out from shelter in a winter storm. A clamorous agony of alarm. They did not howl, or whine; they all but spoke.

"Push off! Give way!" cried the mate. The boat gave one heavy drag and lurch, and next moment shot swiftly from the beach, turned on her heel, and sped. The dogs ran howling along the water's marge; now pausing to gaze at the flying boat, then motioning as if to leap in chase, but mysteriously withheld themselves; and again ran howling along the beach. Had they been human beings, hardly would they have more vividly inspired the sense of desolation. The oars were plied as confederate feathers of two wings. No one spoke. I looked back upon the beach, and then upon Hunilla, but her face was set in a stern, dusky calm. The dogs crouching in her lap vainly licked her rigid hands. She never looked behind her, but sat motionless, till we turned a promontory of the coast and lost all sights and sounds astern. She seemed as one who, having experienced the sharpest of mortal pangs, was henceforth content to have all lesser heartstrings riven, one by one. To Hunilla, pain seemed so necessary that pain in other beings, though by love and sympathy made her own, was unrepiningly to be borne. A heart of yearning in a frame of steel. A heart of earthly yearning, frozen by the frost which falleth from the sky.

The sequel is soon told. After a long passage, vexed by calms and baffling winds, we made the little port of Tumbez in Peru, there to recruit the ship. Payta was not very distant. Our captain sold the tortoise oil to a Tumbez merchant; and adding to the silver a contribution from all hands, gave it to our silent passenger, who knew not what the mariners had done.

The last seen of lone Hunilla she was passing into Payta town, riding upon a small gray ass; and before her on the ass's shoulders, she eyed the jointed workings of the beast's armorial cross.

ISBN 0-935180-79-6